Veil of ℑ

Reading *Veil of Fire* is like feasting on a banquet of rich words and vivid images. Marlo Schalesky's voice is lyrical, and the gripping story is a tale of truth and true beauty centered on a historical firestorm that altered a community forever. It made me think twice about my own fears and prejudices.

—TRICIA GOYER, AWARD-WINNING AUTHOR OF FIVE NOVELS,
INCLUDING *A VALLEY OF BETRAYAL*

Moving. Heartbreaking. Compelling. This beautiful, sensitive story of pain, loss, and, ultimately, healing touched the deepest parts of my heart. Bravo, Ms. Schalesky! Highly recommended.

—LAURA JENSEN WALKER, AUTHOR OF *MISS INVISIBLE* AND
RECONSTRUCTING NATALIE

A truly gifted storyteller, Marlo Schalesky has woven a beautiful tale that confronts readers with truth and the character of God. Her lyrical style and deep characterization will transport you into a story populated with unforgettable characters. If you're brave enough to search, you may even discover answers to some of those hard questions from your own past. This book is one you don't want to miss!

—JUDITH MILLER, AUTHOR OF THE *BELLS OF LOWELL, LIGHTS OF
LOWELL,* AND *FREEDOM'S PATH* SERIES

Veil of Fire is a lovely, well-crafted story of love and loss, redemption and restoration. Marlo Schalesky has written an original, unpredictable story that will stay with me for a long, long time.

—ANNETTE SMITH, AUTHOR OF *A BIGGER LIFE*

VEIL OF FIRE

A NOVEL

MARLO SCHALESKY

RIVEROAK®
Good News in Fiction

COOK COMMUNICATIONS MINISTRIES
Colorado Springs, Colorado • Paris, Ontario
KINGSWAY COMMUNICATIONS LTD
Eastbourne, England

RiverOak® is an imprint of
Cook Communications Ministries, Colorado Springs, CO 80918
Cook Communications, Paris, Ontario
Kingsway Communications, Eastbourne, England

VEIL OF FIRE

This story is a work of fiction. It is based on factual events, and some characters
are based on actual people. Otherwise, all are products of the author's imagina-
tion, and resemblance to any person, living or dead, is coincidental.

Cover Design: The DesignWorks Group
Cover Photos: iStock.com, shutterstock

First printing 2007
Printed in the United States of America

1 2 3 4 5 6 7 8 9 10

"Praise Ye the Lord, the Almighty" by Joachim Neander. (Words Public Domain.)

ISBN 978-1-58919-077-1
LCCN 2007921091

For Mother,

who first introduced me to Hinckley

and the hermit in the hills.

With special thanks

to my wonderful husband, Bryan,

whose support and sacrifice made this book possible.

Thank you for being the man that you are,

a man of integrity, uprightness, and love.

αληθεια

"truth"
from the root meaning "unhidden"

And ye shall know the truth,
and the truth shall make you free.
—JOHN 8:32

1

Sometimes, when the wind blows just right over the fields, I can still smell the spice of her perfume. Sometimes, when the dandelion seeds dip and twirl across the sky, I see the way the silk slipped through her fingers, how the needle flashed in her hands. In and out. In and out. The seam straight, perfect. I pause to listen to the warble of a common loon, and in it hear the soft echo of her laughter. Lilting. Faint. Fading.

Then the sky turns dark. The wind stills. The bird is silenced. And in that moment, I am returned to the day my world burned. The day that changed everything I am, everything I was.

Listen, the silence whispers.

See, the darkness beckons.

So I wait. I remember. And in that quiet, in-between place, she lives again.

***

September 1, 1894

  Darkness oozed through the windows and settled in the crevices of the sewing room. It weighted Nora's shoulders and pressed like a cloth over her mouth and nose. She straightened, drew a deep breath, and coughed.

"You okay, Mama?" Ellie shifted her feet on the chair.

The needle paused in Nora's hand. She glanced up at her daughter standing on the chair above her. "Hold still, punkin, or you'll be tippin' over like a kettle of tea."

Ellie snickered.

Nora grinned into the gray-blue eyes of her daughter. "And no giggling either, or the hem will be crooked." The gray fabric brought out the flecks of dark blue in Ellie's eyes, making them appear old for a girl of twelve.

"You almost done?" Wheat-colored hair bobbed over thin shoulders and dropped over the dress's front, still loose on a chest teetering on the brink of womanhood.

"Just a few more stitches."

"You were giving me that look again."

"Look?"

"You know."

Nora smiled and lowered her gaze. How could she help but look? Among stacks of folded taffeta, Swiss muslin, and pongee, baskets of thread, drawers overflowing with pressed lace, Ellie was the only thing of real beauty in the room. But she didn't know it. Not yet. Nora bent over the dress's hem and pulled the needle through the soft fabric. The silk was smooth to her touch, like the feel of water lapping her fingers on a warm day. Warm, like today. Too warm for September.

The darkness deepened. She squinted at the seam and cleared her throat. "Strange day, ain't it? Like the light's a-choking on the air."

Ellie let out a long breath. "Light can't choke. That's silly."

Nora swallowed her laugh as the needle dipped into the hem. "Then you explain it. Was bright as a bead this morning."

"Well, now it's as dark as … dark as … well, it's real dark."

"Yep, dark as dead coals after a campfire. That it is."

"And it stinks like old fire too."

Nora sat back on her heels, flicked the bottom of the dress, and watched as the silk settled into elegant folds. "Probably just Mr. Strom clearing his land. Don't pay it no never mind." She turned her daughter toward the mirror on the far side of the room.

For a moment, they each stared at the dress's reflection. Gray silk fell in a straight panel in the front and bunched in demure waves in the back. Simple, stylish, wasp-waisted with gigot sleeves.

"It's beautiful, ain't it?"

"The best I've done."

"Is it a traveling dress?"

"Yep."

"Who for? Not that snooty Mrs. Jensen?"

"Be nice."

"Is it?"

Nora sighed. "Not this one, punkin. This one is for someone special."

"Who? Tell me. Miss Winnie? Mrs. MacAllister? Miss Blackstone?"

"No."

"Someone new then? Someone who can pay for an expensive dress like this?"

"This dress I'm giving away."

Ellie gasped. "But, Mama, the others, they won't like that. They'll stop ordering dresses if they know you're sewing a dress for a regular person. You know they will. You always said ..."

"I know what I said."

"But ... then who ..."

Silence settled between them.

Finally, Nora stood and touched the silk with her fingertips. "You'll know when the time comes, child." Her voice lowered. "Everybody will know."

"If you say so, Mama." She rubbed a bit of lace between her fingers.

"Anyone would be beautiful in this dress."

Nora's gaze rose to capture her daughter's. "Clothes don't make the person, Ellie Jean. But people don't know that. Sometimes it's just the clothes they see. Sometimes they see truth only if it's dressed up pretty."

"Is that why you make dresses, Mama?"

Nora laughed. "Come here." She lifted a hand and helped Ellie down from the chair. Then she brushed back a stray hair from her daughter's forehead. "I make dresses so we can eat, and keep this house, and live. But this dress is different. It's special. And it's worth the risk."

Ellie's brows drew together in a knot. "Why?"

Nora ran her fingers over the dress's scalloped collar. "Because this here's a freedom dress. For someone who needs to be free."

Ellie pulled out of her mother's arms. "A dress can't set no one free."

"And air can't choke." Nora's eyes narrowed as her gaze traveled out the window. "But it does. It does today." She reached out and touched her daughter's chin, raising her face level with her own. She studied the clear blue eyes, the wrinkled brow, the bottom lip caught between her teeth. "There are times you see a hurt and make it better. You can be a friend. You can do for another, make their burden a wee bit lighter. But there are other times, dark times …" She paused, allowing the silence to grow long. "Sometimes all you can do is give someone a dress. You remember that, Ellie Jean."

"Okay, Ma—"

A sharp cry sliced through the window. Piercing. Fierce. Inhuman.

Nora spun toward the door.

Ellie grabbed her sleeve. "What's wrong with Meri, Mama?"

The horse screamed again.

In five long strides, Nora reached the front door and flung it open. She rushed onto the porch. A hissing rumble, like a thousand cats spitting from fence posts, assaulted Nora's senses. Flecks of gray floated in the dark air. For a moment, Nora stared at the gray specks, spinning, thickening, drifting onto the porch, the railing, her arms. She touched a flake, rubbing it between her fingers. Dust? No. Ash.

Another shriek pierced the air. Ellie grabbed her arm. Fingers dug into Nora's flesh.

"Mama, look."

Nora whirled. Burning heat slapped her face.

Fire charged across the western field toward her. Like a herd of stampeding bulls it snorted its smoke into the nightlike sky. Bucking, twisting, consuming the stalks of wheat in its path until she could see nothing but the flames and the blackness beyond them. Acres of burning wheat. A hundred acres. A thousand, devoured in a sea of undulating red.

Nora stared into the advancing darkness, smelling the bulls' bitter breath, captivated by their glowing eyes of flame. Suffocating warmth squeezed her chest, drove the air from her lungs. She gasped for breath and stumbled forward. The fire leapt higher, closer, red tongues licking clouds of ash.

"We have to run, Ellie. We have to go." The words came from somewhere beyond her. From some strange place that denied the nearness of the flame.

Ellie stood frozen, her face pale. Ash settled like fine powder on her nose, cheeks, eyelashes.

Nora leaned over and gripped her daughter's face between her hands, forcing Ellie's eyes to meet hers. "Meri's in the barn. We'll ride her out."

Ellie blinked.

Nora's gaze darted toward the town. Even from this distance, she could see fire snaking through the streets, sending up long trails of black smoke. Her stomach churned. Morrison Hotel, Hanson's Opera House, Cowan Drug Store. All gone. Her gaze swung north. There, Brennan's Lumber Mill spat shimmering flames into the sky. And beyond it, the Grindstone River gleamed. A mile, maybe more. But they could make it.

"Mama, are we gonna die?"

Nora grabbed Ellie's wrist and pulled her toward the barn. "Not today. We got a straight shot to the river."

Ellie yanked her arm away. "No, Mama, look."

"Come on."

"No. Not the river."

Nora slowed. Her eyes narrowed, stung. She wiped the ash from them and looked again. *Oh no ...* The river was burning. Flames swirled over its surface and shot ribbons of light into the blackness. *Sawdust from the mill. Oh God ...*

Then she heard it. Two sharp blasts of a train's whistle. The Number Four had come.

Nora squinted through the dimness, searching the west side of town for the shadowed speck that was the train. But the day was too black, the air too thick. The slithering path of tracks ran to the east of her farm. They could follow it, find the train.

"Hurry." She ran to the barn and threw the crossbar from the door. Heat scorched through the thin cotton of her dress. She dared not look back. Dared not see how close the fire had come.

The barn door swung open. Nora rushed through with Ellie behind her. "The bridle. Quickly."

Ellie raced toward the post.

Meri kicked the side of the stall. Her whinny pierced the smoke.

"Easy, girl." Nora edged into the stall. Her heart hammered in her ears.

Meri threw her head, eyes wild.

Ellie thrust the bridle into Nora's hands. The metal was hot against her skin, but not burning. Not yet. Nora shoved the bit into the horse's mouth and threw the reins over her withers.

She hitched up her skirt, then flung herself onto the horse's back. Meri's hoof scraped at the stall's floor. Nora hoisted Ellie in front of her. She kicked open the stall door, and in a breath, Meri surged through the opening, into the barn, out the main door.

There, not thirty yards before them, an inferno raged. Fire blazed from the farmhouse roof, shooting jagged shards of flame to the ground below. Nora sucked in her breath. Ash burned her throat. A moment later, the porch caved inward, losing itself in a ball of fire. Sparks flew upward, bursting with brilliant light.

Ellie sneezed. The sound mixed with the roar and cackle of flame.

Heat seared Nora's cheeks, crept down to her stomach, set her heart afire.

The horse spun and sped from the flames. The ground flashed beneath them. Nora's eyes fixed on the town. Through the darkness, the opry house blazed orange. The school crumbled to nothing but a shell spitting flame. And the depot ... even the depot was burning.

Nora leaned low over Ellie, her body protecting her child from the heat. She peered over her shoulder. Behind them, like a line of soldiers, the fire advanced, swords of flame shimmering, slashing. The branches of the old birch tree glowed red and orange against the sky. Flames crackled, even louder than the hiss of wind in her ears. A sound like bitter laughter, like the cries of devils. Her hands shook on the reins. Tears streamed across her temples. How could fire move so fast?

Another sharp whistle scraped her nerves. They'd never make it. The train was too far, the fire too swift.

Oh God, help ... Ellie ...

Heat blasted Nora's skin. Ellie's body shuddered against her. Her child, her beautiful girl ...

Nora focused again on the town, barely visible through the ash-stained air. Nearer, nearer, the fire at their heels, beside them, before them, ambushing her from every side. She swallowed, the taste of smoke sour in her mouth. With one hand, she rubbed the cinders from her eyes. They were almost there. The horse swung north, racing now along the town's edge.

From the corner of her vision, the Presbyterian church burned like an immense funeral pyre. The steeple flared upward, then crumbled into the flames below. The wind rose like a cyclone, tearing at her blouse, scraping against her eyes. The sky turned black. The air thickened.

Before her, the mercantile's walls crumbled, revealing the store's contents before the whole building burst into flame. She reined toward the tracks. The ties burned in stripes of orange flame.

Ahead and to the left, the livery barn burst into a ball of flame. A horse spurted from the burning door. He galloped wildly down the roadway, his tail held out like a smoking musket, the sound of his hoofbeats lost in the roar of flames.

The blacksmith stumbled from the livery just as the outer walls melted behind him. "Jonas." The name tore from her lips.

The man looked up. Then fell. And the fire consumed him.

Nora ripped her gaze from the sight. Her eyes teared as she squinted through the smoke. Ahead, red flame belched from the depot. And beside it, like a black shadow, the train was pulling away.

Terror stuck in Nora's sternum. Her heels dug into Meri's sides. Faster. Faster. Was that her voice screeching in her ears, ripping through the dryness in her throat?

The fire roared closer, blocking her vision of the town, until she could see nothing but smoke billowing, rails burning in fiery lines, and waves of ash falling so thick that she could taste nothing else, smell nothing but the acrid stench. In a moment, the whole world reduced to a tunnel of smoke, ash, and fire, with hope in the form of a retreating train engine, moving backward along the tracks.

Then in the dimness, figures emerged from the smoke. Screams pierced the darkness. Townspeople ran, dashed toward the train. A man with a bundle in his arms bolted toward her, his face obscured by ash. The bundle wailed. The blanket fell away. Nora's heart slammed against her throat. She reached out. But the man stumbled and fell behind, the baby's cry lost in the roar of flames.

For a moment, she tried to turn back, but Meri wouldn't slow. The horse was wild now, racing with fear as its whip, terror as the spurs that dug into its sides. Wind whipped Nora's hair as the air scorched her lungs. Ellie threw up her arm, shielding her head against the embers that spun past them. Pinpricks of fire jabbed into Nora's face, her hands, her legs. She gritted her teeth against the pain, her eyes focused on the train. They were gaining on it. Closer, closer. They could make it still.

Fire licked at the train's sides. Hooves thundered beneath them. The sound pounded in her head, growing louder, drowning out the shouts of the townspeople, obscuring the inferno's howl.

Meri pulled behind the train, then drew even with the last car. Arms reached from the window openings. White eyes stared from blackened faces. Hands flailed toward them. Mouths shouted words she couldn't hear, couldn't understand. Fingers grabbed for Ellie.

"Mama!" Ellie's cry sank like a dagger in Nora's heart. For a moment she clutched her daughter close, smelled the ash in her hair, felt the warmth of her body against her skin.

Then Nora dropped the reins, reached around Ellie's waist, and thrust the girl toward the train's window.

Hands grabbed Ellie and dragged her inside.

Arms stretched toward Nora. Someone pulled at her sleeve. Meri swerved. The fingers slipped away.

And Nora knew nothing but the sharp embrace of the flames.

2

A single word, a prayer, devoured in the roar of fire. A cry no one heard, least of all the horse and rider who disappeared into the smoke.

For one moment, Josef had believed that God heard him. Out of the darkness, the horse appeared with two figures shining like angels on its back. Salvation had come for Emma Ann. Hope flamed brighter than the fire as the horse raced toward him. He lifted Emma. A woman's arms reached down. But then he stumbled and fell. The moment vanished, the horse with it, leaving nothing but the darkness, the flames, and the terror swelling like a black current in his heart.

Josef clutched his baby close, sheltering her against his chest, feeling the rapid beat of her heart against him. His free hand pressed into the hot ash. Heat burned through the denim covering his knees. Fire leapt around him, like the walls of a cage he could not escape. So, he knelt there, his head bowed, his arms trembling. *Get up. Run.* The commands slithered through him. He blinked, drew a breath, felt the air burn in his lungs.

"Josef!" He heard the scream, like a dart piercing the darkness.

"Maggie?" He raised his head.

And she was there, kneeling beside him. Her face, once flawless, now smeared with black ash, glowed in the flash of fire. Twin trails shone on her cheeks where tears had fled and dried. Her hair, black with cinders, whipped in the wind. Her hand, hot, fierce, gripped his arm. He saw the ring there, a simple silver band. His ring. His wife. His love.

"I'm sorry." He mouthed the words, his eyes searching hers.

She turned away. But not before he saw the horror, the desperation in her gaze.

He reached up, touched the softness of her neck, ran his ash-stained fingers over her cheek. His Maggie. Could she read the love in his eyes? The sorrow? The fear?

She turned her head, her lips brushing his palm. Her eyes closed. Her mouth moved, and he read the words formed there. "I know."

Then the darkness turned black. A billow of smoke rolled over them, blinding, choking him. Emma shuddered in his arms. He huddled over her, waiting for the blackness to lift.

It didn't.

A fireball exploded above him, illuminating the smoke in a single flash. Then another. He staggered to his feet. Maggie's hand found his. He plunged forward, through the smoke, through the ash. A line of fire appeared at his feet. A railroad tie, burning. He hurried forward. A second. A third. He picked up speed, following the tracks. Hot wind tore at his skin.

The world condensed to a cave of blowing smoke, lit only by lines of fire and an occasional burst of flame in the air above. Still, he pushed through, fighting for each breath, each step a victory over wind and ash. They would make it. They had to.

Eerie flashes reflected off the smoke. Heat seared his flesh, blistered his skin. His derby hat flew off, bursting into flame above him. Sparks showered his shoulders and lit the baby's blanket on fire. He smothered the flame. His wife's hand slipped from his. The baby twisted in his arms. He clutched her tighter. Her back stiffened, and he knew she was screaming, though he couldn't hear the sound.

"Shh, Emma, shh." Worthless words, spoken anyway. Spoken to the darkness. He held her face in the hollow of his neck and raced forward, toward the place where the train should have been. The baby's chest heaved against his. He stroked her back.

The depot appeared before him. A husk filled with fire. And beside it, the train was gone.

No! God help us.

Josef stumbled, slowed. A vision filled his mind. Barren dirt, rock, shallow, muddy water. Three acres of it, cursed by the town as an eyesore. But it just might save them. If there was time.

Maybe. Just maybe …

He swerved right.

Another flash illuminated the air. Maggie ran along the tracks. He reached toward her.

"Make for the gravel pit." His shout dissolved in the wind.

Maggie didn't turn. Didn't even look his way.

He moved toward her. The light faded. "Maggie!"

A wagon wheel emerged from the darkness. It spun toward him, its spokes on fire. Turning, twirling. Heat, thick and smothering, rolled over Josef's face. He coughed, choking on ash. The wheel vanished in the smoke.

Then like a monster shedding flame, the wagon leapt from the blackness, three wheels spinning fire, one gone. It flew at him, pushed by a wind that ripped at his sleeves, tore open the buttons at his collar. He jumped aside, shielding Emma with both arms. A flash of fire burst above him. Embers shimmered down. And in the moment of light, he saw her. His wife, struck by the wagon's end, hit and pulled under. It flipped and pinned her, dragging her beneath like a rag doll. The wind drove it further, Maggie with it, caught, pulled into the darkness. A shout wrenched from his lips. Blood pounded in his temples. He turned, raced after the wagon. It tumbled down the short embankment beside the tracks.

He slid down the rubble. "I'm coming. Hold on, Maggie."

The wagon tipped and wedged against the trunk of a tall pine, its branches already burning. Light flamed over the ground, over Maggie, crushed beneath the wagon's side. Breath snatched from Josef's chest as he flung himself toward her. He grabbed the wood with his free arm, yanking, clawing at the burning planks. Heat seared his skin. He gripped the wood harder.

Maggie clutched at him, her fingers digging into his arm.

His hand shook. The wagon would not give, would not move. He needed two arms, but the baby, he couldn't let her go. Maggie tugged at his arm. But he wouldn't look at her; he didn't dare. He rose. His heels dug into the ash as he pulled, pushed, lifted until the veins bulged in his arm. His foot slipped, bringing him to his knees.

Maggie gripped his face, forcing him to look at her. His eyes caught hers, black, with fire reflecting in the irises. But there was no terror there now. Only resolve. Only sorrow. And forgiveness like a cool wave dimming the fire.

"Save the baby." The words formed on her lips. "Go."

"No." Fury flamed within him, burning fear, burning reason. He ripped at the wagon again, his fingers bloody, torn.

Maggie slapped his face.

Pain stung his cheek, tipping him backward. Three fingers rose before his vision, and behind them, her eyes fixed on his. Understanding slithered through him. For three years they tried to get pregnant. Three years of sadness, followed by nine months of hope, and six months of heaven. He shook his head. It couldn't end like this. God wouldn't allow it.

Josef's gaze darted to the baby. Her eyes were closed, her breath ragged.

"Josef—" Maggie's voice pierced the fire's scream, stabbed into him. She pointed.

His eyes followed. There, a sea of fire rolled toward them, swallowing the smoke in its path. And with it, the wind rose to a cyclone.

"Save the baby. For me." She pushed him, shoved him away.

"Please."

The fire roared closer.

He stumbled back, away from the fire's edge.

Maggie covered her face. The wagon shook, broke free. It rolled over her just as the fire enveloped it in a rush of flame.

"Maggie ..." Her name died on his lips. He turned away as ash fell like gray tears, obscuring his vision.

Emma clutched his neck. She trembled against him, her tiny fingers pressing into his skin. He held her tight and stood. Then he ran, with his heart still caught beneath the wagon's fire, burning in the blackness of his pain.

3

Redemption came in the form of a child, in the form of Ellie Jean falling through the train's window and into her arms. A girl to protect, to hold on to, to make up for a sin too terrible to recall. A chance to save someone's daughter. A chance to do right. For Nora's daughter. For another's child. It should have been Rakel.

God …

Arla drew Ellie toward her, her arms a shelter against the heat, the girl a shield against thoughts far more threatening.

"Mama. Mama, come back." Ellie's whimper twisted through Arla's heart.

"Shh, it'll be all right." Arla brushed her hand through the girl's hair. Hair covered in ash, light hair, so different from Rakel's. *What have I done?*

Arla touched her lips to Ellie's forehead. Her gloved finger traced a line of tears on the girl's cheek. "Don't think about it, child. Don't cry." Her voice lowered to a whisper and was lost in the rattle of the train's wheels.

Soot-covered bodies pressed around her as the train continued to move north. Two dozen people, three dozen, crammed together in a space meant for half that many. Elbows jabbed into her ribs. A shoulder dug into hers. She pulled away, pushing against the side of the car, feeling the warmth through the thick metal, the shudder of the train moving backward. The scent of sweat and ash assaulted her. A sickening smell, like manure, but bitter.

The clatter of the car mixed with the rumble of fire outside, and for a moment Arla could no longer hear the sounds of harsh breathing, could no longer discern the choking sobs that rose from somewhere behind her. Heat swirled through the car in waves, until the air shimmered with it.

Arla brushed flecks of ash from Ellie's hair, focusing on the gray specks, and remembering, for an instant, the look on Nora's face as she disappeared into the flames. Sorrow, resignation, peace. Pain stabbed through Arla's chest.

She swallowed, tasting cinders on her tongue. Beside her, Mr. Warner clung to his young son, and beyond them, old Widow McMurray held a frayed handkerchief to her lips. Charlotte Johnson, with ruffled pantalets poking from beneath a torn frock, sniffled at her feet. And in the aisle, Jane Tew and six of her children huddled on the floor, their faces pale beneath a layer of ash. Beyond them sat one Fraser boy and the stylish Mr. Jensen, his velvet-trimmed coat for once imperfect. Those were the ones she recognized, familiar faces scattered in a blur of crushing humanity. Survivors. A remnant from those left behind.

Sweat beaded on Arla's forehead. She dabbed it with her sleeve. A dark smear appeared across the broadcloth, marring the once-perfect cream. She turned her arm until the mark was hidden against the folds of her skirt.

A whistle's blast, faint and sharp, sounded ahead. A murmur raced through the car. "Brennan's Lumber Mill. The mill is burning."

And Arla knew that now all Hinckley was lost.

Rakel ...

The window beside her shattered. Glass sprayed over her arms. A woman screamed. Arla turned, protecting Ellie from the flying shards as a fresh wave of heat washed through the car. A body flew into the back of her seat, flinging her forward. Her shoulder jammed into the seat in front.

Ellie gasped.

"Are you hurt?"

"No."

Another window broke. And a third, exploding inward. Shattered glass spun through the air, reflecting a million points of light. A wail rose from across the aisle, followed by a curse. She pressed her hand over Ellie's ear.

Then the world turned black. Sheets of darkness rolled through the windows and obscured the faces within. And for that moment, nothing existed but the heat, the voices, and the trembling body held against her. *Rakel was this size. Once. Not so long ago.*

A lantern flickered and roared to life at the front of the car. Then another. Shadows swirled over the walls, creating a wicked dance of darkness and light over the people around her. Familiar faces altered, distorted. Arla glanced away.

A burst of light flashed through the windows. Outside, branches flamed, throwing chunks of cinder at the passing train. A giant pine whirled in the fire. Then it fell, its trunk devoured in the smoke. The tracks turned, revealing a dozen lines of flame, upright, leaning into the wind, burning in the blackness.

"The forest is on fire."

Arla heard the words spoken in a hush behind her. Wind broke a thick branch, hurling it toward the train. The car shuddered as the branch hit and sprayed a bouquet of sparks through the windows.

Then another flash.

Arla's stomach heaved. There, in the light, a family of four raced toward the train. Their faces were black with ash. Their mouths were open, shouting, though the fire swallowed the sound. An arm extended. The train passed. And smoke filled Arla's vision.

She closed her eyes. *Why? Why did some live and some die?* She touched her face, wiped the grit from her cheeks.

Words became a jumble around her, meaningless sounds dulled by the rumble of the train and the constant slap of debris hitting the sides. The car quaked and groaned. Arla opened her eyes and pulled Ellie closer. A bowler hat knocked into her, then spun to the floor and was crushed underfoot. A hand grabbed her blouse. A man leaned over her. Shadows trickled over his face, making his eyes wild.

"Morphine." His breath washed over her like old cigar smoke. "I need morphine."

"I have none."

He yanked at her sleeve, tearing the cloth. "We're all going to die. It's the end of the world. The end, I say."

She wrenched her arm free. "Control yourself, sir."

He wavered, swaying on his feet. "Morphine. Help me."

Ellie stared up at him. Her body trembled against Arla's chest.

"I'll die before I burn."

Arla shoved the man away. He tumbled into Widow McMurray, muttered another curse, then fell back to his seat. Arla smoothed her hand down Ellie's back. The dress was too big for her, too fine. A strange garment for a child fleeing the fire. "Don't pay any attention to him, Eleanor." Her mouth brushed the girl's ear. "Fool's got smoke for brains. Not a bit of cinder on him. Come straight from Minneapolis, unless I miss my guess."

A lantern shattered. Half the car plunged again into darkness. Sparks made pinpricks of light on the far side. Then the smoke thinned. There, outside the far window, a farmhouse glowed with flame. And beyond it, fields shimmered with red light.

"The Stroms' place ..." The words fell from Arla's lips. A lump formed in her chest. In her mind she saw them—Josef, Maggie, the new baby. What was the child's name? She couldn't remember. She rubbed her eyes, trying to erase the vision. Maybe they escaped. Maybe ...

The train plunged on. The farmhouse disappeared, giving way to an ocean of flaming trees, whirling in a ghostly dance. Branches, like emaciated arms, reached toward her, burning, always burning. Hinckley lay behind them now. Sandstone would come ahead. But now, there was only the forest, and the fields, all caught in the rage of fire.

A sound, high pitched and strangled, echoed through the car. Wood scraping metal. An eerie song, sung to the wind, with lyrics of death and shame. The walls creaked around them, playing a discordant tune to the branches flying outside.

Ellie whimpered.

Arla held her tighter. *Lord in heaven* ... the words clogged in her mind, turned bitter, acrid. For a moment she held her breath, willing time to stop, reverse, allow her to relive the last hour. But time raced on, clacking with the sound of the train's wheels, roaring with the wind that mocked their escape.

A fiery twig spun through the window and clawed at Arla's sleeve. She batted the branch to the floor. Flame flared, twisting into two eyes, staring, condemning. Then the fire died.

Arla shivered. It knew. The fire knew she shouldn't have escaped. Knew what she had done. Bile rose in her throat.

Could God really forgive? Perhaps. But Rakel would not. Could not. Not anymore.

"I'm afraid, Mrs. Anderson." Ellie's voice broke through her thoughts.

Arla pressed her cheek against Ellie's forehead. "So am I." Her whisper fell, unheard. "So am I. God forgive me."

Then another voice rose from beside her, a voice louder than the children crying, than the man still whimpering for morphine to end it all. "Dear Lord, keep us safe from the fires outside these windows, and from the fires inside our hearts."

Heat flushed Arla's cheeks. Jane couldn't know. No one knew.

Jane Tew raised her head, and for one brief instant, her eyes caught the lantern light and pierced Arla.

Then her head bowed again. "And protect our loved ones who are left behind."

Arla swallowed, a taste more bitter than ash filling her senses. Prayer had always been a comfort, a refuge, a solid place to stand and know that right would triumph over wrong. To know that she was in that right. But now ... She brushed her fingers through Ellie's hair.

"Save our husbands, our wives, our mothers, fathers, children."

The prayer penetrated her, until she could hear nothing but the words and the sound of her hand, rubbing, rubbing the soft silk over Ellie's back.

Ellie quivered against her, but she didn't cry. Not anymore. *Brave child. Good girl. Rakel had been—* Arla buried the thought.

The train slowed. Smoke blotted out the vision of fire and blanketed the world in darkness.

Jane's voice softened. "Amen, Lord. Amen in Jesus."

The door opened. Conductor Harry Powers stepped into the car. Shadows obscured his face. His gaze swept over them, lingering on the Tew family on the floor, on the women at the back of the car, skipping over Arla and Ellie.

A voice burst from behind her. "Why are we stopping? Are the tracks gone? We're all going to die." The words dissolved into a breathless groan.

The conductor pulled off his hat. "Yes, sir, we are all going to die." The answer boomed through the car, drowning the sounds of wind and fire. "But God willing, we will not die today."

"But we're stopping."

Conductor Powers pulled at his walrus mustache. "Stopping? Who said we were stopping?" He smiled down at Jane. "In fact, if you don't mind, ma'am, you could pray for Beach and McLaughlin. They're going to need it."

Jane raised her head, her gaze steady, unflinching. "The brakemen?"

Powers ran his fingers through his hair. "They're riding outside the train, ma'am. With nothing between them and the flames but a couple of lanterns."

A gasp shimmered through the car.

"With the train going backwards, we have no other light but theirs. On their signal alone we know the bridges are safe to cross."

"You mean?" The question escaped Arla in a whisper.

"The bridges are burning."

Silence shot through the car, punctuated by a loud wail.

Jane turned toward Arla. "Shall we pray then, Sister Anderson?"

Arla's breath stopped halfway to her lungs. She couldn't pray. She couldn't. Her prayer would doom them all.

A shrill whistle sliced through the car.

And Arla could breathe again.

Powers cleared his throat. "It means this bridge is safe. For now."

The train lurched forward, then picked up speed.

"Arla?" Jane raised her eyebrows.

Arla bowed her head. Her cheek brushed Ellie's hair. She opened her mouth. But no words came. Instead, her chest heaved. Her breath rasped in her ears. Her lips clamped shut.

Then Jane's voice rose again. "Keep those brave men safe, Lord. Let their lights shine out into the darkness."

And so it went, with Jane praying, the children crying, and Arla clutching Ellie as the train slowed, the whistle sounded, and the train began moving again. Minute after minute, mile after mile, until dark, thick smoke replaced the flames outside the windows.

And then the train stopped.

No whistle came.

Arla held her breath. The others grew silent. Time stretched and twanged across her nerves.

"It's the end, I tell you." A man's voice shrilled from the back of the car.

"Hush." Mr. Warner raised his hand. "Listen."

The car grew quiet again. Feet shuffled against wood. Someone coughed. Voices floated from the car beyond, murmurs, nearly lost in the rumble of wind outside. "Kettle River. Bridge. One hundred and fifty feet in the air. We'll never make it."

Arla leaned forward. Ellie turned in her arms and slithered toward the window. She poked her head through the hole in the jagged glass.

"Eleanor!"

"It's burning, Mrs. Anderson. Burning big enough to see without no lanterns."

Arla joined Ellie at the window. Her eyes searched ahead of them, peering through the smoke and darkness. Then she saw it. The long wooden expanse hovering above a river hidden in smoke. The forest on fire on either side. And the wooden supports burning in long, thin flames. The bridge would never support their weight. But they couldn't go back. Couldn't go over.

Then a whistle.

Dread settled in Arla's gut.

Someone shrieked.

The train started again, creeping, inching over the bridge, until Arla could almost hear the rails breaking beneath them. One yard, two, ten. Smoke rolled through the window. Embers glimmered in the grayness. Wheels turned. The bridge moaned. Ellie's fingers pressed into Arla's arm. Faces stared. No one spoke as bodies rocked with the sway of the train. Mr. Warner pushed across the aisle and watched out the window.

The train crept onward.

A sharp crack resounded through the car. Arla squeezed her eyes shut. Words welled up within her, spilling over. "Not like this, God. Not here. I'm sorry. So sorry. Don't make them pay for me." Her whisper flickered and was swallowed in the waiting silence.

Arla opened her eyes and counted to ten, eleven, twelve. And still the bridge held.

The smoke lessened until she could see, down, down, almost to the river. She turned away. Thirteen, fourteen, fifteen …

"We've made it." A shout rang through the car, followed by a bubble of laughter. The Tew children jumped to their feet and threw their arms around each other. Jane grinned, tears shining on her cheeks. Someone whooped. Ellie giggled.

Arla's gaze swept through the car. White teeth in black faces. A crazy sight. Crazy, and beautiful.

"Look." Mr. Warner pointed out the window. Arla leaned over until she could see the tracks behind them. Flames shot to the sky.

A moment later, the bridge swayed, twisted. And fell. God had heard her prayer.

4

I am caught, captured in a cage of fire. Red and orange and searing blackness. It lunges at me and laughs. It jeers at my helplessness. A black burning. Flame and fury and sharp agony. Darkness eating away at my flesh until pain and nightmare mix, and I can feel no more.

Tomorrow is gone. Yesterday flees. Only this moment remains, then it too burns. The air rushes from my lungs. Abandons me. So I will die here.

Yet I feel no fear. Only the rushing of the wind burning through me. Only the quiet whisper of memory. Only the silent relief that it ends here.

I would welcome it, but for her. But for the one face that holds me to this world, and beckons me to remember, to take one more breath. To dare to face more than flame and fire ...

But the fire is too strong.

It devours me.

And I am lost in searing blackness.

***

If it weren't for the cow, Josef would have believed it was a dream. A nightmare brought on by too much sun and too little breakfast. But even in his wildest musings, he would not dream of the Larsens' cow standing knee-deep in water in the gravel pit while the world was consumed in flame. He wouldn't dream the piercing shriek of his baby girl, the burning heat, the look on Maggie's face just as ... just as ... He closed his eyes.

Water splashed over his head and back. He jolted upright. His eyes flew open. Water dribbled down his chin. He turned to find the minister's wife standing behind him.

"Get to pouring, Mr. Strom." Her voice rose over the thunder of the fire. "No time to waste dreaming or fainting."

"I wasn't neither dreamin' nor faintin', Mrs.—" He'd forgotten her name.

She pushed back a strand of matted hair and tucked it behind her ear. Shadows of fire played off her features, making her look like a creature from some strange nightmare. She leaned toward him. "If you don't want the skin singed off you or the little one, you'd better be getting wet. Pour the water." Her hands formed a bowl and made the motions of scooping and pouring.

Josef blinked twice.

"On the baby, Mr. Strom. Keep the baby wet."

Josef glanced down at his daughter. Her face was red and wrinkled, her mouth opened in a cry he couldn't hear. He touched her cheek with his fingertip. It felt hot, dry. Water. Yes, water. He leaned over and dipped his hand in the water, then smoothed it over Emma's head and chest. Her eyes opened. She gulped and stared up at him. More. She needed more. From somewhere behind and above him, fire exploded in the air, reflecting in the roundness of her eyes. He scooped water faster, wetting her arms, legs, back.

"Yourself, too." The minister's wife placed her hand on his arm and smiled. "You'll be all right now. Just keep up with the water." Her voice, still raised to a shout, grated in his ears. "Everything will be fine."

Fine? The word jabbed at him as she turned away. *Fine?* Nothing would be fine again. Ever. "Maggie didn't make it." The statement sliced the air between them.

The minister's wife glanced back at him, her eyes dark, silent, as if reading his thoughts. "Hope is not lost yet, Mr. Strom."

"I saw her die." The last image of his wife flashed through his mind. "Maggie's dead."

The minister's wife pressed her lips together until they formed a thin line. "Many are." The words sounded strained, forced. "But you are not. Nor is your child."

"How can anyone survive this?" He flung his arm upward, toward the town.

"God always leaves a remnant."

"What?"

Her features softened. "We are the remnant. We will survive."

He gripped her arm. "Why? Why us? Why me?"

"Don't you know?" For a moment, her eyes pierced his, then she removed his hand from her arm and moved away. "The water, Mr. Strom. Keep pouring the water." Her final words shot over her shoulder toward him.

Josef knelt and splashed more water over baby Emma and himself. Mud drizzled down his cheek and dried there. He squatted lower, dipping Emma's legs and back into the pool of mud. He caressed her with the water. Her downy hair, her soft arms, her chest, rising and falling with each steady breath. Why did some live, and some die? Why would a cow survive, and a mother not? What had they done to deserve this?

Josef's eyes were drawn to the darkness above and around him. Blackness and heat and bursts of flame. That was all that Hinckley had become. And here he sat, safe in the gravel pit, while the whole world collapsed around him. So dark. So hot. With the wind howling and fire whipping the sky. And in the middle, a three-acre hole, fed all summer by an underground spring. Ugly. And beautiful.

He glanced around him. Here and there, rocks jutted from the shallow water. The axle of a broken cart tilted across the water's surface. And scattered in groups across the gravel pit were perhaps a hundred survivors, huddled together and pouring handfuls of water over their neighbors' heads and backs. He squinted at a group close to him. Grim faces, covered in ash and soot. Faces obscured in the darkness and unrecognizable.

Josef sank lower into the warm water. Fire reflected off its surface. It sparkled in black waves, splashed with flashes of light. He listened past the sound of fire, listened for the sound of voices in the dimness. None came. Only the moo of the cow, the bark of a dog, the crash of a building falling into flame.

Emma twisted in his arms. He scooped more water and poured it over her. His fingers lingered on her hair, her shoulder, the soft place just behind her ear. She looked up at him, her eyes now wide. Wide, innocent, and unafraid.

"Shh, baby girl. It'll be over soon." He spoke to himself, too softly for her to hear.

A chubby hand patted his chin. Emma smiled.

Josef tried to smile back, but instead his eyes watered. His lips trembled. The baby could smile because she didn't know, didn't realize that their lives had changed forever. She didn't know her mama was gone. What would they do? How would they live?

Emma's brow furrowed.

Josef wet his hand again and smoothed it over her forehead. She was beautiful, precious. The most beautiful thing he had ever seen. She deserved better than this. Better than a mama lost forever. She deserved sunshine and flowers and the sweet smell of rain. She deserved to be more than a remnant.

Heat flared in Josef's chest. Fierce, agonizing, hotter than the fire. How could God do this to him? To her? Did he not see? Could he not hear? What kind of God could look into the innocent face of this child and allow her mother to burn in the flames? It wasn't right. His fist clenched beneath the surface of the water until his fingers dug into his palm. How could there be a God in heaven? There certainly didn't seem to be one on earth. Hell had come, with no one to stop it.

He tilted back his head, his eyes searching the sky. Black ash rained on his face like hot spittle.

How could you do this to us? How could you?

No one answered.

Probably because no one was there.

* * *

Minutes melted together in a long line until at last the fire moved past. Eventually, the sky lightened. Those in the gravel pit waited, breathless. No one spoke. No one moved. Then one lone body ambled to the edge of the pit. All eyes followed. He crawled up the embankment and stood at the upper edge. For one long moment, the air trembled. Josef shivered. Then the call came.

"It's all right. The fire's passed."

Hushed murmurs trickled through the crowd. Someone shouted. Then everyone moved at once.

Josef watched as people scrambled up the slopes of the pit, then stood at the top like posts frozen in winter. Slowly, they thawed and came to life. Women chattered, families hugged, men shouted and stumbled in every direction.

Emma woke, whimpered, then started to squall. Josef touched her forehead. It felt cool, moist, normal. He ran his hand over her arms. She yelled all the louder. He dipped her in the water. She shrieked. He held her close. She struggled against him. Her feet flailed. Her back stiffened. Panic rose in Josef's chest.

"Here." Something cool hit his hand. He glanced down. Half of a hollowed-out muskmelon pressed into his palm. He pushed it away.

Someone shook his shoulder. "It's milk, man. Milk."

Josef turned. His eyes caught those of the minister. "What?"

"The missus says to try this." The minister thrust the melon under his nose. White liquid filled the bottom of the husk.

Josef glanced over the minister's shoulder. There, the minister's wife sat calmly milking the Larsens' cow. One by one the hollow melons were filled and given to the line of children standing beside her. Briefly, she looked up. Her eyes caught his. "Give her the milk, Mr. Strom. She's hungry enough to take it."

Josef pushed the melon against the curled, wailing lips of his daughter. Milk wet her mouth. Her tongue flicked out. The shrieking stopped. Her hand moved toward the melon. He tipped more milk into her mouth. She gulped, sputtered, and swallowed. Liquid splashed down her chin and chest. He settled onto a fat rock and tried again. And again. And again. For an hour, it seemed, he sat there, tipping the melon and watching as some drizzled into Emma's mouth and more dribbled down her front. Eventually, she pushed the melon away and snuggled into his chest. Only then did Josef look around him. The minister and his wife were gone, the pit emptied of people and livestock.

Josef rose and crawled from the gravel pit. His eyes stung with the sight before him. Smoke rose from piles of ash. Houses, trees, buildings, sidewalks, all had vanished. Only the roundhouse remained. Yesterday, Hinckley had been a thriving town. Today, it was gone.

Movement caught the corner of Josef's vision. He turned. There, like an image from a dream, a figure rose from the rubble. For a moment, the person stood still.

Josef called out.

But the figure turned away and disappeared in the lingering smoke.

5

It was her. It had to be.

Nearly two weeks ago Lars Jensen had fled Hinckley with fire at his heels. But now, he was back and standing at the edge of a long trench. He leaned over and tapped his toe into the emaciated corpse at his feet. The body was shrunken, black as coal, just like the dozens of others that lined the death trench to his left and right. His head throbbed with the gruesome images—blackened skulls with hollow eyes, withered limbs like branches of old wood left when the stove has gone cold, twisted torsos with nothing left to tell whether they were once man or woman. Bodies stacked up in a ghastly row. And farther down, a wheelbarrow filled with remains.

Most had been buried already, last week, the week before. But some still remained. Enough. Lars pulled a handkerchief from his pocket and pressed it to his lip. Fat flies buzzed in a lazy circle around his head. He scowled and swished them away. How could flies survive the fire when so many people had not? But life was like that. It wasn't always the good who lived and the bad who died. Death had no favorites. Good thing.

A breeze stirred the ash and sent gray bits swirling over the corpse before him. He stared down at the unrecognizable features. No eyes. No nose. No hair. Nothing that would distinguish it from a hundred others.

It should disgust him to see his wife like that. But it didn't. It was too strange, too inhuman. Yet, it was Agnes all right. It had to be. That was her wedding ring on the thing that was once a finger.

A hand touched his shoulder. He turned to find Josef Strom standing beside him.

"That her?"

Lars pulled the hat from his head. "'Fraid so."

"Sorry to hear it." Strom spoke as if each word were a strain. "Found her on the tracks. Looked to be running for the train. Didn't make it." His voice dropped. "Lots of folks didn't."

Lars nodded.

Strom waited.

Lars rubbed the velvet trim on his top hat. He ought to say something. Say how he had tried to come back for her but couldn't, how he had fought through wind and fire to reach her. How he had striven to save her but failed in the end. But none of that was true. He hadn't tried, he hadn't come back, he hadn't even cared. Even now, as he stared down at the remains of what used to be his wife, he couldn't find the right emotions. Instead, he felt nothing. Nothing at all.

"Hard to lose a wife. Good woman."

Good woman? Hardly. Simpering, stupid thing. She'd only married him for his money. He'd come a long way from the little boy who used to hawk newspapers on the street corners of New York. From the boy whom no one noticed. They'd toss him a coin and grab a paper. But no one looked him in the eye. No one smiled. Or patted his shoulder. Or called him by name. But they asked now. They noticed now. And everyone knew his name. Or at least they knew the name he'd given them. Lars Jensen. A strong name. A good name. A normal name.

Lars brushed a bit of ash from his sleeve. Yes, he'd come a long way. In miles and in money. Here, he was the big fish. He was important. Somebody. Sometimes, Agnes forgot that. Still, he had loved her once, when they were younger, before he'd found out what kind of woman she was.

He placed his handkerchief over his fingers, then bent down and carefully removed the ring from his wife's hand. He wrapped the ring in the cloth and dropped it into his pocket.

"You want we should put her here with the others?"

Lars glanced at Strom. He'd always thought that the man was rather an idiot, lumbering around his farm with that old hat smashed down on his head and nary a word for a neighbor. Even at church people couldn't get more than a "how do" out of him. Yet here he was, stringing together a number of sentences in a row. Maybe the fire changed folks. Maybe things would be different now. Lars set his hat back on his head and adjusted the fur lining of his collar. "Yes, that would do nicely." He smiled. Agnes would have hated that, being laid to rest in a group trench like some kind of common refuse. But she deserved it. And no better.

"Found another body near her." Strom motioned toward another burned corpse a few feet away.

"Who?"

Strom shook his head. "Can't tell."

A chill pimpled Lars' skin. "My daughter?"

Strom shrugged.

Lars held his breath and stepped over to the other body. He squatted down to get a closer look. Relief washed through him. "I can't tell. I don't know."

Strom sighed. "Lots like that. Too burned to tell."

Lars stared down at the blackened mass. "Did they find a necklace on her, a sterling silver cross?"

Strom shook his head. "Didn't find anything. But that don't mean nothing. Grave robbers, or I ought to say body robbers. Come already, from all around. It's a wonder they didn't get your wife's ring, too."

Lars almost reached out and touched the body. Almost, but he drew his hand back. Could that be his daughter? The one he had held as a baby, the one he had taught to fish, to tie knots, to shoot just like a boy.

The one who had grown up to be too much like her mother. Weak willed and foolish. It could be her. The body was the right size. And she had been with her mother.

Ah, Winnie. Why didn't you run when you first saw the flames? It was your mother's fault, wasn't it? Everything was always her fault.

Lars coughed and turned his head from the sight. The Lord gave and the Lord took away. Who was he to question the will of the Almighty? That was what they said, anyway. And that's what he would say too, if anyone asked.

He stood. Maybe it was better this way. Maybe now he could truly start again. Just him and Leif. A man and his son. That's the way it ought to be. With no one interfering. No one knowing the hidden past he had left behind.

Lars turned up his collar and moved back from the trench.

***

Arla stepped from the train into a world gray with ash. No red, no blue, no yellow. Only gray. Gray sky, gray earth, gray future.

After two weeks, she and Ellie had returned to Hinckley. But what a return. If it weren't for the roundhouse, she may have never believed this was her hometown. She'd think she'd stepped out into some gray purgatory. No sidewalks. No street corners. Only the burned stumps of telegraph poles, and a mass of charred rubble.

The opera house where she used to go with her husband before he died of the influenza, the church where she was married, the schoolhouse, Brennan's Store, the town hall—its great bell lying now in the ruins—the depot, the milliner's shop. Everything that represented the way life used to be was gone. Hardly a chimney or a gutted wall remained upright. Only the Eastern Minnesota Railroad roundhouse stood as if untouched, the paint on its sides barely blistered. A single building surrounded by ash.

A chill ran over Arla's arms. She breathed deeply and choked on the sharp smell of ash and something more. Sweet. Sickly. Her stomach clenched. Death.

Arla dug in her handbag and found a lace handkerchief. It fluttered in the breeze as she pressed it to her nose. White lace, stark and feminine, a shocking contrast to the world of gray.

To her left stood rows upon rows of dingy tents, and beyond, a line of railway cars sat piled high with fresh timber. Men, hunch-shouldered and filthy, drove mules with carts full of supplies. A cow wandered down what had once been Main Street. And over it all hung an eerie quietness, broken only by the ring of hammers, the wheeze of grinding saws, and the soft chug of the train behind them.

Most women had not yet returned to Hinckley. Most stayed nestled in refugee houses in Duluth and St. Paul. But not Arla. Hinckley was where she belonged. Where she'd always belonged. *Even now?* The question skittered through her mind. She straightened her shoulders. *Yes, now. Especially now.*

Ellie sniffed.

Arla reached out and pulled the girl to her side.

"It … it's awful, ain't it?"

"What's gone is past." Arla straightened her back. "Hinckley will rebuild, and so will we. You and I. Together. Don't you fret." She squeezed Ellie's shoulder. Ellie had no one now, no family, no relatives, no one but Arla. Yes, all they had was each other. And Arla owed it to Nora, to Rakel, to do right by Ellie. So, they would rebuild. Somehow. Not just buildings, but lives. And this time, she would do things right. This time, it would be different.

Ellie squirmed beneath her touch.

"Shush, child."

Ellie glanced up. Their eyes locked. Then Ellie removed the dress box from beneath her arm and clutched it to her chest.

Let it go. Stop hanging on. The words thickened on Arla's tongue and refused to be spoken. But it didn't matter. Ellie wouldn't let go of that dress. Not now. Not yesterday. Not a week ago. She clung to it as if it were her last treasure. Maybe it was. It was more than many had left.

"Get on now." A voice rumbled from the train behind Arla.

She rubbed her thumb along the fabric on Ellie's shoulder and guided her forward. Behind them, a murmur of low voices accompanied the thud of work boots as men disembarked from the train.

"Ain't nothin' left."

"Lord help us."

"I wonder if ..."

"Well, that's one way to clear the land."

"Don't it stink though."

Someone coughed. Someone gasped. Another groaned. But no one wept. No one cursed. No one sobbed. Nor would they. No, the townspeople of Hinckley would face the future, build from the ashes, honor their dead. And so would Arla. So would Ellie. Somehow, they too would go on.

Arla lifted her feet higher as she picked her way through the rubble. Chunks of cinder, blackened rocks, a rod of twisted metal lay in her path. Once, the streets of Hinckley had been swept clean. Now, there were no streets at all. Only this.

The train's whistle blasted through the air. The sound raised rows of goose pimples on her arms. *Don't think of it. Don't remember.*

"Glad you made it, Mrs. Anderson. And you too, young Ellie."

Arla turned to see Nils Heg, the mercantile owner, behind her. A smear of black ash stained his cheek, and his normally neat shirt was torn at collar and cuff.

"Your family, Mr. Heg?"

He grinned. "Mom and Sis are safe in Duluth. And yours?"

She shook her head.

"I'm sorry." He removed his hat, then twisted its brim in his hands. "Miss Ellie's—"

Her jaw tightened.

Mr. Heg cleared his throat. "Well, they're, uh, they're," his voice lowered to a whisper, "they're laying out the bodies over there." He waved his hand toward a ditch on the edge of town. "For identifying, you know, though there's mostly no way to tell who ... who ... well, you know. I guess you could take a look."

Arla gripped her handkerchief and again lifted it to her nose. "No. Thank you." She shuddered.

"I know it's not pleasant business, especially for a lady like yourself. But you ought to check all the same. We've had some surprises." He turned his head and looked toward the hills. "And some mysteries." His voice faded.

"You haven't seen ..."

He glanced back toward her. "No. No, of course not. Would have said right away, you know."

Ellie tugged on Arla's arm. "Do you think that Mama, maybe ..."

For a brief instant, Arla closed her eyes. Then she opened them and focused on the child. "You were there, Eleanor. You know what happened."

Ellie dug her toe into the ash. "Yes, ma'am."

Arla touched Ellie's chin with her finger and lifted the girl's face until their eyes met. "Miracles don't happen, Eleanor. Not like that."

Mr. Heg leaned toward her. "Beggin' your pardon, ma'am. But they do. Stories are already flying. Amazing stories. Awful ones too."

Arla scowled. "Don't get up the child's hopes." Her voice lowered to a hiss. "She's been through enough already."

Mr. Heg straightened. "Haven't we all?" He sighed and scratched his head. For a long moment, no one spoke. Then he turned toward Ellie and forced a smile. "You like peppermint, Miss Ellie?"

She hesitated.

"Of course you do. What kid doesn't? So, I tell you what. The first peppermint stick I get in my new store will be yours. Just come on in, and I won't do you in the penny for it, either. My treat. And one for Mrs. Anderson, too, if she wants it." He winked at Ellie. His smile wavered.

"Foolishness." Arla spoke the word under her breath. The man had always been silly, ever since their school days, but even more so since his wife died years ago in the same influenza epidemic that took her husband, Grant.

"Ain't no foolishness in a bit of candy." He crossed his arms over his chest. "Is there, Miss Ellie?"

Arla turned on him. "How can you talk about candy when bodies are fresh in the grave and the town lies in ash?"

He raised his eyebrows. "Is there a better time? Folks need something to hope for, especially the children."

Arla dug her fist into her hip. "Look around you, Mr. Heg. We don't need hope. We need hard work."

"That we do, Mrs. Anderson. That we do."

She wagged her fingers at him. "So get to it then, sir."

He stuffed his hat back on his head and strode away. "Don't forget about that peppermint." He tossed the words over his shoulder. "I'm ordering it first thing. Though it might take a bit to get here."

Arla sniffed and turned east. "Come, Eleanor."

Ellie didn't move. "Mama always liked peppermint." She gazed west, toward her homestead.

Arla touched her hand to Ellie's back. "Shh. Don't think on that now. We must move on. Your mama would have wanted it that way." Her voice softened. "We'll be all right, Eleanor. We'll start over. You'll see. There's more to hope for than just a few peppermints." She squared her shoulders. "But right now, we have work to do." Her hand extended toward Ellie. "Come. Let's see what the fire left for us."

She led Ellie down what had once been a street, turned left, and stood where her front door had been. Now, there was nothing but the ash. The fine wooden steps, the beautiful windowed door, the sweeping entry— they were nothing but memory now. *Don't think on it. It was only a house.*

She stepped over a charred board, then made her way through the ashes.

The toes of her shoes brushed through the ruins. Her brick fireplace, crumbled. The mantel, burned and fallen. Her Queen Anne furniture, brought all the way from Boston, gone. The lace doilies, the handcrafted vases, the rugs, the pottery. Nothing had survived. Nothing.

Arla moved to the kitchen area. There, shattered, blackened china mixed with shards of wood in the ash. Her mother's prized set. She leaned over and brushed her finger through the cinders. Something cool and smooth met her touch. She picked it up. A single saucer. Marred, but unbroken. Arla cradled it in her palm, her finger tracing the edges of the yellow rose in its center. Then she stood and searched the ash further. There, she found a blackened jar, a metal milk jug with the bottom seam separated and useless, her washbasin, cracked and unusable.

She took a few more steps. Her heart thudded in her throat. This was where Rakel's room would have fallen. She stumbled backward and squeezed her eyes shut. Bile rose in her throat. *No ...*

Her heel impacted something hard. She turned. A black metal box stuck up from the ash. Her hand shook. She'd seen that box before. It held Rakel's special things—a silver locket from her father, a ceramic bird, a key, and usually, her latest journal. Surely none of that had survived. It couldn't have. Unless ... She bit her lip to keep it from trembling. Unless fate had left them to mock her.

Arla snatched up the box and shoved it into the pocket of her skirt. Maybe she'd look at it later. Maybe she wouldn't. After all, Rakel was gone. It was better to just move on, to forget, to start over.

I didn't do anything wrong. How could I have known? It wasn't my fault.

Arla closed her eyes. Flames rose before her vision. Flames of memory, and accusation. "No." She whispered the word. But the vision came anyway, sickening her, condemning her. She opened her eyes, but the ash had vanished. Instead, a door appeared before her, her daughter's door, locked by her own hand. Locked before she had ever dreamed of the fire.

Words streamed through her memory, echoing from the hollow place where she kept her fear.

"It's nothing you don't deserve."

"Let me out, Mother."

But Arla had shoved the key into her apron pocket. "You stay in there until you learn right from wrong."

"No. Please …"

"You stay in there and pray that God forgives your wicked soul." Her own words, as scorching as the fire. She could almost feel those words on her lips still. Could almost taste them.

The memory shifted. Fire leapt before her vision. And she was in front of the door again. Only this time wild shadows gyrated in an indecent dance against the walls. A shower of cinders pricked her skin. The key burned like a coal in her hand.

She fumbled to fit the key into the lock. Her hand slipped. Metal scraped against metal.

A hiss sounded behind her. She glanced over her shoulder. Flames flickered up the stairs. A beam creaked overhead. Arla shoved the key harder. It twisted in her hand. The end jammed into the door, missing the lock. Horror fishtailed down her back.

"Mother?" The call shrilled from inside the room.

Arla didn't answer. She didn't dare. *The key, the key, why won't it fit?* Her fingers trembled. Her breath came harsh and ragged in her ears. She grabbed her wrist with her free hand to steady it.

"Let me out."

I'm here. I'll save you. The words clogged behind her tongue and refused to be spoken. Sweat poured down her face, blinding her. She wiped at it. The key missed again. Was it the right one? She couldn't see. Couldn't remember.

Rakel's fingernails scraped on the inside of the door. The sound reverberated over the wild laughter of the flames.

The key, oh Lord, the key.

"Mother!"

"I can't, it won't." Tears formed in Arla's eyes and dried before they could fall.

Fire crept toward her. Hot, so hot, its fingers clawing up the stairs. She couldn't breathe. Dared not turn.

Without warning, the shrill whistle of the train sliced through the smoke. Fire shimmied up the wall. The rose wallpaper curled and shriveled. A vase tipped. Glass shattered, reflecting in a thousand points of red fire.

A scream burst from Arla's lips, drowning all other sounds. The key dropped. And Arla's feet took flight, racing, running, pounding toward the back stairs. And suddenly, she heard not the flames, nor the train, nor the wild thud of her fear, but only the sharp cry of her daughter, echoing in her ears.

"Mama, noooooo ..."

And then only gray ash. And she was here again, standing in the ashes, the metal box heavy in her pocket.

If only she hadn't ... If only I hadn't ... the thought dwindled as Arla fell to her knees and gripped the cinders in her hands.

6

There's a monster in the water. It stares at me from a face I don't recognize. Twisted flesh. No eyebrows. A clump of hair straggling across patches of baldness. Eyes as black as bottomless wells. Empty. Cold. Dead. What is this creature in the water?

A breeze shudders through dry branches overhead, tiptoes over the surface of the pond. The monster shivers. I tremble.

With one finger I touch the image. Bits of ash flee away as ripples scamper over the surface, and for a moment, for a single breath, the figure distorts, changes, and I know the truth. I am the monster. Mine are the eyes that stare with black horror. Mine the flesh deformed beyond recognition.

I close my eyes. I don't want to see any more. I don't want to remember. Then I can almost believe it never happened. I can pretend the breeze whispers to me a word of hope. That I am not this misshapen creature crawling along the edge of my pain. But then in the darkness of my mind the flames come again. Biting, searing, a mountain of heat crushing down upon me. And then the blackness, the sickening reek of flesh burning, of white-hot pain, of screams that tear through me and are swallowed by the wild cackle of flames. Fire, like a pack of rabid dogs, gnawing, chewing, grinding my flesh.

I should have died there. But fate laughed too. Or God did. The fire passed. But it burns in me still, deep within, clawing, ripping at my soul. So I search back further, before the fire, before the pain. Thoughts come now, winging through the silence, fluttering against the surface of a mind still swirling with pain. I travel through the dark halls of remembrance. I hear a wild scream, a train whistles, a tree falls. And a face. I can almost see a face. But then the fire roars up and devours memory, and I am here again, kneeling by the pond, staring at the reflection in the water. I lean closer. "Who are you?" My question feathers the surface. But no answer comes.

I thrust my fist through the image. Drops of water splash over the wounds on my arms. Arms once strong. Somehow I know they were. Just as I know they will never be strong again. Will never work in the fields. Will never hold a baby close and feel the gentle rise and fall of her breathing.

Oh God, God, how could this happen to me? How could you allow this horror? Are you blind? Did you not see? Or do you just not care that in one flash, in one moment, my life burned away, and left me with this horror?

I pick up a rock and throw it at my reflection. For a second, the image vanishes, and I'm me again. I see the land stretched out before me, golden with ripening wheat. A hand touches my shoulder. Warm eyes meet mine. We laugh. And the vision skews, wrinkles, and burns like a photograph crumpled and tossed into the flame. There are no kind eyes, no laughter, no fields of wheat. Only murky water, reflecting pictures I don't want to see.

I stand and turn away from the pond. My feet press into earth still warm and white with ash. Before me blackened trunks rise like prison bars. I stumble, my hand reaching for a boulder kissed with black cinder. I pause, listening. The birds are gone, the insects, silent. I hear nothing but the tumble of the stream that feeds the pond and the relentless breeze rattling through the trees, rippling over the water, taunting me.

Then into my world of embers, another sound comes. The whistle of a train. I've heard it before. A sound that brings both hope and horror. A noise that steals my breath, leaves me panting.

I gaze toward the setting sun. Out there, dark ribbons still trail into the sky. Just days ago, or a week, or two, a town stood where the smoke now rises. Hinckley. I remember that. But now there is nothing but the smoke, nothing but the smoldering hulks of buildings made of brick, and a few dozen pale tents scattered like bits of bread over the landscape. A whole town, a whole world, gone, consumed by the beast that birthed the image in the water.

My eyes focus on the train, a black thread in a tapestry of gray ash. And I see that Hinckley is not dead. Not defeated. For those who have survived or returned, the train brings hope in the form of fresh timber, long logs that will rebuild the homes, the hotels, the shops, the churches. And it brings, too, the—thoughts wedge and splinter in my mind—the strong arms, to make things new.

Yes, they will rebuild. The farms, the opera house, even the mill. Without me. It's better that way. No one will miss the creature I've become. No one will even know I lived.

No one but the breeze, the white pines turned black, and the strange monster in the water.

***

Three weeks. Josef had avoided this moment for three long, agonizing weeks. He knew what he would find. Nothing. And that's just what stretched before him now. Everything he had owned, everything he had worked for. Nothing but ash in the wind.

He tucked Emma into the crook of his arm and stared out over the blackened land that was once his farmstead. Charred trunks of white pines lined the northeast edge of his land and obscured his view of the hills beyond. To the west, a breeze stirred mounds of ash into low, swirling clouds. And in between, the ground lay black and bubbled. A pile of black cinders marked the place where his house had stood, and farther on, the warped skeleton of a barn rose dark against the horizon.

Nothing was left. Nothing at all. Except ... Josef squinted his eyes and took a step forward. Was that? No, it couldn't be. Yet, it was. A smile picked at the corner of his lips. There, shadowed by the remains of the barn, sat a small wooden cart, whole and intact. Somehow the fire had missed it.

Josef tipped back his hat and scratched his forehead. *Well, I'll be ...* It wasn't much. Not big enough to haul more than a bit of timber or maybe a bucket or two of water. But it was more than nothing. More than he expected to find. Tomorrow he'd come back and fetch it. Tomorrow he'd bring back one thing that he could call his own.

Emma squirmed in his arms. He leaned over and brushed his lips over her forehead. "Shh." She whimpered and stuck her fist into her mouth.

He rocked her back and forth.

The whimper turned to a wail.

Josef frowned. At times like these, Maggie would have sung to the baby, something about not crying and a lullaby. But he didn't know any of the right songs. The only ones he knew were those they sang in church, and somehow those didn't seem right anymore.

The pitch of Emma's cry rose until the sound became as sharp as nails in his temple. He brushed his fingers over her hair. "Hush now. It'll be all—" He stopped and pulled back the lie. He held her closer, cooed in her ear, bounced her in his arms the way he had sometimes seen Maggie do. Nothing helped.

Great tears tumbled down her cheeks. He wiped one away. Emma turned her head toward his finger.

She's hungry. The words whispered through his mind. Just hungry. *Of course.* She was always hungry. Josef grabbed for the makeshift bottle, already filled with milk. He touched the tip to the baby's lips.

She howled all the more fiercely and batted at his hand.

Josef dribbled a couple of drops onto her lips.

Emma shrieked and pushed at the bottle.

Josef tried again.

Emma kicked her feet.

And again.

Her face turned red.

And again.

She whimpered and turned her head.

And again.

"Come on, Em, it's the best I can do."

Emma stopped wailing and clamped her lips around the bottle's tip. With a long suck, she drew the milk into her mouth and swallowed. Then she stopped.

Josef waited.

Emma's lips quivered.

"Now don't be lookin' at your papa that way."

She sucked some more and paused.

"Oh no." Josef closed his eyes and sighed. He knew what she wanted. For him to talk. Out loud. And for minutes at a time. "It's gonna kill me, you know." All those words would make him dry up and float away on the breeze. "You're turning me into a fool, yammering away to a baby. That's what you're doing, you know."

Emma gurgled and continued to drink.

"Makin' your papa into a crazy man. Your mama wouldn't never believe it. Not by a long shot." He adjusted the bottle. "Your mama now, she was the one who could talk. Talk the ears right off the cornstalks. Talk faster and longer than the preacher on a Sunday morning." Josef smiled. "But her voice was as sweet as an apple pie. And could she sing.

I hope you get her voice, Emma Ann. She could sing those church songs like an angel come visiting from heaven. Sundays won't never be the same again. I suppose that Mrs. Anderson will do all the singing now." He grimaced. "Maybe we just won't go no more. What do you say to that?"

Emma said nothing. But he knew what Maggie would have said. She would have said that she didn't want any daughter of hers to grow up ignorant of the Good News and the Good Book.

Josef tipped the bottle higher. Emma glared up at him.

"I know. I know. We'll have to go. And tomorrow's Sunday." He scowled. "But we ain't got no fancy clothes. Not anymore." He paused and hunched lower over Emma. His voice dipped to a whisper. "You know, I don't see why God cares about fancy clothes anyway. Downright silly." He glanced up. "But don't be tellin' no one I said so. Can't see why a man needs a special shirt for one day of the week. Horsefeathers, I say. And the shoes. What good is shoes that make your toes ache so bad that you sit there on them hard benches thinking about some doggone blistered toe instead of what the preacher's saying? And they wonder why folks argue more when they're going to and from church. Lace a-scratchin', shoes a-pinchin', collar too tight, and breeches so stiff a man can't hardly sit. Now, let him go with his regular clothes and a pair of boots, then he might learn something. Yep, I might learn something." He shook his head. "Don't listen to me, baby girl. Your papa ain't making no sense. Talkin' like some fool heathen, I am. But still, sometimes I wonder ..." Josef sighed.

Emma burped and spat the bottle's tip from her mouth. She grunted and closed her eyes.

Josef slipped the nearly empty bottle into his pocket and turned toward the wagon. "All right then, we'd better be getting back. Promised I'd work on Mrs. Anderson's house some more. If anyone needs a place, it's them. You and me, we can wait. You don't know no different anyway, and me, well, I'm used to makin' do." He leaned closer to Emma's ear. "But just between you and me, that Mrs. Anderson don't know the first thing about makin' do. Tough as a railroad spike, she is, though. And just as sharp." He straightened. "But the Good Book says something about caring for widows and orphans. And we got lots of those now." Josef fell silent. Look at him, talking even when he didn't have to. He had better save up for suppertime. Besides, the thoughts he was thinking now ought not be voiced. Leastwise not to an innocent baby.

He looked away as images of weeping women and stark-faced children washed through his mind. *If God is good* ... He pushed away the thought. He had done enough heathen thinking for one day. Enough for one lifetime. At least that's what Maggie would say.

Josef laid Emma gently in a box in the wagon and tucked a blanket around her. Her eyes drifted open, then shut again. He touched her tiny hand, marveling at the softness of her skin, the delicate curve of her arm against the blanket.

Emma curled her hand around his finger and squeezed.

Warmth shot through Josef's soul. He stood there until her grip grew limp. Then he looked over his land one last time. His gaze fell on the cart. No, he didn't lose everything. He had that cart, and he had something more. Much more. He pulled his finger from Emma's hand and touched it to her cheek. "I won't fail you, baby girl. Won't let nothin' hurt you. Not again. Not ever."

He looked up. Breath caught in his chest. There, among the charred trunks of the northeast trees, stood a person, watching him. A figure robed in black. A figure like death come a-calling.

7

The music calls to me. The melody, haunting and clear. It rises from the tent-turned-church and floats across the ashen air toward me. Like a dream it beckons me to follow. To believe. To close my eyes and forget who I am. What I have become. And so I follow it, down from my hiding place in the hills. Through the black-trunked trees, across the dried-up stream, to the very edge of yesterday. But I won't step farther. I can't. Not anymore. This face, this body, this twisted image of what should have been, has no place in their world. So I huddle here in the shadows, behind a clump of dead pines, and I listen to the music mocking me. I listen to the hum of voices and picture their perfect faces, their unscarred hearts. And something in me shatters. Again.

I know that I can do no more than watch them rebuild, watch as Hinckley rises like a phoenix from the embers. Even now I see the houses, shiny with new lumber, half-built. And bricks stacked high and wide for the new schoolhouse. Beyond is the new mercantile, the new blacksmith shop, and another I don't recognize.

I close my eyes and turn from the sight. Today, there are no sounds of hammers, no grinding of saws, no men whistling or shouting. Just the music weaves through the day, just the song, its sound somehow strange and eerie as it wafts over the barrenness of the land and prods at the bareness of my soul.

I lean forward. I know this song. Know it too well. I cannot hear the words, but I remember them. Praise ye the Lord, the Almighty, the King of creation ... The music pulls the verses reluctantly from my memory. And they are there, in my mind. Persistent. Relentless. Cruel.

Praise ye the Lord, who o'er all things so wondrously reigneth,
Shelters thee under his wings, yea, so gently sustaineth.
Hast thou not seen
How thy desires all have been
Granted in what he ordaineth?

Did God ordain the fire? Did he reign over the flame? Is it he who stole from me everything I once dreamed?

Praise ye the Lord, who doth prosper thy work and defend
    thee;
Surely his goodness and mercy here daily attend thee.
Ponder anew
What the Almighty can do
If with his love he befriend thee.

Goodness. Mercy. Love. The words of yesterday. I believed them once. But not anymore. I press my hand into the torn flesh on my cheek. Is this God's mercy? I brush my fingers over the crusted scabs on my neck. Is this his love?

I glare at the cloud-soaked sky. God, why did you abandon me? What have I done that you would scorn me so? Tell me, what have I done to deserve this pain?

And into my mind comes a memory of a story told when I was a child. A tale of two brothers. There was Jacob, and there was Esau. Jacob, heel-grabber, deceiver, chosen by God. Loved. Esau, firstborn, rugged. And rejected. The Bible says that God loved Jacob, but Esau he hated.

I close my eyes and know the truth. I know who I am now. I am Esau. Unchosen. Unloved. I am Esau, hidden behind a mask of pain.

***

Lars Jensen sat at the back of the tent, surveying the congregation before him. In front, the preacher spouted meaningless words meant to give hope to the feeble hearted. But Lars knew better. A man didn't get ahead by sitting back and hoping for the best. A man pulled himself up by his own bootstraps. He worked, schemed, got rich. Then he got respect. Then he could have anything he wanted. And what Lars wanted now was a woman.

He yanked at his collar as his eyes flickered over the backs of those sitting in front of him. To his right, the Larsen girl sat hunch-shouldered in her seat. Matted blonde hair trailed down her back. Lars turned away. He wasn't that desperate. Not yet, anyway. Beside her sat her fat mother, digging in her ear with her pinkie. He shuddered. Two rows up sat the preacher's wife, all straight-backed and straitlaced.

Lars' gaze traveled to the other side of the tent. There sat the Anderson woman with a girl he thought he knew. What was her name? Swenson? Carlsson? Hansen. Ellie Hansen. He shook his head. The Anderson woman was too old and the Hansen girl too young. So few had come back yet from Duluth, Pine City, and St. Paul. Made it hard on a man. Almost made him wish Agnes was still alive. But no, Leif wouldn't be getting into that fancy school back East if Agnes had lived. They'd refused him before. He'd have thought that being the owner of half the businesses in town would have been enough for them, but they weren't impressed. Yet now, with the devastation of the fire and the loss of his mother, the administrators had decided that Leif had "character." They had decided he might be right for their hoity-toity school after all.

Leif may only be fifteen, but soon he would be ready for college. And a couple of years at this school would get him into Harvard for sure. Leif, his son, his boy, would be the first of his family to ever go to college. He straightened his shoulders. Later in the month, or maybe next spring, a man would come out from the school and interview Leif. A formality only, they'd said. And then Leif would be on his way come September. Lars smiled. The boy would do him proud yet. He glanced up.

Ellie Hansen flicked her hair behind her shoulder.

Lars leaned forward. She was growing up, that one, turning into a woman. Too bad she wasn't a very attractive girl. Took after that mother of hers. Nose too big, hips too scrawny, shoulders like old fence posts. Be hard to find a man for that one. Still ...

Lars shuddered. He shouldn't think those thoughts. He was supposed to have a pure mind. A righteous soul. But the thoughts came anyway. And the need. Just as it had done before.

His gaze slipped to the left and settled on Mrs. Anderson. There was one who had been a fine-looking woman in her day. But that day was long gone. Her daughter, though, had gotten twice her looks, and more.

Lars licked his lips and pulled at his collar again. *Don't think about that.* But he wanted to. He had to. That Rakel Anderson had been something to see. With her long black hair, blue eyes, and curves in all the right places. He closed his eyes. Visions of raven hair and swaying hips danced before him. She was a bad one, she was. A temptress. Luring him to evil. It was her fault, all her fault ... and yet, the fire did him a favor there, too.

Lars opened his eyes. The preacher paced at the front of the tent. He was right worked up now. Voice had even fluctuated a bit. Might wake up a few congregation members if he wasn't careful. Lars scowled. Why couldn't the man stop his yammering and say something useful? Say something that made a difference, something that would tell him how to tame the monster within.

He turned his head.

Ellie Hansen had shifted in her seat and was now staring right at him. He caught her gaze. Her eyes narrowed. A slow smile spread over his face. He'd seen that look before, seen it in eyes the color of the summer sky.

He sat back as the Hansen girl once again faced forward. Maybe her nose wasn't too big after all. Maybe her shoulders weren't too skinny.

Lars frowned. The women needed to come back to town. And quick.

***

The preacher knew. Arla shifted in her seat. He was seeing right through her. Into her heart. Seeing the sin she hid there. Brown eyes pierced hers, then moved left. *Don't look at me. Don't see.*

He was speaking now. Words that said nothing, meant nothing. A breeze ruffled the tent flap behind her. Heat rolled up her back and settled at her hairline. Sweat gathered at her temples.

And still the preacher talked on until his voice became nothing but a steady hum in her ears, a buzzing that grew louder as his gaze swept back toward her. Then he was looking at her again, looking past her, as if just the sight of her would sully him. He didn't know. He couldn't. But then why did his eyes condemn her?

I shouldn't have come. But what choice did she have? Respectable people attended church, even if it was held in a hot tent with makeshift benches that would soon become walls in someone's house. Respectable people combed their hair, donned their Sunday best, and did what was expected. Besides, Ellie needed her religion. She glanced at the girl sitting next to her.

"Sit up straight, Eleanor."

Ellie's gaze lowered even as she did as she was told.

Arla frowned. She hadn't meant to sound harsh. And yet ... She adjusted the dainty, embroidered shawl over her shoulders, then paused. Her fingers twitched. She could reach out now. Could lay her hand gently on Ellie's shoulder. Or touch her cheek, or put her arm around her and draw her close. But she didn't. Instead, she swallowed and tugged at the lace around her wrist. It was too warm for tight lace, too warm for the fine embroidered shawl. But she didn't care. Appearances were important. They should be kept up. Even now. Yes, even here.

"We all have a past." The preacher's voice sliced through her.

Her gaze darted to the front of the tent.

"And for some of you, that past was a good one. Family, home, friends, a good business." His hand motioned toward the open tent flap. "And for others, that past was not as good. Some of you cheated, or lied, or treated others badly." His fist clenched. His eyes swept the crowd.

Arla twisted the end of her shawl around her finger until her skin turned white. No. He couldn't know, could he? No one knew. Except ... Arla's gaze fell on the rough wooden cross at the front of the tent. God knew. The thought lodged in her heart like a stone weight. But he forgave, didn't he? The Bible said so.

A voice whispered through her mind. *Are you certain?*

Arla stared at the dirt near her feet.

He shouldn't. He won't.

But ...

Others, maybe. But not you.

I'm atoning for my mistakes. Ellie ...

You'll never make up for what you've done.

I have to.

You can't.

I will ... I will. I will. I will. It became a chant in her mind, blocking out the voice of the preacher, the murmurs of the people around her, blocking everything but the pounding of her heart in her ears.

"Mrs. Anderson? Mrs. Anderson? Arla!"

A hand gripped her shoulder. The tent jarred back into focus. Arla looked up to see the minister's wife standing over her.

"Are you well?"

It was over. *Thank God.* Arla drew a long, shuddering breath and rose to her feet. Voices swirled around her. Mrs. Petersen murmuring about the sermon. Mr. Lind coughing with a hacking wheeze. Old man Johansson asking his wife about supper. A group of young people discussing when the schoolhouse would open again. Everything was as it should be. Normal. Reassuring.

"Mrs. Anderson?"

Arla blinked. "Yes, thank you. I'm fine."

A couple of mill workers shuffled past. "A new future, preacher said." The taller one jabbed his finger in the air as he spoke. "God's doing a new thing."

The shorter one shook his head. "New? Ain't nuthin' new at my place but the wood planks. Same old, same old."

"That preacher knows how to give a man hope, though, don't he? No point dwelling on what's done and gone. New days, that's what I say."

Arla reached toward Ellie. *New days ... new hope.*

"You're sure you're well?" The minister's wife placed a hand on her arm. "I can tell Mr. Strom that you're ill."

"Mr. Strom?"

"You agreed to watch his baby this afternoon, remember?"

"Oh yes, of course."

"But ..."

"No, I'm fine. It's just the heat." Arla pulled a handkerchief from her reticule and dabbed at her neck.

The woman smiled. "I understand. It's hard. You lost so much."

Arla's jaw tightened. "We all did. I no more than others."

The woman patted her arm. "Rakel was such a special girl. We mourn her loss."

Arla pulled away. *Special* ... yes, that was the term. Special was another word for odd. Rakel was special all right. Arla gave a curt nod to the minister's wife. "I will return shortly for the Strom child." She turned and hurried up the aisle with Ellie. Sweat stung the back of her neck. Words beat in her mind. *Special. Strange. Peculiar. Abnormal.* Where had she gone wrong? Where had she failed? She'd done her best to raise a proper girl. She'd taught the child all the right manners. Introduced her to all the right circles. Given her all the right opportunities. But Rakel was always a little different. It wasn't Arla's fault. She'd done her best to do right by the girl. So then why had it turned out so badly? Why had she failed in the end?

Arla steered Ellie out of the church and turned sharply toward the tent they called home. The girl's long hair, pulled together in a simple blue ribbon, rippled down her back and shone in the morning sun. For a moment, Arla longed to reach out and touch it. But she quelled the yearning. This time, she would do things right. She would be sure not to make the same mistakes again. But what were those mistakes? How could she be sure that she wouldn't drive Ellie away as she had done with Rakel?

The answer came, just as Arla had known it would. The moment she had found Rakel's journal in the remains of her house, she knew she would have to face the words written there. She knew they would tell her what she needed to know, and more. Perhaps more than she could bear. *No, I can't. Not yet.* But her objections were meaningless. She had to know. Had to find out where she had gone wrong.

Arla paused before the tent opening. Her fingers touched Ellie's shoulder. "I have a few things to attend to, child. But there's no need for you to stay inside. Go out and see if any of your little friends are about. I'll call you when it's time to return for the Strom baby."

Ellie frowned. "Go? Go where?"

Arla looked out at the ash-strewn town, past the new mercantile, beyond the old roundhouse, across the trenches where so many were buried. The few bright new buildings stood starkly against the black ruins of what had been their town. So much was gone. So little had been rebuilt. Ellie was right. There was nowhere to go. Nowhere to escape from the grim reality of what their lives had become. Yet, the journal called. And she must face it alone.

"Please, Eleanor."

Ellie lowered her gaze. "Yes, ma'am." Her shoulders hunched as she turned and slumped away.

Arla watched her go. *Come back. Save me.* The words flared within her, and died, unspoken. A moment later, Ellie turned a corner and disappeared.

Time inched forward. Still, Arla hesitated. She counted to twenty. Twice. Then she entered the tent. The flap dropped with a thud behind her. She held her breath and listened. Silence. Pure, ugly silence. She stretched out her hand. Her fingers trembled. *I can't. I must.*

Twin canvas cots lined each side of the tent, and between sat a small wooden trunk. Arla tossed her reticule onto her cot and knelt in front of the trunk. Her palm brushed the rough exterior. A moment later, she leaned over and lifted the lid. It was there, she knew it. Down beneath the green cotton dress, beneath the single pair of stockings, beneath undergarments, the ribbons and lace collars.

She closed her eyes and reached to the very bottom of the trunk. Her fingers closed over the small journal. Her stomach clenched. *Do I dare?* With a quick movement, she drew out the book. It shook in her palm. *Help me.*

She ran her hand over the cover, then slowly, carefully, opened it to the first page. *19 April 1894.* Her gaze fell to the opening line. Words jumped out at her, searing into her mind.

Arla slammed the book shut and threw it back into the trunk. A chill raced over her skin. She should have known better. She should have never tried. She pressed her palms into her eyes and rubbed. But the words remained, emblazoned across her vision.

MAMA HATES ME. I KNOW SHE DOES.

Arla fell onto the cot and sobbed.

8

Josef was going to hell. He knew it. And he didn't care. If he had, he would have stopped all the blasphemous thoughts that had been going through his mind during the church service. He would have hung his head and told God that he was sorry for any doubting. But he wasn't sorry. Not at all.

Heat radiated up his neck and settled in his temples. He mopped the sweat at his hairline then stuffed his handkerchief in his pocket.

And still the preacher droned on. "Casting all your care upon him." He extended his arm toward the congregation. "For he careth for you."

God cares? Josef nearly choked on the thought. God let Hinckley burn. He let good people die. He let children become orphans, women become widows, and worse. What kind of God would do that?

Josef ground his foot into the dirt floor. The last hymn still rankled in his memory. Mercy, goodness, love. The words had stuck in his throat like the bones of a northern pike.

Just weeks ago, Maggie had sung them all, and what good had it done her, or him? She'd sung, she'd believed, she'd trusted. Just like he had. But where was God when a wagon came tumbling out of the flames? Where was God in the smoke and darkness? Vanished. Absent. Gone.

Josef twisted his hat in his hand and clutched Emma tighter. No, he wouldn't sing today, or next week, or ever. In fact, after this service, he was done with church for good. Forever.

A memory came to him. Of him striding up to the front of the church, kneeling down there at the altar, giving his life to the Lord. "I'm yours, God. Whatever you want for me. I'm your man now." He'd said the words, and he'd meant them. Every one. But that was ten years ago, when he was little more than a boy. Now that church was gone, consumed in the fire. And that boy was gone too. Lost the moment a burning wagon had tumbled into the darkness. Josef shifted in his seat.

Finally, the preacher stopped jabbering. The people stirred. Josef lifted Emma from his lap and bolted up the tent's middle aisle. A moment later, he thrust the tent flap aside and rushed out. A warm breeze ruffled his hair. He shoved the hat onto his head and hurried toward his tent.

"Mr. Strom?" The voice of the minister's wife called out behind him.

New sweat broke out on Josef's forehead. He couldn't turn. Couldn't let her see the doubts beading on his face. He had to escape. Get away now, or else she would know. Everyone would know.

In his arms, Emma cooed. He glanced down at her sleeping face. For once, she wasn't crying for milk or mama. And he wanted to keep it that way.

Footsteps thudded on the soft ground behind him. "Mr. Strom, wait." A hand touched his shoulder.

He paused. "Baby needs to eat." He threw the words between them, not revealing the thoughts behind them. *Leave me alone. Don't ask me no questions. I ain't gonna talk.*

The minister's wife glanced from Emma to him.

The baby's soft snore made him a liar. His cheeks flushed. He used to be an honest man. He used to be a lot of things.

A slight smile brushed the face of the minister's wife. "I understand."

His gaze dropped.

Her voice turned gentle. "Mrs. Anderson will be back shortly to look after Emma. By the time you feed the baby, Mrs. Anderson should have returned."

Josef let out his breath. He stole a glance at the minister's wife.

She pushed a strand of graying hair behind her ear. "We all have questions, Mr. Strom." Her murmur barely reached his ears.

His mouth opened, but no sound came.

She patted his arm. "Go home. Take care of your baby. I'll send Mrs. Anderson around when she comes."

Josef nodded, still unable to form the words he now longed to speak. Does everyone doubt? What is faith in the face of tragedy? How can anyone still believe? How can I?

The minister's wife withdrew her hand, then waved to another woman. "Mrs. Larsen, I have your cabbage." She threw Josef a glance and hurried away.

At that moment, Emma began to cry.

Guess I'm not a liar after all. Josef pulled the blanket away from Emma's chin and strode to his tent.

A half hour later, just as the minister's wife had promised, Mrs. Anderson appeared outside his tent. He pulled back the flap.

Mrs. Anderson smoothed the hair around her temple. "Good day, Mr. Strom. I can watch the baby now."

Josef held back the flap as Mrs. Anderson entered. "You, uh, feeling all right?"

She paused. Her brows drew together. "I'm fine. Why?"

Josef looked away. "Eyes. Red." Had she been crying? What could possibly make a woman like Mrs. Anderson cry? He didn't want to know.

"It's just the ash. I'm somewhat sensitive." Her voice wavered.

He knew it was a lie. But he accepted it anyway. Folks needed their privacy. And he needed his. Without a word, Josef retrieved Emma from a basket in the corner and handed her to Mrs. Anderson.

Mrs. Anderson stood there and stared at him.

Josef stared back. What did she want? Was she expecting sympathy?

Or for him to question her about her lie?

Her brows knit together. "You have no instructions for me, Mr. Strom? About the baby?"

Josef stuffed his hands into his pockets. The baby, of course. Instructions. "Um, well …"

Mrs. Anderson glanced around the tent.

Josef followed her gaze. A pair of cinder-streaked pants lay across the cot. A pile of dirty diaper cloths was stacked in one corner. A crust of dried bread sat on a chipped plate. And Emma's blanket lay half on the floor, half in her basket.

Without a word, Mrs. Anderson plucked up two clean diaper cloths and Emma's bottle.

Awkward silence stretched between them.

Josef grabbed his hat. "I'll be back in a few hours then."

Mrs. Anderson gave him a curt nod. "I shall take the child to my place. She'll be there when you return." With that, she turned and stepped from the tent.

Josef watched her go, then crumpled onto his cot. Maybe Mrs. Anderson was right. She didn't say so, but he could read it in her eyes. This tent was no place for a baby. A child needed a home, and clean clothes, a cradle, and … and … and so much more than he could give her. He shifted on the cot. Paper crinkled in his pocket. He reached in and drew out the folded relief form that he had put there a week ago. *I can't. I won't.* He tossed the paper onto the cot. He wouldn't be beholden to some state commission. He didn't need no help. He sighed. But Emma did.

Slowly, Josef picked up the form again and held it up until it was even with his eyes. Letters swam before his vision. He wiped his hand over his forehead and turned the paper toward the light. Bold, black letters ran across the top of the page.

R-E-G-I-S-T-R-A-T-I-O-N B-L-A-N-K.

He repeated the letters, but they made no sense to him. It didn't matter, though. He needed only to fill out the lines. That's what the man behind the desk had said. He could do that. At least, he hoped so.

Josef grabbed the stubby pencil the man had given him and stepped outside the tent. Dim sunlight reflected off the form, illuminating the column of words running down the left side of the sheet. He focused on the first word, his mouth forming the sounds. En-ay-em. Name. That was easy. He knew how to write his name. He sat down on a log and balanced the paper on his thigh. With slow precision, his fingers formed the letters. Then he glanced down to the next question.

Wife's Name. Josef clutched the pencil tighter. He could spell her name too. M-a-g-g-i-e. His hand trembled. The paper shook. He pressed the pen harder against the sheet. Then he wrote what he knew he must. D-e-d. For a moment, he stared at the word, his stomach twisting. Then he moved on.

Children. Just Emma. Only her. And now, that's all there would ever be.

Josef looked down the rest of the page until he saw a word he recognized. Needs. Needs? They meant things like milk, bottles, cereal, baby clothes. But what Emma really needed was a mother. Her mother. And neither God nor the state commission could help them there. No one could.

Josef shoved the pencil into his pocket. Then he crumpled the paper and threw it on the ground. What good would it do to fill it out now? It wouldn't bring Maggie back. It wouldn't make things right.

"Whoa there, Josef. What are you doing?"

Josef glanced up to see Nils Heg driving up in his wagon. The man's chestnut mare came to a halt beside him.

"Hullo, Nils."

Nils jumped down from the wagon. "That wasn't your relief form, was it?"

Josef scratched his head. "Don't need it."

Nils clapped Josef on the back. "We all need help, Josef. Especially you, with the little one." He leaned over, picked up the paper, and smoothed it against his leg. "Give me the pencil."

"We'll do just fine. There's others who need more."

Nils looked at him for a long moment. "Is there?"

Josef's answer caught in his throat. *It won't do no good.*

Nils sighed. "I know, it isn't fair. You're left without a wife. Emma without a mother." His gaze drifted to the play of shadows on the cinder-strewn ground.

Josef didn't respond. How could he? He knew how he was supposed to act, how he was supposed to feel. After all, loss was a part of living. Things happened. Life changed. Tragedy struck and left you breathless. But you took it as it came, and you didn't grumble. You didn't question. You endured. Silently. Stoically. That's how it was done in the old country, his papa always said, and that's how it was done here, too. A frost came and took out your crops. You made do. The sickness came and took a loved one. You accepted it. No tears. No complaints. Life could be worse. You did not rail at the heavens. You didn't blame or curse. You squared your shoulders and went on. That's how his father, and his father's father before him, had taught him to live. But it wasn't working. Not for Emma, and not for him either. There had to be something more. Some secret that hid just beyond his understanding. Something that would loosen the ache in his chest, silence the questions that beat inside his head. But that something, he knew, wouldn't be found in any baby clothes or bottles, or anything the state commission could provide.

Nils lifted the paper and placed it on the footboard of his wagon. Then he plucked the pencil from Josef's shirt pocket and poised the instrument over the page. "Come, Josef, let's fill it out. Can't hurt."

Josef turned his head away without answering.

"Needs." Nils tapped the pencil on the paper. "Let's see. You could use some clothes for the baby, I suppose. And some, um, changing cloths." The pencil scribbled over the paper as he spoke. "Then some timber and seed and maybe the lend of a plow to start up your farm again." He paused. "Anything else?"

Josef shook his head.

"One more question, then I'll hand this in for you. What property do you have left? Was anything spared?"

Josef grimaced. "Just a cart. Maggie's old gardening cart."

"A cart? Are you certain?"

"Saw it up at the farmstead yesterday. I know it ain't much."

Nils placed a hand on Josef's shoulder. "I was up to your place just this morning." His hand dropped away. "I'm sorry, Josef. There was no cart."

No cart. He should have known. Josef clenched his fists and glared into the sky.

* * *

Shame. It wells up in me, spilling over like bile. Shame, screaming at me in the form of this ramshackle cart that I have claimed as my own. It is a small cart, one wheel broken, one side singed with flame. Still, for it I have sacrificed my last shreds of dignity.

It is one thing to take from a stranger, and another to steal from a friend. But I have done neither. I have done worse. I have taken from a man who needs it more.

I told myself he would be glad for me to have it. I told myself he would forgive me if he knew. But how can I say that? How can I know? I don't know. But I took it all the same.

Strange how easy it is to despise the wicked, until you become one. But I knew that.

With one hand, I reach out and touch the handle. The wood is old and dry, brittle. I lean over and place another branch in the cart. I fill it until sticks are heaped far above the edge. It holds so little, but it holds enough. Enough to make me into this thing I have become. If only my mama could see me now ... What would she fear more? The face or the person behind it? What do I fear more?

I lift my fingers and feel the wounds. I touch the still-raw scars on my half-burned cheek. I touch the pain, and in some ways, I savor it. It tells me I am alive. But what a life. Pilfering carts, stealing food, rummaging through half-burned remains for clothes black with cinders and stains, scurrying along the edges of others' lives like some kind of filthy rat. I hate it. I want to die.

And yet I live. I protect this thing that is now my life as if it is precious. I build a shack to live in, from wood licked with flame, from boards stolen from relief cars in the night, from bits and pieces dug up in the ash. I find clothes. I sneak food. I take what I need, and loathe myself for it. In my private way I fight a battle I'm destined to lose. I fight for hope. But all I find are ashes and cinder and memories too black to recall.

Sorrow, unworthiness, shame lodge like a stone in my chest. And I remember what could have been. Once, I dreamed of land and of family, of strength and laughter and love. I dreamed of faces around a dinner table, of crops growing golden in the sun, of warm lefse on Christmas mornings. No one made the traditional potato flatbread better than Grandmama. Even now I can almost taste the butter melting within its rolled folds. But that's all lost now, burned in a fire that seared more than my skin.

Now, I have no past, no future. Only this moment. Only this fear.

The world goes on. But I do not. I am caught here, in this place between who I was and what I am. I long for what I can never have. And I curse the longing.

Once, I walked among them without fear. I sang. I prayed. I did what people do. But I am no longer one of them. What am I, then? Who is this

*creature created in fire? I am no one. I am nothing. A shadow? A ghost?
A monster?*

*No. There are more than scars that separate me from them. Now, there is
this thing called shame.*

***

Ellie Jean knew them boys were up to no good. She could smell it in the
air. She wrinkled her nose and sniffed. Or maybe that was just the scent
of boiling cabbage drifting over from the Larsen tent. Ellie hated boiled
cabbage. And her feelings about them boys weren't a whole lot different. She narrowed her eyes and peeked out from behind the watering
barrel. Sure enough, there they were, huddled behind the new mercantile store with their heads bunched together like a pack of wild dogs
gnawing a bone. They were planning something. A frog slipped slyly
into her pocket? A spider in her shoe? This time she was going to find
out before it was too late. This time, she'd know about the slimy green
snake before it slithered out of her bag. Her teeth clenched. This time,
she'd be ready.

A breeze stirred up the ash dust and sent it dancing in tiny swirls
around her feet. Ellie held her breath and stifled her sneeze. She wasn't
going to let them boys know she was here, even if she had to swallow
a hundred sneezes. She looked up. The glow of the sun shone dimly
through the murky air. It hadn't seemed clear in a long time, not since
the fire. They'd done so much in town. Already the mercantile was up,
and some houses, too, the schoolhouse started, the trains running
good and regular again. But the ash remained. And the dim old yuck
in the air. And she was sure she could still smell the scent of burned
wood, now mixed with boiling cabbage. The fire had touched everything, changed it. Changed every single thing, except maybe them
awful boys.

Ellie leaned forward, straining to hear their words. But they were just out of earshot. She held her breath again, this time to listen.

"Ghost ... night ... shirt."

Shirt? Ellie bit her lip. They weren't making no sense. She was missing the important stuff. Her brows furrowed as she leaned farther out from behind the barrel. Ned's lips were moving. That big bully was yammerin' up a storm. And that meant trouble. He slicked back his sandy hair and rubbed his ugly freckled nose.

Leif laughed. Ellie glared at the boy with dark cropped hair. They called him a black Norwegian 'cause of his hair, she guessed. But it was a better description of his heart. Weren't nobody blacker. She was betting it was him who caught the snake last time.

Her gaze flitted over the other boys. Gunnar and Gregor, the twins. Karl and Evan. Evan wasn't so bad when he was alone. But he wasn't alone near enough. Together, them boys were just evil. At least Ellie thought so, no matter what Mama had said.

Ellie glanced back to Ned and Leif. Leif was talking now, his mouth moving as fast as the afternoon express. And he had that hard, stony look on his face. Even Mama didn't have nothing good to say about Leif when he looked like that. Thought he could do anything he wanted 'cause his papa was rich. Made a bundle of money back East, someone said. But he wasn't so rich anymore. No one was. Not since the fire.

But that hadn't humbled Leif none. He just kept going on about 'surance money and his papa's investments. Said they were just as rich as ever. Said his papa was putting up the new schoolhouse and buying books and tablets and pencils for everyone, all with his own money. Might just have to think nicer thoughts about him if that were so. Ellie crossed her arms. But still, Mama had said to stay away from both of them. Especially the father. "He's got a smile on his face and the devil in his eyes," Mama used to say. Ellie wasn't sure just what that meant, but she believed it. Mr. Highfalutin-Bigwig made her feel like spiders was crawling up her insides, with or without the new schoolhouse.

She sighed. Why that fire took some and left others folks could do without, she couldn't figure. And here was Leif, getting his old gang back, and most likely filling their ears with all manner of lies and tall tales.

She would know what them lies were if she could only get a little closer. Her gaze slipped to the woodpile just to the left of the mercantile. If she could just get behind that without them seeing her, she could hear everything. But if they found her spying ... She squashed the thought. They wouldn't find out. She'd move real fast. Now, when no one was looking.

Ned's head swiveled toward her. She bolted back behind the barrel and pushed her shoulders into the rough wood. Her breath grated in her ears. They were going to hear. She pressed her hand against her mouth. It didn't help. It was like Mama always said, "The easiest way to breathe loudly is to try to be quiet about it." Ellie drew a long, slow breath and listened for footsteps. None came. She peered around the barrel again. The boys' heads had returned to their tight circle.

The soft thud of horse's hooves and the creak of wood on metal caused Ellie to turn. There sat Mr. Heg atop a rickety wagon. He slowed his horse. The wagon creaked louder. Ellie pressed a finger to her lips just as Mr. Heg touched his hat in greeting. His eyes slid toward the group of boys, then back to her. With a slight nod, he smiled and jiggled the reins. His horse moved past. Just as the wagon drew even with the barrel, Mr. Heg spoke in a low murmur. "Got that peppermint on order." He threw her a quick wink. "A whole box of it."

Ellie grinned up at him.

Then Mr. Heg clucked his tongue, and the wagon lumbered by. Ellie watched him for another moment, then returned her attention to the woodpile. She could make it. She had to.

She counted to three. None of the boys looked back. She counted again. They still didn't move. Neither did she. *Come on, Ellie Jean, you've gotta do this.* She counted to three, to four, to five. Then she dashed toward the woodpile. Two seconds later she was hidden behind the wood. She dropped to the ground. Her foot kicked a rock. It skittered from behind the pile and pinged against another stone.

Ellie crouched lower and screwed her eyes tight shut.

"You hear something over there?" Evan's voice sent shivers down Ellie's back.

There ain't no one here. No one but the wind.

Ned laughed. "What, you scared, Evan? Oooo." His voice rose an octave and cracked. "Maybe it's the new ghost."

Ellie smiled and opened her eyes. She could hear perfectly now. Them boys wouldn't get away with anything this time. She'd make sure of that.

"Ain't no ghost." Evan's tone turned harsh. "It's not even night. Ghosts only come out at night."

"Then what are you jumping for?" That was Karl. Ellie could tell by the way he slurred his words.

"I ain't jumping."

"Aw, shut up, will ya?" Leif's voice rose above the murmuring of the other boys. "Haven't I been telling you? There is no ghost."

Ellie shifted her position until she could see the boys through a crack between logs.

"Sure, you've been saying so. But my mama says she seen him a-haunting over there among the graves." Gunnar waved his hand toward the death trench at the end of town.

"So?"

"And what about all them things gone missing?" Gunnar's brother, Gregor, stood up straighter and jabbed his finger toward Leif. "Papa's missing a pair of pants—taken right from the clothesline, they were. And old man Olsen's missing some boots. Didn't your father say he was missing a hammer, Evan?"

Evan nodded. "A twig basket was left in its place."

Gunnar leaned forward and lowered his voice to just above a whisper.

"I heard tell that Mrs. Olsen got a pie snitched right from her tent. And a carving of a bird was right there where the pie had been."

Leif crossed his arms over his chest. "What would a ghost need with a pie?"

Gunnar shrugged. "Who knows?"

"It isn't a ghost."

"How do you know?" Evan's soft question barely reached Ellie's ears.

Yes, how do you know? Ellie squinted through the crack. Was that doubt on Leif's face? Was it fear? She had seen something too. At night, a shadow on the side of the tent. A figure, moving in the moonlight, silent and stealthy. But when she'd peeked outside, no one was there. A ghost? Maybe. But whose?

Gregor made a fist and thumped his leg. "I'm telling you it is a ghost. My papa saw a light up the hills just last night. He thinks it's the ghost of someone burned up in the fire."

Ellie's heart thudded in her chest. Could it be? Maybe? Mama?

Leif's voice raised to a shout. "And I'm telling you it's just some man. And I aim to find out who. Today."

A man. Ellie dug her fingers into the ash at her feet. Then it couldn't be Mama.

"Maybe it's a monster."

"Don't be stupid."

"I ain't stupid."

Leif pretended to cough.

Gunnar slugged Leif in the shoulder. "You shut up."

Leif chortled. "So who's coming with me?"

"Me."

"Us."

"Me too."

And me. Ellie gritted her teeth. She'd be there. Somehow. If there was a ghost, she wanted to see it. She wanted to know.

"Not me." Evan brushed his foot over the ground and avoided Leif's gaze.

Leif shoved his hand against Evan's chest. "What? You scared?" He turned toward the others. "Evan's scared of the big bad ghost. Gonna go hide behind Mama's skirts."

Evan's chin shot up. "I ain't scared of no ghost."

"Then why aren't you coming? 'Fraid the ghost'll get you?"

"That ghost ain't nothing compared to my papa. Papa says we're shuckin' corn tonight, and I'll get a skinnin' if I'm not there. I'm not getting no skinnin' for a man or a ghost."

The other boys nodded.

Leif shrugged. "Forget it then. The rest of us'll go."

Ned rubbed his hands together. "When?"

"Twilight."

"I thought you said night?" Gunnar frowned.

"Evan said that."

"Oh."

Leif wiggled his fingers. His voice lowered to a breathy whisper. "Twilight, that gray time between day and night, when spooks walk free and living folks can see them. Woooo ..."

"Stop that."

Leif's voice returned to its normal tone. "Twilight's when I saw him yesterday."

"You saying you seen him? Honest?"

Leif's gaze slid toward Gunnar. "'Course I did. Seen him at the back of the mercantile." His tone again turned spooky. "It was in this very spot."

Gunnar shivered. "Right here?"

"Right here. And I'm betting he'll come back again tonight. We'll wait behind that woodpile."

Ellie jumped back.

"Then what?"

"You'll see. I'll be ready." Leif opened his coat.

The boys gasped.

Ellie pressed her eye to the slit between logs. For a moment, her breath left her.

There, tucked into Leif's belt, was a bright silver pistol.

9

Guns, and ghosts, and gray shadows. Ellie could think of nothing else as she hid behind the mercantile and waited for the sun to dip below the horizon. Her dinner of boiled cabbage rumbled in her stomach. She pushed her fist into her gut and peeked around the corner.

No one was there.

No ghost. No boys. Not yet.

Ellie waited.

The sharp ping of a hammer echoed through the air and mixed with the sound of men shouting in the distance. Soon, two mill workers ambled by carrying a load of timber. Then a dog trotted past, its tongue lolling to one side. Across the way, a horse swished its tail and snorted.

And still Ellie waited.

The sun dropped lower in the sky. And lower. And finally vanished. The sound of the hammer ceased. The men quieted.

Ellie crossed her arms over her chest. Where were they? Stupid boys. Dusk had come and was almost gone. She dug her heel into the ground and squatted down. Couldn't count on nobody to do what they said these days. Folks promising that everything would be all right when nothing was all right. Preacher making promises about the God of all comfort when all she was feeling was miserable. And now them boys. Not that she wanted to see their awful selves, but it was better knowing where they were than having them sneak up on her. Better if they just came while she was ready for them.

Another minute passed. The scent of sawdust coming from the stack of crates beside her made her eyes grow heavy. She rubbed her hand over her face and squinted. Was that someone coming? No, it was just a shadow. She sighed and allowed her gaze to wander over the town.

There, the first rays of moonlight scattered over the land and covered the scars of the fire. She looked out past the street, past the long line of tents, past the railroad cars heaped with fresh timber. If she looked long enough, she could almost believe the fire never happened, could almost believe everything was as it had been. Except for one thing. Except for the big old hole in her heart where Mama should have been.

Mama ... Ellie closed her eyes. Mama used to walk down this very street with fabric tucked under her arm. Fat bolts of blue cotton. Narrow strips of soft silk. Folds of crinkly taffeta. If Ellie concentrated hard enough she could almost hear Mama humming the way she always had when coming from town. All the way down the long streets she would hum some old hymn, then she'd dance up the steps, throw open the door, and place her fabric carefully in a basket. After that, she'd tell Ellie all about who she'd seen and what they had said. Sometimes, she'd brush Ellie's hair while she told her stories.

Ellie leaned her head against the wall of the mercantile and tried to remember how Mama used to brush her hair in long, soft strokes. It wasn't at all like the quick, rough movements of Mrs. Anderson. No, Mama's hands had been gentle, one on the brush and one smoothing Ellie's hair. Then the light would grow dim, the lantern would flicker, and Mama would pause, look up, and smile. "Make us some tea, Ellie love," she'd say. "You pour while I set up the sewing for tomorrow."

A little later, Mama would close the sewing basket and pat a spot on her lap. Ellie loved to crawl up and snuggle in. Them moments when they sipped tea together were the closest thing to heaven that Ellie figured she'd ever know. Especially now. Now, there'd be no more kisses on the forehead. No more stories shared over tea. No more soft strokes from the brush before bedtime. No more nothing. Except the memories.

Ellie ran her fingers through her hair and pretended it was Mama's brush. Slow and steady, the bristles just touching her scalp. She opened her eyes. Fingers just weren't the same.

Something rustled behind the woodpile. Ellie jumped. A log shifted. She held her breath. A cat slunk from the logs and leapt onto a pile of timber. Ellie breathed again.

Then the hiss of voices slithered toward her. She squatted behind the crates and peeked out.

They had come.

Four black silhouettes slipped behind the woodpile. She could hear their arms bumping one another, their feet kicking the logs. And then the whispers began.

"I don't see nothing."

"Shh."

Feet scuffled over the ground. Then silence.

Ellie's heart beat faster. A minute passed. And another.

"Ain't no ghost. I told you."

"Shut up."

"He'll come."

Ellie's calves began to cramp. She stretched out her legs. Ash stirred at her feet. It was no use. No one was coming. Or maybe there was no ghost at all. Maybe it was only a story, or a figure from a dream. Maybe she should just forget what the boys said and sneak away. Go home now before Mrs. Anderson came looking for her.

Ellie stood and shook out her leg. She inched along the wall of the mercantile.

Then she stopped. A shadow moved. Goose bumps rose on her arms. She leaned forward and peered into the street. Was it? Could it be? A figure emerged from the night. It stumbled toward her. One slow step, then another, with its left foot dragging behind. Ellie stared at the hunched shoulders, at the head covered by the hood of a dark cloak.

A ghost? Or just a man?

It crept forward, lit only by the lantern hanging outside the mercantile. The light cast a thousand rippling shadows over the dark cloak, yet failed to illuminate the figure within.

Ellie's arms trembled. Her breath rattled in her ears.

The ghost paused.

Ellie crouched lower.

His head tilted up. Light glimmered off black eyes. Human eyes. Hurting eyes.

Ellie caught her breath.

For a long moment, the ghost-man gazed into the light. And for a longer moment still, Ellie watched those black, silent eyes. Eyes that weren't mean, or evil, or even spooky. They were scared, and tired. Sad eyes, shining in a face shadowed by night. And in them, Ellie could see reflected all the awfulness, all the loss of the whole town, of Ellie's whole life.

Her hand gripped the side of the building until the rough wood dug into her flesh. *Poor ghost. Poor man. It ain't your fault this happened to you. It ain't any of our faults. Bad stuff just happens. Folks get hurt. People die. And others are left with holes on their insides where happy used to be.* Ellie rubbed her fingers over her chest. Things would get better, though. They had to. She glanced over to the woodpile. Only the top fringe of Ned's hair was visible over the logs. Yes, things would get better. But not if them boys got their way. Someone had to stop them. The town didn't need no more hurt. Didn't need no more dying. Or being afraid. And that meant someone had to save that sorry figure in black. But how?

The ghost-man lifted a hand and pulled the cloak's hood tighter around his face. And again, his eyes were hidden in the shadows. He stepped forward.

Ellie chewed her lower lip. She could shout, leap out from behind the mercantile, and wave her arms hard to warn him away. She could, but then the boys would see her. They'd turn on her instead.

A chill swept over her skin. *Go. Run away. They're waiting for you.* She concentrated on the words, shouting them in her mind. But the ghost-man kept coming. One slow step after another. Right toward the woodpile and them wicked boys.

Ellie glanced up and down the empty street. Somebody had to come. Someone who the boys wouldn't cross. Maybe Mr. Heg would ramble down the road. That would chase the ghost away. Or Mrs. Anderson would come a-looking for her. She would scare anyone. Or the preacher. Or a mill worker. Or anyone. *Please God, send someone to save that poor ghost-man.* Ellie waited. God would hear.

But no one came.

The ghost shuffled closer.

Behind the woodpile, the boys shifted positions. At any moment they would leap out.

Surely someone would come first. Someone had to.

Closer.

God?

Ned's sandy blond head rose from behind the wood. A hand reached out and grabbed a log.

No!

Too late.

Light glinted off a stone near Ellie's feet. She stared at it. Could she? Did she dare? She leaned down and clutched the rock in her fingers. The rough surface of the stone pressed into her flesh. She rubbed her thumb over the sharpest edge. A mark of black ash smeared her skin. She looked up at the ghost one more time.

He was still coming. Step, hobble, step. A pathetic figure robed in night.

She had to stop him. The rock grew heavy in her hand. Ellie lifted her arm, and paused. She couldn't. She had to. It was the only way. She drew back her arm and threw the rock at the ghost-man.

The stone hit the ground and skittered to the ghost's feet.

He stopped and turned.

Go back. Don't come no closer.

For a second, it seemed he heard her and understood. But then he started forward again. Step, hobble. Step, shuffle.

Ellie picked up another rock and threw it. Harder this time. This one hit, clunking off the front of the ghost-man's cloak.

He shivered and halted again.

Ellie pressed her lips into a thin line. She knew it. It weren't no ghost after all. It was only a man. The rocks proved it. Rocks would go right through a ghost, but they struck solid on the man. He was just a person. A strange person. But one who didn't deserve what that scheming Leif had planned for him.

The man took one more step.

Ellie reached for another rock and threw it. Then another, and another.

The man stopped. His shoulders rounded. His head turned toward her. And in that moment, the full light from the lantern shone in the man's face.

Ellie gasped and dropped the rock in her hand. The face was no face at all, but a mass of twisted red flesh. Horror clawed through her chest. It weren't no ghost. It was a monster. Horrible. Deformed. A creature out of some awful nightmare.

She stumbled backward and grabbed up the stone.

His eyes caught hers. Those wide, suffering eyes. They looked right into her and filled her with their pain.

The rock trembled in Ellie's hand. She couldn't throw another stone. Couldn't make those eyes hurt any more. But she had to. For his sake. And for hers.

Ellie straightened, steadied her hand, and threw another stone.

* * *

It comes at me from the darkness. A small stone. A simple rock. And in it, all my fear, all my pain. It skitters at my feet. I pause and stare. Where has it come from? What does it mean? Another follows, and strikes me. Shock ripples through my body. And I know. It comes from a human hand. It means that I am not wanted. I am feared. I am hated.

Despair clogs in my throat, and I choke on it. Is it not enough to be burned and crippled? Is it not enough to be cast aside? Why? Oh God ...

I stand here and don't know what to do. Where do I turn? Do I run, and starve? Do I turn away and hide in the darkness? Do I face the one attacking me? Do I dare? I step forward.

Another rock comes, and another. Then I see her. And I know her face. It can't be. Not her. But it is. For a breath, our eyes meet. No. Don't you know me? Don't you see that it is me? Please ... look past what I have become.

Her face pales, washed white in the lantern light. For a moment, I think she knows, I think she sees. But the moment passes. She only sees the scars. Only sees the monster I've become. And I recognize her revulsion, the horror reflected in her eyes.

I long to reach out my hand, to shout that I am not this monster. That I am human. Just a person. Just like her. But my hands are still, my mouth silent.

She wouldn't believe me anyway. She couldn't. Even I can't.

So I stand here, waiting.

Her hand shakes. But she doesn't drop the stone. It comes at me. I cannot move. Cannot flee. It hits me, and sets my feet free.

I run.

In my mind, I see the rocks still coming. They fly at me from all sides. They have faces that sneer. Eyes that accuse. Mouths that shriek at me that I don't belong.

The place where the rock hit me stings. But the pain is slight, so little compared to what I have endured. I barely feel the stones on my body, scarcely know that they've hit. But I feel them in my soul. They strike my flesh and bounce away. They leave no mark. But inside, something is bleeding, aching, something beyond healing.

They know who I am, unloved.

God, why do you hate me? Why won't you love me? Why won't someone love me? Is it because of what I've done, or what I've become?

Wind rushes in my ears. I hear nothing but the rumble of it. And I know the rocks have stopped. But I don't pause. Don't turn. I can't.

All I can do is run.

My leg throbs. My chest beats.

Someone is coming. I hear their pursuit. I want to yell, bellow, scream. But I don't. I only run.

The pounding of feet behind me. The roar of voices. A call. A shout.

Then a shot splits the night.

* * *

"Run. Run away." Stone after stone flew from Ellie's hand toward the retreating back of the ghost-man. "Go." Her shouts echoed in her ears. Loud. Harsh. But it didn't matter now. It was too late. The boys had seen her. Seen him.

Ellie lurched back. A crate tipped beside her. Bits of sawdust scattered across the ground and glowed in the moonlight.

With a savage roar, four boys erupted from behind the woodpile. They raced toward her. Faces, red and narrow-eyed, swarmed before her vision. A fist raised. An arm cocked back.

Ellie screamed and dashed into the street.

And still they came, their voices making a cacophony of sound around her. "There it is."

"Told you so."

"Do you see him?"

Footsteps thudded behind her.

"What's she doing here?"

"Get him."

"Get her."

"Hurry."

"It's getting away."

"Stop him."

Ellie tripped and lurched forward.

Someone rushed past. A hand shoved into her back. She fell. Her ankle twisted beneath her. Ash flew into her eyes, into her mouth. She spat it out. "Leave him alone." The words tumbled from her lips. "Don't!" She staggered upright. Pain shot up her leg.

Two more bodies pushed past her and swerved right. She swayed on her feet. "Stop it."

The boys only ran faster.

But the ghost-man was running too. His image grew smaller. He was almost gone. Almost free.

Ellie clenched her fists.

Someone yelled. Another whistled.

Then Leif's voice punctured the air. His words came sharp and clear. "I'll stop him."

Ellie turned.

Silver glinted in the moonlight.

"Nooooo!" She reached toward him.

Leif's arm shook. "Get down, fool."

Ellie froze.

A shot exploded into the air. Pain pierced her side. She spun backward, doubled over, and dropped to her knees. The world tipped.

And then came sickly silence.

10

The lantern flickered. Shadows shuddered over the tent walls. Arla laced her fingers beneath her chin and stared at the wooden trunk between the cots. Now was the moment. Ellie was gone. The Strom baby slept quietly in a basket in the corner. No one, nothing, kept her from opening the trunk, retrieving the journal, and again facing what Rakel had written there. Nothing, except the horrible hammering of her heart.

Arla stood and adjusted the wick on the lantern. The light flared brighter. *I can do this. God help me, I must do it. I owe it to Rakel. I owe it to myself.* She straightened her shoulders, crossed the tent, and lifted the trunk's lid. There, the journal lay askew with the cover bent back and three pages wrinkled beneath it.

With shaking hands, Arla lifted the journal from its place and smoothed the pages. Her finger traced the clear, slanted writing. *Rakel …*

Strange how this was all she had left of the daughter she had fed and clothed, fought with and loved, for nineteen years. Just this skinny little book with its memories and accusations. Just these pages that began with words that shredded Arla's soul. *Mama hates me.*

How could everything have gone so wrong? The fire had taken Rakel. But Arla had lost her long before that. Somewhere between pinafores and grown-up pleats, Rakel had slipped away; had become the person who wrote those terrible words that still ricocheted in Arla's mind.

But with Ellie, maybe God was giving her a second chance, a chance to do things right. And this time, things would be different. Arla would cherish her, protect her, redeem the mistakes she'd made before. This time, there would be no locked room, no fire, no regrets. Ellie would be safe and happy. And nothing would go wrong.

Arla lowered herself onto her cot and tilted the book toward the lantern light. She focused on the words, dark against the page.

MAMA HATES ME. I KNOW SHE DOES.

Arla's breath shuddered in her chest. For a moment, she could read no further. How could Rakel write those words? How could she think them? *Oh God, help me …* Arla pressed her knuckle to her lips and focused on the next sentence.

OR MAYBE HATE IS TOO STRONG A WORD.

Arla trembled. *Yes, Rakel. Too strong. Much too strong.*

MAYBE IT'S MORE THAT MAMA JUST DOESN'T NOTICE ME UNLESS I'M DOING SOMETHING WRONG. AND APPARENTLY, I DO WRONG QUITE OFTEN. I SMILE TOO MUCH OR LAUGH TOO MUCH OR CRY TOO MUCH. I AM NEVER WHO SHE EXPECTS ME TO BE. I AM NEVER THE DAUGHTER SHE WANTS. NEVER THE DAUGHTER SHE WANTS TO LOVE.

Tears gathered in Arla's eyes. Rakel had always been fierce, stubborn. But unloved? Unwanted? Never. Hadn't Rakel known that? Hadn't she realized that everything Arla had done was because she loved her daughter? Loved her, and wanted what was best.

IT HAPPENED AGAIN THIS MORNING. WE WENT TO CHURCH AS WE ALWAYS DO ON SUNDAY MORNINGS. WE SANG OUR SONGS, THE PREACHER PREACHED, AND WE DROPPED OUR COINS IN THE OFFERING PLATE AS IT PASSED. IT WAS SUCH A NORMAL SUNDAY, WITH THE SUN GLITTERING IN THE WINDOW AND THE PEOPLE SITTING STRAIGHT AND SCRUBBED IN THE PEWS. IT SHOULD HAVE BEEN A DAY LIKE ANY OTHER. BUT IT WASN'T.

Arla searched back through her memory, but could think of nothing special that had happened on April 19. She couldn't even remember anything unusual that had happened in all of April. Now August. August was different. That was when everything changed. But she wouldn't read about that. Not yet. April was difficult enough.

Her gaze again lowered to the page.

I HAVE NO IDEA WHAT THE PREACHER SAID TODAY. I DON'T KNOW WHAT VERSE HE READ OR WHAT MESSAGE HE BROUGHT TO OUR CONGREGATION. BUT I DO KNOW THAT I SAW LOVE TODAY. I SAW WHAT FAMILY OUGHT TO BE. I SAW WHAT I'VE MISSED ALL MY LIFE.

Oh Rakel ... Arla paused and wiped the wetness from her eyes. Had it truly been so awful? Had Rakel never been happy, had she never felt cared for?

THERE, TWO SEATS IN FRONT OF US, SAT MR. STROM, WITH HIS BROAD SHOULDERS CRAMMED INTO THAT FANCY COAT, AND MAGGIE, LOOKING ELEGANT AND CAPABLE EVEN THOUGH SHE WAS ONLY WEARING A PLAIN COTTON FROCK. HE LOOKED AT HER AND SMILED. THEN SHE LIFTED AN UNGLOVED HAND AND BRUSHED HIS CHEEK. A SIMPLE GESTURE. QUICK. GENTLE. I GLANCED AWAY AND SAW MAMA LOOKING TOO. HER BROWS WERE KNIT TOGETHER IN A FROWN. HOW COULD SHE FROWN AT SO PERFECT A PICTURE? HOW COULD SHE SCOWL IN THE FACE OF SUCH TENDERNESS?

Was I frowning then? Arla touched a finger to her forehead and rubbed at the wrinkles she found there. She didn't remember frowning. Didn't remember even seeing Maggie touch her husband's face. But it was just like Rakel to make something out of nothing. Just like her to believe the worst without cause.

THEN MAGGIE SHIFTED IN HER SEAT. AND THERE, IN HER ARMS, LAY THE MOST BEAUTIFUL THING I'VE EVER SEEN. THEIR NEW BABY DAUGHTER, WITH A PINK BLANKET TUCKED UNDER HER CHIN. I WATCHED THE WAY MAGGIE LOOKED AT THAT BABY, WITH LOVE BRIMMING IN HER EYES AND SOFTNESS PAINTING HER FEATURES. NO WONDER MR. STROM COULDN'T KEEP HIS EYES OFF HER AS HE LEANED OVER AND ADJUSTED THE BABY'S BLANKET.

Ah, yes, the baby. Arla did remember the baby. And how Rakel had looked at that child. She had often wondered later if that had anything to do with what happened in August. She had wondered, and even accused. But she never asked. Why didn't she simply ask? She should have. She could have. But now it was too late.

HOW COULD I HELP BUT GO UP TO THEM AFTERWARD? HADN'T WE PRAYED FOR THAT BABY FOR THREE LONG YEARS, ME AND NORA AND WINNIE? HOW COULD I HELP WANTING TO HOLD THE BABY, JUST FOR A MOMENT, AND FEEL HER WARMTH IN MY OWN ARMS? MAGGIE DIDN'T MIND. SHE SMILED SO SWEETLY WHEN SHE HANDED LITTLE EMMA TO ME.

AND I WAS CAREFUL. SO VERY, VERY CAREFUL, AS I STOOD THERE AND GAZED INTO THAT PERFECT LITTLE FACE. THE PINK BOW MOUTH, THE PORCELAIN SKIN, THE DELICATE EYELIDS FLUTTERING IN HER SLEEP. HOW MY HEART POUNDED AS I HELD HER. HOW MY SOUL THROBBED WITH THE LONGING.

IF ONLY ... IF ONLY ... DARE I SAY IT? DARE I WRITE THE WORDS HERE AND MAKE THE WISH REAL? IF ONLY I HAD A BABY TOO. I WANT A CHUBBY

HAND TO WRAP AROUND MY FINGER, A SMALL FACE TO GAZE UP INTO MY OWN. I WANT TO SIT IN CHURCH WITH A HUSBAND AT MY SIDE AND A BABY IN MY ARMS. THEN IT WOULDN'T BE JUST MAMA AND ME ANYMORE. THERE WOULD BE SOMEONE NEW. SOMEONE WHO DIDN'T CARE HOW I DRESSED, WHAT I LOOKED LIKE, OR IF I SANG OFF-KEY. IF I HAD A DAUGHTER, I WOULD LOVE HER. AND SHE WOULD LOVE ME.

Pain lodged in Arla's chest. *I did love you, Rakel. I always loved you.* But love wasn't enough. Rakel had needed something more. Something Arla didn't know, didn't understand.

I DON'T KNOW HOW LONG I HELD THE BABY. BUT MAMA SAID IT WAS TOO LONG. SHE FROWNED AT ME, GAVE ME THAT LOOK THAT SAID I'D DONE WRONG. JUST BY HOLDING A BABY. HOW COULD JUST HOLDING A BABY BE WRONG?

The page ended. Arla ran her fingers over the words one more time. Her vision blurred. *I wish you knew how much I loved you. I wish you had known it before you died.* She sighed. *It was for your own good. Always for your own good.* But Rakel wouldn't understand. She never did. Never had.

Arla turned the page.

GOD, PLEASE HELP MAMA CHANGE. HELP MAMA UNDERSTAND THAT—

A shot shattered the silence. Then a shout. A scream. The pounding of feet. Arla dropped the journal and rushed out into the night. A dozen pale faces shone in the moonlight.

Rakel. No. Ellie. Where was Ellie?

Her gaze flew down the street. There, a boy stood, smoke still curling from the gun in his hand. For a moment, he didn't move. Then he turned and fled.

Arla lifted her skirt and ran after him. Then she saw it. A figure crumpled in the street. No. It couldn't be. *Ellie?* She raced toward her.

Voices blurred in the darkness.

"Who was that?"

"Is someone shot?"

"That boy had a gun."

"What's going on?"

"Who is it?"

Arla reached Ellie and fell to her knees beside her. She touched the child's face, white, stark in the glimmer of lantern light. "Eleanor? Eleanor!"

Ellie's eyes fluttered open. "Mama? Is that you?"

Arla's heart constricted. *No. I'm not your mama, but I want to be.* She looked away and sniffed. "Yes, child." Then she leaned over and gathered Ellie in her arms. "Mama's here. It'll be all right."

"I hurt. My side."

Arla lifted her hand away from Ellie's back and saw fingers stained red with blood.

* * *

Josef kicked a rock in his path. Nils had been right. The cart was gone. Just one more frustration in this already maddening day. As if having to endure that church service wasn't bad enough, the seam had split on his boots, he found spit-up on his shoulder, and worst yet, Mrs. Larsen had cornered him on his way out to the farmstead.

Oh, it wasn't as if he hadn't seen her coming. You could hardly miss her, with her pumpkin-red hair and dress to match. He thought of ducking behind a tree, but the fire had burned off all the branches. He considered striking off across the field, except there was that culvert he couldn't cross. He even tried turning around and pretending he didn't see her, but Mrs. Larsen refused to be fooled. Just as he started back along the path, her voice reached out and grabbed him.

"Josef Strom!" Her squeal halted his escape. "There you are, you silly man."

Reluctantly, he turned back toward her.

She bustled up to him, her cheeks pig-pink with exertion. "Wherever have you been hiding yourself, you naughty boy?" She slapped his arm with the handkerchief in her hand.

Josef tightened his jaw.

Mrs. Larsen leaned into him and grinned. Her breath wafted into his face. Cabbage, and onion. He tried not to breathe.

"Lucky thing I came upon you here. Been hopin' to catch you for weeks now. Got a little secret for ya, I do." She winked at him.

Secret? Josef narrowed his eyes.

Mrs. Larsen giggled. "Look at you." She put her hands on her hips, tilted forward, and squinted up at him. "Ya look like a rabbit caught in the lantern light. Buck up, now. I got fine news." She paused, as if expecting him to say something. She should have known better.

Finally, she sighed. "Well, I'll tell ya anyway. Charlotte Johnson's got eyes for you. But don't be telling that you heard it from me." She thumped her chest with her thumb. "So what do you got to say to that?"

Josef grunted.

"That it? Charlotte's a fine-looking woman. Got all that curly blonde hair, and good wide hips for the childbearing." Mrs. Larsen swung her own hips from side to side.

Josef backed away.

Mrs. Larsen frowned. "What's wrong with you, man? You have a baby, you need a wife."

"I had a wife."

"Can't see no man takin' proper care of a wee one. That there's women's work."

Josef turned away and stared out over the treetops. It wouldn't have been so bad if it were the first time someone had said something. But Mrs. Petersen had mentioned a cousin in Pine City, Mr. Bremer his sister in Minneapolis, and Mrs. Biddle some widowed daughter of a friend's sister. Why couldn't they understand? He didn't want another woman to try to replace Maggie. The last thing he needed was another mouth to feed. But would they listen? Of course not.

"You come on over for some cabbage soup tomorrow at suppertime. I'll invite Charlotte." Mrs. Larsen's voice broke into his thoughts.

Josef glanced back toward her. "Can't. Busy."

"Busy? With what?"

Josef didn't answer.

"Well, the next day then. And don't say you're busy. Can't be too busy to look after that baby's future, can ya? Tuesday night, supper. And don't you be late." She patted him on the arm. "You can thank me later."

But Josef wouldn't thank her. And he wouldn't be coming for supper. Not on Tuesday, not on Wednesday, not a month from now or two. He didn't want no wife. All he wanted was that fool cart.

Now, Josef rubbed his hand over his face to drive away the memory of his encounter with Mrs. Larsen hours before. He needed to just forget it. Move on. Think of other things. Things like who could have stolen Maggie's cart. Who ... and then he remembered. A figure cloaked in black watching him from the edge of the trees. A person just waiting for him to leave. He punched his fist into the palm of his hand and glared into the darkness. *Of course*. If he ever saw that man again, he'd ... he'd ... well, he didn't know what he'd do, but he'd do something.

Josef strode down the path away from his farmstead. Gray twilight darkened to night. Eventually, the town came into view. There, spots of lantern light shone over half-built structures. Tents, dirtier now than when they were first erected, still stood in jagged rows. Timber-filled freight cars lined the tracks. He glanced left. There, a few townspeople moved in the streets. He could barely make out their shadowed figures. Three, maybe four. No, five people cluttered the street. He narrowed his eyes. Something was wrong.

Muted voices drifted toward him. Someone was shouting. Another shouted back. Two pushed past a third. Another leapt forward behind them.

Josef's gaze swept over the scene, then focused on the fifth figure, wrapped in a black overcoat. The man raced toward him with an awkward, limping gait. Could it be? It was. He knew it. He quickened his pace. He'd seen that strange, black-cloaked figure before. But this time, Josef was ready. This time, he wouldn't let the man get away.

He veered left and broke into a run.

The sound of a shot blasted through the night.

A shudder rippled through Josef's frame, but he didn't stop. He would catch that man. Make him pay for his thievery.

The cloaked figure swerved.

Josef followed. The distance closed between them until the man skidded to a halt just ten yards in front of him.

Josef slowed, ready for a fight. He raised his arms.

The man stumbled backward. "You!" The word rattled between them.

Josef lunged forward.

The man turned.

And there in the distance, lit by a circle of lantern light, lay a child, fallen in the street.

11

For a moment, I am free. Then he is there. A burly figure wrapped in shadow. He comes at me from the darkness.

I swerve.

He turns too.

What does he want? To capture me? But why? Can't he hear my fear? Can't he sense my pain?

The shot. I still hear it in my mind. And I wonder if another is coming. The one with the gun will catch me. And this time, he will not miss.

But I can't escape. Can't get past this man before me.

He slows.

I stop.

And I know the set of those shoulders. The tilt of his head.

"You!" The word escapes me in a gasp.

He stares at me.

Does he know me? Does he guess who I really am? He mustn't. I can't let *him. I must escape. Turn back. But they are there. Behind me. I can't go forward. I can't go back.*

I turn. But they aren't there. Somehow, my pursuers have vanished. And then I see a crumpled mass in the street. A person? Oh no. Not Ellie.

I forget about the man behind me. I forget about those who were chasing me. I run toward her. Faces flash around me. Voices buzz. But I don't care. Not anymore. I must reach her. I must know …

But someone else is running too. A woman, with skirts gathered up in one hand. She reaches Ellie first.

I stop and press myself into the shadows.

The woman kneels beside Ellie. She gathers her in her arms. And I hear her weep.

Ellie stirs. Her eyes open. Words stumble from her lips. "Mama?"

Sweat breaks on my forehead. I tremble and cannot move closer.

The woman looks up. Across the distance, our eyes meet and clash. She drops her gaze. "Yes, child. Mama's here."

My jaw tightens. My fists clench. Pain shoots up my arms, across my face. How could you? How dare you?

Words force themselves from my mouth. "She is not your daughter."

Does she hear me?

Her eyes raise again. They search the darkness where I stand. Is that fear I see on her face? Or fury? She spits words toward me. "What do you know? Who are you?"

Who am I? I want to laugh. I want to cry. But all I do is turn and run away.

And I don't look back.

* * *

Lars Jensen pulled back the heavy drape and glanced outside. "There's nothing there now. Are you sure you saw it, Robert?" He let the drape fall and turned back around.

Robert Larsen paced in front of the massive brick fireplace. Flames crackled in the grate. "Saw it last night, I did. Clear as a white bean in a black cat's—"

"I know the saying."

Robert nodded. "There was a light up there in those hills, no mistake. And today I saw something moving out there."

Lars ran his hand over the upholstery on his new wingback chair. His house was one of the first to be rebuilt. He had to cash in some of his investments to do it, but it was worth it. Two stories, and when it was finished, it would have rich oak floors and more rooms than he needed. The preacher had called it lavish, especially when the train arrived with a load of furnishings all the way from New York. But it was important to keep up appearances, especially if that man from Leif's school came a-calling.

"We gotta do something." Robert made a fist and punched his palm. "Too many things gone missing. Too many questions. Too many accidents. It's that ghost. I know it."

A cat meowed in the next room. Then another. And another.

Robert started. "How many of those things you got in there?"

Lars glanced toward the kitchen. "Four or five. Strays, you know, from the fire."

Robert shook his head. "Can't say as I can stand cats."

A calico meandered through the doorway and toward Lars. It stopped and rubbed along his leg. He reached down and scratched it behind the ears. The cat purred.

Robert cleared his throat. "As I was saying 'bout that ghost ..."

Lars straightened. "I've told you. There is no ghost."

"I saw it."

Lars picked up the cat and tucked it against his side. "What you saw is a light in the hills. A light that shouldn't have been there, to be sure. But only a light."

"Ain't that enough? Tells us there's something out there. Something we need to protect against."

"Do we?"

"Sure we do, before anyone else comes to harm. You know how old man Whitworth says someone's been tamperin' with his saw. Almost cut his arm off last time he tried to use it. Will Swenson swears he saw something go into his tent. His dog went missing after that and never did come back. And Billy Benson tried riding up there in those hills last week. Horse got so spooked it pretty near threw him down in a ditch and trampled him. If that ain't the doings of a ghost, I don't know what is."

"Could be a man."

"It ain't a man. It's something else. Something bad." His voice rose and cracked.

Lars strode to the kitchen and placed the cat inside. He closed the door, came back, and poured himself a shot of vodka. Then he offered one to Robert. "So, what do you propose?"

Robert downed the drink in one gulp. "I say we get up some men and go after it. Hunt it down."

"And when you find it?"

"I don't know. Bring it in, I guess."

"Bring in a ghost?"

"Well ..."

Lars set the shot glass on the table and smiled. "One thing I've learned is that you don't go hunting for something if you can make it come to you instead."

"But how—"

The creak of the door silenced both men.

Lars turned.

Leif's head poked through the doorway. His eyes met his father's.

"Son?"

Leif dropped his gaze and slipped through the door. Without another glance, he hunched his shoulders and headed toward the stairs.

Lars raised his voice. "What have you been up to, boy?"

"Nuthin'." Leif stopped and glanced toward Robert. "What's he doing here?"

Lars' eyes narrowed. His tone hardened. "Don't be rude. You been up to no good?"

Leif's face flushed.

Robert cleared his throat. "I gotta go anyway, Lars. The wife's got cabbage on, and she'll cook it down to nothing if I'm not back in time."

Lars nodded. "We'll talk again. Soon."

Robert grabbed his hat and coat and hurried out the front door.

A full minute passed before Lars again turned to his son. "I can see you've done something. So, tell me now."

Leif jabbed his toe into the floor. "I didn't do nuthin', I said."

Lars crossed the distance between them in two strides. He grabbed Leif's arm and spun the boy toward him.

Something flew from Leif's waistband and clattered on the floor. Lars bent over and picked it up. His pistol. Firelight flickered off the silver barrel, shone off the ivory handle. His knuckles whitened as he turned and shoved the weapon under Leif's nose. "What are you doing with this?"

"I ... I ..."

Lars ran his finger over the gunpowder residue on the muzzle. His voice sharpened. "Don't lie to me."

Leif backed away. "I just, I just wanted to show the boys. That's all."

"It's been fired."

"I had to. It was there, the ghost." Leif licked his lips. "I mean, the man. The one everyone's talking about. I saw it."

"And?"

"It was coming at us. I had to do something." His gaze slid away to the left. "I was just trying to protect the town."

Lars laughed. "Trying to be a hero, were you?" He tucked the gun into his belt.

Leif dropped his head.

"Look at me when I'm talking to you."

Leif's eyes slipped up to meet his.

"You're no hero. Don't try to be." *Not like this, anyway.* It was too dangerous. Too risky. If Leif had succeeded … Lars shivered. Shooting someone, even if it was just a "ghost," wouldn't look good to the people at the school back East. If they heard about that, they might just change their minds about the boy's character. Good thing Leif was such a bad shot.

"Yes, sir." The words came out in a low mutter.

Lars straightened. "So, you missed then?"

"Yes, sir."

A long silence stretched between them. Lars turned away. There was more. He could tell by the way Leif fidgeted with the hem on his sleeve, the way he rubbed his nose with his index finger, the way he stood with his shoulders rounded and his head listing to one side. Leif's mother used to do that. It meant she was hiding something. But Lars knew how to get the truth from her. He always had. And he knew the same technique would work with her son. He rubbed his knuckles with the palm of his hand. "You'd better tell me everything. Now."

Leif's voice shook as he spoke. "I think, I think …" The next words tumbled out in a rushed whisper. "I think I mighta shot Ellie Hansen."

Lars spun back around. His insides went cold. It couldn't be. He'd heard wrong. He had to. Leif couldn't have … not after all his plans, all his work. "You didn't … She isn't …"

Leif stumbled backward. "I was aiming for the ghost. The man. And she jumped up in front of me. It weren't my fault."

Lars stepped forward. His hands balled into fists then loosed again. "It was an accident. I swear."

"There are no accidents." Lars drew back his hand and smacked Leif's face. A single blow. Well aimed. Well timed. He deserved worse. If he knew, if he only knew …

Leif fell against the wall behind him. A tiny speck of blood welled at the corner of his mouth. Tears rose in his eyes. "Pa … please. She ain't hurt bad. At least, well, I don't think so."

"You didn't stay to find out?" He forced the words from between clenched teeth. This wasn't happening. It couldn't happen. Not now. Not after he'd planned so carefully and worked so hard. He had to make this go away, make it disappear. That way the school people wouldn't find out. They would never know. "Did anyone see you?"

Leif wiped his mouth with the back of his hand. "Well, Ellie did." The admission was no more than a whisper.

Cold fear settled in Lars' gut. He'd done everything for the boy. Given him everything a father could give. Clothes, food, a name, a reputation. Handed it to him on a silver platter. Handed him a place of respect, of honor. And opened doors for him that he, Lars, had never even dreamed of when he was a boy. Leif had it all. And one stupid mistake wasn't going to take that away.

And not only that, he'd worked hard to gain his standing in this town. For himself, and for Leif. He wasn't going to lose that either. If the town found out, if there was a trial … that would be even worse than the school finding out. There were too many secrets hidden in his past. Things only Agnes had known, and Winnie, too. But they were gone, buried, and his secrets with them.

Lars drew a deep breath and closed his eyes. He would make this problem go away. He would make that Ellie girl go away. For Leif, and for himself. He leaned over until his nose was an inch from Leif's. "Remember this, boy; if you're going to do wrong, do so in secret." The words hissed from between clenched teeth. "Only a fool shoots someone in the open for all to see."

"I didn't ..."

"You'd better hope not."

Leif shrank back and ran the back of his arm over his face. "Yes, sir."

Lars spat on the floor. Coward. Idiot. Fool of a boy. Like his mother. Do something stupid and whine about it afterward. But ... he took a deep breath. Things were supposed to be different now. Better. He wasn't going to rant and rave and do something he'd regret. He wasn't going to lose control. Lars pressed his fingers into his temples and lowered his voice to an even tone. "Go."

"What?"

"Get out of my sight and go to your room. I'll take care of this. I'll make it go away."

"Pa?"

"Go!"

Leif scuttled up the stairs and disappeared.

Lars shook his head. Somehow, he was going to have to teach that boy how to be a man, how to stand on his own two feet. But first he'd have to save his reputation. He was good at that.

He had done it before, and no one ever knew. Except her. And now she was dead. And he was safe. One mistake. That time, his. This time, Leif's. But he would take care of it. He would make it disappear just as he had done then. And no one would ever be the wiser.

***

Flame spun through Ellie's mind. A face shifted, distorted in the fire. Strange. Unrecognizable. A monster, with twisted red flesh and wide, shining eyes. It plunged toward her.

Ellie screamed. Heat burned her throat.

Claws stretched from the fire. Reaching, contorting, scraping hot air.

A shriek pierced her senses. Hers? Or the monster's? She didn't know. Didn't care.

She tried to escape, but couldn't.

The monster lunged, then withdrew, then lunged again. Farther, closer. Churning heat. Roiling fire.

"Get away from me."

Heat seared her hand. She looked down. There, a rock burned, glowed red with flame. She shouted and tried to throw the stone from her. It stuck fast, burning, burning, sending fire up her wrist, her arm, her chest.

"No." A yell ripped from Ellie's throat. She jolted upright. Pain shot through her side. Her breath grated in her ears.

"Eleanor?"

She blinked.

The fire withdrew, then disappeared. Her breathing slowed. Before her, the tent flap shivered in the breeze. The glow of sunlight drew a thin line around the opening and cast beads of light onto the dirt floor. Her hands pressed into her cot, damp now with sweat. She gripped the fabric and squeezed her eyes shut.

It wasn't real. Not the flame. Not the fingers. Not the face in the fire. *Just a nightmare, just a dream ...*

"Shh, child. Lay back now."

Hands pressed into Ellie's shoulders and guided her back to the cot. A cool rag touched her forehead. And the fire retreated, down from her neck, her chest, and settled in her side.

Ellie's eyes fluttered open. Above her, Mrs. Anderson's face came into focus, driving away the image of the monster in the flames.

Mrs. Anderson tried to smile, but failed.

Ellie turned her head. *Where am I?* Her mouth formed the words, but no sound came. She wet her lips. "Where am I?" This time, her voice reached a croaking whisper.

"Right here. You've been right here."

She groaned. "What happened?"

Mrs. Anderson dunked the cloth into a bowl of water, wrung it out, and again dabbed Ellie's forehead. "It seems you were shot."

"Shot?" Did the monster shoot her? He had claws, not a gun. And there was fire. Lots of fire.

Mrs. Anderson held a cup up to Ellie's lips. "Hush now, child. Everything will be all right. Drink this."

A trickle of hot tea slid down her throat. Tea, reminding her of Mama. She pushed the cup away. Pain throbbed in her side. Bad pain. Like someone was digging at her with a hot poker. She reached down.

Mrs. Anderson caught Ellie's fingers before they reached her side. "No. You mustn't touch it. The doctor has dressed and bandaged you. You'll heal, in time."

Bandage? Heal? Then Ellie remembered. Leif and the gun.

Her eyes fixed on Mrs. Anderson. She wet her lips. "Ghost?" The word tumbled weakly from her mouth.

"Shh ..."

Ellie spoke again, louder this time. "Ghost? Ghost-man?"

Mrs. Anderson stood up.

Ellie grabbed her sleeve.

"Did he get away?"

"Who?"

"The ghost-man."

Mrs. Anderson removed Ellie's fingers from her sleeve and turned aside. "She's talking nonsense again, Doctor. Something about a ghost."

A man's voice drifted from the corner of the tent. "The laudanum will start working soon."

Around her, the tent began to spin and blur. Ellie rubbed her eyes. Her hand fell back to the cot. Fire flared around her again. And the monster appeared once more, his mouth open, one arm reaching toward her.

Ellie ran.

The fire followed.

And then, out of the flames, someone called her name. "Ellie ... Ellie ... come back."

She stopped. Turned.

And there stood Mama, with a halo of flames, and fire reflecting in her eyes.

12

Lars had just grabbed his velvet-trimmed coat when someone banged on the front door. He paused and smiled. Two days. It had taken them two full days to come for Leif. He'd expected them to come that night, but they hadn't. And that meant they didn't want to come at all.

He took a moment to straighten his collar and smooth his hair. A glance in the mirror in the hallway told him that it didn't help. That little bit of hair still stuck up in the back, and his collar wouldn't lie just right. From a distance he looked fine. But up close, well, he could see the imperfections. He'd waxed his mustache, but it still didn't look as neat as those he saw in the magazines. He bought all the right clothes, but somehow they didn't seem to fit right. And the gray at his temples was supposed to give him a look of authority, but today it seemed only to accentuate his age. He tried a smile. No, that wouldn't do. He drew his eyebrows together. That was better. He ought to look concerned, caring. He narrowed his eyes. Yes, that was a look that communicated how seriously he took the incident.

A knock sounded again on the wood.

Lars pulled back his shoulders and walked to the door, not too quickly, not too slowly. Calm. Controlled. He needed them to believe him. Trust him. He opened the door.

Outside stood the sheriff, his face red, his hat tipped to one side.

Lars opened the door wider. "Sheriff, come in, I've been expecting you." He took the man's hat and hung it on a hook near the door.

"Sorry to have to come, Lars." The sheriff knocked the mud off his boots and stepped inside. "You know what happened in town a couple nights ago?"

Lars stifled a snort. Of course he knew. He knew everything. More than the slow-witted sheriff at least. And more important, he knew who saw what, and what it took to adjust their memory. A few dollars, a few comments, a few well-placed questions. After all, it had been dark. Even that fool boy Ned was now sure Leif had been only acting to protect the girl. Sometimes he thought that people could be convinced of anything. And swear they saw it with their own eyes. Except the girl. She was the only one who could still accuse his son.

The sheriff waited.

Lars put on his look of concern. "Leif told me about the accident."

The sheriff shook his head. "Well, I don't know about no accident. Some said your boy shot a girl right there in the street, then he ran away. We can't just let that pass, you know. No matter who he is."

Lars pulled at the corner of his mustache. "Those folks are mistaken then. I'm sure if you asked them again ..."

"Don't need to ask them. I'm asking you."

Lars frowned. "Of course Leif ran home. To get me. To get help. What any good boy would do."

"To get help, you say?"

Lars nodded. "Of course, Sheriff. And as anyone will tell you, I went right out, as soon as he told me. By the time I got there, though, the girl had already been moved. She's all right, I'm told. The bullet just grazed her?"

The sheriff scrubbed his head with his hand. "Lot more than a graze, sorry to say."

A chill raced through Lars. "She's not, not ..."

The sheriff pulled at his ear. Then he shifted his weight from one foot to the other.

Lars cleared his throat. The man needed to stand still. It was hard to concentrate with him hopping about like a jaybird on a hot stone.

"Naw, she'll be fine. In time. Got a lot of healing to do. Gonna need a good doctor, too."

"Of course, I'll pay for all that. Whatever she needs." And he'd do more. He'd already made plans. Soon, the girl would be gone, and he wouldn't have to worry about her any longer.

"Mighty good of you."

Lars motioned toward the parlor. A black kitten trotted through the doorway and disappeared into the next room. "It's the least I can do. Come, have a seat." He guided the man into the parlor and to the wing-back chair near the fire. Then, he poured two shots of vodka and handed one to the sheriff.

The sheriff turned the shot glass in his hand, then set it, still full, on the table. "Justice has to be done, Lars. The boy's got to face up to what he did."

"What he did? He didn't do anything wrong. The boy was just trying to protect that girl from a ghost. It's just too bad he's such a lousy shot."

The sheriff grinned. "Ain't that the truth. Poor kid couldn't hit the broad side of a barn. Last summer—"

"Can't punish him for bad aim, can you, Sheriff?"

The sheriff stared at Lars for a long moment, then his voice turned thoughtful. "Don't suppose we can. That Gunnar kid did say that they saw the ghost, and it was coming on quick toward the girl."

"Yes, to attack her." Lars' fingers tightened on the glass in his hand. Clear liquid sloshed against the rim.

The sheriff pulled at his chin. "Might be."

"Leif tells me it would have killed the girl, if it weren't for his shot."

"Shot almost killed her."

"Now, Sheriff ..."

"Well, it coulda."

Lars grimaced. "But it didn't. A simple mistake. The boy takes the gun to show his friends. That creature appears and attacks an innocent girl, and Leif tries to fight it off, but the bullet ends up missing. The creature breaks off its attack, and the girl is hurt but alive. Good thing the boy had the gun, I say."

"Maybe ..."

"The one truly responsible is that monster in the woods."

The sheriff stood and sighed. "Don't I know it. Folks been pestering me to go find that thing. 'Hunt down the ghost,' they say. 'The town's not safe.' As if there ain't a hundred other things to do, what with all the rebuilding, and relief trains, and everyone needing something. I'm only one man."

Lars led the sheriff toward the door. "Don't you worry. I'll get some men together soon, and we'll go find out what's hiding in the hills. You just leave it to me." The last thing he needed to do was hunt down a ghost. The trick would be to look for it without finding it. It was too convenient to have an obscure figure on which to blame everything that went wrong. If he had his way, the monster in the hills would remain a mystery forever.

"You're a good man, Lars. Thank you."

"And I'll make sure the girl is taken care of too. I have some friends in St. Paul who'd be happy to take her in."

"Can't ask for more than that."

No, you can't.

The sheriff ambled toward the door and grabbed his hat. "Glad we got this cleared up."

"So am I. You take care now, and say hello to the missus." Lars patted the sheriff on the back, then shut the door behind him. His smile grew. In a week, Leif's misdeed would be forgotten, or better yet, remembered as a fine act of heroism. The school would never find out the truth. And the townspeople would forget their questions. There would be no trial. No digging about in the past. No shame. All he needed to do was get rid of the girl. For good.

And to do that, he need only send a telegram, and call in a favor.

***

"You aren't planning on stealing that jar of beans, are you?"

Arla heard the voice behind her and turned. "Nils Heg." She drew herself up to her full height. "How dare you suggest—"

Nils chuckled. "Don't worry, I have plenty more." He swept his arm toward the rows of shelves lining the mercantile. Barrels of potatoes and salt pork, baskets of cloth, and boxes full of who-knew-what sat to one side of the store. In the middle, where Arla stood, were the shelves filled with jars of beans, sauerkraut, and a few pickled beets.

Arla set the jar back onto the shelf and wagged a finger at Nils. "I have never stolen a single thing in my life, and you know it."

Nils threw back his head and laughed. "You never could take a joke, Arla Mae."

She put one hand on her hip. "That's Mrs. Anderson to you, sir."

"You betcha, Mrs. Anderson." He gave a quick bow.

Arla frowned. "Besides, how would you know?"

"Know what?"

"If I can take a joke."

Nils chuckled again and tapped his temple. "Well, I do recall that time back in school—"

"Oh no. Don't you dare bring that up—"

"When someone, and I won't say who—"

"I know it was you."

"Accidentally opened the outhouse door—"

"It was no accident."

"Just as—"

"Not another word. I mean it."

Nils sighed. "Okeydokey, you win." He turned and straightened the bean jar on the shelf. "But they were such pretty bloomers." He said the last words under his breath.

"Oooooh." Arla pulled off a glove and slapped Nils' arm with it. "You hush. What a time to be bringing up that awful memory. You should know better. Times like these and all."

Nils put up his hands as if to ward off Arla's blow. Then he rubbed his chin. "I don't know. No better time, I'd say, to do a little remembering. Those were good days."

Arla shook her head. "Some good, maybe, and some bad. But they're gone now. And the old schoolhouse is too."

"New one's gonna open in not too many weeks, don't you know. Will Ellie be well enough by then?"

Arla grimaced. "I hope so. But Doc isn't certain." She glanced out the door and into the street. "I fear for infection. I just can't believe …"

"I know. Leif says he didn't intend to shoot anyone except some ghost, some monster. Says he only brought the gun to show to his friends. Says it just went off, and he didn't even see Ellie."

Arla watched a stray dog dart down the street. The town was full of dogs these days. Dozens of them, with no homes, no owners. Running wild. Just like those boys. "I know what Leif says. But I wonder … Do you believe him?"

Nils shrugged. "His papa's putting a lot of pressure on everybody to believe him."

"I believed Leif's father before." She shifted her gaze to the window as her eyes focused on another time.

Nils laid a hand on her shoulder. "You all right? You look pale."

A shudder rippled down Arla's back as she refocused on Nils and forced her thoughts back to the present. "Tell me, Mr. Heg, do you know anything about this ghost they're talking about?"

The smile faded from Nils' face. "Only the rumors."

"I've heard talk too, and Eleanor, well, she keeps raving about some ghost-man."

Nils' voice turned hard. "I don't believe in ghosts."

Arla's eyes narrowed. "Of course not." She didn't believe in ghosts either. Only silly, weak-willed women believed in such foolish things. Ghosts. Pah. And yet, there was that form in the shadows. That cloaked figure who spoke words she didn't want to recall. Not a ghost, but a man. Of course he was a man. And one she hoped never to see again.

Nils leaned his forearm on a shelf and glanced out the window. "Sometimes things aren't as they appear, Arla Mae. You remember that."

Arla took a step backward. "I should be going. Eleanor ..."

He shook his shoulders as if he had gotten a chill. A strand of graying hair fell over his forehead. "I'm sorry. I didn't mean to be rude."

Her voice lowered. "You're never rude."

His gaze snapped back toward her. A smile again crinkled his eyes. "Here, take this to Ellie." He turned, plucked a stick of peppermint from an open jar, and handed the candy to Arla. "I made her a promise, you know."

"I know. I was there."

"Well, tell her she can have as many as she wants just as soon as she gets well enough."

"I will." Arla stared down at the striped candy in her hand. Peppermint. Crazy man. As if a stick of candy would make things better. As if that would somehow make the hole in Ellie's side heal up. It was absurd, ridiculous. But Arla tucked the candy into her pocket anyway.

"And don't worry, I'll add the beans to your order and have it sent up right away." His voice was subdued.

"Thank you, Mr. Heg."

"You're welcome, Mrs. Anderson." He moved away and returned to his place behind the counter.

For a moment, Arla watched him and wondered. Then she shook her head and walked out the door. Mud stuck to her shoes as she sloshed down the street toward her tent. That Nils Heg. She smiled to herself. He was a good man. Honest. Kind. If only she had married someone like him instead of Grant Anderson. But Grant was rich and handsome and everything a girl could want. Everything except faithful.

Arla sighed. She'd made plenty of mistakes in her lifetime. With Grant, with Rakel. But she wouldn't make them again. She looked up into the sky, dark now with rain clouds. *Lord, help me not to fail again. Help me to start afresh.*

Her gaze dropped. And there, illuminated by a single ray of sunlight stood the skeleton of her new house. Arla paused and soaked in the sight. So far it was only framed walls and an open roof. But soon, in just weeks, she hoped, it would be a real house, with a wood floor instead of dirt, and solid plaster walls, a kitchen, and—a smile quirked her lips—an outhouse, too. The house wouldn't be very large. Less than half of what she'd had before, and no second floor. But she was glad for that. She didn't need more. Just enough for her and Ellie. Just enough to start their new lives.

Arla turned a corner and made her way back to her tent. She pulled back the flap.

"Doctor." A gasp escaped her. "What are you—" She spotted a second man standing behind the doctor. She rushed toward the far cot. "Eleanor. Is she okay?"

The doctor reached out and grabbed her arm. "She's fine, Mrs. Anderson."

The second man cleared his throat.

The doctor scowled and released his grip. His hand fell to his side. "I mean, of course, she's as well as can be expected, under these conditions."

Arla looked into Ellie's flushed face and knew the child was only feigning sleep. She turned and positioned herself between Ellie and the men. "These conditions? What do you mean?"

The doctor glanced around the tent. "Please, don't make this difficult."

Arla pressed her palm to her chest. Her pulse quickened. What were they saying? Why were they here? If Ellie was okay, then why ...

The second man twirled his mustache, then stepped forward and removed his hat. "Mrs. Anderson, my name is Dr. George Fenray, PhD, administrator at St. Luke's, in charge of," he cleared his throat again, "charity cases, among other things." He extended his hand.

Charity cases? Why ... Arla stared at his hand and stepped backward.

The doctor motioned toward the empty cot. "Please sit down."

"I don't need to sit."

The doctor crossed his arms. "I told you this wouldn't be easy." His muttered words barely reached her ears.

Arla trembled.

Dr. Fenray moved toward Ellie, his eyes never leaving Arla's face. "Let us be frank with one another, shall we?"

Arla remained silent. Something was happening. Something awful. Something she had to stop before it was too late.

"Hmmm." Dr. Fenray tugged at his mustache again. "I shall get right to the point. We have concluded that these conditions are no place for a wounded child."

"No." The denial rushed from Arla's lips.

Dr. Fenray didn't pause. His voice grew louder. "Therefore, we have arranged to take the girl to St. Luke's in Duluth for treatment."

Arla swayed on her feet. She reached out and placed her hand on Ellie's shoulder. "No. She needs to stay here. With me."

The doctor touched her sleeve. "I'm sorry, Mrs. Anderson."

She lifted her chin. "Then I'll go with her. I'll pack our things." She moved toward the wooden trunk between the cots.

"No, ma'am. We have no room for you."

"But, I'm—"

"No."

"But ..."

"Ma'am." She heard the warning in his voice.

Arla widened her stance. "Then she's not going."

Dr. Fenray stepped forward. "She is going. Today."

"Please."

"Are you her mother?"

"I'm ..." Arla choked back the words.

"I didn't think so." Dr. Fenray shoved his hat back on his head, then shifted the coat draped over his arm. "We'll be leaving on the Number Three. Please have the girl ready to depart."

Without another word, the men turned and quit the room.

Arla stood frozen to the spot, her gaze fixed on the tent flap. *They can't. How can they?*

"Mrs. Anderson?" Ellie's voice floated from the cot behind her.

"Yes, child."

"I'm afraid."

Arla closed her eyes. "So am I, Eleanor. So am I."

***

Winter is coming. I feel it in the sharpness of the air, hear it in the dimming song of the crickets. Winter, with its snow and ice and wicked winds. I will face it alone.

The mallet is heavy in my hands as I stand in front of this mean little structure I will call my own. One window. Four walls. A roof. A door. All made with stolen timber, built with a stolen mallet, brought on a stolen cart.

I swing the mallet again. An awkward movement. But I swing it anyway, as if by doing so I can ward off the thoughts that hiss through my mind.

You will never survive the winter.

You will die alone.

No one knows.

No one cares.

No one ever will.

And so I keep company with them, these merciless thoughts of mine, as peg by peg, board by board, I construct this thing that will be my home. Or my prison.

It is hidden here between hills and large stones. Hidden by the trunks of dead trees and the steep slope of earth. No one comes here. There's no reason to. So I am safe. Or so I believe.

In the distance, a train's whistle blows. I straighten and stretch my back. If I look just right, I can see it out there, a black snake with smoke billowing from its head. It whistles again, then starts down the long tracks away from Hinckley. The Number Three, I think, making its way to Sandstone, then on to Duluth.

I wonder who is on that train and where they are going. Will they see things that I've only dreamed of? Will they meet people and call them friends? Once, I had plans too. I wanted to get on that train and see places I've never seen. Cities with bright lights, plantations dotted with magnolias, plains filled with buffalo. I wanted to see it all, and then head out West. They say there is land that stretches past the horizon, and mountains that scrape the clouds. They say you can scoop gold from the rivers and drink dew from the sky. They say you can travel forever. Or at least far enough to leave yesterday behind.

But I didn't leave. Not in time, anyway. And so it's too late. I am caught here, with this ramshackle hut to shelter me, with memories I want only to forget, and this face that defines the monster I am. This is all that is left. Some boards. And burned flesh. And the embers of hopes that died in the flames.

Yes, winter is coming. Will I live to see the spring?

13

Ellie dreamed of Mama every night for a week. Mama hemming a man's trousers, Mama stirring soup in a kettle over the fire, Mama gazing out the window saying how Papa was as gone as the autumn leaves in winter. And Mama sitting there in her sewing chair with the dove gray dress draped over her lap telling how it was for someone special. It was the last thing Mama ever made. And Ellie had left it back in Hinckley. Left it there, along with everything else that mattered.

She squirmed in the hospital bed. Everything here was wrong. The sheets were too thin, the pillow too squishy. And the smell, it made her eyes water. But she was better. The pain in her side was only a dull ache now. The nurses said she was healing up real good. She had to be careful though, or the stitches would split. Then she'd never get out of here and back home.

And one thing she knew. Mama would have wanted her to hightail it back to Hinckley. The dreams had convinced her of that at least. That ghost-man was haunting her dreams still. Mama and the ghost. Every night it was the same. A monster in the fire. Mama calling out to her. A ghost weeping. And Mama beckoning her to come. No matter how the dreams started, they always ended with Mama calling. Just last night Ellie had woke up with the sheets balled up under her and her side throbbing like some old Indian drum.

She smoothed the sheet around her and pressed her head back into the pillow. She had to get back to Hinckley. Had to figure out the mystery of the ghost-man, and had to make right what she'd done by throwing them rocks. That poor ghost could have been anyone. Could have been Mrs. Larsen's son, Ben, lost in the fire. Or Mr. Lind's brother, or one of them workers at Brennan's mill. Could have been the blacksmith, or the milliner, or the barber. Whoever it was, Ellie needed to do her part to help. Mama would have wanted it that way. Mama would have said that Jesus has got no feet now but ours, so we had better get moving. Mama always said that. Read it in a book somewhere, way back when.

Ellie wiggled her toes beneath the sheets. Only problem was it didn't look like this set of Jesus' feet was going anywhere soon. She rubbed her eyes and looked around the hospital room. White walls, white sheets, gray floors, and some strange silver instrument near the narrow bed. Nothing to look at but a single, bare-leafed tree swaying outside her window. Nothing to think about but how she ought to be getting home. But every time she asked, Doc just shook his head and murmured, "In due time, in due time."

As if her thoughts had conjured him, Doc knocked on the door, then poked his head into the room. "How you doing, Little Whisker?"

Ellie grimaced. Doc had been calling her that ever since he told her Leif's bullet had missed her kidney by a whisker. "Feelin' like going home now, Doc." She tried to sit up but failed.

"Now, now, you just lay on back." He strode over to the bed and pressed a hand against her shoulder. "How's the side, any more pain?" He lifted the sheet and poked at the bandage covering her wound.

Ellie winced. "Don't feel nothing."

"Oh?"

"All healed."

His eyebrows raised.

"I want to go home."

Doc sat on the edge of the bed and looked into her face for a long time. "Well, about that ..." His gaze slid away from her toward the window. "That's a good-sized sugar maple out there, isn't it? I don't know as I've really noticed it before." He paused. "Did you know that ever since 1876 the Canadians have put maple leaves on all their coins? I took a trip to Toronto just last summer, and—"

"I don't much care about Canadian coins, Doc. Or about Toronto either. I care about Hinckley. I want to go back home. Now."

"Yes. I know. But you see ..."

Ellie twisted her fingers around the sheets.

"With your mama gone ..."

She clutched the sheets harder.

"You need someone else to take care of you."

"Mrs. Anderson said—"

Doc unraveled her fingers from the cloth and patted her hand. "I know. It was very well meaning of her, but Hinckley—"

"Is being built again."

"It'll never be what it was."

"I want to go back."

"It's too dangerous. And Mrs. Anderson can't—"

"It ain't her fault."

"It's no one's fault, Ellie."

No one's, 'cept that dumb Leif's.

Doc stood. "Let's start over, shall we?"

Ellie nodded. "Okay."

Doc smiled. "You see, the real reason I've stopped in to your room today is because there's a very nice couple who have come to see you."

"Me?"

"Yes, you." He reached over and tweaked her nose. "They are the Coles. They have no children, and they live in St. Paul. Mr. Cole is a philanthropist. Do you know what that is?"

Ellie frowned. She didn't know what a phil ... philan ... whatever was, but it couldn't be good. Mama had called Leif's father something like that once, and her face had gone all red when she said it. "Ain't that what you call a bad man, a man who steps on his wife?"

"Steps on?" Doc paused, then chuckled. "Steps out on, you mean. No, that's a philanderer. Mr. Cole is a philanthropist. It means he gives money to people who need it."

Ellie folded her hands on her lap. "Oh, well, that's all right then. But what's it got to do with me? Is he going to give lots of money to the folks in Hinckley?"

"Not exactly." Doc grinned and turned toward the door. His voice raised. "Mr. and Mrs. Cole, please come in now."

Ellie's eyes widened.

A woman dressed in a fancy silk traveling outfit with thin gigot sleeves glided into the room. She glanced at Ellie, then attempted a smile. Behind her came a short man in a business suit. He looked everywhere but at Ellie. Down at the floor, at the walls, out the window, at his shoes. Then he gave a little cough.

Ellie frowned.

The two stopped a few feet from the bed.

No one spoke.

Finally, Mrs. Cole took one step forward. "Hello, Ellie Jean." Her voice came out as smooth as water. "Do you know who I am?"

Ellie eyed the woman over the long expanse of sheets. She noted the perfectly manicured hands, the flawless tailoring of the traveling dress, the slight hint of rouge. "No, ma'am. I don't recall ever seeing you before."

Mrs. Cole touched her fingertips to her chest. "My dear, I'm your new mother."

Ellie choked.

***

The cold soaks into my bones. My breath makes misty circles before me. Snow powders the ground like a sprinkling of sugar on rolled lefse. I try not to shiver, but I do anyway.

The branch in my hand quivers. I hold it still, waiting, watching the line that travels from the end of the stick into the water. I have never been much of a fisherman. I have never liked the taste of fish. But I am learning to like it now.

The wind has vanished. Here, next to the lake, nothing moves but the slow lapping of water. Nothing speaks but the waves against the shore. All is quiet, still, eerie. And I wonder, have I ever heard such silence before? I am used to noise. To people bustling about town, talk and laughter, the clip-clop of horses' hooves, the barking of dogs, the distant buzz of the saw at the lumber mill. But that's all gone now, replaced by the nothingness of a windless day, the chill of a cloudless sky, the silence of being alone.

I would have never thought that I would miss it. But I do. I miss the predictable variety of the days. I miss the chatter at Sunday picnics. The sound of milk sloshing in a bucket on Monday mornings. The music drifting from the saloon on Thursdays. The shouts of the children as they raced home from school on Friday afternoon. Strange how I miss all the things I once disregarded. Strange how the silence has changed me.

So I sit here, waiting for a fish to bite, wondering if this is all my life will ever be. Food, shelter, and old memories. What else is there for me? Day after day, month after month, year after year, will there be nothing to break the monotony of this life of solitude?

I tip my head and stare into the cold sky. Where are you, God? Where is the life you have for me? There has to be more than this. Even for one unloved, there is surely more than this.

The end of my stick plunges toward the water. I leap up. The line darts left, then right. I tug, release, and pull again. The line strains. I step away from the water's edge and lift the stick higher, higher, until the end rises from the surface. And there, dangling from the hook, I see the gray flash of a northern pike.

I rush toward it and grab it with both hands. It thrashes. I tighten my grip and look into eyes round and unblinking. I stare at it. It stares at me.

And I see that we are the same. Both captured, caught on a hook not of our own making. For a moment, I think I will free it. For a moment, I imagine what it would be like to swim free.

But then I remove the hook and throw the fish into my basket. I will eat well tonight. And for now, that is enough.

***

Moonlight slipped through the crack in the curtains and drew a thin line across the quilt on Arla's bed. She traced the line with her finger and sighed. It was no use. She had been lying here for hours. But sleep would not come.

She rose and pulled back the curtains. Hinckley spread before her. Moonlight shone off the new buildings as if someone had painted them with a brush dipped in silver. The laundry, a saloon, the milliner's shop. And between them, the ground sparkled white with frost. Hinckley had risen from the ashes, and so could she. But it was hard, oh so hard, to do alone.

Arla closed the curtain and turned away. The glow of embers in the fireplace cast a soft sheen over the bedroom. She stooped and lit a candle from the coals. Light flared over the room. She ran her hand over the footboard of her new bed, then touched the trunk below it. A new mahogany bureau, dressed with crisp lace and a white washbasin, covered one wall. And beside it sat a high-backed chair with a tapestry seat. The chair had just come two days ago. It was supposed to be like the one handed down from her grandmother. But this one was too dark, and the tapestry too stiff.

The chair had come with the armoire she had bought for Ellie's room. Now the armoire sat empty in the room across the hall. Empty armoire. Empty room. Empty bed. Empty heart. Arla closed her eyes. It wasn't supposed to be like this. Ellie was supposed to be here, not in some hospital in Duluth. How she missed the girl, with her thick black hair and ... no, not black, brown, light brown like wheat in the summer. Arla opened her eyes and rubbed her fingers over her forehead. Ellie's hair was neither thick nor black. She had to remember that.

She stood and gripped the mantel above the fireplace. Her gaze fell on the journal she had set there. *Rakel.* Her mind had been filled with Rakel these past days. She haunted her dreams, invaded her thoughts. Simple things brought her to mind. Yellow chintz pillows purchased from the mercantile reminded Arla of Rakel's favorite color. A song hummed by a man on the street brought to mind a time when Rakel had sung the same song. And purple wildflowers, she didn't even know their name ... Arla stared at the bouquet she'd placed on the mantel. *The flowers. Of course.*

She groaned and touched a finger to the petals. Now she knew why she'd picked them. It had seemed no more than a whimsical act at the time, something to buoy her spirits. But it was more than that. She should have known.

Arla plucked a single flower from the vase and brushed it beneath her nose. The fragrance tickled her senses, and a memory burst into bloom. Rakel had been maybe seven at the time. It was the beginning of spring, and the flowers had just begun to dot the fields. Arla had just dried the last plate and placed it in the cupboard when Rakel burst through the door.

"Look, Mama, for you." She thrust a fistful of purple into Arla's chest.

Arla looked at the broken stems and partially crushed petals.

Rakel grinned. "Aren't they pretty? Take them."

Arla balanced the flowers in her fingertips and held them at arm's length. And that's when it happened. A fat white spider crawled from between the petals. Arla screeched and dropped the bouquet. Flowers scattered everywhere.

But Rakel didn't flinch. She squashed the spider with her heel, picked up the flowers one by one, and took them away. Those were the last flowers Rakel ever brought home.

Arla crushed the flower she was holding and threw it into the fire. She hadn't thought of the spider incident in years. And she didn't want to think about it now. Every memory accused her. Every thought of Rakel brought her face to face with her guilt.

She reached out and touched Rakel's journal. *Maybe you were right about me. God help me, maybe I am the monster you saw.* She took the book, sat back on the chair, and opened the pages.

15 May 1894

THE LAST OF THE SNOW HAS MELTED. SPRING HAS COME. THEY SAY SPRING STARTED WEEKS AGO, BUT I WON'T BELIEVE IT UNTIL THE LAST BIT OF WHITE IS GONE.

Arla skimmed through more ramblings about the weather, until she spotted her name.

MAMA WON'T ALLOW THAT.

Arla backed up to the paragraph before. There, Rakel's script had become looser, more loopy. She again began to read.

SOMETIMES I WONDER WHAT'S OUT THERE, BEYOND THE HILLS OF HINCKLEY.

Is St. Paul as big as they say? Are there really places where you can walk all day and only find strangers on the streets? Most people would hate that, I suppose. But not me.

What would it be like to go where no one knows me? Where no one expects a thing. Where I am just Rakel Anderson, with no history, no past, no prejudices.

It can never be like that in Hinckley. Here, I am the wild one. I am the one who runs shoeless in the hills. Who throws off her stockings and wades in the river, who smears mud on her face and pretends to be an Indian. The town will never forget that.

Arla smiled. She remembered that episode too. Rakel had been too old for such games of make-believe. But that didn't stop her from galloping down the street, whooping like an Indian on the warpath. The town was scandalized, Arla horrified. But it didn't seem so terrible now. It was just Rakel, unpredictable, capricious, passionate. But she didn't stay that way. Not at the end, anyway. In August, she changed.

Arla turned the page and continued to read.

I suppose they're right about me. Maybe I am crazy. But it's because I just want to live, to breathe, to be free. I want to run and sing and dance when everyone else is standing still. But Mama won't allow that, of course. I'm supposed to be a lady. There are roles we must fulfill, Mama says. We must act a certain way, behave like everyone else.

Arla lifted her gaze from the journal's pages. Was it really so wrong to be normal? Was it really so terrible to be a lady? Maybe it was. At least for Rakel. She again dropped her gaze to the page.

Sometimes I just want to scream for everyone to stop pretending. I

ALMOST SCREAMED TODAY. THERE WE WERE AT THE SUNDAY PICNIC EATING COLD CHICKEN WITH PICKLED BEETS WHEN MR. JENSEN RIDES UP ON HIS PERFECTLY GROOMED STALLION. THEN UP RIDES THAT FILTHY SON OF HIS, LEIF, ON SOME SHINY NEW MARE. I DON'T KNOW HOW WINNIE CAN STAND IT, HAVING A FATHER AND BROTHER LIKE THAT. 'COURSE HE WON'T BUY HER A HORSE, OR LET HER RIDE ONE EITHER. WELL TODAY ANYONE WITH HALF AN EYE COULD SEE THAT THOSE HORSES WEREN'T GOING TO GET ALONG. THE ONE WAS THROWING HIS HEAD AND SIDESTEPPING EVERYWHERE. THE OTHER KEPT SNORTING AND LIFTING HER TAIL. THAT STUPID LEIF COULDN'T EVEN CONTROL THE OLD NAG HE USED TO HAVE, SO WHO COULD EXPECT HIM TO TAME THE MARE?

BUT OF COURSE EVERYONE JUST SMILED, TIPPED THEIR HATS, AND SAID, "HOW DO, MR. JENSEN?"

DIDN'T TAKE BUT A MINUTE FOR THE MARE TO THROW LEIF AND PRACTICALLY TRAMPLE THE STROMS WITH THEIR NEW BABY. GOOD THING MR. STROM WAS QUICK ON HIS FEET.

AND EVEN THEN FOLKS LIKE MAMA DIDN'T SAY A WORD. THEY JUST FLUTTERED THEIR FINGERTIPS AT THEIR COLLARS AND SAID, "OH MY, IS EVERYONE ALL RIGHT?"

IT WAS SICKENING. SOMEBODY'S GOT TO STAND UP TO THAT MAN. TELL HIM THAT HE CAN'T GO ACTING LIKE THE FOLKS OF HINCKLEY ARE HIS TO TREAT ANY WAY HE PLEASES. SOMEDAY, MAYBE I'LL TELL HIM. SOMEDAY … SURE, SOMEDAY, WHEN THE SKY TURNS GREEN AND FAT PINK PIGS FLY ACROSS IT.

Arla shuddered and closed the book. She covered her face with her hands. *I'm sorry, Rakel. I didn't know. I didn't guess.*

But she knew now. Pigs had flown. And if she guessed right, they had found their wings in August.

14

Josef straightened his collar and glanced down at the baby in his arms. "You want to see what a fool looks like, Emma Ann? Well, take a good look. Ain't ever been a bigger fool than the one standing right here." He adjusted Emma's blanket and stamped the snow off his boots. "This might just be the stupidest thing I've ever done."

Emma reached up and patted his cheek. "Da-daaaaaa." She squirmed and let out a burp.

Josef chuckled.

Sounds drifted from the other side of the closed door in front of him—the squeal of a mouth organ, Mrs. Larsen's screechy voice, and the rumble of other voices responding.

He raised his hand, but didn't knock. There was still time to slip away, to escape home and shed these ridiculous go-to-meetin' clothes. He could say the snow was too thick, or Emma had the sniffles, or his wagon broke. But then he wouldn't be able to ask about the man in the black cloak. Rumor was that Robert Larsen knew something. That he'd seen something up in the hills. And Josef aimed to find out what. The image of the black-garbed man had haunted him since the night of the shooting. And the more he thought about it, the more he wondered. Who was he? What did he want? And what had he done to make those boys so scared that they'd shoot a girl? Something wasn't right. The hunched shoulders. The hidden face. What would make a man hide himself in the hills?

Josef sighed. Was it worth a night of socializing just to find out more about the mystery man? Probably not. But he couldn't stay out on the porch forever. Besides, if he ran away now, that Mrs. Larsen would just continue to hound him. She was worse than some blood-sucking mosquito. Already she had hunted him down at the blacksmith shop, nearly pounced on him outside the mercantile, even found him out at the creek when he was trying to have a wash. Weren't no hope in trying to escape her. But if she thought he was going to cozy up to some strange woman, she had another thing coming. He weren't that crazy. Not yet, at least.

"We don't need no one else, do we, Em? We're making it just fine on our own." Of course it was a lie, but he wanted her to believe it. He wanted to believe it too. Especially tonight. "May as well do the deed. Get the worst of it over with." Josef ran his fingers through his hair, then rapped on the door.

"He's here." Mrs. Larsen's shriek sent shivers down his spine. He stepped back as the rattle of her feet sounded on the wooden floor inside. A moment later, the door flung open.

"You came." She clapped her hands together. "Oh, how wonderful. Do come in. Quickly now before that sweet cherub freezes." She clucked her tongue at Emma. "How's the bee-bee? Such a good punkin'." She opened the door wider.

Josef stepped through and drew a deep breath. Lutefisk. The house reeked of the pale fish. And of course, cabbage. He should have guessed.

"Give me that coat now. Make yourself at home." She grabbed his coat and hung it on a hook by the door next to a fancy Eton jacket and cottage cloak. Then she bustled him down the short hallway. "Baby growing so big, isn't she? Such a little doll. Looks like her mama." Mrs. Larsen paused to tickle Emma under the chin.

Emma pulled away and batted at the woman's hand.

"That you, Strom?" A booming voice shot from the sitting room. "Get yourself in here before that woman of mine has you married off to the stranger in the kitchen."

Josef shivered and swerved toward the sitting room.

Mrs. Larsen stopped to scowl at her husband. "Robert Larsen, you just shut your mouth. Charlotte ain't no stranger. She's the cousin of your mother's best friend's daughter. Practically family."

Josef cringed.

Robert grunted. "She's got a squint."

Mrs. Larsen threw her dish towel at him. "Shh. She'll hear you."

"Don't suppose there's anything wrong with her ears." He motioned to Josef. "But maybe the man don't care if the woman can't see but a foot in front of her nose."

Actually, Robert was right. Josef didn't care. He didn't care if she could see or hear or smell. He didn't care if she had donkey ears growing out of her head. He wasn't interested. Not now. Not ever. Sure, it got lonely when the winds blew out there at his new little house on the farmstead. Sure, he wished for company when the windows rattled and hot water bubbled on the cookstove. And when Emma started to crawl … Oh, how he missed Maggie then.

For a moment, the Larsens' sitting room faded away, and all Josef could see was Emma with her little bottom in the air as she rocked back and forth like one of those funny black bugs. The first time he saw it, he'd laughed out loud. It had been a long time since he'd laughed. It was a good feeling. One he wished he could have shared. But not with a new wife. Especially not one related to Mrs. Larsen.

"You okay, Strom?"

Josef refocused on the man in front of him.

"Come, sit by the fire till supper's ready." He gestured to a chair near the box stove. "And you, woman, go get the food on. Man will be much more receptive to your schemes on a full stomach."

Mrs. Larsen tapped her foot, then turned and marched to the

kitchen. Her muttered words floated back to the sitting room after she had gone. "Man needs a good woman. Should be thanking me. Ain't right he's out there all alone. And the baby ..."

Robert sighed. "Every woman's a matchmaker. It's in their blood."

Josef smiled and set Emma on the rug on the floor.

Robert whistled.

A shaggy brown dog trotted in from the other room.

"New mutt. Kids named him Max. Baby like dogs?"

Josef shrugged.

"Dog likes babies. Good with 'em too."

Max lay down by Emma and nestled his head in her lap.

Emma giggled and buried her hands in the dog's fur.

Robert laughed. "See, you don't need a wife, Strom. You just need a dog."

Josef reached down and patted the dog's head. "Plenty of them running around town now, since the fire."

"Shame, ain't it? Families gone. Animals don't got no homes."

Josef cleared his throat. The time had come. "They aren't the only things running around."

For a moment Robert looked into Josef's eyes, and Josef returned the gaze. "So, you want to hear about that, do you?"

Josef nodded.

"Was nigh on a fortnight ago, I'd reckon. Saw a light flickering up in the hills. Thought it might be more of those fool relic hunters digging around for stuff left from the fire."

Josef grunted. People had been coming from all over. From St. Paul, from Duluth—even all the way from Wisconsin—for months, trying to get "a piece of history," they said. Stealing silly things like burned-up pots and washing boards, tin plates and melted coins. Getting in the way of honest folks trying to rebuild their lives.

"But it weren't no relic hunter."

Josef leaned forward and rubbed Max's head. "Who was it?"

"*What* was it, you mean." Robert shuddered. His voice dropped to a whisper. "Creepy thing, crawling out of the shadows, all covered in black." He leaned forward. "Headed right toward town. Toward our families, our young 'uns."

"A man in a cloak?"

Robert sat back and frowned. "A man? Maybe. Some's been saying it's a man. And some's been saying it's a ghost. But I say it's a thing. A monster."

"A monster?"

"Ten feet tall. Claws like a hawk." Robert curled his fingers and scratched at the air. "And eyes that'll freeze your blood solid."

Josef raised his eyebrows.

Robert nodded. "If it comes back, me and some of the boys are aiming to find out just exactly what that creature is."

"Then what?"

Robert rubbed his hands against the arms of his chair. "Then we'll do what needs to be done to keep us all safe, that's what. Look what happened to that Hansen girl. That Ellie." He jabbed a finger in the air. "That was the creature's fault, it was." He shook his head. "Fire did enough damage. We don't need no thing preying on our children too."

Josef looked away. The monster was nowhere near Ellie Hansen when she was shot. He knew that well enough. "Let me know next time you see it."

"Why, you want to come?"

"Maybe."

"We won't abide no monsters." Firelight gleamed in Robert's eyes. Shadows flickered over his features. "Not in this town."

Josef looked into the man's face and shivered.

***

Loneliness is a living thing. It feeds in the night and grows fat on the darkness. I listen to it whispering in the breeze and slithering through the silent corners of my hut. It crouches in the shadows and waits to devour me.

I pray for the dawn.

But there is only night.

I clutch my worn blanket and speak into the emptiness. "Leave me alone." But I am alone. Completely, utterly alone.

I try a song. "Round and round the cobbler's bench, the monkey chased the weasel ..." My voice stutters and dies. It's a silly tune. Too weak to beat back the night.

So the silence comes again, eerie and unbreakable. I huddle on the hard ground and tuck the blanket tight under my chin. I close my eyes. But sleep evades me. The nights are long. Haunted by a hundred doubts, a thousand fears.

How long can I live like this? How long can I survive with loneliness as my only companion, silence as my only friend?

God, what have you done to me? Why have you left me alone?

I open my eyes and stare through the window into the moon-stained night. The stars are gone. The trees are only black silhouettes against an endless sky. In the distance, a dog howls. And snow begins to fall.

***

Josef flicked the reins over the horse's back and adjusted his seat in the wagon. He breathed out and watched the white mist hover then swirl behind him. It had been a long night. He'd paid for the information he'd gathered about the monster in the hills. Paid with three hours of yammering by Mrs. Larsen and Miss Johnson.

"Do tell us about your new farmhouse, Mr. Strom."

"Was it built with relief funds, Mr. Strom?"

"How big is it again, Mr. Strom? Two rooms? Three?"

"Is it as drafty as this one?"

"They say you brought in a brand-new cookstove from Minneapolis."

"Are you planning to plant corn again? Or only potatoes?"

"Mr. Hill has wheat. Will you plant wheat?"

"Will you have cattle?"

"How many head?"

"How far is the house from the stream? Or do you have a well?"

And so the questions came, one after another, until his head was spinning from them. Not that he needed to answer. They didn't seem to notice that he did little more than grunt, nod, and shake his head at the appropriate intervals.

If it weren't for Emma, it might have gone on forever, the women jabbering, Robert shoving in lutefisk and cabbage and muttering, "Yer gonna kill the poor man with all that talk," and, "He ain't no fat beef cow to be looked over for the slaughter, you know." But Emma had saved him.

Josef glanced over at the baby in the basket beside him. Dark lashes fluttered against pink cheeks. He tucked the blanket in around her. She was sleeping so quietly, so peacefully, just as if she'd never spat potatoes all over Charlotte Johnson's brand-new silk shawl.

Josef smiled. Not that the relentless Miss Johnson hadn't deserved it. He hadn't insisted that she feed Emma. He hadn't placed her on the woman's lap and pushed the spoon into her hand. Quite the contrary. But she had been determined to show her wifely qualifications. And show them, she did.

The grin widened on Josef's face as he remembered how he had allowed Emma to poke at his potatoes with the fork. He had known she was finished eating, but Miss Johnson thought better.

"Oh goodness, do let me," she'd said.

And that's when the trouble began.

"I know how to feed a baby, Mr. Strom." She snatched Emma out of his lap and settled the baby on her own. "I feed my sister's little Jacob all the time, you know. He's such a hearty boy. Simply loves potatoes. Can't get enough of them."

Josef watched as Miss Johnson prattled on and on, all the while pushing the mashed potatoes into Emma's mouth. Of course, he could see that Emma wasn't swallowing. Her cheeks got fatter and fatter while Miss Johnson talked about her sister, her nephew, their home in St. Paul, their cat, their dog, and some strange pet bird they'd purchased last Christmas.

Josef tried to warn her. He'd put up a hand and opened his mouth to talk, but she kept right on until an explosion of potatoes erupted from Emma's lips.

Spuds had flown everywhere, over the table, over the floor, and all over Miss Johnson's fine new shawl.

"Oh, I say. I never ..." Miss Johnson's face turned a truly awful shade of scarlet as she flicked potatoes from her bodice.

Josef shook his head and jiggled the reins again. Of course she'd never, and she should have admitted that before. But she hadn't. And she paid for that omission.

He chuckled as he envisioned Miss Johnson again, with potatoes in her hair, on her neck, dribbling down her front. Nope, he wouldn't be seeing her again. And if he was lucky, word would get around and he would receive no more unpleasant invitations, even from Mrs. Larsen. And that, perhaps, would make the whole evening a success.

Josef closed the top button of his coat and pressed his hat down farther on his head. Sometimes people were harder to endure than a skunk at feeding time. Sometimes he wished he could just hole up with Emma in their farmhouse and never have to go through another social supper, another church service, another Sunday picnic full of gossiping women again. Sometimes ... He paused.

What would make a man hide himself in the hills, he had asked. What would make him slink into the shadows? Maybe he knew the answer. Maybe it wasn't such a mystery after all.

Josef stared into the dark hills as a thin drizzle of snow drifted from the sky. Somewhere out there, there was a man, or a monster, who chose to stay in the darkness. Who stole carts. Who frightened children. Someone who, perhaps, just wanted a moment of peace.

And soon, even that would be taken.

15

Arla stood on her tiptoes and hung a bit of mistletoe above the doorway to Ellie's room. She glanced at the cream bedspread, the white bureau, the stuffed bear that sat on the rocker. Everything was perfect, shiny new and ready for Ellie to come home. Arla clenched her hands in front of her. *Let it be soon, Lord. Please ...*

Any day now the train would bring Ellie home, or a telegram would come telling Arla she could come and take the girl back to Hinckley, or a messenger would arrive to let her know the day and the hour of Ellie's arrival. And when that happened, everything would be ready.

Arla turned from Ellie's room and strode down the hall. A bit of silver tinsel shone from the mantel, and below it hung two fat stockings made from red wool. In the corner, a tall fir tree stood waiting for white candles. Ellie would help her place the candles, and together they would light them on Christmas Eve. A box of green and red beads and a roll of string sat beneath the tree, and hanging in the window were fancy snowflakes cut from white paper.

The smell of gingerbread wafted from the kitchen. Arla had never before made gingerbread for Christmas. There were always too many parties to attend, too many people to impress. At least when Grant was still alive. Cookies and stockings and shiny decorations had never seemed important. Until now.

Arla stepped into the kitchen and tied an apron around her waist. She glanced at the four keys hanging from the hooks on the wall. Four bright, shiny keys that fitted the four bright, shiny locks on the front door, the back door, and the two bedrooms. Arla shivered. Some things never changed. Like locks on bedroom doors. Her mama had always insisted on them, said they made folks safe. And Arla continued that tradition. But the lock hadn't made Rakel safe, not by a longshot.

It wasn't the lock that killed her. It was—

Stop it! Arla pressed her hands to her ears. She wouldn't think of that now. The locks were there, just like Mama said they should be. It didn't mean she had to use them. It didn't. Did it?

Heat radiated from the oven. She wiped her hand across her upper lip and forced her attention back to the gingerbread. It would be ready soon. And if God answered her prayers, Ellie would come home to fresh cookies in the cookie jar.

A knock sounded from the door. Arla caught her breath. She rushed to the window. Could it be? Already? She peeked through the lace curtain. It wasn't.

Instead of Ellie or a messenger, the freshly scrubbed face of Nils Heg met her gaze. What was he doing here? Arla leaned closer to the window. And whatever was that in his hand?

She scowled, moved to the door, and opened it. There Nils stood with a silly grin on his face and a glass vase filled with peppermint sticks in his fist.

He held out his arm. "Merry Christmas, Mrs. Anderson."

She put a hand on her hip. "Whatever is this?"

He bent in a mock bow. "A bouquet of hope, of course, for the ladies of the house."

"Hope?" She motioned inside. "Come in."

Nils pulled off his hat, tucked it under his arm, and stepped inside. "They're for Ellie, for when she returns." He sniffed the air. "Something smells good in here."

"Gingerbread." Arla closed the door, then touched Nils' sleeve. "Have you heard something? About Eleanor, I mean."

Nils shook his head. "No. I just figured ..."

She sighed, took Nils' hat and coat, and hung them on the coat rack. "Neither have I."

Nils glanced around the house, his gaze pausing on the bright tinsel, the stockings, the box of beads. "But you're expecting to. Soon." It wasn't a question.

Arla led him down the hall toward the kitchen. "Of course. I've been praying."

"So certainly God must answer?" He tossed the question between them, then sat down at the kitchen table.

Heat flushed Arla's face. "I would hope so."

"Why?"

Arla straightened the dish towel near the basin. "I go to church. I say my prayers. I read the Good Book."

"So you deserve to be heard?"

Arla studied the water droplets in the kitchen basin as a hundred memories flashed through her mind. *Deserve? Hardly.* "I don't deserve a single thing." The words slipped out in a whisper. She turned and sat in the chair across from Nils.

He smiled. "You're right. You don't."

"Nils Heg." She crossed her arms and glared at him over the table. "Did you come all this way over here to make me feel worse?"

He chuckled. "Guess I did."

She shook her head. "If things weren't bad enough, now I've got a madman visiting me."

"Guess you do."

"You stop that."

"Stop what?"

"Agreeing with everything I say."

"I thought women liked that."

"What do you know about women?"

He tipped back in his chair until the front legs lifted from the floor. "Nothing. Absolutely nothing."

She clasped her hands together. "Well, you'd better just hush up there then."

His chair returned to the floor with a thud. "Guess I better." He rapped his knuckles on the tabletop. "But I just can't seem to. I've been doing a mighty lot of thinking lately. Wondering, questioning really."

Arla stood and turned her back toward Nils. "No good ever comes from questioning, you know."

"Who says?"

She crossed her arms. "Well, um, I don't know. We're supposed to have faith. And faith doesn't question."

"Why not?"

She spun back around. "Nils Heg, are you trying to make a fool out of me?"

He clenched his fist. "Don't you ever wonder, Arla Mae, why this fire came? Was there a reason? Or was it just a bit of bad luck?"

Luck? She didn't believe in luck. So what was it then? Her voice lowered. "No, not luck."

Nils leaned forward until his face was level with hers. "Then why? Tell me why."

Punishment. The word stole through her mind. But it wasn't true, was it? The fire wasn't her fault. It wasn't payment for what she'd done wrong. What they all had done wrong. She deserved the fire, and worse. But Rakel hadn't. Rakel hadn't deserved to die.

"Is there an answer?" Nils' voice cut through her thoughts. "Do you think we can know why?" He laced his fingers beneath his chin. "What if bad things just happen? What if that's just life this side of heaven?"

"Then what good is God?" The question was out before she could stifle it. How could she say such a thing aloud? Maybe he didn't hear.

Maybe he was too lost in his own musings to pay attention to her blasphemous words.

Arla turned and opened the oven door.

"That's some fine-looking gingerbread."

"Would you like some?" Her voice quivered. She slipped the spatula beneath a cookie and slid it onto a plate. Then she snuck a glance at Nils. He smiled.

She smiled back. He didn't hear. He couldn't have.

He took a cookie and bit into it. "Mmmm, it's real good. What goes into it?"

Arla took a bit for herself and nibbled the corner. She wrinkled her nose. "Some ginger, molasses, flour, and salt."

Nils reached for a second cookie. "I see. Some sweet, some bitter, and a whole lot of heat." He held the cookie up to the light. "I think I know the answer to your question."

"Question?" Her hand trembled. He had heard. What must he think of her now?

"I propose that God is a gingerbread maker."

Her gaze flew to his. Was he taunting her? Making fun?

Nils stared at the cookie. "Yes, maybe that's what really matters."

She snatched the cookie out of his hand and dropped it onto the plate. "You are crazy. God doesn't make gingerbread."

Nils stood and took back the cookie. "Maybe I am crazy ... or maybe I'm not." He grinned and walked toward the door.

Arla grabbed the plate and followed.

"But either way, I do love gingerbread." He saluted her with the cookie in his hand.

Before he could reach the outer door, a knock came from outside it.

Arla hurried forward. "Who is it?"

Nils opened the door. "It's Evan." He stepped out. "Can I help you, son?"

Arla glanced around Nils to see the boy holding out a bit of paper.

"Telegram for Mrs. Anderson. Just came in."

She set the cookies on a table near the door, then wiped her hands on her apron. "I'm here."

Nils took the paper from Evan. His eyes scanned the words.

"Is it about Eleanor?"

Nils' brows knit together in a frown. "Yes."

Arla let out her breath. *Thank God.* "When is she coming home?"

For a moment, Nils didn't answer. Then he handed her the telegram. "I'm sorry, Arla."

She stared down at the paper. The words swam before her vision. Adoption. Coles. St. Paul. She dropped the telegram and slumped into the chair behind her. She raised her arm. "Why? God ..." Her hand hit the table.

Pain ricocheted up her shoulder as the gingerbread fell and scattered across the floor.

* * *

My hands shake. My body trembles. I lick my lips, tasting the raw fury. How could they? How could they go on as if nothing happened? How dare they praise the fire that devoured my dreams? That took everything and left me with this. A monster's face. An outcast's life.

But then, Angus Hay always was an optimist. Only he would start up the newspaper again and make it twice its former size. Only he would add children's stories, adult serials, tidbits about science, just as if life could return to normal. Just as if ... as if ... as if no one cared whether I lived or died.

I stare at the newspaper in my hand. It is days old now, found alongside the road, pages missing. But the front page is still intact. The Hinckley Enterprise, it reads, December 19, 1894. And there, in bold print, words commending the fire. I force myself to read the screaming headline and the paragraph beneath it.

15 YEARS WORK IN 15 MINUTES!!

The fire ... did in 15 minutes what it would have taken the husbandman 15 years to accomplish. All nature is with us; it seemingly knew our needs, and came to clear the land. Come and see; no word can tell the opportunity afforded the farmer here since the fire ... Hinckley with her enterprise and energy will welcome the industrious home-seeker, but spurns the approach of a drone; industry only may enter here.

Opportunity. Enterprise. Energy ... Destruction. Devastation. Despair. I grip the paper in tight fists and tear it from top to bottom. It flutters to the ground and lands facedown. I kick it. Once. Twice. And stub my toe on a stone.

I bite back my cry of pain. It serves me right, standing here like a madman stomping a bit of paper. Am I insane? Maybe. Sometimes I think I am.

I stoop, pick up the paper, and tuck it under my arm. It will make good kindling for the night. Then I turn toward home. Toward the woods and hills. Away from the town that once welcomed me.

They can start their lives again. They can skate on the Grindstone River. The Odd Fellows can build their hall at the Brennan Lumber Company site, the children can return to school, the saloons can serve their spirits, the lumberjacks can have their fistfights on the street corner.

They can hang their mistletoe, light their stoves, decorate their Christmas trees, eat their baked hams. They can gather, and sing, and laugh. Their

lives can return to the normal ebb and flow of work and family. And
maybe, someday, they'll forget that the fire ever came. They'll forget what it
took from them. They'll forget what they lost.

But not me. I will never forget. For me, there will be no Christmas. Not
now. Not ever. No skating, no tree, no ham, no mistletoe. This life of exile
is all I will ever know. And soon, I will forget that I once skated, I once
stole a kiss under the mistletoe, I once laughed at the antics of children.

God, how could you do this to me? How could you hate me so? Why must
everything remind me of all that could have been and will never be? Why
do I have to live this life you've forced on me?

Oh God, I want to go home.

* * *

Darkness curled around Ellie like a fuzzy blanket. She closed her eyes and
listened to the early morning sounds—breezy snores from the bed next
to hers, groans from the far side of the room, and the click of footsteps
approaching, just as she knew they would.

She steadied her breathing. In, out, in, out.

The footsteps paused, then continued, paused, then stopped at her
bedside. In, out. In, out. Slowly, steadily.

A pen scratched on paper. The nurse cleared her throat.

In, out. Don't move. Don't look.

The nurse moved on.

Ellie waited. The nurse would stop at the next bed, and the next.
Then she'd go on down the hall, just as she did every morning. Twenty-
six seconds after leaving the last bed, she'd be too far away to hear Ellie
getting up. Twenty-six seconds, a moment, an eternity, and then it would
begin. Now. This morning. It had to be. Or the Coles would take her
away.

They were coming at noon, they'd said. Yesterday, the nurses could talk of nothing else. They just kept on jabbering about how excited she should be, how lucky she must feel, what a blessed little girl she was to be adopted by the Coles. Just as if she shouldn't care that the fire had come and taken everything she knew, everyone she loved. Just as if Mama hadn't ...

The door creaked. A swath of light splashed into the room. Then the door closed. Twenty-six seconds. Ellie counted. One, two, three. The footsteps faded down the corridor. Four, five, six. *I won't let them take me, Mama.* Eleven, twelve, thirteen. *I'm coming home. Somehow.* Seventeen, eighteen, nineteen. She sat up and swung her legs over the side of the bed. Pain fishtailed up her side. Her heart hammered in her chest. *Please, God, help me.* Twenty-five. Twenty-six!

Ellie held her breath. And heard nothing except for the woman snoring beside her. Even the groaning had stopped.

Her fingers moved toward the drawer of her bedside table. Quietly, she opened it and pulled out the clothes they had placed there yesterday. She slid the dress over her head, the pantaloons over her legs. The shoes were silly, impractical, but they'd have to do.

Moonlight glowed through the window and shone on the ribbon for her hair. She brushed her fingers through the tangles, then tied up the short tresses.

Someone snorted. Ellie jumped. The snoring came again, soft and even. She had to get out. Fast. Had to make the train to Hinckley. It was more than four miles to the West Superior station, the only one that had a train leaving this early in the morning. At least she thought so. The woman three beds down had talked about how she took the early train from West Superior to St. Paul every third Thursday to visit her sister. And if it went to St. Paul, surely it would stop in Hinckley. Surely it would take her home.

Ellie grabbed her coat from the bedpost, tiptoed to the door, and peeked out. A lantern flickered at the far end of the empty hall. She stepped through the doorway. Her shoes clunked on the floor. Voices shot from around the corner.

"They're arriving at twelve."

"Better get her ready early."

"But the doctor said ..."

Ellie whipped off her shoes, held them in her hand, and raced down the hallway. Four turns, three sprints, and two close calls later, she was standing outside the hospital with the air turning white with her breath. Bits of snow dripped from the sky overhead. She brushed her palm over the thin bandage on her side. Already the wound throbbed.

A carriage spun around the corner. Ellie darted into the bushes. A hunk of snow fell and splattered on the sidewalk in front of her just as the carriage stopped before the hospital. A doctor stepped out, glanced her way.

Ellie pressed herself farther into the bushes. Her breathing grew shallow. *Keep going. Don't come this way.*

The doctor shook his head, then entered the hospital. The carriage rolled on.

Ellie gathered her coat closer around her neck, put her shoes back on, and started down the road. After a mile, her head buzzed with the pain in her side. Her breath came in heavy gasps. But she kept on. One step after the other. Down one road, turning onto another, across an empty lot, down a hill, over a bridge.

The sun had not yet tipped over the horizon, yet the city was beginning to wake. The warm smell of baked bread drifted through the streets. The clang and shuffle of newspapers being delivered in big bundles filled the air. Doors slammed. Street cleaners whistled songs as they scraped snow with their shovels. Somewhere to her right came the piercing shrieks of a cat fight. And still she walked on.

Above her, the stars grew dim. The moon faded. On a porch beside the road, some kind of retriever stood and shook all over. Mama always loved retrievers. Ellie paused and wished she could run up and pet the dog, wished she could hold his cheek to hers and feel his soft pant against her skin. She sighed. "I miss you, Mama." Her whisper echoed in her ears. "I miss your laugh. I miss the sound of your humming while you sewed. I miss your prayers for me at bedtime." She gave the dog a final glance, then moved on. "I miss the way you made me feel safe and loved and happy."

In the distance, a train whistle blew. She quickened her pace. "But I'm coming home now, just like you'd want me to. I'm going to make it. Somehow. Some way."

She touched her fingers to her side. The hole was supposed to be mostly healed by now. But it still hurt something awful when the stitches stretched. Or when she walked too far. And today was definitely too far.

Despite the chill of the day, sweat beaded on Ellie's forehead. She wiped it away. The air seared her throat and lungs. Ice stuck on her shoes. She took a deep breath. She couldn't smell the bakeries anymore. Couldn't hear the songs of the street cleaners. Just the harshness of her own breath filled her ears, and the thud of her feet on the frosty ground.

On and on she trudged, until the stars vanished and the sky turned sickly gray. And then, finally, the train station appeared through the morning mist. Ellie hurried forward. Down the street, up the stairs, into the station. There. She almost laughed. She was not too late. The train still stood by the platform. Black smoke still puffed from its engine. Faces looked from the window. And ... yes. This time Ellie did grin. There, about to board, was a man in a fine top hat and silk coat. She needed only to step up behind him and it would look to anyone spying that she was his daughter. Then, maybe, she'd be able to board without anybody asking questions. That was the plan, anyway. And she prayed it would work.

Ellie strode up to the man and stood just behind him. He didn't even glance back as he moved closer to the train. Just three more steps and she'd be on. The man boarded. Two more steps. She lifted the hem of her dress. One more.

"You, girl." The shout came from somewhere behind her.

Ellie turned.

A man in a blue uniform pointed right at her.

16

I don't know why I'm standing here, my feet cold with ice, my breath making thick mist before me. The morning sun has not yet risen to paint the snow with a blinding brightness or to show the branches around me hanging heavy with white. I wrap my arms around myself and blink away the moisture that freezes on my lashes. Why have I come? Have I not been punished enough?

Yet, somehow I've been drawn here, to the light that shines from the window into the near-dawn darkness, to this hollow where I stand and stare into that window not my own. I gaze into another world. And see a piece of heaven.

A fire tumbles in the cookstove. Warm light dances on the walls. A bit of garland hangs over the far door next to a tree topped with a silver star. Bread is on the table, and a fat yellow candle. An old banyan overcoat hangs from a hook on the wall. And there, gripping the chair leg in chubby hands, is the baby, is Emma.

I reach out and see my reflection moving dimly between the shutter slats. I pull back.

He is there. He has not seen me. Has not noticed the shadow behind the glass. He squats near the far wall and motions to the child. His arms are out, welcoming, urging her to come. His lips move. I can read the words. "Come on, baby girl, walk to Papa."

Little Emma takes one tottering step, her fingers still touching the chair. Then she takes another. Her arm stretches. And another. The chair is now behind her. In three fast steps she's reached her papa and falls into his arms.

He laughs.

She giggles.

He pulls her into a big bear hug. For a moment, they roll on the floor together. And I can hear their joy. Then he stands and sets her next to the chair again.

I move closer to the window. I feel the warmth. Can they see me here? I hope not. I am hidden by shutters and shadow, and the lingering darkness of just before dawn. But I can see them. I see too well. Oh God, why have I come?

Once more he kneels near the wall, his arms out, waiting. His face glows with a smile. His eyes shine in the firelight. His fingers wiggle. "Come, little one. Papa's waiting."

Emma takes one cautious step, followed by four fast ones. Then she's in his arms again. A squeal of delight. A rumbling chuckle.

My eyes burn.

They try a third time, and this time she doesn't hesitate. She throws her arms out and quicksteps to her papa. He grabs her up and tickles her tummy. She howls and squirms in his grip. Then she wraps her arms around his neck and kisses him.

My throat closes.

Family. Trust. Love. A child trusts her father's presence. She trusts his care. Did I ever trust that way? Did I trust my father? Did I trust God? Maybe. But trust vanished long ago. Long ago I fell. Fell, and shattered. Where were the arms of protection then? Where are they now?

Let go of the chair.

The words come into my mind. Challenging. Haunting.

Let go? How can I let go? I have no chair, no warm room. I have nothing except my despair.

I lean forward. Closer, closer, until my fingertips brush the glass. A chill races through me, a coldness that has nothing to do with the snow, nothing to do with the frigid air. If only ...

Emma sits on the floor. A streak of gray light slips through the window and touches off her golden hair. She looks toward the glass and waves her arms. Does she know I am here? Does she sense me watching?

She shoves her fist into her mouth, then takes it out and studies it. Her brows dimple.

My heart constricts. I never thought she would look so much like her papa. But she does.

He stands and moves toward the door opposite me. He opens it and disappears from my view. What is he doing? Is he coming here?

I push back, ready to run.

But I don't run. Something holds me here. I wait for footsteps. I wait for a shout. I wait for fear.

The door opens again. And he is there, inside the house once more, with a grin splitting his face and a rope in his hand. He calls Emma's name and steps to the side.

I catch my breath. There behind him, with a shiny red bow tied around its neck, is the ugliest dog I have ever seen. A shaggy coat with splotches of brown and white. Lopsided ears, tongue lolling. It's just a pup, I think, for it has that gangly look of legs and feet too big for a body not yet caught up.

But Emma doesn't care. She claps her hands, then stretches her arms wide.

Her papa leads the animal toward her. He looks up.

I leap backward. Has he seen me? Am I found out?

His gaze fixes on the window.

I tremble and dare not move.

Then he looks away.

I breathe again. I am safe. I am invisible. I am a shadow and no more.

Inside, the dog barks.

* * *

The man in the uniform raced toward Ellie. "You there, wait."

Ellie whirled back around.

"Stop." Footsteps pounded behind her.

With a strangled cry, she leapt from the platform toward the open door of the train. Her foot caught on the step. She rolled, her hands scratching metal as she clambered aboard. Heat seared her side. She glanced down. Blood seeped through the fabric of her dress.

A hand grabbed her arm. She shook free, then rushed up the steps into the belly of the train. Her shoes rattled on the metal floor. She pushed through another door and dashed down the aisle of the seating car. Only then did she glance back. But no man followed. No blue uniform, no pointing finger, nothing but a woman with a small suitcase and a young son.

Ellie stumbled forward. The shriek of the train's whistle filled the air. Then the train began to move beneath her. She tipped forward, bumping into a hard seat back. The train's interior blurred and spun. She fell into a seat beside the window. *I'm almost free. I've almost made it.*

She stared out the window as the depot passed. There, on the platform, the man in the blue uniform watched the windows. His eyes caught hers, then he was gone, swept behind her as the train picked up speed.

The city passed in a flash of gray and white. Soon, rows of buildings were replaced with trees with pale trunks and deep green needles. Streets gave way to bare maples and rocks covered in snow. Ellie leaned her forehead against the glass. *I'm coming home, Mama. I'll be there soon.* She touched her hand to the stain of blood at her side. It wasn't much. It would dry. The wound would heal. It had to.

So why did it hurt so much? Why did her eyes refuse to focus? Why had her throat gone dry?

Her stomach rumbled. Shoes scuffed along the carpet in the aisle behind her. She sank lower in her seat. The conductor? Was he coming? No. A moment later, a young man sauntered past and sat next to the woman with the little boy.

Ellie's eyes fell closed. She was safe. At least for now. Her seat jiggled. Someone coughed. Around her drifted muted conversation from the other passengers. A man talking about the price of something called es-car-go in the East. A woman filling her neighbor's ear with the recipe for mince pie. A boy singing about the sidewalks of New York. And, toward the front of the car, the young man muttering something about Hinckley and the fire. Ellie kept her eyes closed as she focused on the man's voice.

"I tell ya, I'm gonna get me something."

The woman beside him answered. "Been all picked over by now, don't you think?"

"Naw. That old fire burned four hundred square miles if it burned an inch."

"In four hours, they say."

"You can't pick over that much, even in four months. I'll find something."

"Johnny and me's going out there for a picnic. Going to see how much they've built up. They say it's coming along right fine."

Ellie gritted her teeth. Sightseers and relic hunters. Like buzzards, they were, flocking down on Hinckley after the fire, digging through the remains of people's lives, taking anything they fancied. She'd thought they'd all come and gone by now.

"Want something for my girl for Christmas." The man's voice came again. "My brother found a doll. Clothes all burned away, but only a smudge on the porcelain face. Don't suppose I'll get so lucky though."

Lucky? Ellie cringed. She had a doll before, before the ... Red hair, pale cheeks, a blue gingham dress that Mama had made. How could he speak of some girl's doll like a prize?

"Mementos, you know." The man's tone sharpened. "They'll be worth something someday. And me and my girl will be able to say we got some from the big fire of '94."

Stop it! Stop. Don't you see? Don't you know? The words screamed through Ellie's mind. That doll belonged to a little girl. She's probably dead now. Or her family is ... or her mama. Ellie opened her eyes and found them wet with tears.

The young man leaned forward in his seat. His hands darted to and fro as he spoke. "Probably have to settle for some coins or a tin plate though. Good stuff's gone by now, like you say."

Ellie shuddered and looked away. There was nothing you could say to folks like that, Mama always said. Some folks just couldn't see other people's pain even if you smashed their face in it and rubbed. She sighed. Weren't no use fretting about it. Weren't no use ... the voices faded. Weren't no ... her vision tunneled. Weren't ... her eyes closed.

* * *

"Hush, boy." Josef patted the dog on its head. He strained to hear any strange sound. Was that a twig snapping? A footstep? Or just the wind in the branches outside?

The hair along the dog's neck bristled as it let out a low growl.

Josef frowned and looked toward the window. Did the shutters move? He strode over and peered through the glass. Nothing. Just snow and dark sky and still-black tree trunks. He turned back around.

The dog now lay on its back with Emma rubbing its stomach.

"Ahhh. Ahhggg." Emma giggled.

Josef went over and knelt beside them. "Does Emma like her new doggy?" He scratched the animal under the chin.

"Ahhh. Ahhggg." She pounded the dog's head with her palm.

The dog grinned, then licked her wrist.

She snatched it away and squealed with laughter.

Josef ran his fingers down the dog's back. "Well, what should we name you, boy?" He chuckled. "How about Patience?"

The dog wagged its tail.

"No? Survivor? Too long?"

The dog pushed its nose against Emma's arm and cuddled up to her side.

Josef sat back against the wall and crossed his arms over his knees. The dog was a good choice. Jacobson had been right about that. Rumor had it that its owner was lost in the fire, just like so many others. And now there were dozens of homeless animals roaming the streets. Dogs, cats, goats, chickens, even a donkey.

The preacher man had said once that animals running loose would be a sign of the end of the world. If that were the case, the end might be coming soon. Josef had certainly thought so when the fire descended. But now? Well, now he wondered if that wasn't just another fool story. Like the ones that said God cared about folks, that he took care of them. Weren't no one taking care of him and Emma but him. And a scraggly dog.

Jacobson said the animal was good with kids, despite its scrappy appearance. He stood right outside the saloon and swore that the dog was just what Josef needed. "That Billings boy had the dog in the house with the babies and weren't no problems," Jacobson had said. "Good guard dog too. Scare off coons and bears, and," the man winked, "and even nasty ghosts, they say." He clapped Josef on the shoulder and guffawed.

Josef had almost walked off then, but Jacobson stopped him. "Aw, come on, give me a dollar and he's yours."

Josef had given the dog one last look. "A dollar? You crazy? He ain't even yours."

"Been feeding him, haven't I? Keeping him all domesticated and trained, haven't I?" Jacobson put out his hand and wiggled his fingers. "That's worth something, ain't it?"

Josef reached in his pocket and pulled out a quarter. "Twenty-five cents." And that was too much for the scruffy mutt. But then the dog had rubbed its head against Josef's hand and looked up at him with those big, ugly eyes. And Josef had known it was the dog for him and Em.

"Deal." Jacobson snatched the coin, handed Josef the dog's rope, and winked again. "Forgot to tell you, he ain't house-trained." The man flipped the coin in the air, then pocketed it. "Good luck to ya." With that, he turned and sauntered down the street, leaving Josef standing there with the rope in his hand and a mutt panting at his side.

"Beware of ghosts." The man shouted over his shoulder, then he laughed.

Ghosts. Even now, the word still echoed in Josef's ears. There weren't no ghosts. He paused and glanced toward the window. Or maybe there were.

Emma laid her head on the dog's stomach and sighed. She closed her eyes.

The dog lay there, with his big floppy ears twitching and his tongue hanging to one side.

Josef reached out and petted its head. "There ain't no ghosts, are there, boy?" He smiled. "That's it. I think we'll call you Ghost. That way, you'll be the only one."

A log tumbled in the fire. Josef could see the sparks fly and fade through the cracks around the stove's door. He got up, opened it, and poked at the embers with a stick. The fire would go out soon unless he added another log.

He grabbed his coat and stepped outside. The first rays of dawn streaked the eastern sky. Gray light splashed over the snow. He moved toward the woodpile on the other side of the house. He filled his arms with wood, then paused. The window. What was that beneath the glass?

He tramped across the ice. Breath rushed from his lungs as the logs tumbled to the ground. Could it be? It was.

There, outside his window, was a line of footprints pressed into the snow.

17

The noonday sun splashed through the window. Ellie jolted upright. Was she late? No. There up ahead was Skunk Lake. She shivered at the sight of the shallow, marshy water cut in two by the train trestle. From her window, she could just see the west side.

Hundreds of people were saved there, Mr. Heg had said. Even now, Ellie could see the way his eyes had flashed, could hear the way his voice quickened, as he told how an engineer named Jim Root had backed the train up a whole six miles from Hinckley to the lake. 'Course, it weren't really a lake. It was just a stinky hole, filled with black mud and water.

Ellie wrinkled her nose. Ugly thing it was, especially now. But Mr. Heg said it was the prettiest lake in the whole wide world. Said he never seen nothing so beautiful. And when the fire had come in three big waves and showered down sparks and cinders all over it, he was right thankful for having even that bit of smelly water. But then the wind died down and black flakes drifted from the sky like manna in Bible times. And Mr. Heg was saved.

Ellie pressed her face against the window and watched the lake draw near. It was frozen over now, the blackness frosted with white snow.

What if Mama and me had come north instead of south? If we had tried to catch that train instead of the other ...

She gripped the folds of her dress in her fist as the lake dropped behind her. There were still a lot of ifs. Still too many maybes. Perhaps there always would be.

Minutes later, the train pulled into the new depot at Hinckley. The wheels gave a loud squeal just as the conductor opened the far door and started down the aisle.

Ellie leapt up and sped off the train before the man could reach her.

"You there. Girl."

The call faded as she jumped onto the platform and rushed away from the train. She looked over the town. In just the few weeks since she'd been gone, Hinckley had changed so much. New buildings rose out of the snow, houses lined the streets, the tents were mostly gone, and smoke curled from chimneys all around.

Ellie hurried away from the depot and down the street. She glanced down at her side. A small amount of blood still seeped through her dress. *I'll be all right. I just gotta make it to Mrs. Anderson's house. She'll take me in. She'll be glad ...*

Her vision tunneled again. She rubbed her hands over her eyes. *Focus, Ellie Jean. You're almost there.* Her steps slowed. Her dress scraped over fresh blood. *It don't matter. I walked miles before.* But the stitches hadn't split then. *It'll be fine.* She pressed her fingers into her side. *Just a little bit farther.*

She turned a corner and spotted Mrs. Anderson's house ahead. It was a simple white structure with a covered porch in front. She quickened her pace. Was that ...? Yes, it was. A bit of mistletoe hung over the door. Ellie smiled. She could make it. Just a few more steps. She stumbled over a stone in the road. Pain shot up her side. She paused and caught her breath. *I'm almost there.*

A sound came from behind her. A cry. Or maybe a sob.

Ellie turned. There, in the shadows next to a building, stood the figure from her dreams. The man in the black cloak.

For a moment, Ellie froze.

Then the figure moved toward her.

And Ellie forgot that she had come home to solve the mystery of this man. She forgot she wanted to find him. She forgot everything except the single image of a mangled face covered in shadow.

A yell gathered in her throat. She swallowed it and tried to run, but her feet wouldn't move fast enough. He was there, behind her. She could sense him. She had to go faster. Faster. He could catch her soon.

She swerved. The house was just in front of her. If she could make it to the door, turn the knob, get inside ...

She bolted up the steps.

He was coming. Was that a voice? A shout? Her toes banged into the top step. She fell. Pain exploded in her side. Her breath came in short pants. The sky whirled and spun. Her eyes closed.

Mama ...

Something soft slipped beneath her head. She tried to open her eyes, and failed.

Mama ... help.

The world fell away as a gentle hand stroked her brow.

* * *

A storm approaches. Black clouds billow in from the north. The air tingles. The sky turns dark.

I shiver. My cloak trembles with me. I should hurry. But I don't. I hate being here, in this town that calls me a ghost, a monster, and worse. And yet the sound of their voices calls to me, the rumble of lives lived together. How long has it been since I've spoken to another person? How long since I've felt human touch? Here, I can almost believe I am part of them again. I can almost imagine what it would be like to be normal.

Yet, I come now, in the late morning when the town is quiet. Men are inside with their work, women tucked away in their homes, animals curled

*up beneath steps and porches. The streets are empty but for a few horses tied
outside the saloons. All is still but for the whorls of smoke from a dozen
chimneys.*

*No one is here to see, to notice a figure creeping along the edges of the
buildings, skirting streets, stealing through shadows. Yet my heart thuds
all the same. And my mouth is dry.*

*Was that a curtain fluttering? A movement behind the window of the
house across the road? Was that the sound of footsteps? Or a wagon
creaking? Is it worth the risk that I will be seen, captured? And what
would they do to me if they caught me at last?*

*My gaze darts down the road. First right, then left. And I scurry across.
Two more blocks, and I'll reach the mercantile. I hope that today there will
be a little box left behind the store. There has been one every Tuesday for a
month. I think it is left for me. I pray it is.*

*Voices tumble from a building on my left. Laughter, and song. I pause
and inch closer. Then I see them. A room full of squirming schoolchildren,
and Miss Craig wandering between them. Bits of yellow straw line the
floor. And on the desks sit shining new toys. A doll. A painted truck. A
pocketknife. A stuffed dog. Gifts sent from afar. Tokens that someone out
there cares. For them. But not for me.*

*Yet their laughter infects me, and I find myself grinning. My fingers
touch my face. How strange to feel the stretch of a smile, the wrinkles
around my eyes as my lips lift. I step closer. Little Chloe has opened a pink-
dressed doll. Matthew has a tin whistle. Jake and Elizabeth are running
in circles at the back of the room. Another group is singing a carol. For a
moment I join in, my voice low, the words only murmured.* All is calm, all
is bright … Christ the Savior is born …

*Sweet voices. Innocent. I close my eyes and savor them. Savor the hope they
offer.*

Then I back away. Their voices follow me, pushing me down the street. I turn one corner, and another. And someone is there. In the road.

I skid to a halt. My breath hisses in my ears. I press myself into the gray darkness alongside the blacksmith shop. Inside, a hammer pings on the anvil.

Don't turn around.

My hands touch the rough wood of the blacksmith's wall. I hold still. So still that tiny snowflakes sift from the sky and settle on my sleeves. And I watch the girl in the road.

Her gait is slow, her steps unsteady. She stumbles.

I gasp.

She turns.

And I see the stain. Red. Blood. For a moment, my breath stops. Ellie! I rush toward her.

Her face blanches as she turns and flees.

I follow. "Come back. I won't hurt you. It's me." The snow takes my words and flings them back at me.

Ellie doesn't stop. She veers left. Down the street, toward a row of houses.

I chase her, not knowing what else to do. She needs me. Needs help. I've almost reached her, can almost grab her arm. "Wait."

She hurtles toward a house, along the walkway, up the steps. And falls.

I cry out. Then I am at her side. I take her in my arms, hold her close to my chest.

Her eyes are closed, her breath labored.

I stroke her cheek, brush the hair back from her brow. "Shh, shh, it'll be all right." My voice grates in my ear. Ugly and harsh.

She groans.

And I want to weep.

Then comes the sound of footsteps. And the door is flung open before me.

***

Arla sat with the journal on her lap. Outside, the sky turned gray. Already the snow fell, making white mounds on the windowsills. A cold day. A quiet day. A day when memory came out to play.

She took out her handkerchief and wiped her cheek. Beside her lay a box filled with mistletoe and garland. Yesterday, the sprigs had decorated the house. Today, they sat in a useless heap, awaiting the fire. It was silly to put the ridiculous stuff up all over her house. She should have known better. They were probably part of some heathen tradition anyway. Besides, she'd only put up those things for Ellie, for Christmas. But now there would be no Ellie. There would be no Christmas. God had taken away Arla's second chance, and she didn't know why. Why did bad things happen? Why did life have to be filled with pain and mistakes and heartache?

Arla gripped the journal in her hands. "Talk to me, Rakel. Tell me what I should have done. Tell me why God took you from me, and took Ellie. Tell me why he left me alone."

Arla opened the journal and continued reading where she'd left off the night before.

30 May 1894

HE WATCHES ME. I FEEL IT. AND SHIVERS GO UP MY SPINE. I SPIED HIM AT CHURCH PEEKING OUT AT ME UNDER THOSE AWFUL, HEAVY EYEBROWS. SURE,

HE WAS HOLDING THE SONGBOOK, AND HIS LIPS WERE MOVING, BUT HE
WASN'T SINGING THAT SONG.

Heavy eyebrows. Arla leaned forward. She turned the page and
continued.

HE KNOWS I HATE HIM. AND I'M GLAD HE DOES. HE SHOULD KNOW THAT
SOMEONE AROUND HERE KNOWS WHAT A ...

Arla coughed and skipped over the next word.

... HE IS. HE CAN'T FOOL EVERYBODY. THE WOMEN ALL TITTER AND BAT THEIR
LASHES. EXCEPT FOR ME. AND NORA. AND MAGGIE. WE KNOW. NORA
SAYS A MAN CAN'T HIDE WHAT HE IS FROM GOD. SHE SAYS GOD KNOWS
EVERYTHING. AND I SUPPOSE HE DOES. BUT I WONDER. HOW CAN HE KNOW
AND STILL LOVE?

Ah, here it was. The question without an answer. Rakel had asked
Arla the same thing back in May. But Arla had shushed the question. Just
as she had shushed Rakel's queries so many times. *It wasn't because I
didn't care, Rakel. It was because I didn't know. I'm sorry ...*

It was a sunny day in May. Bright light poured through the window
and reflected off the water in the basin. Arla had been washing dishes as
Rakel dried.

Arla handed a plate to Rakel. "Good sermon today."

Rakel paused. The dish towel dangled from her hand. "Do you really
think so? I found it, well, rather dull."

Arla sighed. "Oh Rakel, not again. Why is nothing ever good
enough for you?"

Rakel pursed her lips and didn't answer.

"What did the preacher say wrong this time?"

"Nothing."

"Then why can't you just enjoy his message and be happy?"

"Is that what I'm supposed to do?"

This time, Arla fell silent. She scrubbed at a bit of potato stuck in the bowl.

"Is that what you do, Mama?"

Is that what I do? Of course it is. That's what everyone does. Folks listened, nodded, and appeared interested. Then they went home and ate a good meal. That's what decent folks did. That's what was expected.

"How can you?"

Arla scrubbed harder at the bowl. "What?"

"Not wonder."

She slapped the bowl back into the water. "Wonder what? Why the sky is blue? Why grass is green? Why the sermon wasn't better?"

"No, that's not what I mean."

"Then what do you mean?"

"Don't you wonder how, if God knows everything, I mean everything, how he still loves us?" She stopped wiping dishes and looked Arla straight in the eye. "Or does he?"

"Of course he does." She had said the words quickly, but Rakel's question stuck in her mind then just as it did now. And so the doubts were born. *God knows. Does he still love? God is holy. I am not. God will punish. He must. He has to.* Maybe that's why she lost Rakel, and Ellie too.

Arla's gaze dropped back to the journal.

I WISH HE WOULD GO AWAY. I WISH HE WOULD LEAVE HINCKLEY AND NEVER COME BACK. I WISH I COULD LEAVE ... MAYBE, MAYBE IF WHAT NORA SAYS IS TRUE ...

There was a change in the writing then, as if Rakel had stopped and then started again later.

ARE QUESTIONS WRONG? ARE THEY EVIL? BUT HOW CAN I NOT ASK? HOW

CAN I NOT WONDER? GOD, DO YOU ONLY LOVE US WHEN WE ACT AS WE

SHOULD? DO YOU STILL LOVE US WHEN WE DO WRONG, WHEN WE CHOOSE

POORLY? DO YOU STILL LOVE US WHEN WE SIN?

Then in tiny letters in the margin, almost illegible, were written five simple words. "I think maybe you do."

Arla closed the book and pressed it to her chest. *God, now I'm the one wondering. I'm the one asking. Do you—*

Something crashed on the front porch. Arla leapt up. A rattle of footsteps. The scuffle of heavy boots. She dropped Rakel's journal onto the table and hurried to the door. Someone was there. She could see a shadow through the window. Not a person, but a thing—dark, squatting at the edge of the steps.

She reached for the handle. Did she dare? She held her breath and flung open the door. And there it was, all in black, hovering between the porch and stairs.

"What are you—"

The thing moved, looked up.

And Arla saw what it held in its arms. "Eleanor. How?" Her gaze shot to the creature in black. White rage erupted in her chest. A scream ripped from her lips. She flew at the thing, pounded into it, her fists flying.

The creature fell back.

Arla scratched at the arms, the hood, the hands. "Get away from her, you foul creature. You devil!" With each word, her arms swung at the figure, her fists beating its head, its body.

It crawled away, its arm lifted over its head in defense.

Fury filled Arla's vision until she could see nothing but a blur of black cloth. She grabbed the creature's leg with one hand and beat its back with the other. "I hate you. Get away from us. Get away, I say." This time, things would be different. This time, she would protect the one she loved. No one would hurt Ellie. No one.

The creature tore away from her grip. It staggered to its feet and rushed down the steps.

She picked up a flowerpot from the porch and threw it at the figure's back.

A cry burst from the cloak as the pot hit its mark.

"Don't come back. Don't ever come back."

The creature looked back only once. And in that moment, Arla glimpsed the face of a monster.

18

The shriek shredded Josef's nerves. Emma! He raced toward the house. It came again. Shrill and piercing. Josef threw open the door and lunged inside.

Emma lay on the floor, the dog on top of her.

"No!" The shout burst from him. He dove at the dog.

The animal looked up. Saliva dripped from its lips.

Josef gripped the nape of the dog's neck. Then he saw Emma.

Her face was scrunched with laughter. Her cheeks shone wet with dog kisses.

He relaxed his hold.

Emma squealed again. "Daaah. Daaah." She giggled and reached out her arms.

Ghost wagged his tail as Emma grabbed his face and pulled herself up.

Josef's pulse slowed. He patted the dog's head. "Okay, boy. Good Ghost." He turned and picked up the wood he'd dropped at the door.

Ghost nuzzled Emma's neck, then rolled over on his back.

"You like your new doggy, Em?" He scooped her up and planted a kiss on her forehead.

"Daaahhh."

Josef walked to the far window and flung open the shutters. There, the footprints still dented the snow. Someone had been watching him, watching them. A shiver snaked over his skin as he followed the tracks with his gaze. Were they headed to town? Or would they turn again toward some hidden destination in the trees? Already a light snow sprinkled over the prints. Soon, they would disappear beneath the powder. Josef pressed his fingertips against the glass and envisioned a dark figure standing on the other side. Goose bumps rose on his arms. Why had the man come here? To spy? Or worse?

He turned from the window. He needed to follow those tracks. He needed to know, for certain. He glanced down at Ghost, now sitting up with his ears forward.

"You coming with me, boy? To protect Emma?"

No one would threaten his family. Not even some mystery figure dressed all in black. Not even some ghost-turned-man. He'd find the monster and make him pay.

Josef settled Emma in her crib and placed the blanket around her. Then he tossed a few more logs into the fire.

"Waaaaa." A cry rose from the crib.

Josef shut the stove's door and turned around. "Not again, Em. Please."

She sat up and stuck out her bottom lip. Fat tears formed in her eyes as her lip began to quiver.

Josef ran his hand through his hair. "Ah, now don't be looking that way. You know you have to have a nap."

"Waaaaa."

He sighed. "Oh, all right. You lay down and close your eyes, and I'll tell you a story."

Emma clapped her hands.

"Lay down now."

He leaned over the crib and guided her back in place.

Emma looked up at him with wide eyes. Then she smiled.

Josef smiled back. "Be a good girl and close your eyes." He reposi-
tioned the blanket over her.

She blinked and stuck her thumb in her mouth.

Josef shook his head, then settled in a chair near the fire. The dog
curled up at his feet. "See, even Ghost is sleepy."

"Da-da-daaaa."

"Hush now. Shh."

"Daaaa ..."

Josef sat back in the chair. "Once upon a time many, many years ago,
there was a farmer who grew potatoes in a country far away. The potatoes were good. But the land was hard, and the nights were so cold that
ice crept under the door and made patterns on the floor."

Emma cooed.

Josef leaned back, closed his eyes, and continued. "So the farmer
packed up his wife and his two small sons and came all the way to the new
world." His voice grew softer. "It was a long journey, by boat, by carriage, by foot. But the man and his family kept on."

Emma yawned.

"The man wore out three pairs of boots walking westward before he
found a new home. He settled in the Red River Valley, up there near the
border of North Dakota, right 'bouts near Fargo, and there the soil was
rich and plentiful. The man farmed the land and grew potatoes as big as
Ghost's head." He leaned over and rubbed the dog behind the ears.
"And the sons grew up and were happy."

Emma's eyes drooped shut.

"But then one day a sickness came. And the farmer went on to
heaven." Josef's voice hardened. "And then a bad thing happened. A
thing that should never have been." He paused.

Emma squeaked.

He tilted forward and brushed his fingers over her hair. "Shh, baby
girl. Go to sleep." His gaze fixed on the slats of the crib. His vision
blurred. "One day, the older son got into a card game, and he lost the

family farm." Heat rose in his chest. Even now. Even after all these years. "And so the younger son had to leave his father's farm. He traveled east and finally came to Hinckley. He worked hard in the lumberyard, earned a spot of money, found a little plot of land, and then he farmed potatoes just like his papa. Potatoes as big as a man's fist, but not as big as a dog's head." Josef made a fist and held it up. "And he was happy again ... for a little while." His voice lowered to a whisper. "Then a fire came." He fell silent.

Emma sighed in her sleep.

Josef stood and snuffed out the candle on the table. Then he tucked the blanket closer around her shoulders. "I'll be back soon, little Em. Sleep well." He turned to Ghost and patted his leg. "Come on, boy. We've got a ghost to catch."

The dog stood and trotted to Josef's side.

Josef threw on his coat and hat, then opened the door. Wind whistled through the opening and scattered wisps of snow over the floor. He turned up his collar and stepped out into the cold.

Ghost followed.

Snow fell in small flurries, obscuring his view. He looked toward town, but could see only dark tree trunks against white snow, rocks covered with fine powder, and the gentle roll of the land toward the creek in the distance. He hunched his shoulders and headed toward the prints on the east side of the house. A moment later he found the tracks and followed them into the trees.

Ghost trotted beside him.

The prints led east for a few hundred yards, then turned south and curved through the trees. Bits of blackened bark scattered over the snow like cracked pepper over potatoes. Overhead a bird chirped. A branch shook, sending a handful of ice to the ground below.

Then the tracks shifted again, this time heading straight for the frozen creek bed. The snow fell faster, making the tracks no more than slight indentations in the whiteness.

Josef paused and squatted down.

The dog whined and pushed his nose into Josef's hand.

Josef glanced behind him. Already his homestead was lost to sight. Even the trail of smoke had vanished behind the snow-filled sky. He should go back, but the tracks led on. Just a little farther. A few more yards, and maybe, just maybe, he'd find where the ghost-man was hiding. And this time he wouldn't let him get away.

Josef stood and continued toward the creek. The prints grew shallower. The snow fell harder. And still he pressed on until he reached the stream's northern bank. There, the footprints disappeared.

He stopped and squinted into the whiteness. West, then east. Nothing but snow and shadow.

Ghost rubbed against his leg and whined.

He patted the dog's head. "Just a little farther. The track may pick up again on the other side." But it was too late. He knew it. The snow was falling too heavily now. If there were prints, they'd be filled. He hadn't been quick enough, hadn't been smart enough. He should have done more, sooner. And now …

The hair stood up on the back of Ghost's neck. A growl sounded in his throat.

Josef froze.

The growl deepened.

A branch snapped.

Ghost backed toward him, his lips curled, his teeth bared.

A form appeared out of the whiteness. Tall. Gray. It took shape. A wolf.

Josef ran.

Snow pelted his face. Wind deafened his ears. He threw his arm across his forehead and raced on. The edge of the creek was there somewhere, but he'd lost it. Was it ahead or to the right? And the wolf? He didn't know. He glanced over his shoulder. His foot struck a stone.

Then snow was everywhere. In his eyes, his mouth, his ears. He tumbled forward. Down. Twisting. His shoulders striking ice, making it fly around him. The earth tipped. The creek bank. For a moment, the frozen water flashed below him, then white filled his vision again. He toppled down the bank. Legs contorting, hands unable to stop the wild descent.

Something smacked into his shin. Pain shot up his leg. Then he was lying on the creek's frozen surface. He could see nothing. Hear nothing. Feel nothing but the fierce throb of fire in his shin.

He tried to stand, but failed.

The snow deepened. Cold seeped into his bones. His thoughts blurred. What was he doing out here, in the cold and snow? Where was he? Where was home?

Home ... Emma ... Alone.

He had to get up, get home. The fire, it would go out. And then ... then ... Josef pushed himself to his feet. He took a step forward. His leg buckled. And he fell again to the ice.

Emma ... I have to get up.

But it was cold, so, so cold.

Get up.

His eyes closed.

Get up.

Just a minute.

Get up.

I need rest.

Emma ...

Then out of the whiteness came a frantic barking.

***

Arla fell to her knees beside Ellie and cradled her in her arms. Snow slanted from the sky and spat onto the porch. She brushed the flakes from Ellie's coat and smoothed back the girl's hair with her fingertips. "It's okay, Eleanor. You're home." She lifted her head and stared at the place where the monster had disappeared into the whiteness. "Everything's all right now."

Ellie's hands trembled.

Arla took them and pressed them to her chest. The girl's skin was cold, like the scales of a fish pulled from beneath the ice. "Wake up, Eleanor. Open your eyes."

Ellie's lashes fluttered.

"Let's get you inside." Arla wrapped her arms around Ellie's shoulders and waist, then lifted her to a sitting position.

Ellie's eyes opened. "Where did it go?"

"What, dear?"

"The angel." Her head turned toward the street. "Didn't you see it? It was here. I know it."

Arla shuddered. "There was no angel." *Only a monster.* She pulled Ellie to her feet and took her inside.

Wind blew through the open door and slammed the knob into the wall.

Arla shut the door behind her, then laid Ellie on the couch. She knelt beside her. "What happened to you, child? How did you get here?"

Ellie leaned her head against the pillow and stared at the ceiling. "Can I stay, Mrs. Anderson? I want real bad to stay here with you."

Warmth flooded Arla's chest. She reached out and squeezed Ellie's arm. "Of course you can." She smiled for a moment, then stood and went into the kitchen. There, she found a rag and dipped it into the warm water already on the stove. A moment later, she returned to the main room and wrapped the cloth around Ellie's hands. Visions of the telegram, of the doctor in Duluth, flitted through her mind. But she didn't ask about them. She didn't dare. Besides, none of that mattered now. Ellie was home. Somehow she had come back.

"I ran away."

"Hush now. We don't need to talk about that." Arla removed Ellie's shoes, then wrapped the warm rag around the girl's feet. *I don't want to know. I don't want to hear.*

"My side hurts. I think I broke the stitches."

"Let me take a look." Arla opened the buttons on Ellie's dress and pulled back the fabric.

"Is it bad?"

"No, just torn open a bit. You lie still, and it will be fine." Arla took Ellie's hand in her own and smiled. "We're going to be just fine, you and I. Now that you're back. Now that you're home."

Ellie tried to sit up, then winced and lay back down. "They won't come looking for me, will they? They won't make me go back?"

Arla looked out the window into the whiteness of the falling snow. The pane rattled in the wind. "Not today, child. No one's coming here today."

Ellie sighed.

Arla stood. "I'll get us some tea. That'll warm you right up. Then we'll get you into some fresh clothes." She patted the girl's arm, then retreated to the kitchen. No one would come for Ellie today, she told herself again. Arla took two teacups from the cupboard and placed them on a tray. But tomorrow ... who knew about tomorrow?

Eventually, someone would come for Ellie. Someone would see her, would realize that she was here. And they would take her. Again.

No. Arla gripped the tray until her knuckles turned white. That couldn't happen. She wouldn't let it. Not this time.

She let go of the tray and poured tea into the cups. No one had seen Ellie arrive. No one knew. Except the monster.

Arla looked down the hall toward Ellie's bedroom. Then, she glanced through the kitchen doorway to the keys on the wall.

* * *

It was a mean thing she'd done. Ellie knew it. Mrs. Anderson thought it was because of her that Ellie had come home. And Ellie had let her think just that. It wasn't right. But she'd done it anyway. How could she tell Mrs. Anderson that she'd only come home to find a ghost? To hunt down a dream?

Mama wouldn't approve. Mama always said you had to be straight as a needle with folks, not all crooked like a buttonhook. But, well, sometimes it weren't so easy.

The hiss of boiling water sounded from the kitchen. Ellie glanced toward the open door. There, she could just see the curve of Mrs. Anderson's skirt as she traveled from stove to table.

Ellie shifted on the couch. Her gaze fell to a book lying open on the small table in front of her. She picked it up and opened it. Rakel's journal. Ellie would have known that handwriting anywhere. When Ellie was younger, Rakel had written stories for her. And there was always that certain slant to her words, and the funny way her *T*s curled up at the end. Ellie turned to a place near the end where a page was bent. A word caught her eye, and before she knew it, she was reading a dead woman's private thoughts.

24 August 1894

> SHE'S MAKING IT FOR ME. I DARE NOT SAY MORE IN CASE MAMA FINDS THIS JOURNAL. MAMA CAN'T KNOW. SHE'D RUIN EVERYTHING. SHE'D MAKE ME STAY. SHE'D MAKE ME REPENT. BUT I'M NOT GOING TO. NOT THIS TIME. NOT AGAIN.
>
> BESIDES, IT WILL BE DONE SOON. AND THEN EVERYTHING WILL CHANGE. EVERYTHING.

Ellie paused. Who was making what? And why did it matter? She glanced toward the kitchen. And, more important, why didn't Rakel want Mrs. Anderson to find out?

Dishes rattled in the other room. Ellie frowned. Maybe there was something about Mrs. Anderson that she didn't know. That nobody knew. Except Mama, and Rakel. And they were both gone.

Ellie riffled the pages of the journal, then continued reading the entry.

SHE'S AN ANGEL FOR DOING IT. SHE WOULDN'T HAVE TO. AND I KNOW IT'S HARD WORK. BUT, SHE'S MORE THAN AN ANGEL. SHE'S A FRIEND. A REAL FRIEND. LIKE THE KIND THEY TALK ABOUT IN THE BIBLE.

She turned the page.

AND BECAUSE OF HER, I'M GOING TO BE FREE. TRULY, HONESTLY FREE. MAMA THINKS SHE'S STOPPED ME. BUT SHE HASN'T. WE HAVE IT ALL PLANNED OUT.

The entry stopped abruptly. Ellie studied the words on the page. *Free? Could it be?* Memory stirred. Mama had said something about freedom, something about someone being free. Could it have been Rakel? But why would she need to be freed? She'd had her mama, at least, and a good house, and plenty to eat. Wasn't that enough?

Maybe it wasn't. Maybe that's what Rakel and Mama had been talking about in those weeks before the fire. Rakel had come to the house often then. She'd come to help Mama sew. But then she stopped coming. She stopped, and Ellie hadn't seen her again. Something had happened. Something bad.

Ellie unfocused her eyes and turned her face toward the window. She could almost see Rakel there, sitting at the table in their old farmhouse. A bit of black ribbon twined through Rakel's fingers. She held a needle in one hand. But she wasn't sewing. Instead, she was looking out across the fields, away from town, away from everything.

"What do you think is out there, Nora?"

Mama flicked out the hem of the dress in her lap and continued sewing. "Same thing that's everywhere, I suppose. Land and trees, folks and families."

"It can't all be the same."

Mama smiled. "Every place has its own unique beauty." She smoothed the soft fabric with her fingers. "Even Hinckley."

Rakel grimaced. "You know what I think of that."

Mama pointed her needle toward the puff bonnet in Rakel's lap. "If you don't keep going, that capote will never get done."

Rakel sighed and dipped the needle through the ribbon into the cloth. "I could stand it here, I guess, if things were different."

"How different?"

Rakel had paused and wrapped the ribbon around her finger. "I have this vision of what my life should be. A husband, children, a farm."

"Just like Maggie?"

"Well, like her maybe. But not so dull." Rakel grinned then. "All that, plus adventure, travel, faraway places."

Mama laughed. "You can't have it all, Rakel."

Rakel jabbed the needle through the ribbon. "Right about now it seems I can't have any of it."

"Perhaps not yet."

"Not ever?"

"I don't know."

"Who does?"

"God."

Rakel huffed and threw the bonnet onto the table. She stood and paced the room. "Then tell me this. Why must life hurt? Why can't it be what I dream?"

"Life is what it is."

"Then where is God?"

Ellie had held her breath then, waiting. Surely Mama would scold Rakel. Surely she'd tell her not to ask questions like that. But Mama didn't scold. She didn't even scowl. She just smiled with that funny little smile that she'd wear whenever she knew a secret. She just smiled and kept on sewing. That's when Ellie knew that Mama and Rakel had a real

friendship. One that went beyond "how do?" and chitchat over afternoon tea. "Some friendships are like flowers," Mama always said. "They
bloom real pretty for a time, then they die away. A few, though, are like
trees. They grow through the years and stand strong, even through a
storm." That day, Ellie saw that Mama and Rakel were like two oaks.

Finally, Mama spoke. "Do you know what this dress is going to be,
Rakel?" She held up the fabric in her hand.

Rakel shook her head.

"It will be a grand ball dress, like the ones you see in the catalogs.
You can't tell it now, of course. Now, you can only see today's stitches,
and yesterday's."

Mama was going somewhere with this conversation. Ellie knew that
look.

Mama picked up a part of the fabric that was all bunched up. "Some
of it looks bad now, but in the end, when it's part of the whole, the gown
will be beautiful." She raised her eyebrows. "That is, if I don't give up."

Rakel twined the ribbon tighter around her knuckles. "What does
that have to do with my question?"

"God is the dressmaker."

Rakel snorted. "Well, mine isn't fitting very well."

Mama laughed. "It will. In the end, it will. I promise."

Ellie frowned and stared at the journal in her hand. Mama had
promised. But it hadn't come true. Rakel had died. And so had Mama.
Their dresses, half-formed, were left unfinished.

And maybe that was the real answer. Sometimes life just doesn't turn
out the way we expect it to. Sometimes all the stitches go awry.
Sometimes a fire comes and—

"Eleanor?"

Ellie jumped and shoved the journal beneath her.

19

I cannot see for the tears streaming from my eyes. Cannot hear for the blood pounding in my ears. I run as if devils pursue me. And maybe they do. Devils in the form of vicious words still tearing through my soul. Hateful claws that ripped at me and left their mark. Fists that pummeled me until I fled.

But the fists are gone. The claws have retracted. And still I run. For the words remain, shouting in my mind, driving me down the street, through the alley, across the railroad tracks.

Today, no train comes. No whistle blows. No black smoke makes dark stains against the white sky. There is nothing but the silence. The snow. The memory of hate that twisted familiar features and made them new.

"You devil. You foul creature."

How could she abhor me so? She, of all people. How could she not know? How could she not see? What have I done to earn her scorn? To earn the hatred of them all? Is it only because of this distorted face, this twisted and burned body? Or is it more? Have I somehow become the shadow they fear?

I will never go back. Never. If I must live as a hermit for a hundred years, I will never let them hurt me again. I will never let her.

For a moment, for one final time, I glance back. But the town has vanished behind me. The streets have been swallowed in snow, the buildings sheeted in white. It's gone. All gone. And I am alone.

My feet slow. I can run no longer. Ice whips in my face as I weave through the stumps of trees and head north. Toward the wilderness. Toward the dismal shack that I now call home. Miles stretch between me and it. Miles of cold. Of frost. Of wind-driven snow.

I stop, then stumble forward. Or is it back? I am lost. Adrift. Abandoned.

And the storm blows around me. I see nothing but the whiteness. Hear nothing but the wind and the sound of my own breath, panting. Where am I? Where has the world gone?

My coat is too thin. The snow too heavy. I will die out here. Alone. With no one knowing. No one caring.

I sink down to my knees. And the snow welcomes me. I grip it in my hands and feel the sting of it against bare flesh. It will claim me soon. Take my warmth. Steal my breath. Make me its own. But what does that matter now? Why should I care? I have lost everything. Everything. There is nothing left. No hope. No dreams. No peace.

I lie down and curl up in the snow. They will find me here in the spring. The snow will melt, and here I will be. Will they know me then? When they peel back the layers of cloth that hide my scarred body, pull back the hood that covers my misshapen face, will anyone recognize who I used to be?

God, it is over. I am finished. I cannot live this life you have forced on me. I cannot walk this path of pain. I cannot live in their hate.

I close my eyes. My breath slows. The darkness comes.

Then a dog barks.

* * *

Arla threw the pillow on the floor, then stuffed her hand between the cushions of the sofa. It wasn't there. She shoved the sofa to one side. Not there either. She tipped the table, dropped to her knees, and ran her fingers over the rug. It wasn't anywhere. But it had to be. She'd been reading it when she'd heard the scuffle on the porch. A journal just couldn't vanish into the air.

But what if it had? Was it really such a loss? Wasn't it better not to read it, not to remember? She'd thought she could find answers in Rakel's final words. But so far, they had brought only pain and guilt.

Arla sat on the edge of the sofa and stared into the flickering flames of the fire in the grate. Warmth billowed from the small blaze. She reached out until the heat brushed her palms. Strange how fire could be so warm and comforting when contained, when kept within its bounds. But let it loose and nothing could stop the destruction. Memory was like that. It had to be managed. There were so many things better forgotten. So much that ought to be buried before it burned out of control.

What would happen if she let the fire loose? Would she be consumed? Lost forever in a conflagration of guilt, of regret? Or maybe, just maybe, the fire would set her free.

As it set Rakel free.

Arla's hands dropped to her sides. Where did that thought come from? It was crazy, but it was true, too. Rakel had been so unhappy in those last months. And now she was in a better place. She had to be. Now, she was free.

Suddenly, a memory flashed before Arla's vision. A picture of Rakel staring out the window, her back rigid, her eyes unblinking.

"You can't keep me here forever, Mama."

Arla straightened the sheets on the bed and smoothed out the wrinkles with one hand. "I don't intend to."

"Then why do you lock the door?"

"I have to. You know that."

"When I leave here, I'm never coming back."

"You aren't leaving."

"I am. Someday."

Arla snapped the bedspread into place and plumped the pillow on the bed. "Unless some fairy comes to the window and spirits you away, you're staying right here until you get your head on straight. No more tomfoolery, no more making up tall tales." She paused and jabbed her finger toward Rakel. "And no more barefaced lies about the good folks of this town. You hear me?"

Rakel turned. Even now Arla could see the deadness in her eyes, the stiffness of her face. Then Rakel turned back to the window.

"You'll thank me one day. Soon as you confess what you've done and make right the fibs you told."

"I didn't lie."

Arla pursed her lips and gave a final flick to the bedspread. "Stubborn." She muttered the word under her breath. "Always have been, always will be. Nothing I can do about it. Lord knows I try. Yes, he does."

And that's when Arla noticed the journal lying open on the table. "What's that?"

A smile had quirked Rakel's lips, then faded. "The truth." She turned and faced Arla one last time. "Or a lie. You decide."

You decide … The words still haunted her. Truth or lie. She didn't know anymore. Hadn't known for a very long time.

Arla shook her head, then searched beneath the end table. She needed that journal. Needed it, and hated it too. She stood and retraced her steps to the door.

It must be here. It's got to ... oh no.

The creak of the wardrobe door echoed from Ellie's room to the parlor. Arla paused to listen. Pattering feet. The soft, almost inaudible rustle of sheets. Then silence.

Arla turned and raced down the hallway.

***

Ellie balanced on the edge of the bed and fished her hand under the pillow. There it was. She pulled out Rakel's journal and set it on her lap.

The lantern flickered on the bedside table. The oil was getting low. If she was going to read more, she'd have to do it now.

For a moment, she held her breath and listened for Mrs. Anderson. But she heard nothing. No clanking of dishes from the kitchen, no footsteps down the hallway, no creak of a door opening across the way.

She slipped out of bed, tiptoed to the door, and quietly closed it. It wouldn't do to have Mrs. Anderson wandering by and seeing what she was doing. 'Course, Mrs. Anderson might not care if Ellie read Rakel's journal. Maybe she'd be glad that someone wanted to remember her daughter. Or maybe she wouldn't like it one bit. And that was a chance Ellie didn't want to take. Not when reading the words of Mama's best friend was the closest she was going to get to hearing Mama again.

Ellie squeezed the book to her chest and moved back toward the bed. Halfway there, she stopped beside the open wardrobe door. Inside hung the gray dress that Mama was making when the fire fell. It was such a beautiful dress, even now with a burn mark on the sleeve and the hem ragged. She touched the hem and let the fabric slip through her fingers like water. She'd never seen a softer gray, a more perfectly turned collar. Now, it was all she had left of Mama. Just this dress and the tidbits in the journal. She sighed, closed the wardrobe door, and returned to the bed.

"What story will you tell me this time, Rakel? One about monsters and giants? Or princes in faraway lands?" Ellie smiled. If she knew Rakel, it would be about monsters and warrior women who fought like men. "Just tell me about Mama, please. Tell me what you once saw."

Ellie snuggled down into the covers and opened to a random entry in June.

MAMA WEARING PANTS. GEESE FLYING NORTH FOR THE WINTER. MEN TAP-DANCING ON THE MOON. ME WINNING A COOKING CONTEST. THEM THINGS ARE MORE LIKELY THAN WINIFRED JENSEN FALLING FROM A HORSE.

BUT THAT'S WHAT SHE SAID SHE DID. THIS TIME. HIT HER CHEEK ON A ROCK, SHE SAID. THAT'S HOW SHE GOT THAT TERRIBLE BRUISE BELOW HER EYE, THE ONE THAT SPREAD ALL THE WAY UP TO HER TEMPLE. THAT'S WHY SHE WINCED WHEN SHE WALKED AND TREMBLED WHEN I GRABBED HER WRIST. A TERRIBLE FALL, SHE SAID. BUT IT COULD HAVE BEEN MUCH WORSE.

I'LL SAY IT COULD HAVE BEEN WORSE. WINNIE JENSEN DOESN'T HAVE A HORSE. NOT THAT HER PAPA ISN'T RICH ENOUGH. HE'S JUST NEVER BOUGHT HER ONE. SHE FORGOT THAT I KNOW THAT.

Ellie scratched her head. She remembered that strange bruise. A queer shape, it was. But then Winnie was always coming over with bruises. Real clumsy, that Winifred Jensen. But she was Mama's friend, and she ordered the most expensive dresses. So Mama had said it weren't nice to notice certain things. That Ellie should just ignore them. But it was hard to ignore a big purple splotch that spread over half of a person's cheek.

She turned the page and continued reading.

I TOOK HER TO NORA'S, LIKE I ALWAYS DO WHEN SHE'S HAD ONE OF HER FALLS. WE MADE HER SOME TEA WITH PEPPERMINT, JUST LIKE USUAL, AND

WAITED AS SHE SIPPED AND STARED BLANKLY AT THAT LITTLE DENT IN NORA'S
KITCHEN TABLE. YOU'D THINK NORA WOULD GET THAT FIXED FOR ALL THE TIME
WINNIE SPENDS STARING AT IT. BUT THAT'S PROBABLY WHY NORA LETS IT BE.
WINNIE'S GOT TO HAVE SOMETHING SURE, SOMETHING RELIABLE, IN HER LIFE.
EVEN IF IT IS JUST A DENT IN SOMEONE ELSE'S TABLE.

Is that what she was doing all that time at Mama's table? Just staring
at a mark in the wood? Why, that was downright silly. Rakel was making
Winnie sound like some kind of a fool. And they were supposed to be
friends. It didn't make no sense. No, not a lick. Winnie wasn't crazy.
Quiet maybe. And a little dreamy. But there was nothing wrong with
that.

Ellie closed her eyes and remembered how the sun would shine off
Winnie's yellow hair, making her look almost pretty. She'd had a closet
full of Mama's dresses. Wouldn't have no one else make them. Just
Mama. And whenever money got a little tight, it seemed it would come
time for Winnie to need a new gown.

Mama always said that God was providin'. But sometimes it seemed
that it was Winifred Jensen doing the providing. Ellie never could figure
how one woman could need so many dresses. Too bad they never made
her happy.

And then that horrible fire came and took all Mama's beautiful
dresses, and took Mama and Winnie Jensen too.

Ellie sighed and dropped her gaze back to the journal.

IT'S ALWAYS THE SAME. WE SIT. SHE SITS. WE ASK A FEW QUESTIONS. SHE
DOESN'T ANSWER. AND FINALLY SHE SAYS, "THANK YOU SO MUCH, YOU JUST
DON'T KNOW HOW MUCH I ..." THEN SHE CATCHES HERSELF AND RUNS OUT.

TOMORROW IT'LL BE LIKE NOTHING HAPPENED. SHE'LL COME WHILE WE DO
THE SEWING, AND MAYBE SHE'LL PICK UP A NEEDLE AND TRY A FEW STITCHES
HERSELF. WE WON'T ASK ANY MORE QUESTIONS. AND SHE WON'T GIVE ANY
ANSWERS. NOT THAT SHE NEEDS TO. WE KNOW THE TRUTH.

BUT WHAT ARE WE TO DO? WE'RE ONLY WOMEN AFTER ALL. THAT'S WHAT NORA SAYS. WE'RE ONLY WOMEN.

YET EVEN WOMEN CAN ONLY TAKE SO MUCH.

The door burst open.

Ellie dropped the journal.

Mrs. Anderson stood in the doorway with her mouth contorted, her face glowing like a hot coal. Her finger jabbed toward Ellie. "You! How could you, when I, when I—" The words sputtered to a halt.

Ellie flicked the sheet over the journal.

Mrs. Anderson's gaze shot to the bed. Her jaw tightened. She stormed toward the bed and ripped back the sheet. Her fingers closed over the journal. "I knew it." The accusation spat from her lips.

Ellie shuddered.

Mrs. Anderson shoved the journal under Ellie's nose. "Why did you steal this? What did you read?"

Ellie looked down, away, refusing to meet the gaze that would impale her. Her voice shook as she spoke. "I didn't steal it. I just, I just ..."

"Tell me the truth. What lies did you read in here?"

Ellie shrugged her shoulders. "Nothing. I mean, I just read a little about Mama, that's all."

"Mama? Your mama?" Mrs. Anderson straightened and thrust the journal into her apron pocket. "I'm your mama now."

Ellie swallowed. "No, ma'am, you're not." The words were no more than a squeak.

Mrs. Anderson's hands curled into tight balls. "Don't you contradict me. Don't you ever ... not again." Her voice turned low, strained. She whirled toward the door.

Ellie could see the stiffness in her spine, the slight tremble of her shoulders.

Then the words came again, all thin and wispy, as if she was breathing them out between teeth that refused to unclench. "I give you the roof over your head, I feed you, I take care of you. And don't you ever forget it, Rakel!"

Ellie's eyes widened.

Mrs. Anderson stomped to the door and slammed it behind her.

A moment later came the click of a key turning in the lock.

***

The sound brings me to my feet. It echoes in the whiteness. Draws me from my despair. It comes again. A simple bark. A whine. A howl in the blinding nothingness of blizzard snow.

I fling my arm over my head and stumble toward the sound. One foot after the other, slogging through this jungle of falling ice. On and on I go as the barking becomes clearer, closer. My breath freezes on my lips. Snowflakes catch on my eyelashes. I pause. But the barking continues, pulling me through the trees toward it.

I try to call out, to whistle, but my lips won't form the sounds. And then it is there, a dark shadow against a backdrop of white. It sees me, and silence falls. I move forward. It moves not at all.

"Here, boy." I force the words from between frozen lips.

The dog does not come. But neither does it run away. It simply sits. Then it whines again, a forlorn cry that reaches to the recesses of my soul.

I rush forward, and the whining ceases. My fingers ache with cold as I hold out a hand toward him. He pushes his nose into my palm. Warm breath feathers my skin. I sink to my knees and bury my fingers in his fur. His eyes look into mine. And for the first time since the fire, I see into another's face and find no fear there. I almost laugh. I almost cry. But instead I rub my hands over his neck and sides. "What's wrong, boy?" The question comes out in a croak. I touch his legs, feeling for the wetness of blood, for evidence of injury. I find none. "What is it?"

He whines again and shoves his nose beneath my elbow. I take his chin in my hands and look again into those deep brown eyes. I search them, and they search me.

Then I remember. This face. This dog. I saw him just this morning. He was safe then, home. So how ...

Another sound comes, breaking through the muffle of falling snow. A human sound. Like a groan. Or a cry. Or a muted call.

I gasp. The dog is not alone. He is out there. In the snow. Waiting.

He mustn't find me. I turn to escape. But the dog is beside me, pressing against my legs, blocking my flight. He whines again, and looks toward the sound of the man.

I cannot. I won't.

A sharp bark.

No!

He licks my hand.

And I am undone. I will help him find his master. I will take him to the man who would capture me if he could. "Where is he, boy? Show me." I place my hand on the dog's head and follow as he guides me through the falling snow.

A moment later, we are at the edge of the creek's bank. The snow thins, and I can see down the bank, to a splotch of brown against the whiteness at the bottom.

It is him. I know it. But snow covers his legs, his arms.

I sidle down the bank. Chunks of ice dislodge and race before me to the bottom. They strike him, but he does not cry out. Does not even move.

Fear slithers through my gut. My feet slide out from under me. Snow flies so thick that I cannot tell where the air ends and the ground begins. Then I am with him. Beside him. My knees buried in the snow.

I brush my fingers against his cold cheek. His eyes are closed. His chest still. I take his icy hand in my own.

"Wake up. Come back."

He doesn't move.

I have come too late.

20

Lars rubbed the blade of his knife over the sharpening stone. The sound of it lulled him. Scrape, swish, scrape, swish. Steady, even strokes. The blade glistening in the lamplight, his hand firm on the stone.

He paused and held the knife up in the light. The ivory handle gleamed white, with carvings so intricate that he couldn't make out all the details. Even now, after all these years, its beauty still pleased him. He ran his finger over the warm ivory. *It's mine. It always will be.*

He'd told Agnes that the knife belonged to his father; it was a memento, he'd said, from a trading trip in India. But that was a lie. Or rather a fabrication. The knife had indeed come from India, and a merchant had brought it. But it hadn't come from his father. He didn't even know who his father was.

Lars lifted the blade and blew warm breath across its surface. Then he took a cloth and wiped it until it shone. He tilted the knife until his image reflected from the surface. He had changed much since he'd first glimpsed himself in the silver. Almost forty years ago. When he was seven. Only seven. But he still had the same dark hair, the same green-blue eyes, and the scar that he had gotten that day.

His eyes narrowed as he remembered. He'd found the knife in the trunk of his mother's latest lover. There, among the soiled shirts and a smelly coat the knife had gleamed. He remembered how his eyes had gotten round and big as he looked at it. How his breath quickened. How smooth and rich the ivory felt in his hand. How the shininess of the blade entranced him. He had sat on the floor with the knife in his hand and taken a few practice jabs. And that's when *they* came in. His mother and that man. Him laughing that ugly laugh. Her giggling with eyes red and watery. They stumbled toward him. The man's hands all over her, hers gripping a bottle. They never saw him. He was right there. But they didn't care, didn't even bother to look.

His grip tightened on the knife's handle. How could they not have noticed him? A seven-year-old boy playing with a knife. But they had noticed him a moment later. Just as soon as they tripped over him and the knife slipped and fell into the man's foot. Lars had gotten two black eyes, a broken arm, and the scar that night. And no one cared, not Mama, not that man, no one but the little orange kitten he'd found three weeks before in the alley behind the slaughterhouse.

Lars rubbed the place on his cheek where the scar still shone. Still, after all these years. Funny how he remembered every detail of that day, yet he couldn't recall the man's name, or what he looked like. He was only a shadow, a mist, a darkness that had stained his life and then vanished forever.

But he'd kept the knife. Lars placed the weapon carefully back in its holder on the wall. It reminded him of how far he had come. No one could threaten him now. No one could hurt him. He was respected, trusted, admired. Noticed. And that was all he wanted, except ... he frowned. No, it was better not to think of that, not to dwell on what had happened in August. The knife hadn't helped him then. Not at all. But that was past, forgotten.

He straightened his collar and watched how the lamplight danced over the wall. *It was one mistake. One sin.* He wouldn't make it again. He couldn't. After all, she was dead. And temptation with her.

And now, everything was as it should be. He glanced at the telegram on the table. It announced that Mr. Whitehall from the school back East would arrive next week to interview Leif. In a week, the process would be over, Leif would be accepted to the best school in the country, and in time he would be admitted to Harvard. Lars smiled. It would feel good to say that his boy was studying back East, and better yet to mention the name of Harvard and watch people's eyes turn round with awe. His boy. His son. Everyone would respect him then. Everyone would notice.

Lars smoothed the telegram with his fingers. Two weeks ago, he'd opened his new bank on Main Street. Last week, his restaurant opened. This week he'd been honored for his donation to the new school. And next week, well, that would be the best of all.

The coffeepot gurgled from the other room. He picked up the telegram, put it in his pocket, then strode over to remove the pot from the stove. He poured the thick liquid into a cup and took a gulp. It was good. Strong and black, just the way he liked it.

From the front room, a door slammed.

Lars set down his cup just as Leif's voice shouted from the other room. "Pa? Pa, where are you?"

Lars stepped through the door. "What are you doing home, boy?"

Leif pulled off his fur cap and stomped the snow from his boots. His cheeks and nose shone red. "Miss Craig sent us home early on account of the snow. They say a blizzard's coming in."

Lars walked to the window, pulled back the curtain, and looked outside. The snow slanted in heavy clumps, obscuring all but the dim outline of the garden fence and the new wagon that sat beside it. "All right then. Get on up to your room."

"But Pa, I saw her."

Lars dropped the curtain and turned. "The girl of your dreams?"

"No. Ellie Hansen."

Lars' stomach dropped. Ellie Hansen? Impossible. He'd had it all arranged. Her care. Her adoption. Everything. "Don't you be telling tales to me, boy."

"I'm not, Pa. I swear it."

Lars crossed his arms. The boy was imagining things. He had to be. "How could you see her? I thought you were in school."

Leif's cheeks turned even redder. "I was. Well, I mean, I was just taking a little break. Me and the boys ..."

Lars drummed his fingers on his arm. That boy was going to ruin everything yet. "Yes?"

"I saw her. Getting off the train and stumbling down the street."

"You're sure it was her?"

"I am."

"Where did she go? Did you follow her?"

Leif rubbed his nose and stared down at his feet. "Well, no."

Lars raised his eyebrows. Fool boy. Didn't he realize what was at stake?

"Miss Craig came out just then and spied us. Took Gunnar and Gregor by the ears. I had to go too." He paused. "So what are we going to do, about Ellie I mean?"

Lars stared at his son for a long moment. All it would take was for Ellie Hansen to start talking, to start telling everyone that Leif had shot her intentionally. If that rumor got around ... Well, he hated to think what the man from that fancy Boston school would think then. Lars scowled. And what if folks started asking other questions, started remembering how another girl had made accusations not too long ago?

And then they'd start probing. Looking into his past. It was bad enough when Agnes discovered the truth, bad enough when she told it to Winnie. But it had stopped there. And now he was safe. From Agnes, from Winnie, and from that black-haired siren. He didn't need any more enemies.

No, people didn't need to start remembering. Wondering. Digging around in the past. And he didn't need another girl causing trouble either. Especially not nosy Nora's daughter. No. He wouldn't let that happen. Couldn't take the chance. Leif would go to his school. Lars would maintain the respect of the town. And maybe, once Leif was off to Boston, Lars would even run for mayor. He'd always wanted to. And now, maybe, was the time. He just had to make sure that Hansen girl didn't cause trouble. That is, if she really were back in town after all.

Lars rubbed his hand over his chin. "Don't worry, son. I'll take care of it. I'll take care of everything." He again reached out and pulled back the drapery. Now, even the fence and wagon were hidden by the driving snow. Even as he watched, the snow grew heavier. He backed away from the window and glanced at the knife on the wall.

Control. Admiration. Respect. He took down the knife and balanced it on one finger. Yes. Respect. It would take more than one girl to ruin his plans for himself and for Leif. More than one girl. More than one blunder. More than one sin.

***

He's heavier than I expected. A mass of weight pressing me into the snow. But I don't care. I won't leave him. I dare not.

He may be dead. He may not be. But he's cold. Oh so cold.

I fling his arm around my shoulders and take a step forward. My foot sinks. Another step. My legs shake. Another, and I stare up the short bank of the creek.

I grit my teeth and blink the ice from my eyes. Slowly, so slowly, I drag him up the bank. His feet make twin channels in the snow, mine deep punctures that reach nearly to my knees. And then we are at the top. The dog is waiting. He yips at me, then sniffs at his master. He circles, once, twice, and takes his place at my side. He starts west.

"No, boy. Not that way." The words sound strained, muffled by the driven snow. I draw a stinging breath. My calves ache, my chest burns. Already.

But it's not far. A hundred yards to the north, and a hundred more east. Along the line of burned pines. I can find it from here. I've done it a hundred times. In the dark before dawn, in the snow, and in the blindness of my pain. And I will do it now.

So I turn and start north. Slow steps, too slow, too small, too few, pulling him alongside me, wishing that I were stronger, bigger, faster. I've wished the same before. Snow falls in thick sheets. My breath freezes on my lips. Beside me, the dog whines. I glance down at him, his back hunched, his ears flattened, his head bent against the onslaught of ice and snow. "It's all right, boy." The wind snatches my words and throws them to the ground.

My grip weakens. I stumble, and his arm slips from my shoulder. I try to grab harder, but my fingers will not obey. They are too cold. I am too cold. I shift his weight. The dog bumps against my leg. North. North. Fifty more yards. Then east. North. Then east. North ...

The words pound in my head, guiding me through this world of ice. Of silence broken only by the rattle of my breath, the thud of my footsteps in the snow. On and on I trudge with his weight heavy on my shoulders. I see nothing but white. And the shadow of trees cloaked in snow. But I know these trees. I know this wood. It is mine. It always has been.

He groans.

My breath comes faster.

He moves. Just a little, a tiny jerk of his shoulder, a twitch of his arm.

And I want to shout, to leap for joy. He is alive.

But I can't. My lips are frozen, my legs like stones.

He groans again. And this time I pause.

His arm slides from my shoulders. He sinks back to the snow.

I set him against me and press my hand to his neck. There, I feel the slow pulse of blood. I lean closer. "Wake up! Josef!" The snow mutes my voice. I loosen the scarf around my neck and shake him. His head jolts back and forth. I grip his face in my hands. His skin is like ice. His cheeks drained of color. "Josef!" His eyes flutter open, and closed again.

I pull him to his feet, but his leg buckles. Again, he crumples to the snow. Once more I tug him up. One leg stiffens. The other hangs useless, bent. I lower him to the snow and roll up his pant leg.

A shudder runs through me. His leg is swollen, his skin a mix of purple and white. I touch his shin, pressing my fingers along the bone.

He gasps, and falls silent. I can feel it there, the bone broken halfway between the knee and ankle. I could splint it. But not here. Not in this storm.

"Josef! Josef, wake up." I fire the words at him like pellets from a shotgun.

His head falls back. His eyes stay closed.

I rub his hands between my own, blow my warm breath on his fingers and face. For a moment, I think he will respond. I brush back his hair, wipe the snow from his forehead and collar. And still he is quiet, unmoving.

My chin drops to my chest. Josef. Come back. *I have not the energy to shout it again, to make myself heard again in this awful wasteland of snow. I stand and grab his arm.*

But then he is reaching for me, one hand searching through the ice-filled air. He finds me, grabs my cloak. He pulls me toward him until I am kneeling beside him, my face just inches from his. But he doesn't see me, doesn't look, doesn't even open his eyes. His face tilts up. Snowflakes fall on his cheeks, whiten his lashes.

I see the skin torn on his lips as he forces them open again. He speaks a single word. "Emma."

And my heart goes cold.

***

Emma!

Josef shot upright. Pain pulsed up his leg. He reached down to grab his shin, but his hand closed instead around two thin planks of wood. He threw back the blanket covering him. The bottom half of his leg was held tight in a makeshift splint. His gaze darted around him. Four crudely built walls. A single window. One door. A bare dirt floor. An empty peg on the wall. And fire leaping in a rough rock fireplace, with Ghost asleep on the rug before it.

A couple of pots sat by the fire. Josef leaned forward. One was empty, the other filled with water. He picked up the filled pot and dipped his finger in the liquid. Cold. Like snow just melted. He lifted the pot to his mouth and took a drink. He shivered as the water stung his lips. He licked them and felt the dry cracks.

How long had he been out in the snow? And how did he find himself here in this miserable shack? Ghost had been with him then, too. He remembered the dog barking. And then the snow fell heavier. And the cold. Bitter, bitter cold. Drowning him, smothering him, wrapping him in a world of white. He should have died then. But someone, something appeared out of the falling snow.

That someone had brought him here.

Josef took another sip of water. "Hullo?" His voice cracked. He tried again. "Hullo?"

No one answered. Not even Ghost.

He swung one leg over the edge of the cot. It didn't matter where he was, or how he got here. All that mattered was Emma. He had to get back to her. Now. He spied his boots, sitting by the door. He glanced at his feet. They were covered in what looked like long underwear. His toes throbbed with a dull ache. That was good. If they ached, they were still there. They would be all right.

Josef tugged his splinted leg over the edge of the cot, then pressed his swathed feet to the floor. He shivered and forced himself to stand. Pain coursed up his leg, making him dizzy. He reached out and steadied himself on the wall. Then he tried to take a step. But his leg buckled. He spun sideways, his shoulder crashing into the wall. He gritted his teeth and tried again.

With his hands on the wall and his leg dragging behind him, he pulled himself toward the door. One tottering step. Pain twisted his stomach. Two. His throat closed. Three. He reached the door and flung it open. A blast of cold and snow slapped his face. He caught his breath and squinted into the storm. White. Nothing but white. Snow slanting. Snow falling. Snow swirling in eddies of frozen ice. No trees, no rocks, no sky. Only a blizzard of white.

Josef turned and retched into the snow. But nothing came. Only a trickling of the water he had just drunk. He wiped his mouth and stepped back. His body shook. His vision blurred.

It was so much like the fire. Though white instead of black. Cold instead of hot. But just as deadly. *Em, oh Em.* He had to get to her. Had to stoke the fire, warm her milk, change her diaper. She would freeze when the fire went out.

Snow swirled in through the open door and landed on his nose and eyelashes, spat over his cotton-clad feet. He trembled again. *I could try. Maybe I could find my way.* He looked out into the falling snow. But which way would he start? Was his house north or south or west? Not that it mattered. He couldn't tell north from south anyway. There was nothing. No sun, no landmarks, no paths. Nothing to tell him which way he might go to find home. To find Emma. He couldn't even find his way a hundred feet.

Josef groaned and slammed the door shut before him. He ran his fingers through his hair. The dampness of melting snowflakes wet his hand.

He tottered back to the cot and fell down on it.

Emma ... Somewhere out there his little girl was all alone. All alone, and crying for her papa. He couldn't just sit here and do nothing. But he couldn't go out in this storm either.

He closed his eyes. *Not again. Don't do this to me again.* He was helpless. Useless. Powerless to save the one he loved. What good was he as a man? As a father? A vision of his little house flooded his mind. There, he could imagine the fire growing dim. He could see the way it sputtered in the stove, how the logs would crumble, fall, and turn to red embers. One minute. Five. And for a moment longer, they would glow dull orange. And then, with a final puff, the fire would die. Emma would wake. He could almost hear her cry. Soft at first, then growing louder. Sharper. More desperate. As the house grew colder, and colder, and colder. And soon, the cries would fade to a whimper. And then ...

No! Josef pressed the heels of his hands into his forehead and sought to erase the images from his mind. But he couldn't. They were too real. Too terrible. Too reminiscent of the images from his dreams.

He shuddered and gripped the blanket in his fist until his hands ached with the pressure.

"God, oh God ..." The prayer tore from his throat as his eyes blurred with tears he would not shed.

"God ..."

The God he had scorned.

The God he had blamed.

The God who had failed him once before.

"Help her. Please ..."

A log fell in the fire. Sparks shot upward. And something broke in Josef's soul.

21

Arla stood with the key trembling in her hand. *Not again. Please, not again.* But life had somehow conspired to bring her back here, to the locked door, the shiny key, and the fear that had driven her to it. She squeezed the key and dropped it into her pocket. So like before.

She had thought that the fire had changed everything. Everything, it seemed, except the condition of her soul.

She stumbled across the hall into her own room and sank down onto the chair by the fire. It wasn't fair. It wasn't right. The edge of the journal dug into her ribs. It was one mistake. Only one. Or was it?

Arla lifted her chin and stared out the window. The drapes were pulled open, and she could see nothing but white outside, nothing but snow. *Rakel always loved the snow …*

She pulled her knees to her chest and wrapped her arms around them. If only she could go back, before everything. Back to when she was a little girl in pinafores, with a mama who loved her and a daddy who didn't deceive.

"Mama, what am I going to do?" The whispered words fluttered from her lips. But no answer came. Only the silent falling of snow, the soft thud of it on the window, and the faint whistle of wind against the pane.

Mama couldn't help her anymore. Mama was dead. And so was Daddy. And now there was no one left who could take away the pain. Only God remained. Only God, and this book that spoke of her shame.

Arla shivered. What if Ellie had read what she had done? What if she knew the depths of Arla's sin? Ellie would hate her for certain. Then there would be nothing to fill the emptiness in her soul. "Oh God, what am I going to do? Why can't I escape what I've done? Is there no hope, no future, no forgiveness?" She glanced down at the book.

Truth or lie. You decide.

Rakel had spoken those words. At the time, Arla thought they were spoken out of spite, to punish her. But what if they weren't? What if they were not a punishment but an invitation? An invitation to read and reflect. Could she? Dare she? Yes, it was time. Time to remember, even though there was no way to make amends.

Arla dabbed her fingers under her eyes and dropped her feet to the floor. She leaned over and lit a candle. Then she opened the book and turned page after page until she reached the dreaded date in August. Here, the ink sat thick on the page, as if Rakel had written every word with slow precision.

MAMA IS SENDING ME INTO THE DEVIL'S LAIR. SHE DOESN'T KNOW IT, WON'T HEAR WHEN I TELL HER. SHE SAYS HE'S ASKED TO SEE ME. I BET HE HAS. I'M A BAD INFLUENCE ON HIS DAUGHTER, HE SAYS. I WISH I WERE. I WISH SHE WOULD LISTEN TO ME WHEN I TELL HER SHE HAS TO GET AWAY FROM THERE, HAS A RIGHT TO PROTECT HERSELF AND HER MAMA. I TELL HER SHE DOESN'T HAVE TO SIT STILL AND TAKE IT. I TELL HER SHE SHOULD STAND UP FOR WHAT'S RIGHT AND NOT LET HIM GET AWAY WITH IT ANYMORE.

Arla rubbed the goose bumps from her arm. That's where it had started, with Lars Jensen confronting her, demanding that she keep her daughter in hand. He said they were stirring up all kinds of trouble over there at that seamstress's house. Said Winifred was a good, obedient girl until she met up with Rakel and the others. They were a strange four-some—Nora, Maggie, Rakel, and Winifred. Arla wasn't sure she liked the friendship any more than Lars Jensen did, but what harm could come of it? What harm. If only she had known.

"You control your daughter," Lars Jensen had shouted.

She couldn't control Rakel, and she knew it.

"Or I will."

It was then that Arla should have spoken, should have said, "What do you mean?" or "Mind your own business." A good mother would have said those things. A good mother would have asked more questions, would have done what was needed to protect her daughter. But Arla had done nothing. Nothing at all.

"Keep her away from my Winifred."

"They are grown girls, sir." Weak words, then and now.

"You are still her mother, are you not?"

No answer.

Then Lars Jensen leaned close, his jaw set and his eyes like button-holes. "A failed mother at best."

She made no response. No gasp, no denial. Nothing. It was as if she hadn't heard it. But she had. And she could hear him now. Still. Those words slithering through her mind, accusing, condemning.

He turned away. "You will send your daughter to my house after the noon meal. I will speak to her myself."

So Arla sent her. One didn't cross Lars Jensen. No one did. No one … except perhaps Rakel. She glanced down at the journal and continued to read.

BUT HOW CAN SHE STAND UP TO HIM? HOW CAN ANY OF US?

There was a fat blot of ink on the page where Rakel had let the pen sit without writing. Then the words started again.

I SUPPOSE I'LL FIND OUT. I'M GOING THERE THIS AFTERNOON. MAMA SAYS I
HAVE TO. SHE SAYS I MUST MAKE AMENDS FOR WHATEVER WRONG I'VE
DONE. EXCEPT I HAVEN'T DONE ANY WRONG. IT'S HIM WHO'S DONE IT. AND
I'M NOT GOING TO STAND BY AND LET HIM HURT HER ONE MORE TIME. NOT
ONCE MORE. I SWEAR IT.

The entry stopped. Arla's vision blurred. *Why, Rakel? Why couldn't
you just let well enough alone?* But Rakel was never one to live in peace.
Was never one to simply accept the way things were and be content. If
nothing were wrong, she would make something up. That's why Arla
hadn't believed her when she came home. That's why she had her doubts
about what happened next.

Rakel had left right after the noon meal. She had returned an hour
later. But what a return. Her sleeve was torn, her hair loose, her lip split.

"What have you done?" They were the first words out of Arla's
mouth. Words of shock, accusation. How she regretted them now. But it
was too late to take them back. Then and now. Too late to erase words
spoken in haste.

Rakel's face had hardened. Her shoulders grew rigid. "You would."

"What?"

"Take his side."

"Whose?"

Rakel looked at her, looked through her, as if not seeing her at all.
"He's going to pay. Pay for what he did to me, and to Winnie." Her eyes
widened, turned wild.

"Calm down."

For a moment, Rakel's gaze focused. "You sent me there. You did it."

"You're talking crazy."

But her eyes shifted again, moved to the rifle that hung over the
door.

Arla's gaze followed. "No." The gun was loaded. Had been ever
since Grant died years ago. "Rakel?"

"Never again."

The words were only a breath, but they echoed in Arla's ears, pounded through her heart.

Rakel took a step toward the door.

* * *

The wind blows white. The sky is vanished. And still the snow spills down. Unrelenting. Uncaring. An eerie nothingness that numbs my soul. My arms ache where I tore strips from my sleeves to bind his leg. My lips are chapped and frozen. My lashes thick with ice.

Yet I push on, dragging his cart behind me, counting every step from my door to his. A thousand steps. And more. All I know is the whiteness, the cold, and the knowledge that I must not fail.

So I continue, with one arm flung over my forehead, and the other pulling the cart behind me. I think only of her, of little Emma. Alone, cold, and crying. All that matters is that I get to her. Whether I am human or monster. Unloved. Despised. Accepted. Rejected. It has all dropped away. Only the snow remains. And Emma somewhere beyond it.

A few more yards, a few more feet. My hand throbs on the cart's handle. My calves sink deep into the snow. And I see a shape, a rock dark against the whiteness.

I pause and dare not cry out. My arms shake as I reach toward it. A strange shape like a finger pointing upward. I have seen this rock before. There is the stick I placed on top. There are my footprints already half-buried in the snow.

My head spins. My stomach turns. I am lost. I have failed her. Failed him.

Oh God …

I fall forward. Snow fills my nose. I blow it out. Tears freeze in my eyes. I grip the snow in my hands and let it sift through my fingers. God, help me. I can't do this alone. I cannot find my way. Please ...

I wait. There is no voice in my mind. No whisper of hope in the wind-driven snow. No flash of understanding, or welling of warmth in my soul. So I stand. What can I do but go on?

God, if you're out there ...

My grip tightens on the cart's handle as I leave the rock behind me. Ten steps, twenty, fifty, a hundred. I do not see the rock again. Two hundred. A row of trees appears out of the whiteness. Two hundred and twenty. I catch my breath. I know these pines. I have stood in them before, watching him, watching them.

The skin on my cheek pulls tight. The snow lessens. And I see it. A dark shadow in the shape of a house. A trickle of smoke from a chimney. I run forward, stumbling, tripping, sloshing in the ice. A laugh gurgles up from my chest and splashes against the snow. I've made it. Somehow, I've found the way.

I stop and glance back. There is nothing but snow. I am alone. Yet not alone. I feel him here. God in the storm. God present in the silence.

For one single breath, I reach out my hand. Then I turn toward the house and hurry on.

A moment later, I am at the door. Then I am through it.

She is there, standing in her crib. Her face wrinkled, her wail filling the air. Fat tears roll down her cheeks. "Da-da-da-da!"

I yank the cart through the door, then slam it shut. The air is cool, but not yet cold. The fire is dying, but not dead. I drop my snow-covered cloak and rush toward her.

"Shh, baby girl, hush now." I coo the words as I lift her from her crib.

I look into her face.

She looks into mine.

I draw her close.

She grunts and stops crying.

Then I do what I have yearned to do for so long. I kiss her cheek, I brush back her hair, I dry her tears.

She sneezes.

I laugh.

She giggles.

I turn and see the diaper cloths stacked neatly on a bench near the stove. And beside it a pail filled with milk. With the baby tucked against me, I stoke the fire and warm her milk. Then I change her diaper.

We will wait out the storm here. Afterward, I will take her to her papa. But for now, for now she is mine. All mine.

I sit in the rocker and settle her on my lap. Outside, snow and wind buffet the house. Inside, we are safe, warm, happy. My feet ache as they begin to thaw. But I don't care.

She sucks her bottle and looks up at me with wide eyes. She smiles and keeps sucking. Then her hand reaches toward me. She touches my scars. Touches them and does not recoil.

My lips brush her hand. And for the first time since the fire, I am glad that I survived.

***

Outside, the storm subsided. Inside, it had just begun. Arla laid the journal on her lap and turned her face toward the window. A few white flakes
brushed against the pane. Wisps, really, remnants of a storm passing.

It was different on that day in August. Then there was no snow, no
cold or wind. It was hot, and as dry as jerky left too long by the fire.

Sweat had trickled down Rakel's temple, glistened in a shaft of light
as she stepped toward the rifle over the door.

Arla knew what her daughter planned, knew it in a flash of fear and
understanding. And she had to stop it, stop the insanity. At least that's
what she told herself afterward.

"Come with me. Hurry."

Rakel paused, turned. Then she blinked. "What?"

"Come quickly to your room. There's something there you must
see."

Rakel glanced at the rifle. "Not now."

Arla moved forward to grab Rakel's arm. "It has to be now." Her
fingers closed over Rakel's wrist.

Rakel winced. "Don't touch me." For a moment, her tone turned
hollow. She stared at her hand. "You don't know, do you? If you knew
what he did ..."

Arla dropped her grip. What Rakel was insinuating couldn't have
happened. It didn't.

"Mama, he—"

"Hush, child. Don't talk about it."

"I have to. He's got to pay."

"He will. But now you have to come with me." She brushed her fingertips over Rakel's arm. This time, she didn't object.

"He's fooled everybody long enough."

"Yes, of course." Arla led Rakel down the hallway.

"I'm going to tell everybody."

No you won't. "Here we are." She drew Rakel into her room. "Just
sit there on the bed."

Rakel sat.

"You believe me, don't you, Mama?" Rakel tilted her face up and speared Arla with a glance.

She shook her head. "There's nothing to believe." And before Rakel could answer, Arla stepped out of the room, shut the door, and locked it.

Now, months later, Arla stood and touched the key in her pocket. A different key, a different door, a different girl. She shivered and closed the drapes. But even that couldn't shut out the memory of Rakel's shriek. It couldn't muffle the way her fists pounded on the wood.

"He's gotta pay, Mama. Mama, Mama ... How could you?"

That cry had torn through her, shredding her soul. It still did. After all these months, she could still hear it.

Arla picked up the journal again and turned the page.

SHE'S BETRAYED ME. SHE'S LOCKED ME IN. NOW, I'M THE ONE WHO MUST ESCAPE, WHO MUST FIND A WAY TO GET FREE ...

She stopped and clutched the book to her chest. A sound came from across the hall. A scraping of a chair against the floorboards. The creak of wood. And a choking sound, like a child weeping.

I can't do it. Not again.

But they'll come. They'll take her away.

I can't.

Arla closed the journal and stepped into the hallway. She pulled the key from her pocket.

A knock thudded on the front door.

She paused.

A voice came. "Mrs. Anderson, Mrs. Anderson, open up."

The key fell and jangled on the floor. They had come for Ellie already.

22

Arla Anderson. Why did every problem always come down to a confrontation with Arla Anderson? It had been different when Grant was alive. They'd all been friends then. But Grant was gone, and that Arla was no more than a fool.

Lars trudged down the snow-filled street toward Arla's house with Leif beside him. Gentle flakes still drifted from the sky to obscure his view. All around him, new buildings were smothered in fat layers of white. The mercantile, two saloons, his bank, his restaurant, the church, and even the new school building. Houses, their roofs heavy with snow, their chimneys breathing lines of black smoke, lined the side streets.

So much had been done, rebuilt, since the fire. And most of it was his doing. He had organized the state commission relief efforts, he had donated, he had marshaled the workers, even the lazy ones. The town would still be in ashes if it weren't for his leadership. But no one would remember that. Not if they found out who he really was, what he'd really done. And that was sure to happen if word got around that Leif shot that girl on purpose. That's all folks would be talking about. He could almost hear the whispered questions, the quiet comments made behind raised hands. What kind of father would raise a son like that? What kind of man would let such a son get a hold of a gun? What kind of person was Lars

Jensen anyway? And if they asked that question, if they bothered to find out the answer, he would be ruined. Then not only would Leif be rejected from that fancy school in Boston, Lars would lose everything he had worked for here in Hinckley. That he could not allow to happen. Not this time. Not ever.

Lars sighed and adjusted his collar. People were fickle, their memories of good were short. He could spend years building up his reputation, and all it would take was a little rumor, a whisper of sin, and it would all be forgotten. Folks were just waiting to bring him down, just itching to scorn him. To discount him. He knew it. But he wouldn't give them the chance.

That Rakel Anderson had tried to ruin his reputation before. She'd threatened and railed. But he'd taken care of that problem, and he'd take care of this one too. But this time, he'd maintain control. This time, he wouldn't sin.

Lars brushed the ice off his shoulders and squinted through the snow and the mist made by his own breath. The Anderson house was just ahead. He could see the snow-lined steps, the gleam from the windows, and the lights shining behind them. He straightened his back and coughed. Arla would listen to him, would listen and obey. She always had.

This is how it started before. The words whispered through his mind. He pushed them aside. That was a different time, a different problem, even a different house.

And yet, sweat broke on his forehead. Just like that day. But that day was hot. This day was cold. He loosened the scarf around his neck.

"Everything will be fine. It's nothing like that time." The snow snatched his words and tossed them in the air.

"Did you say something, Pa?"

"Hush, boy."

Remember …

It was a different person.

Remember ...

A different problem.

Remember what happened last time you tried to silence a girl.

"Shut up!"

"I did, Pa."

"What?" Lars pressed his fingers into his temples and rubbed. But the memory couldn't be rubbed away. It came anyway, sneaking around the edges of his mind, taunting him, accusing.

Afterward, he'd told Arla that the girl had tried to seduce him. And she had. Just the way she moved her hips when she walked, the way her eyes flashed.

Lars licked his lips.

How could he have known what she'd do that day? How could he have predicted that she'd provoke him like she did? It was her fault. All her fault. He'd only asked her to come to his house for a talking to. Just wanted her to stop putting fool ideas in Winifred's head. Winnie was a gullible girl. She needed discipline, guidance. And he gave it to her. He was a good father, and a good man. He deserved people's respect, their notice.

Lars opened the top button of his coat. He'd only wanted her to stay away from Winnie. That was all. And to make that happen he was only going to bully her a little, make her afraid enough to keep away. He had never intended more. Never planned on it being more than a threat.

But there she stood, with her black hair, her flashing eyes, her sneering face. She stood accusing him, in his own home, his own den. Saying he wasn't fit to be a father, not fit to be a man.

"Stay away from Winnie," he'd said.

"*You* stay away," she hissed. "Don't think we don't know what you're doing. We all know. And we aren't going to put up with it anymore."

He'd almost laughed. Empty threats. Idle. "She's my daughter. I will do with her as I see fit."

"No you won't. Not if I can help it." She wagged her finger at him like an old schoolmarm.

"Who do you think you are, little girl?"

She lifted her chin then, flung her long hair behind her shoulder. "I'm not a little girl."

No, she wasn't. His breath faltered.

Then everything changed. He knew he had to get her out of there, had to get free of her before she said another word. He tried to send her away. In fact, he'd already started walking toward the door.

But then she spoke one more time. Said things that should never be uttered. It was her fault what happened next. He would have never done it if she hadn't goaded him.

"You aren't good enough to be her father."

Lars turned.

"You are a lowdown, weak, useless excuse for a man. You strut around this town acting like you're somebody. But I know what you are. And soon everyone else will know too."

He remembered how he moved toward her. Slowly, so slowly. For that moment, his fury contained.

"And when they do, you remember that it was this little girl," she jabbed her finger into her chest, "who brought you down." With that, she reached up, grabbed his ivory-handled knife, and ripped her sleeve.

"What are you doing?" She should have known by the tone in his voice. She should have realized.

"I'm making you pay." She turned her back and took the pins from her hair.

Lars reached out, grabbed her arm. Even now he could hear the sound of the fabric as it tore farther. "Stop."

"You don't matter anymore, you despicable nobody." She looked away.

Rage erupted in his chest. "You will look at me." His voice echoed through the room as he spun her toward him. "Don't you dare ignore me."

She faced him then, but her eyes slid, slid away just like he'd seen a thousand times as a boy. And then he did what he should not have done. She fought him, cut him once. But it didn't matter. She wasn't strong enough. And when he was finished, he made her look at him, made her look straight in his eyes. He saw the hate there, saw the loathing.

"You will not say a word." He spat the command.

"I won't have to."

For a moment, he stared into her face and knew she was right. But then, before she could take her revenge, the fire had come. And he was free again.

Until now.

Lars pulled off his coat, raised his hand, and pounded on Arla Anderson's front door.

***

Fire burned through Josef's mind. A wheel of flame, spinning, undulating, whirling in tongues of red. Then a face, melting, glowing, eyes like coals, features that shifted with each flame. Hands reached toward him.

Then came a high-pitched whine. He reached up to press his palms to his ears, but Emma was in his arms. She twisted, writhed. Then the whine came again, turning to a shriek as he lost his grip and the baby fell, tumbling, turning, lost in the fingers of flame.

"Emma!" A yell ripped from Josef's throat. He jolted upright. *Emma* ... He blinked. The fire faded and became a small flame in a makeshift grate.

The glow of sunlight drifted through the window and cast beads of light onto the dirt floor. His hands pressed into the cot, damp now with sweat.

Then the whine came again. And this time, he recognized it. Ghost, only Ghost, clawing at the door and whining to get out.

"All right, boy, I'm coming." Josef glanced out the window. The snow had stopped. He could get to Emma now. He grabbed his coat at the foot of the cot and stood. The room whirled.

He tipped forward and stumbled. His head knocked against the wall. His leg buckled, sending him spinning to the floor. Pain shot up his thigh and twisted in his gut. *Not again.* He shook his head to clear it.

The dog whined louder. His paws dug at the door.

Josef pulled himself up, one hand on the cot, the other pressed against the wall. He staggered to the door and flung it open.

A gasp burst from his lips. He jolted back.

A man stood outside the door. A man in a black coat, with hood drawn, his face shadowed and bound in a thick scarf.

Josef gripped the door handle to keep from falling back. It was just like the image from his nightmare, except the claws were hidden, and this man was smaller, slighter, than the monster in his dream. He swallowed, opened his mouth, but said nothing.

Then without a sound, the man opened his coat.

Josef caught his breath. There, little Emma was tucked within, held snugly against the man's chest with a blanket tied as a carrier. Her fingers were stuffed into her mouth, her eyes closed, her mouth making sounds of lazy sucking.

"She's well. Fed and changed." The man's voice rasped against the scarf around his face. "Fell asleep on the walk back." The words came haltingly, awkwardly, as if the man was unused to speaking.

Josef steadied himself against the doorjamb, then reached out and gathered Emma in his arms. His throat tightened. "Thank you. Sir." And his words were just as awkward, just as halting.

The man coughed. "Better get on inside." He cleared his throat, and his words flowed more quickly, smoothly. "Let me take her while you get back to the cot. You shouldn't be on that leg."

Josef inched backward. It was such a normal thing that the man said. There was nothing spooky, nothing ghostlike, in the words, nor in the man's grip as he held Emma and helped Josef hobble back to the cot.

"She's grown in the last months."

Josef looked up from his seat on the bed. Who was this man? He glanced at the man's eyes, strange eyes surrounded by red skin and no eyebrows. Haunting eyes. Eyes marked by fire.

Who are you?

The man turned his chin until his eyes were hidden from Josef's view. Then he placed Emma back in Josef's arms. A moment later he had hurried back out the door.

Josef held Emma to his chest and waited for the man's return. A man. Not a ghost. Not a monster. Just a man who must have been burned in the fire. And burned badly enough to not want to go home. He shivered. This man, this hermit, could be anyone. A neighbor, a friend, someone he'd sat beside in church, someone he'd eaten with at a picnic.

Ghost yipped, then pushed his nose toward the baby.

Josef reached down and patted the dog's head.

Ghost's tail thumped hard against the cot as he rubbed alongside it. His body wiggled as he licked Emma's foot.

"She's all right, boy. We all are." *Thanks to a man we've all hated, thanks to the one we named the Hinckley ghost.*

Josef leaned over and kissed Emma's forehead. He had been wrong about the man. So very wrong. If it weren't for him ...

The man came back through the door.

Josef straightened. "Look, sir, I'm sorry about ..." The words faltered on his lips as he saw the cart. His cart. Maggie's cart.

The man pulled it into the hut and closed the door. "Thought you'd need some things." The cart was piled with Emma's blankets, diaper cloths, bottles, food, everything he would need to keep her safe and happy. "Didn't figure you could get home yet through the snow. Not till your leg's healed a bit." The man turned his back toward Josef and brushed the snow from his sleeves. "You'll want to eat something. I reckon you're a touch light-headed from hunger."

Hunger? He hadn't even thought of hunger.

The man pulled off his gloves and stamped the snow from his boots.

Josef watched the scarred flesh ripple as the man reached for a jar of beans from the cart. Narrow hands, the skin puckered with a mishmash of red and white. There were new cuts there, scabs of wounds barely healed. Josef frowned. Weak hands, but strong enough to carry him through the storm, to protect Emma from the cold. Strong enough to pull his cart through miles of powdered snow.

And here it was. The cart. The same one he'd seen in his field. The same one that had gone missing. The same one that had caused him to shake his fist at the heavens. Words stumbled from his lips. "That's my cart."

"I know." He could hear the smile in the man's voice, despite its hoarse tone.

The man turned toward the fire.

Josef set Emma on the cot. She grunted and rolled onto her side, her fingers still in her mouth, her eyes still closed. Then he scooted to the edge of the bed and reached toward the cart. His fingers touched the rough surface. Two extra set of clothes for Emma. All the milk, plenty of blankets and food. *I was so mad. So sure ...*

The man threw a log into the fire. "Don't suppose you ever thought to see it again."

Josef ran his hand over the cart's surface, then plucked up a blanket and laid it over Emma. *Not like this. Never like this.* It was just a cart. A silly little thing that meant nothing. Yet, it had been the final proof that God had betrayed him, had turned his back and left him with nothing. And here it was back again, back just when he needed it most. "How? Why?" He muttered the words under his breath.

The man spoke without turning, his voice like a saw on new wood. "There is no why."

Josef shifted on the cot and stared at the man's back. The black fabric bunched beneath the shoulders and fell nearly to the ground. *No why? What did he mean by no why?*

The man squatted and jabbed a stick into the flames. "Why did the fire come? Why did so many die? Why was I left like this?" His hand fluttered toward his face. "Why. Why. Why. And there are no answers." He turned and opened the can of beans.

The scarf had loosened. Josef pressed his lips shut to keep from making a sound. Firelight glimmered off a misshapen cheek, off a mouth pulled and twisted with scars. Then the shadows fell again, and Josef could see nothing but the glow of light reflecting in the man's eyes.

The man dumped the beans into a pot and returned to the fire. "Why is a fool's question. And only fools can answer it."

Josef settled back on the cot and scowled. He'd asked why a million times. Did that make him a fool?

"No answer is ever good enough."

He rubbed his chin. What if the man was right? What if there was no answer to why? Did that make God unjust? Did it make him wrong? Josef had thought so. Had accused him of that much, and more.

"Unless you can read the mind of God."

The man was talking crazy now, saying things that didn't make no sense. Maybe being out here in the woods all alone, having no one to talk to, had made the man funny in the head. Maybe it had driven him mad. Read the mind of God. No one could do that. Josef paused. But in a way, he'd expected to, hadn't he? And when he couldn't, he'd answered the why for himself—because God didn't care, because God was cruel, because God had failed to do what was right.

Josef watched as the man stirred the beans, listened as the spoon made scraping sounds against the tin. This man had struggled through a blizzard to save him, and not just him, but Emma, too. He had dragged that cart through snow and rock so that Josef could have the things he needed to take care of his daughter. This man, whom he had deemed a monster. This man, whom he had hunted and despised. This man, and God, too.

The man kept stirring the beans, slowly, methodically. "Not why, but who. Who caused the fire? Or who allowed it?" The man's tone sharpened. "Tell me. Who?"

Josef didn't answer.

"Who?"

Josef's voice trembled. "God."

The man nodded, and his tone returned to normal. "Caused or allowed?" He turned his head. Firelight again reflected off shadowed eyes. "Does it really matter?"

Yesterday, Josef would have said yes and meant it. It mattered if God caused this atrocity. It mattered, and it made him to blame. But now, now he wasn't so sure.

"Either way he could have stopped it. But he didn't."

And so we live with the consequences? No questions? No doubts? Is that faith? Maggie would have said so. But maybe Maggie was wrong. Maybe faith was something else entirely.

The man stood. "Though he slay me, yet will I trust in him?" He shook his head. "From the book of Job. But I don't know if I believe it."

Josef tilted forward. Maybe the man wasn't crazy. Maybe he wasn't crazy at all. "Who are you?"

The man pulled the cloak's hood farther down over his face. "Don't you know?"

Josef looked closer.

"I am Esau."

***

I tremble as I speak the name: Esau. Unloved. Unwanted. Esau. Will he understand what I mean? Will he know of what I speak?

"Esau? Don't remember no one by that name." He scratches his head.

I catch the movement from the corner of my eye as I turn back toward the fire.

He leans forward. "Did you live down south of town?"

I shake my head. He doesn't know, doesn't understand.

Yet I savor his words as I watch the steam rising from the pot of beans. How long has it been since someone has spoken to me as a friend? How long since another has listened to me and responded? I had forgotten the pleasure of an exchange of ideas, how it feels to speak and have someone answer. Things I had taken for granted. Things I never knew I'd miss.

I pour the warm beans into a cool pot, find a spoon, and hand them to him. His hand brushes mine. I stop.

Then he reaches out and touches my arm. "Thank you kindly, Esau." Simple words. A casual touch. It means nothing, and everything.

I stare at the spot where his fingers contacted my scarred skin. Once, I had thought I never wanted anyone to lay a hand on me again. But I was wrong.

He has touched me. And suddenly I am almost ... almost human.

23

Ellie dried her tears and jiggled the door handle. She pressed her ear to the door. Nothing. She wiggled the handle again, then held still and listened. Still nothing. But wait. No. There *were* voices out there. Or at least one voice—Mrs. Anderson's, coming from the direction of the front door.

Ellie raised her fist to beat on the wood, but then she paused. Maybe it was better to be still and try to listen. Better not to let folks know she was here. She moved to her right and pushed her ear against the crack between the door and jamb. Then she scowled. She could hear the hum of voices well enough, but it wasn't clear enough to understand. Stupid door. If only she could open it just a crack.

She tried the knob again. Whatever was Mrs. Anderson thinking to lock her in? There was something about that journal, something that made Mrs. Anderson awful mad, or awful scared. Ellie turned, crossed her arms, and rested her back against the door. It was silly, really, locking her in when there was a window right there. If she really wanted to, she'd just open the window and crawl out. 'Course with her side like it was, that wouldn't be a whole lot of fun. But, well, it was good to know there was a way out in case something went wrong. In case—

A sharp thud interrupted Ellie's thoughts. She dropped to the floor and set her ear against the crack at the door's bottom.

This time, she could hear Mrs. Anderson's words.

"Don't you dare step one foot inside this house. I won't have it. You're not welcome."

Ellie leaned closer. Not welcome? That was odd. Mama would have said that to not invite someone in was terrible bad manners. It seemed strange to think of Mrs. Anderson not having good manners. Why, Mrs. Anderson always said please, thank you, and how do you do. She wore hats in public and even held out her pinkie when she sipped her tea.

Something creaked. The hinges on the front door maybe? That was it. Maybe the thud was someone pushing the door all the way open so that it banged against the wall. Mrs. Anderson wouldn't like that, 'specially not if it had made a mark on the new wallpaper.

Mrs. Anderson's voice grew louder. "I told you she isn't here."

Ellie bit her lip. Gracious, had they come lookin' for her already? If they found her, they'd send her back. She couldn't have that. Couldn't let it happen. She glanced toward the window.

"I can't imagine why you'd be here asking me about her. She was taken on the train weeks ago. Go talk to that doctor friend of yours if you want to know where she is."

Ellie rocked back on the heels of her hands. They *were* talking about her. And Mrs. Anderson was lying. Ladies never lied. That's what Mama said. A chill raced over Ellie's skin. She had to get away. Had to run before whoever was at the door found her out. She bit her lip. But if she went out the window now, they would see her. Then she'd be done in for sure. *Sorry, Mrs. Anderson. Sorry I got you in trouble too.* She pressed her ear to the bottom of the door until the skin hurt.

Mrs. Anderson's voice grew shrill. "Don't you threaten me, sir."

Another thud echoed down the hallway.

Ellie's heart beat faster. She leapt up and bolted to the window. *Shh* ... Her hands shook as she opened the pane. Slowly, quietly, inch by inch the window opened. She stuck her head out.

"Bring her on out, and we won't have to involve the sheriff." A man's voice boomed from the front porch.

Mrs. Anderson answered, but now Ellie couldn't make out her words.

Then the man spoke again. "Why, for kidnapping, of course."

Ellie gasped.

"Serve you right, too."

Land sakes. That was Leif's voice. Ellie pulled her head back inside and balled her hands into fists. How dare he. That no-account, good-fer-nothin' ... She ground her fist into the windowsill. Why didn't they send him away after what he'd done to her? *If I weren't afraid of getting caught* ... For a moment, Ellie envisioned herself jumping out the window, running over there, and pummeling that awful Leif into the ground. He deserved it. That, and more. Here she was with her side all hurting, stuck in this room with someone hunting her down, trying to send her away, and all this time that rotten Leif was walking around scot-free. Something ought to be done.

"I can't protect her again, you know."

Weaselly, whiny voice. Dumb boy. And what was this crazy talk about protecting her? Why, that cowardly, lying ... he couldn't mean ... he didn't mean ... Ellie pushed the window up farther. Was that the fool story he was telling everyone? Well, he was as crazy as a loon, and so was everyone else if they believed him.

The man's voice came again, and this time Ellie recognized it. Mr. Jensen. Of course. "Leif knows what he saw, woman."

Mrs. Anderson must have stepped out onto the porch, because Ellie could hear her now. "We can't always believe our children, can we, Mr. Jensen?" There was a sharpness in her tone, a bitterness that Ellie didn't understand.

Lars' voice hardened. "No, we can't."

Ellie sat on the floor under the window. She had to get away. Mrs. Anderson's house wasn't safe. They would find her and send her back to

Duluth before she could find out about the ghost. Before she could tell them all the truth about what Leif had done. Before she could make him own up to it. She wasn't going to let that happen. Not by a long shot. She would have to get out. But not now. She would wait till they were good and gone. Mrs. Anderson would hold them off this time. But next time? No, she couldn't count on Mrs. Anderson again.

She wrapped her arms around her knees and frowned. She had to be smart now. Couldn't just get all mad and do something dumb. Rakel had done that. At least that's what Ellie suspected. She had done something, anyway, and it had turned out bad. That had to do with Mr. Jensen too. And that's why she would have to be extra careful now.

Ellie stepped back from the window. She remembered that day. It was August, and the fire came soon after. Mama knew something bad was gonna happen. Ellie could tell 'cause Mama's face was mighty pale as she stared out the window after Rakel left. So pale that Ellie wondered if Mama was sick.

"She's going." Mama's voice shook as she said it.

Ellie remembered how she had stopped sewing the seam on her doll. "Home?"

"No. She's going to confront him about Winnie. Today." She picked up a bit of lace and twirled it in her hand.

Ellie jabbed the needle into the doll's arm. "Well, that's good, isn't it? Someone ought to do something."

But Mama didn't answer. She just kept twisting that bit of lace around her finger until the edges made white marks in her skin. Her eyes never left the window.

That was the last time Ellie had ever seen Rakel. The very last time.

She grabbed the bottom of the window and started to pull it closed. This time, things would be different.

"I'll be keeping an eye on you, Mrs. Anderson."

Ellie's hands grew still on the window.

"And I on you. Good day." The door slammed.

She pulled the window tight, dried the sill with her sleeve, then quietly crawled into bed.

Moments later, the door opened. She yawned and sat up. "Oh, hello, Mrs. Anderson." She smiled and stretched her arms. "I was just having a little rest."

***

He lies there sleeping, his mouth open, his arm flung out. Emma sleeps too, tucked beside him. I see their chests rise and fall. Steady breaths, deep, calm. She smiles in her sleep. He snores. And I almost grin.

Almost.

They will not sleep forever. And when he wakes, what shall I do? Hours ago I jabbered with less sense than a magpie at midday. But it's been so long since someone has listened, and these thoughts in my head keep tumbling about even when there's no one to hear, no one to understand. He must think me mad. Must think that the loneliness has made me dotty. Maybe it has.

I jab my stick into the fire to stir the coals. Above the flames, stew is cooking. Rabbit meat, some herbs, an old turnip snitched last week from someone's wagon. But the rabbit is fresh. Strange how even the small animals have returned. Rabbits, mice, insects. I would have thought them all gone. But they live. And I with them.

I test the stew. It's nearly ready. The meaty aroma fills the shack. Seems all I do is feed him. Fill his stomach with food. Fill his ears with talk. I stand and wipe my lips. Then I close my eyes and listen to the gentle snoring.

It is true. He is here. I am no longer alone. At least for now. I have imagined this moment for so long, the moment when I would share a meal with another and they wouldn't shrink back in horror. When I would

speak, and they would listen. When they would speak, and the words would
not be filled with hate and fear. Imagined it, yet never believed it would
be.

So why am I afraid? Do I fear that I will blink and they will be gone?
That they will be but figments of a dream that vanishes upon waking? But
I'm awake already. Only they sleep. I smile. I am the dream then. This
cabin, this face, this monster. They will awake and I will disappear, and
all will be as it was before.

I turn back and look at them. A man and his child. Loved and loving.
Don't wake up. *I dare not whisper the words.* Don't leave me alone.

I step toward them. My hand reaches out. I will touch him and be sure.
Just a tap to make sure he's real. He won't notice. He won't wake. My
fingers tremble.

I touch the hem of his pants, the bare skin on his ankle.

His snoring halts.

I look up.

His gaze captures me, and I cannot move, cannot even breathe.

* * *

Lars strode down the street, his fists clenched in his pockets, his jaw set.
He would not lose control. Not out here. Not in the open where anyone
could see. But if that boy did one more stupid thing ... All he wanted was
a quiet life of respect, and the best of opportunities for his son. Just like
any good father. Just like any good man. Was that asking too much? But
first that Rakel girl, and now this. They were making him sin. Making
him be a man he didn't want to be. He hated it. But what choice did he
have?

He turned and glanced back. The mist from his breath fogged his vision.

Behind him, Leif dragged his boots through the snow and refused to meet his gaze.

Lars yanked at the scarf around his neck. "Get up here, boy. And pick up your feet."

Leif hurried to catch up. "Don't, Pa." He hunched his shoulders and dropped his chin until his hat shadowed his features.

"Don't what?"

Leif shivered. "Don't be mad. Maybe she ain't there. Maybe she went somewhere else. You'll find her."

Lars stared at his son. "Find her? I don't need to find her."

"But ..."

"She's there. In that house."

"Mrs. Anderson said ..."

Lars shook his head and quickened his pace. "Don't be an idiot, boy."

Leif fell silent.

Stupid boy. Of course the girl was there, and probably listening too. Arla was a fool for denying it. But she would do as he wanted in the long run. She had before and would again. He just had to give her a day or two to think about it. Maybe send the sheriff to her door, or maybe ... Lars pulled his hand from his pocket and rubbed his chin. Yes, maybe he needed only to remove her from the picture and take what he wanted. Then no one would be the wiser. But how?

His gaze slid over to Leif. "So, boy. Do you have a plan?"

Leif hesitated and glanced up. "No, Pa, I don't have no plan."

His voice grated against the dryness in his throat. "You just figure you'll let the Hansen girl be, and maybe she won't say anything? Maybe Mr. Whitehall from that Boston school will come next week and think you're the most admirable boy he's ever seen. Maybe he won't hear that you shot a girl. Maybe everything will be fine."

Leif dropped his gaze. "Oh, um, well."

"Are you willing to take that chance?"

"I guess not."

He laid his hand on Leif's collar. "Chance is a fickle mistress, boy. And women are more fickle yet."

"What?"

Lars sighed. The boy was an imbecile. "You don't leave things to chance, especially when it comes to women."

Leif pulled his hat down farther over his eyes, then shoved his hands deeper into his pockets. He glanced at Lars, then looked away.

Lars grimaced. "You did a stupid thing, boy. Now I'll have to take care of it. And I will. Soon."

Leif kicked a bit of snow. It flew up before them. "I'm sorry."

Sorry. They were always sorry. Winnie. Agnes. Leif. His mama. He was sick of it. Sick of their sideways glances. Sick of their excuses. Sick of their muttered words of apology. Why did those closest to him always have to disappoint him? Why did they always let him down?

Oh, once he'd trusted people. He'd trusted Mama. "Charlie will take you fishing tomorrow," she'd say. But of course Charlie never did. "Sam's gonna get you a new pair of shoes." But he'd have to wear the old ones until his toes grew right through the front. "George says he'll take you to work today, teach you how to be a businessman." But that's not what George taught him. Not by a long shot.

And Agnes, he'd trusted her, too. She'd promised to love, honor, obey. But he'd caught her sneaking around. Caught her making eyes at the milkman. Caught her in more lies than he cared to recall. Agnes was sorry, of course. So sorry, just like everyone else.

This time, Lars kicked the snow in front of them. Silence settled, broken only by the soft crunch of their footsteps in the snow. On they walked through town as hunks of ice tumbled from the rooftops and made mounds of white against the buildings below. The sky cleared until Lars could look through the space between houses and see the place where the town had buried the unknown dead. Agnes was there, and Winnie, too.

"I miss them. Mama, and Winnie." Leif's voice rose quietly from beside him.

They were only women. Lars stiffened.

Leif slowed and winced, as if expecting a blow.

And yet, so do I. He frowned. Was it true? Surely he didn't miss Agnes. He couldn't miss her. But Winnie? Yes, sometimes he missed Winnie. She'd been such a pretty little girl, with those big, round eyes, and wavy hair. And a laugh like church bells ringing in the distance. A delicate little thing, she was. She got tougher as years went on. And quieter. Much quieter. But sometimes, sometimes in those later years she would still laugh.

Leif snuck a glance in his direction. "She said something strange to me, just before the fire."

"Who?"

"Winnie." Leif swallowed. "She said she'd miss me." His chin shot up until his eyes locked with Lars'. "How did she know, Pa? How did she know the fire was coming?"

"She didn't. At least ..." Lars grew quiet. Winnie had been planning something, there in those last days. He'd suspected it. Something that never happened because the fire had come first.

"Hey there, Jensen." A voice called out behind them.

Lars stopped and turned to see Nils Heg standing in the doorway of the mercantile.

Nils smiled and motioned for them to come. "What are you doing out in this weather? Come on in, have some coffee."

Lars waved his hand at the man. He wanted to get home. But Nils could be useful. Especially now. He grabbed Leif's shoulder and started toward the mercantile.

"Quite a storm we had." Nils leaned his shovel against the shop's wall. "Hope nobody was caught out in it."

Lars knocked his boots against the step. "It'll make for good skating on the Grindstone though."

Nils grinned. "I do love to skate."

"I overheard Mrs. Anderson saying how she'd like to have a go at it herself."

"Arla?" Nils laughed. "That'd be the day."

Lars leaned against the rail in front of the shop. "I hear tell ladies get right softhearted when a man takes them for a winter picnic." He looked up into the sky and squinted. "Give it a day or two, I'd say, and we'll be getting a fine, sunny day for skating. You should think of taking advantage of that opportunity."

Nils took off his hat and scratched his head. "You may be right. I just might do that."

"It'll be your lucky day. I got a feeling." He motioned toward the store. "I'll even watch the shop for you."

Nils paused. "You'd do that?"

"What are friends for?"

Nils chuckled. "You're a good man, Lars Jensen." He picked up his shovel and dug it into the snow

Lars cracked his knuckles. "A few days then. And don't take no for an answer."

24

Ellie was shamming. Arla knew it. The girl could pretend she'd been sleeping, but there was no mistaking the glint in her eyes, the flushing of her cheeks. Had she heard Lars Jensen's threats? Did she know they had come to send her back?

Arla reached up and rubbed the back of her neck. What could she say? How could she soften the knowledge of what Lars Jensen meant to do? She looked at Ellie, her eyes wide, feigning innocence. Looked, and words failed her.

I'm tired of this.

She swallowed and glanced away. What could she say that wouldn't be a lie? She was weary of lies, of secrets and deceptions. So weary of people uttering a blessing when they meant a curse, of smiling when she wanted to cry, of innuendos, hidden plans, whispered accusations. Tired of the life she had lived, of the woman she had been for so long.

A frown wrinkled Ellie's face. "Is something wrong?"

Arla opened her mouth to answer, to say, "Of course not, everything's fine." The words were there, ready to be spoken, just as she had said them so often before. *Everything's well. There are no troubles. Just lie back down and rest. Nothing will go wrong.* But the words wouldn't come. Not this time.

"Mrs. Anderson?" Ellie rubbed her eyes and pasted on a smile.

Just like Arla herself had done a thousand times. A million. Just as she'd done all her life. And as her mama had done before her. "Don't pay no attention to that, Arla Mae," Mama used to say when Grant came home drunk. "Look the other way. Put on a happy face. Every cloud has a silver lining." She'd believed it all. But not anymore. She couldn't stand it for one more moment.

So Arla stood there, staring at Ellie's fake smile, staring and staring, with the door handle in her hand, and her stomach wiggling like a worm inside her.

I can't do it. I can't pretend anymore. She gripped the door handle so tight that her fingers ached. *I won't.* She lifted her chin, forced herself to speak. "Yes." Her voice came out in a strained half-whisper. "Something is wrong."

Ellie sat up straighter.

The truth, say it. She couldn't. She had to. *Mr. Jensen knows you're here. He threatened me, and I'm afraid. I don't know what to do. I don't know how to keep you safe.* The words rattled in her mind. *Oh God, please … don't make me say it aloud.* "Mr. Jensen knows you're here." It was all she could manage, all she could admit.

Ellie's legs slid over the side of the bed. "What are we going to do about that?"

Arla let go of the door handle, pressed her thumb into her palm and rubbed, rubbed, rubbed the skin, as if she could rub away the awful feeling in her gut. "I don't know."

"I can't stay."

Her throat closed. Her gaze flew up. "You have to." Her vision blurred, and for a moment she saw another girl, another time. "You stay right here until I figure out what to do." She stepped back into the hall, slammed the door, and locked it again. Then she fled to her bedroom.

The fire still danced in the grate. The coverlets still lay smooth and crisp. The curtains were still open, the journal still lay on the table where she had left it.

Arla dropped onto the chair and closed her eyes.

Help me.

You must face it.

No.

Face the truth.

Oh God …

She reached over and took the journal in her hand. Then she opened it, and read.

31 August 1894

IT'S ALMOST READY. ALMOST. AND THEN THERE WILL BE NOTHING SHE CAN DO TO STOP ME. IN A DAY, MAYBE TWO, NORA WILL COME. AND SHE KNOWS WHAT TO DO TO FREE US BOTH. ALL I NEED IS THE DRESS.

Arla's gaze shifted to the closed door across the hall. The dress. That dress? Even that, then, was a reminder of her sin. She sighed and forced herself to continue reading.

THEN WE CAN ESCAPE TOGETHER. WINNIE AND ME. WE'LL BE SISTERS, WEALTHY GIRLS TRAVELING TO SCHOOL OUT EAST, OR WEST, OR WHEREVER WE CHOOSE TO GO. I JUST NEED A RICH GIRL'S TRAVELING DRESS, LIKE ONLY NORA CAN MAKE. WINNIE HAS PLENTY OF MONEY, AND IN TIME, I MAY TAKE IN SOME SEWING. WE'LL BE ALL RIGHT. AND WE'LL BE FREE. JUST AS SOON AS THE DRESS IS FINISHED.

So that's what they had planned. To run away. Arla blinked. She should be angry, hurt, something. But instead she was just sad. Sad for Rakel, sad for Winnie, sad for herself.

I DON'T CARE IF MAMA FINDS THIS JOURNAL NOW. SHE CAN'T STOP ME.

MAGGIE IS GETTING US TRAIN TICKETS. WE'LL TRAVEL TO ST. PAUL, AND THEN, WHO KNOWS? AND WHEN WE GET FAR ENOUGH AWAY, I'LL MAYBE JUST WRITE A LETTER HOME TO MAMA. I'LL TELL HER EXACTLY WHAT THAT SCOUNDREL DID TO ME. SHE WON'T LISTEN NOW. SHE HEARS JUST BITS AND PIECES AND MAKES ME HUSH. BUT MAYBE SHE'LL LISTEN ONCE I'M GONE. MAYBE FOR ONCE IN HER LIFE SHE'LL HEAR ME AND FACE THE TRUTH. THE REAL TRUTH, NOT THE KIND THAT'S ALL DRESSED UP FANCY SO THAT IT LOOKS GOOD. BUT THE BARE, BALD, NAKED TRUTH.

Arla shuddered. *I should stop. I shouldn't read on.* But she did. She dropped her gaze and kept reading.

OR MAYBE I WON'T BOTHER WITH A LETTER. I'LL JUST LEAVE THIS JOURNAL BEHIND.

Then Rakel had continued in big, bold letters.

IF YOU FIND THIS, MAMA, I HOPE YOU READ IT. I HOPE YOU READ IT WITH EYES OPEN AND MOUTH SHUT. BECAUSE THIS IS WHAT LARS JENSEN DID TO ME. THIS IS WHAT YOU REFUSED TO BELIEVE.

Arla read the next paragraphs with her eyes open, her mouth shut, just as Rakel had wanted. She read the truth, undressed, uncovered, bare, and shameful. Ugly. Every detail, from the tearing of Rakel's blouse, to the slash she'd put on his neck, to the ... to the ... Tears filled Arla's eyes and spilled onto the page. Tears that would not stop, but kept coming until she could no longer see the written words.

Then it ended. She turned the page. There was only one more entry. One final paragraph written on another day. But Arla couldn't bear to read that. Not now. This was enough. Too much to bear.

She closed the journal and placed it on the table, stared at it, then dropped her face into her hands. She had been so wrong. If only she had known. But she did know. In her heart she knew exactly what had happened that day. She just hadn't wanted to face it. She hadn't wanted to believe.

God, forgive me …

***

"Esau?" Josef sat up.

The man jumped back. "I'm sorry." He turned his back, hid his face.

But not before Josef got another glimpse of his eyes, round now, wide. There was something strange, familiar about those eyes. Something that tugged at his memory and made him sad.

"I've fixed you something more to eat."

Emma rolled over and continued sleeping.

Josef tucked the blanket more firmly around her, then turned back to Esau.

The cloak still covered the man's shoulders and back and reached all the way to his calves. He squatted by the fire and stirred something in a pot. Josef watched the way his arm moved, the way he leaned over just a bit and sniffed the steam coming from the pot. It was something so like a kid would do.

Josef pushed his legs over the edge of the bed and tilted forward. "How old are you?"

Esau stopped stirring. His shoulders stiffened beneath the cloak. "Why does it matter?"

He *was* young. Early twenties maybe. Too young to be condemned to a lifetime as a hermit. Too young to have his chances burned away. "Why do you stay out here?"

Esau scooped something from the pot and put it into the same bowl that Josef had eaten from earlier. "They hate me. All of them." He held the bowl out. "Stew. Rabbit."

Josef took the bowl.

The man snatched his hand back and hid it in his cloak. For a moment, his gaze darted toward the fire, then his voice rattled as he spoke again. "I am a monster, remember?"

Josef shoved a spoonful of stew into his mouth. "I'm not afraid." The words came out garbled.

The man smiled, or at least Josef assumed he did. "Everyone else is." He paused. His voice dropped to a whisper. "Sometimes I am too …"

Josef swallowed the stew and cleared his throat. "Come back to town. Folks'll understand. They just need to know—"

"I can't."

"Can't stay out here all alone either. Shouldn't."

The man turned back toward Josef, and he could tell that he was searching his face, though the shadows hid the man's features. "You know what they say. I've heard their mutterings. I've felt their curses."

Josef didn't answer.

"Every bad thing that happens in that town is blamed on me. I drowned Mr. Johansson's calf. I stole Mrs. Petersen's pie. I tore down Mr. Bremer's barn. I caused Mr. Lind's sickness. I took Mr. Jensen's old coat."

"Did you do those things?" The question was muffled by another bite of stew.

The man chuckled and held out the flaps of his cloak. "Some of them." He wrapped the coat back around himself. "But I had my reasons."

Josef grunted.

The man crossed his arms over his chest and lifted his chin until the firelight almost lit his features. "Tell me this, Josef Strom, what right do they have to hate me? What right do they have to cast blame?"

He wanted to say that they didn't hate, they didn't blame. But it wouldn't be true. How many times had he heard someone mutter about the ghost in the hills? How many times had he done the muttering himself?

"I thought it was my face. But how can it be? Only a few have even seen me. And yet, yet ..."

The pain in the raspy voice, the hurt spoken in every word, made his own throat tighten. *How could they? How could we?* But they had. They'd made assumptions, they'd flung accusations. And they'd believed every one. "It's the Hinckley ghost," Robert Larsen had declared with such authority. "Threatening our families." And that Lars Jensen. How many times had that man claimed that the monster up in the hills was to blame? Especially when Ellie Hansen was shot. That was Esau's fault too. All laid at the door of the ghost-man. Even though his own son had held the gun.

So they blamed and hated and shook their fists. But who among them all had sought out the ghost to see if it were truth? No one had reached out, no one had taken the time to discover who the ghost really was. If they had ... If they knew ...

"They don't know who ..." Josef stopped and shuddered. Who. Not why. But who. It all came down to that. He'd made those assumptions. He'd thrown those accusations. He'd done it all, and not just to Esau, but to God himself.

He dropped his gaze. "I'm sorry." And he was. Sorry that he had hated, sorry that he had blamed. He'd been so sure, so full of anger, of hurt. How could God take his wife? Why did he let it happen? If God was God ... If God was good ... He'd asked the questions, flung them toward the heavens in his rage. But he'd never sought after the who. Not really. What if, instead of assuming he knew, he'd gone tromping through the burned forest to find and sit with and listen to the God he thought was to blame? Would that have mattered? Would it have made a difference? He scraped the clay bowl with his spoon. Maybe. It had made a difference with the man before him. All the difference in the world.

He glanced up. "Come with me to town."

The man shook his head. "I have come. And they chased me away."

Josef ate the last bite of the stew and handed the bowl back to Esau. "If they just knew—"

Esau interrupted him. "They don't want to know." He squatted back down by the fire and ladled more stew into the bowl.

Josef lowered his voice and spoke to Esau, and to God as well. "I do … At least, I do now."

The bowl slipped from Esau's grip and broke into pieces. He reached down, then gasped and pulled back his hand. A thin line of blood shone on his finger.

Josef pushed himself up, wobbling on one leg. He reached toward Esau. "Here, let me see." He leaned over and took his hand. Such a thin hand. Young, and …

The man yanked it away. His hood fell back. Light from the fire shone off a patch of long hair. The man threw the hood back over his head and backed away.

Josef stared and stumbled forward. He grabbed the hand again.

"No." Esau tried to pull from his grip.

Josef tightened his grasp. With his other hand, he pulled back the man's sleeve and touched the slender, delicate arm, ran his fingers over the soft flesh not touched by fire.

"Don't …"

He turned the hand, brushed the unscarred wrist with his palm. His eyes rose and searched the face before him. Skin pulled and scarred. A face so burned that it was unrecognizable. Even now. Even when he stood only inches away. He reached up, slowly, gently, and removed the hood.

The eyes before him filled with tears.

He put a finger under the scarred chin and lifted it.

"Please … Josef."

He touched the cheek with his thumb. "You're not Esau." His voice caught in his throat. "You're a woman."

25

His eyes search mine, and I look away. I don't want him to see me. I don't want him to know. Already he has seen too much, knows too much.

I pull from him and back away. "Don't tell. You mustn't." The words spill from my lips and splash between us.

But he doesn't answer, doesn't respond.

My shoulders bump into the wall behind me. I lift my hand, clutch the cloak tighter around my neck. But it is too late. He has seen me. He knows what I am.

"Why?"

His question startles me. I drop my hand and press it into the wall behind me.

"Why do you hide?"

A hundred reasons flash through my mind. Fear. Shame. Sorrow. But I say none of them. Instead I raise my chin, harden my jaw. "There is no why."

He laughs. Actually laughs. And my heart twists within me. His eyes twinkle. "Then who?"

Who. I tremble. No. I won't tell him that. I can't.

He steps toward me.

I shrink away. "Don't hurt me."

He stops. His smile fades. "I won't."

I dare not look at him. My mind believes. My heart cannot. I've been hurt before. I've held promises in my hand and watched them burn away. I've trusted, only to be betrayed. I've dared and been disappointed. And I've seen all hope turn to nothing but ash.

His hand touches my sleeve, then withdraws. "Come back with me. To town."

He doesn't know what he asks. He doesn't understand. But his voice is so gentle, so kind, that I almost look up, I almost agree. Almost forget the thing that I have become.

"They're wrong. I was wrong."

I shake my head. "No." It is all I can say. A single word meant to convey all my pain, all my guilt. I want to say more. I want to shout at him to go away, tell him that he doesn't understand, that he can't. Does he not see that I am a horror, an abomination, a monster? I am the ghost they all fear, the shadow they hate. I am why they lock their doors, why they watch out their windows, why they won't go out at night. I will not go back.

"It'll be different this time."

His voice turns soft, and I know he's thinking of when he caught me in town. That time, rocks were thrown, a pistol brandished, a girl shot. "They'll hurt me."

"But your family."

Family. The word is like a dagger in my chest. Family. If only he knew. "I am dead to them."

"You're not dead."

"Aren't I?"

He takes another step toward me. I cannot run. Cannot hide. If he gets closer he'll know. He'll see me for who I am.

God, help me. Spare me. Spare him.

The baby wakes and cries.

I dart around him and hurry to the cot. I pick her up and coo in her ear. "Shh, sweetie. It's all right."

She sniffles and stops crying. Her hand bats at my nose. She gurgles and blows raspberries. Then she smiles into my eyes, and asks me no questions, tells me no lies. With her, I am safe. With her ...

I turn, and he is there. So close behind me that I can hear his breath, see the golden flecks in his eyes. He speaks not a word, but I can read his gaze. Who are you?

Don't ask me. Please ...

I turn away and pray in the silence.

***

A woman. The ghost is a woman. That fact cut through Josef's mind like a plow through a dry field. She could be anyone, anyone at all, even ...

His mind caught and held. She couldn't be. She might be. Was she? He'd seen the wagon roll, seen her vanish in the flames. But still ...

He watched the way she held the baby, tucked against her hip, just like Maggie used to do. But Maggie would sing. Or at least hum. This woman only spoke, a little whisper, and then she made no sound at all. If it were Maggie, would she sing? Even when her voice had been burned by the fire?

Josef stepped close behind her. If he could study her face, look closely into her eyes, he would know. He started to reach out.

Before he could touch her, she turned away, hid her face from his gaze.

Maggie wouldn't have done that. But then again the fire had changed everybody, everything.

Josef backed away and sat on the edge of the cot. His leg throbbed. But now he was glad, glad he had followed the footsteps in the snow, glad he had fallen down the bank, glad he had been found by this hermit in the hills. If he hadn't, he'd never have found out. He cleared his throat. He would have to go slowly, carefully. He'd have to set her at ease. But he had to know.

The woman cooed and kissed the baby's ear.

Emma giggled.

"That's a good girl." The woman murmured and clucked her tongue the way he'd heard Maggie do a hundred times.

He held his breath. *Slow ... Easy ...* He'd have to draw her out. Casual words, simple conversation. Could he do it? He had to. "So, you build this place yourself?"

She nodded. "I watched the rebuilding in town." Her words came cautiously at first, then flowed more quickly. "So I knew what to do."

"Good work."

"For a woman?"

He didn't say that. At least, he didn't mean to. "No."

"No?"

This wasn't going at all like he'd hoped. Why couldn't women take a simple compliment?

"You wouldn't expect a woman to be able to build even this?" For some reason she was smiling now. He could tell by the lilt in her voice.

"I've learned how to do a lot of things since the fire."

He bet she had.

"Like stealing carts."

His gaze flew to her face. She was teasing him now. She had to be.

"You don't need to say anything. I read it on your face."

He looked down at his feet. He had thought no such thing. At least, well, not exactly anyway. He glanced up and tried again. "Good house. Solid."

She chuckled. "If you want more stew, you only need to ask."

"What?"

"You don't need to flatter me."

"I wasn't ..."

She held Emma with one arm and ladled more stew into a bowl with the other. Then she handed him the bowl. "My eyes are still good. I can see what this place looks like. But then, it was only built by a woman."

"That's not—" He stopped and sighed. He never had been good at small talk. Last time he'd tried he'd made a fool of himself too. That time was just days before the fire. He'd come into the house when Maggie had those women over. Odd group, it was. The seamstress, that Anderson girl, and Lars Jensen's daughter. But no, the Anderson girl wasn't there. Not that time.

It was just the three of them, if he recalled. They were all sitting close together, talking fast and quiet like. Suppertime, it was. But there wasn't any food on the table, nothing cooking on the stove. Strange, because Maggie was good at that kind of thing.

He had stomped his feet on the mat as they all looked up at him. He stopped stomping and stood still.

They kept staring.

"Oh Josef." Maggie gasped and leapt to her feet. "I didn't ... I'm sorry."

He closed the door behind him. "It's all right, sit on down with your friends."

She didn't sit.

He was aware of the sweat stains under his arms, the dirt on his collar, the bits of dried chaff stuck to his pants. He sneezed.

"Josef?"

He jumped, and his gaze flew to the ladies, still looking at him. "Oh, um, good evening then, uh." Then he stood there, knowing he ought to be saying something polite, knowing that a gentleman would greet them with proper words. He figured he ought to say something about the weather. Folks always talked about the weather. But it was hot, dry, just like every other day that summer. But it was all he had. "Mighty hot out."

Maggie's gaze darted to the metal pitcher on the table. "Oh no, it's all gone. I gave it … we had …"

His brow furrowed as he listened. What was she talking about? He hadn't said nothing about a pitcher. But then he understood. She thought he was asking for a drink, and there was none left. That's not what he meant. He was just trying to … He sighed. Out loud.

Maggie took a step toward him. Her hands shook. "I'm so sorry, Josef."

"I didn't mean—" But the words stuck in his throat. His dry throat.

Maggie licked her lips. "Joe, dear." She never called him that. "We're, um, all out of that tea you like so well." She gestured toward the pitcher. "If you could just take me into town tomorrow."

"I wasn't plannin' on going in."

"Please."

"I'll just pick up what you need."

"No." Her voice rose and cracked. "Mr. Heg has several kinds. You don't know which one."

His brow furrowed. "Oh, all right then."

He put his hat on the hook by the door and tromped past them to the kitchen. As he got there, he heard Maggie whisper. "I'll take care of it. Tomorrow."

Funny how that incident came back to him now. Maybe it was the way his stomach felt all twisted up then, like now. That feeling when he knew what he said wasn't right, but he didn't know how to smooth it over. Or maybe it was because every time he tried to say something simple and polite he ended up asking for something. It had to be something about women. They were always thinking he said what he didn't say, even when he hardly said anything at all. Or maybe it wasn't women. Maybe it was just Maggie.

She'd hurried those ladies out of his house and got him a big cup of water. He'd thanked her and taken her to town the next day just like she asked. But, now that he remembered it, it didn't seem that she'd come back with tea. In fact, she hadn't gone into the mercantile at all. He'd gone to see the blacksmith, and she had gone ... Where had she gone? Josef rubbed his chin. He never did find out, but she was headed in the direction of the train station.

"You go ahead and eat that stew." The hermit's gravelly voice drew him from his thoughts. "I can always make more." She sat on the floor now and spooned broth into Emma's mouth.

Josef watched her blow gently on the stew in the spoon. She held it toward Emma. "Say ah." She made her mouth into an "O" just like Maggie used to do.

Emma opened her mouth, swallowed the stew, then opened again for more.

"Ah ..." Another spoonful. Just at the right pace, spoon tilted, not a drop spilled.

"You got a way with babies."

The woman glanced up. Her gaze caught his. Hers shadowed, dark. And yet ...

A bit of stew dripped from the spoon. "No. I'm not ..."

Josef stood. It couldn't be. It had to be. He had to know. "Maggie?"

26

Sunlight dances through the window of my shack. Warm, inviting, bright against old snow.

It's time. I know it. And he knows it too. The cart is packed, his leg bound for the journey. I will take him home today. Him, and Emma, too. And then …

I can't think of what will happen then. Can't think of what it will be like to come back here. Alone. Cook a meal again and eat it. Alone. Speak to no one, be with no one, weep with only the walls to see me. Today it ends. The companionship, the friendship, the illusion that someone cares.

And yet, what if …

I push the thought from my mind, but it lingers there anyway. Beckons me. Whispers of a dream that I never thought could be. Not for me. Not anymore. But what if …

For three days I have avoided his question. For three days we've spoken of harvests, of picnics we both remember, of the time old Willie Wallace fell into the well. We've commented on Emma's appetite, the new schoolhouse, *and how the town has risen from the ashes of its past. We've spoken of God, of sorrow, and the meaning of faith.*

But in all that, I've not answered his question. I've not told him who I really am. Soon, though, I will be able to hide no more.

The name hangs between us. Maggie. A good wife, a good mother, unblemished, pure. Beautiful. Maggie. I loved her too.

Tears gather behind my eyes. He deserves better. He deserves her back. He deserves more than a monster. He's an honest man, and there are not many. I know that. And I know that I have nothing to offer him, nothing to ease his pain. But what if …

I stand here, with my back to him, and stare out the window into the blinding brightness. Stare, with tears heavy in my eyes, fear pressing in my throat.

He touches my shoulder. "It's time to go." *I hear the question in his voice, and the hope.*

I dare not turn, dare not look into his face. No! *My mind shouts the word. My tongue sticks to the roof of my mouth.* Don't leave me alone!

"Come."

My heart beats so loud that I can barely hear past it. I glance behind me. He is holding out his hand, reaching toward me, asking me silently the question I must not answer.

"Come."

In that single word, I know he is offering me everything I ever dreamed, all I ever imagined. Love, family, future. Even me, even this monster, if only I say I am Maggie.

I can't.

What if ...

What if I give him what he wants, what I want? Can I? How could it be wrong?

What if ...

I'm weary of hiding.

What if ...

I look into his eyes and lay my hand in his.

***

"I can't go, Nils. I simply can't."

That fool of a man stood on Arla's doorstep with his ice skates in one hand and a basket in the other. Steam rose from the basket, carrying the scent of roast chicken and freshly baked bread.

"Just for an hour, Arla Mae. It won't hurt."

Arla smoothed the hair at the back of her neck, then twisted a few loose hairs around her finger. "It's such a bad time."

He raised the basket and grinned. "I have rhubarb sauce. Your favorite."

Her mouth watered. "I can't just go traipsing off any time I please. I have ..." She crossed her arms and forced herself not to look over her shoulder toward Ellie's room. "... responsibilities." She swallowed. "And so do you."

Nils raised his eyebrows. "Ah, but Jensen's looking after the store for me this afternoon. Says he doesn't have to be at the bank this afternoon, or the restaurant. Good man."

"Jensen? Lars Jensen?" Her voice hardened as she said it. *That horrible, awful, despicable ...*

"Yes. So come on."

She frowned. What was that man up to? Still, if Lars Jensen was at the store, then he wouldn't be coming here. Not today anyway. And that gave her a little more time to figure out what to do. "Well …"

"Come on, don't say no." He set down the ice skates and held out his hand to her.

She grimaced. "I hate to skate."

"You don't have to."

"I'll need a coat."

"I can wait."

"I don't know."

"I do." He waved toward the hall. "Now go on, get your coat, and let's go. The bread won't stay warm forever."

Arla uncrossed her arms and shook her head. "You're a persistent man, Nils Heg. I don't know why you bother."

"Don't you?"

She gave him a quick glance, then pushed the door closed, turned, and hurried down the hallway. She paused at Ellie's door. "Eleanor, Eleanor dear, are you awake?"

A muffled reply came from inside. "Of course I am."

Arla leaned closer to the door and continued in a whisper. "I'm going out with Mr. Heg. I'll be back in an hour or so."

Ellie didn't respond.

"Did you hear me?"

"Unlock the door." Footsteps pattered across the floor.

Arla moved back. Her voice softened. "You know I can't do that." She paused and placed her hand on the knob. "Mr. Jensen won't be coming today anyway. He's at the mercantile. You're safe."

Again, silence met her words.

Arla straightened. "Well, I'm going now. I'll maybe bake you some nice cookies when I get back. How would you like that?"

No answer.

Arla sighed. Ellie was angry with her of course, but if she unlocked the door, the girl was likely to run off and be seen. She kept talking about that Jensen boy and how the truth ought to be told. But now wasn't the time for that. Better if she stayed hidden here, at least until Arla figured out what to do.

The front door creaked open. "Are you coming there then, Arla Mae?"

Arla stepped into her bedroom and called over her shoulder. "I'll be right there." She grabbed a coat from the hook in her wardrobe, then hurried out again.

As she stepped from the house, Nils offered his arm. She took it and allowed him to help her down the steps and into his wagon.

"Jensen said the ice is perfect at the Grindstone." Nils flicked the reins over the horse's back.

Jensen. The very name turned her stomach. Evil man. Showing a respectable face, calling "how do" to townsfolk, smiling, pretending, when all the time he ... he ... he knew what he'd done. Arla made a sound deep in her throat.

"You all right there?"

"I suspect the ice is too thin on the Grindstone for any decent skating."

"Jensen said—"

"I don't care what that awful man said." The comment burst from her in a hiss.

Nils threw her a glance. "Something got into you today, Arla Mae?"

She clamped her lips shut. Respectable women didn't speak like that. Respectable women smiled and said gentle, controlled words. Respectable women ... She paused. Respectable women pretended. Her hands clenched in her lap. *I am not like that horrible man. I don't, I can't, I wouldn't ...* And yet, she had done wrong too. Done it, then smiled and called "how do," and covered up her sin.

The horse turned a corner and trotted faster. A moment later, the Grindstone River came into sight. Sunlight shone off its surface in a blaze of white light. It glittered there like a ribbon of pure silver. Pure, clean. It was hard to believe that just months ago it had held nothing but death. So many had died when the sawdust caught fire on its surface. So many had run to it for safety, so many had believed it was clean. But the truth had revealed itself in fire, and even the river could pretend no more.

I am the river. She died because of me. Arla pressed her fingers to her temple. *Don't think about it. Don't ... No, I've not thought for too long. It won't go away. It can't.*

Nils stopped the wagon along the bank. "Here's a good spot. We'll have a bite right here. Are you warm enough?" He reached for a blanket and placed it over her legs. Then he looked out over the ice. "Fine sight, don't you think?"

Don't be fooled. I am the river. How many will pay for my lies?

He picked up the picnic basket and set it on the seat between them. Then he opened it. "Always loved the Grindstone in winter. All sparkly and smooth. Have to be careful though. Ice isn't always as thick as it looks."

The horse snorted.

It isn't as it looks. I am the river. I can pretend no longer.

"I hope the tea is still warm." He opened a jug and poured liquid into two mugs.

Then he pulled two perfectly round rolls of bread from the basket. They had stopped steaming.

"Rakel always loved your bread rolls." There, she said her name. Said it out loud. And now—

"You miss her."

Did she? Yes, in her way. But Rakel wasn't really gone, not fully. She'd left the journal, a witness to the truth, a witness to everything Arla had not wanted to believe.

"Terrible tragedy. But there was nothing you could do. So many were lost."

Arla turned in her seat and faced Nils. "Wasn't there?"

"Of course not. How—" He stopped. "Arla?"

She looked into his face and saw him as she had never done before. Kindness wrinkled the skin around his eyes. Gentleness lifted the corners of his mouth. His nose turned red. His breath puffed in white clouds. Why had he brought her here? Why did he care? She scooted away from him. He had always cared, hadn't he? Ever since the outhouse incident, he had always been there with a smile and a kind word, all through school, all through those terrible years with Grant, through her widowhood, through the fire and the grief and the rebuilding. But what would he think now, if he knew the truth? If he saw beneath her glittering surface to the dirt that ran beneath? He wouldn't have asked her here today if he knew what she'd done, if he knew what she was doing even now.

"Arla?" He reached out, touched her sleeve. "You're pale."

He would hate her if he knew. The kindness would turn to shock. The gentleness would melt away and leave only disgust. His eyes would widen, his mouth fall slack. Then his lips would curl. Just like Grant's used to do.

"Are you okay?"

"No." The truth. It seemed strange to speak it, even in only a word. No. When the expected answer should have been yes.

Nils waited.

Arla again met his gaze. It was time. Time to show the river for what it really was. Time to tell the truth at last. "I'm not the woman you think I am."

His expression didn't change. "Aren't you?"

She swallowed. "Please, Nils, don't make this harder."

He held up a roll and took a bite.

She watched him chew. "I killed her. I killed Rakel because I was too afraid to let her go." She folded her hands in her lap and stared at her fingers. "Something terrible happened to Rakel, but I wouldn't believe it. I didn't want to. So I locked her in her room. And when the fire came, I ran away."

"Oh, Arla ..."

"But it's not just that. I've always run away. I've never faced who I am." She lifted her chin and looked out over the river. "I am a coward, Nils Heg. I've cared more about myself than those I said I loved. I've cared so much about what others think that I let Grant cheat on me. I let another man hurt my daughter. I did nothing. Because I was afraid that everyone would see, that I would see, that I was not the wife, nor the mother, that I pretended to be."

Nils remained silent.

"And now, I'm doing it again. Eleanor is locked away in my house. Locked there because I don't know what to do, don't know how to save her. Locked up because I'm afraid to do what I must." Arla paused and wrapped her arms around herself. "And now, what am I going to do? What can I do?" Her voice dropped to a whisper. "Help."

Still, Nils said nothing.

Arla glanced at him, waiting for the change in his face. Waiting for the revulsion, the distaste, the disappointment.

Instead, the corners of Nils' mouth quirked in a tiny smile. "What you can do is eat your chicken."

"What?"

"It's getting cold."

Hadn't he heard her? Her big confession? The revealing of her sins? How could he just sit there and smile, just sit and chew that big mouthful of bread, like nothing had happened.

"I heard you. And I'll help you take care of what I can."

"But ..."

He handed her a bread roll. "Truth be told, I'm proud of you, Arla Mae."

"Don't tease me, Nils. Not now."

"I'm not." He reached out and brushed his knuckles against her chin. "This is the first time in all these years that you've been real. It's the first time you've even asked for help."

"Why would you help me now, now that you know what I've done?"

Nils picked up the reins and jiggled them. "Did you think I didn't already know?"

"You couldn't ..."

The horse lifted his head and whinnied. Then Nils clucked his tongue and pulled on the right-hand rein. "I didn't know about Ellie, but I did know about Grant, and about Rakel."

"You never let on. Never."

"Neither did you."

"But it's bad, Nils, very bad what I did."

"Yes."

"And you knew."

"Yes."

"And you were still kind to me."

"Yes."

"I don't understand." The words bubbled up as a cry from her heart. She'd been sure, so sure that her sin was hidden, covered. Yet, he'd known all along. How could he, and still care?

For a long time, Nils didn't answer. He simply flicked the reins and guided the horse along the riverbank. Light danced off the ice of the river and shed long shadows over the remnants of burned trees at its rim. The trees, once black, were dressed now in a covering of snow. But she knew the truth, the scars were still there, underneath, on the trunks and in her soul. He knew it too, and yet ...

His voice came then, gentle and strong. It washed through her, brushing aside the remnants of her fear, uncovering the last of her shame.

"You know why, Arla. Because I've loved you."

She closed her eyes.

"Loved you in all your mistakes and foolishness. Even in your lies and deceit."

"You never said a word." Her voice trembled in a low whisper.

"How could I? Until you were honest with yourself?" He urged the horse to trot. "I can't love a mask. I can't love a lie." He turned and pierced her with his gaze. "But I do love you. I always have."

One question, one word, slipped from her lips. "Why?"

Nils laughed. "Because I've been loved that way too." He glanced toward the sky.

And in that moment, Arla was no longer ashamed.

27

Maggie? A chill raced down Josef's arms. *Maggie?* It had to be. Why else would she put her hand in his? Why else would she quiver when he touched her?

But she did tremble, and she wouldn't look into his eyes. Why? Was she still afraid? How could she be? If it were really her.

He wanted to believe it. Wanted it more than anything in his life. But he was afraid to believe. Afraid not to.

If only she'd look up. Then he would know for certain, wouldn't he? Couldn't he read it in her eyes? Couldn't he see it there, shining beneath burnt lashes?

Maggie?

He wanted to sweep her into his arms, tell her how much he'd missed her. He wanted to, but he didn't. He'd never been good with words, never been able to really tell her how he felt about her. *Maybe that's why … No.* He stopped his thoughts and stared down at the scarred fingers in her hand. Better not to think about those things. Better not to wonder.

She withdrew her hand and stepped away.

He dared not follow. He'd have to go slowly now. Win her back little by little, show her he still wanted her. It would take time, but he'd do it. And then everything would be all right again. He'd have a wife. Emma would have a mother. Everything would be like it was before.

Not everything.

He frowned. It didn't matter. He didn't care. Not about the scars. Not about the strange change in her. Not about the cloaked figure they all had thought was a ghost. This was Maggie, his wife. Maggie risen from the dead. His Maggie.

Is it? Truly?

It must be. He reached out and touched her chin, raised it toward him. *Please. For Emma. And for me.*

She closed her eyes and turned her face away.

Tell me it's you. Tell me, so I can be sure.

But she didn't speak. Didn't even open her eyes.

Still, it all made sense now. The stealing of his cart, the footprints outside his window, the watching from the trees. If she were Maggie, he would understand everything. Except why she had hidden, why she hadn't come home. That didn't make any sense at all.

She pulled from his grip and turned toward the loaded cart. "We should go. Now." Her voice shook.

He didn't move. *It's me. Just me. You don't have to be afraid.*

But she was. He knew it by the way her breathing came in stuttered spurts as she picked up Emma and nestled her into the cart. He knew by the way her gaze skittered over the floor. Knew it by the way she avoided touching him as she pulled the cart out the door before him.

He had time. Time to ease her fears, time to help her reenter her old life, with him. He didn't need to push. Not now. Not yet.

Without a word, he followed her outside. The topmost layer of snow had melted the day before then frozen again during the night. Today, it had a hard cover of ice, so that the little cart slid easily over it. He tucked his makeshift crutch under his arm and hobbled after the cart.

She glanced over her shoulder. "Be careful."

Josef nodded. The crutch sank into the snow deep enough to keep him from slipping. But he wouldn't make quick progress. She could go and return three times before he managed to hobble the mile or so to his home.

She again turned back toward him and continued trudging across the ice.

Emma laughed and clapped her hands as the cart dipped into a rut then shuddered over a bit of rocky earth. Sunlight glinted off the snow and sent shards of light into Josef's eyes. He squinted and limped forward. *Home.* They were all going home. And if all went well, it would be a real home again. With him, and Emma, and Maggie. *Please, God* ...

Over an hour later they were at his front door. Emma had tipped sideways and was now asleep in the fold of her blankets. The woman pulled the cart up to the house, then gathered up Emma and went inside. When Josef joined them, Emma was already in her crib, still asleep.

He leaned his crutch against the wall, bent down, and started a fire in the stove. After a few minutes, the crackle of new flame spun shadows onto the walls. He poured water into a kettle and placed it on the stovetop.

As he worked, she took the things from the cart, brought them in, and placed them where they belonged—the remainder of Emma's milk in a bucket of snow on the table, blankets in a basket near the crib, the remnants of stew in a pot beside the stove. Then she straightened. "You should be fine now."

Josef blinked. "You're staying, aren't you?"

A shiver rippled her shoulders. "You can keep the stew pot. I know it isn't much."

"Don't want the pot. I want—"

"Shh." She put up her hand. "Don't say it."

"Maggie?"

She shook her head. "You don't understand."

"Help me then."

She turned and gripped the door handle in her hand. "I can't." Her chin dropped toward her chest.

Josef frowned. Something was wrong. And it shouldn't be. She was back. She was home. And yet sadness hung over her like that ugly black cloak she always wore. And it darkened his heart too. She should be happy. He should be happy. Unless … Josef swallowed and rubbed his eyes. That day before the fire came, that day when she had headed off toward the train station … *what if?* He shuddered. What if she had been buying a ticket there? What if she'd been planning to take Emma and leave him?

He looked at the woman before him. *Were you planning to leave me, Maggie? Is that why you lied?* But she'd loved him, hadn't she? And he loved her. *But you didn't tell her so. Not enough anyway.* He should have told her. Should have made sure she knew how much he valued her. He reached a hand toward her. "Stay."

Her back stiffened. "Josef …" Her voice was so low that he could barely hear it. Then the door opened.

"Please."

For a moment, she paused.

Nothing moved. Not a breeze from outside, not a single wisp of snow, not a hair, nor even a fold of her cloak. "I … I need to get a few things. I'll come back. Tomorrow."

Josef took a step toward her. "I don't care about the scars." In fact, he almost loved her more with them than without. The fire had changed her. The old Maggie wouldn't have said those things that challenged his soul, that beckoned him to deeper places of thought and faith. The old Maggie would have supplied a "why," however shallow. The old Maggie would have never fought through a blizzard to save him. "They don't matter."

She raised a hand to her face, touched her cheek. "They matter to me."

Emma cried out. Josef turned to see her stuff her fingers in her mouth and suck them. She rolled over and kept sleeping.

When he turned back around, Maggie was gone. He limped to the door. There she was, almost to the tree line.

He lifted his hand and shielded his eyes against the glare of the snow. For a moment, he thought he saw her pause. Thought she might glance back. *Don't go, Maggie. Come back to me.*

Instead, she wrapped her arms around herself and kept walking.

"Maggie … I love you." He spoke aloud, but she didn't stop, didn't turn. And then she disappeared into the trees.

* * *

Poor fool. Lars pulled back the curtain and watched Nils and the Anderson woman pass by in the wagon. The man had a grin on him like a fat cat before a saucer of cream. And she was smiling too, a stupid, coy smirk like the kind Agnes used to wear. "Cultured women always smile like this, Lars dear," Agnes once said. And he'd believed her. But not anymore. That was the smile of a woman hiding something. A woman who would lie straight to your face and expect you to believe her.

The Anderson woman glanced away and touched her fingers to her hat. Agnes had a hat like that. Tiny thing. Worthless. She touched the brim that way too. With delicate fingers just brushing the satin.

Lars let the curtain drop. He remembered those days well. The days of false smiles and fancy hats. The days of racing hearts, flattering words, hidden lies. And carriage rides in the snow.

He turned his back to the window and closed his eyes. He could almost hear the clop of the horse's hooves on the cobblestone streets of St. Paul, could almost feel the crunch of snow beneath the carriage wheels. It was a day like today, bright and cold and beautiful, with breath fogging the air and stinging his throat. A day with sunshine so bright it made your eyes bead up and your skin smart. Agnes wore a coat of deep brown with fur fluffing around her ears. Her cheeks shone pink, her eyes wide. Then she smiled that same secret smile. "Oh Lars." His name rushed from her lips in a breathless whisper. Her fingertips fluttered to her hat, then to his arm.

His heart thudded in his chest.

Then it began to snow, just a light feathering of perfectly formed crystals. They drifted onto her nose, sprinkled the brim of that ugly hat. She tucked her hand in the crook of his arm and looked at him with those soft brown eyes surrounded by black lashes. And when she spoke, her voice was like butter on warm toast. "I admire you so, Lars Jensen. You're so clever. So strong. So smart." She lowered her eyes. "And handsome, too. How do you do it?"

And that's when he asked her to marry him. Right there in the carriage, with the snow falling, and cold painting her cheeks the color of candy. He should have known better. He should have realized.

Lars sighed and opened his eyes. He was a wiser man now. He knew what women were like. Knew what they could do to a man. He stepped from the window and wandered through the store. He passed the rows of pickled vegetables, the bolts of multicolored cloth, a row of eight-dollar harnesses, a jar of peppermint sticks, a bin of shiny buttons.

He paused and scowled. *Women.* They were all full of light and flattery, batting their lashes, smiling, making a man think thoughts he ought not think. He ran his fingers through the bin of buttons, grabbed up a handful, and squeezed. Some were round, some square, with different colors, sizes, materials. But they were still all buttons. And women were still all women. Give them a little time and they too would fall away and betray you, leave you exposed. You'd catch them batting their lashes at another man, smiling that special smile at him, whispering how you were nobody, nothing. Saying that you were common. And just like buttons, women needed to be tightly bound. He threw the fistful of buttons back into the bin and turned toward the door. It was time to take care of one of the loose buttons now.

Lars grabbed his coat and put it on. Then he stepped out the front door, locked it, and strode down the sidewalk. The street was mostly empty today, with only a couple of horses swishing their tails outside the barbershop, and one dog darting into an alley. Every door was tightly shut—the milliner's shop, the new cigar store, the hotel, smaller than the one built before the fire. Everything was smaller, simpler, plainer now. The fire had done that, had changed everything. Much had been rebuilt, but it would never be like it was before.

He turned a corner and saw Arla Anderson's house up ahead. He hurried toward it. If all went as planned, the Hansen girl would be on the next train out of Hinckley, and the Coles would be waiting on the other end. And this time, she wouldn't come back. This time, all his worries would be behind him.

Women ...

Lars glanced right and left, then took the steps up to the door two at a time. For a moment, he paused and looked behind him. No one was there. He grabbed the door handle, turned it, and smiled. She hadn't even locked the door. He pushed it open and slipped inside. This was going to be easy.

He closed the door behind him, locked it, and crept down the hall.

***

Footsteps were coming. Heavy, hard. Nothing like the quick, light steps of Mrs. Anderson. It was him. It had to be.

Ellie grabbed the coat from her bed. *I waited too long.* Her breath came in quick spurts. Her gaze flew to the window.

Across the hall, a door squeaked. The footsteps paused.

Then the sound of boots came again. The soft thud of heel on wood. *No. No, no, no, no.*

Without a sound, she tiptoed to the window. *Go away. Ain't nobody here.* Behind her, the door handle rattled. She bit her lip. Locked. He couldn't get in. Couldn't get at her.

Something smacked against the door. Something big, strong. A shoulder maybe? Or a booted foot.

Ellie's hands shook as she pushed opened the window. *Leave me alone.*

The thud came again. The door creaked and groaned.

She put one leg over the sill.

Then from behind her came the sharp crack of splitting wood.

28

Pain shot through Lars' shoulder as he slammed it into the door again. *Stupid girl.* Why couldn't she just stay where he'd sent her? She would have been rich and comfortable, and far away. But she came back. And now he had to deal with her. He drew back and pressed his palm against the doorjamb. One more hit. Right near the knob.

He lifted his foot and kicked the door just below the handle. The wood splintered. He kicked again. And this time the door banged open.

He rushed inside. "Look here, girl—" He stopped. The room was empty.

She was here. She had to be. Ugly flowered wallpaper glared at him from all sides of the room. Big, gaudy roses. Like faces, sneering. He shook his head and glanced over the room. The rumpled bed, the stockings cast over a chair in the corner, the pillow lying on the floor. It wasn't like the Anderson woman to keep a messy house. It wasn't like her at all.

Lars moved toward the west wall. There sat a long bureau, with a shiny washbasin on top. Water glinted from the basin. He reached over and touched the water's surface. Cool, but not cold. His eyes narrowed. The wardrobe. Of course. He hurried toward it and flung the doors wide. Nothing. No girl crouched in the corner, not even a coat or a gown or a lacy pinafore. He frowned.

"Where are you, girl? Come out."

Silence.

"I won't hurt you."

He strode to the rumpled bed, dropped to his knees, and looked beneath it. Again, nothing. He stood and ran his hand over the sheets. Gray fabric peeked from a pillowcase. He pulled it out and found a silk dress and a clean pair of stockings. *Strange ...*

His fingers touched the soft silk. It reminded him of something. Of someone.

Winnie ...

His throat tightened. Winnie had a dress just like this, didn't she? A traveling dress. But then, she had dozens of dresses. Of course this one would remind him of her. It didn't mean anything. It was just a dress. Just a bunch of cloth. He shook his head, but the image of Winnie stuck with him. She wouldn't have liked what he was doing now. She had been fond of the Hansen girl. *I have to, Winnie. You understand. We'll all be better off. The girl will be in St. Paul, and your brother will be safe. It's best this way.*

Lars pinched the bridge of his nose and sighed. He was going crazy, talking to a dead girl, doubting himself over a bit of gray silk. No, he had to find Ellie Hansen. Find her, and dissipate the threat. He stuffed the dress back into the pillowcase. It was odd to find a dress there. It was almost as if ... as if someone had been planning an escape.

A tickle of cold air brushed Lars' cheek. He turned toward the door, then toward the window. It was closed, except for a two-inch gap at the bottom. The curtains swayed in the slight breeze.

Lars threw the pillowcase back onto the bed and stepped toward the glass. *Why, that sneaky little ...* He peered into the day. Sunlight glared off the snow and into his eyes. He threw open the window and leaned out. There, beneath him, were two indentations, each the size of a child's foot. And moving away were prints spaced far enough so that he knew she'd been running. The prints were fresh, the sides unmelted.

He slammed the window shut, raced from the room, and bolted out the front door. She couldn't have gotten far. He would catch her, and fast. He leapt down the steps and out into the street. Then he paused and looked left. Nothing. And right. He let out his breath. There, in the distance, a figure in a blue coat turned a corner and slipped out of sight. He clenched his fists and ran after it.

A few moments later he reached the corner. Ahead, the figure swerved and ran northwest. She was quick, but not quick enough.

The rumble of a wagon on the street behind him caught his attention. He stopped and glanced back. The horse came into sight. And then the wagon.

It was Nils and that Anderson woman. He threw himself into the shadows of the milliner's shop. Why were they returning already? They should have been gone for another hour at least. He held still and watched them through the mist of his breath. It wouldn't do for them to see him, especially since he was supposed to be tending the mercantile, especially since, if asked, he would need to say he'd been there all this time.

Lars waited as the wagon passed. But he needn't have worried. Nils and the woman had eyes only for each other. And what was that? Did she have her hand on his arm? Were their legs touching? *Ah, Heg, you poor fool.*

He lingered for ten seconds longer, then moved out of the shadows. By then the figure of the girl was gone. He loosened the scarf around his neck and again ran in the direction where he'd last seen her. Five minutes later, he reached a clump of burned stumps at the edge of town. There, he paused. He never was a good tracker. But he wouldn't have to be. He straightened and took a deep breath.

Little fool. There, as clear as arrows in the snow, were a line of footprints crossing the railroad tracks and heading straight into the hills. Straight toward the place where Robert Larsen had once seen a strange light.

Lars stuffed his hands in his pockets and followed the prints.

* * *

That nasty Mr. Jensen must have wings growing out of his feet. 'Cause he was coming on right quick after her. Ellie glanced over her shoulder only once. And there he was, flying over the railroad tracks and squawking like some old vulture. "Ellie Hansen. Come back here now. No use—" His voice turned to a distant rumble as she slid down an embankment and raced off through the trees.

He was a bad man. Evil. Like them wicked kings Preacher told about in the Bible. She couldn't let him catch her. She couldn't, or else ... Her breath pushed past the sharp stone in her throat and made a cloud that puffed before her, then streamed away behind. Into her mind came a vision of Winnie. Winnie with strange bruises, and excuses that didn't make no sense. And Rakel. She'd gone to see Mr. Jensen too. And then she disappeared. And no one ever saw her no more. He'd done that, that bad Mr. Jensen. He'd hurt Winnie and made Rakel vanish. Would she disappear too if he caught her? Would she be like mist that twirled away in the wind and was no more?

Her heart pounded in her ears, throbbed in her chest. Snow sloshed into her shoes and froze her toes cold. She wiped her nose with the back of her hand and darted between the tree trunks. Pain twisted in her side, maybe from the old wound, or maybe it was just a regular old stitch like she used to get when she ran to town. She'd already run farther than that now. But she couldn't stop. He was still coming. She knew it. Though she couldn't hear him anymore.

You can't slow down, Ellie Jean. Keep on now.

If she ran far enough she might lose him. Then she would hide and never go back. She'd miss them, Mrs. Anderson, and that nice Mr. Heg with his peppermint sticks. But it would be all right. If that ghost-man could live out here in the woods, so could she. Maybe she'd find him, and they could live together. She'd help him, and he'd help her. Maybe that's what them dreams meant. Maybe that's why God sent them from Mama.

Ellie climbed up a knoll, turned toward the sun, and sprinted toward the icy creek bed. Shadows from the trees darkened the ground before her in long strips. A moment later, she plunged down to the frozen creek, then up the bank on the other side. At the top, she paused.

I don't hear nothing. He ain't coming.

Beside her, snow plopped onto the ground from the branches above. A bird twittered in the distance. But there was no voice calling. No sound of following footsteps.

Ellie pushed her palm into her side and hobbled toward a clump of trees. One tree had fallen, and now its thick trunk lay sideways on the ground. Maybe, if she worked fast, she could dig a hole next to that fallen trunk, a snow cave deep enough to hide in.

She hurried toward the fallen tree. Around it, broken branches were strewn across the snow. She stopped to gather a few in her arms. When she reached the tree, she dropped the branches, fell to her knees, and began to dig alongside the horizontal trunk. In a moment, her fingers turned cold, her skin smarted. But she kept digging until her hands hit frozen earth. The hole was maybe two feet deep, with the back side flush against the fallen tree.

She jumped inside and crunched down until her knees squashed against her chest. Still, the snow came up to her shoulders and no further. She bit her lip, then grabbed the broken branches and carefully placed them over her, with one end leaning against the top of the trunk behind her, and the other sitting on the snow in front. It took five branches to completely cover her and the hole she had made. But they were too straight, too perfect. She reached up and skewed them so they looked more natural. The needles poked through her gloves, stabbed at her frozen skin. The tree must have fallen in the recent storm, because the needles were still green and full. Full enough to hide her beneath them.

She shivered. *I'm safe. He won't see me here. No one will.* Cold seeped through her coat as she peeked out between the needled branches. A few feet away, a blue jay hopped across the twig-covered ice. Her breathing slowed. Not even the bird knew she was here. She could hide this way forever, or at least long enough. Maybe she could build an ice house like Evan said folks did way far away in the North. And she could find berries and roots like bears did. She would remember to never eat the white ones or the red ones. 'Cause you never knew about the red. She would miss school though, and Sunday picnics in the summer, and, and ... the dress. Ellie clapped her hand over her mouth. She had left the dress. But Mama would understand. Mama would know it was more important to get away. Then maybe, after awhile, she could—

The blue jay squawked and flew away. A figure rose from the creek bed. Mr. Jensen. Like some kind of devil rising out of the earth.

Ellie pressed her hand harder over her mouth. *Don't breathe too loud. Don't make a sound.*

Mr. Jensen brushed a bit of frost from his shoulder, bent down, and stared at something in the snow.

Her hand shook. Her eyes widened. *Oh no, no.* Now she could see them too. Her footprints clear in the snow. Leading him right to her.

He looked up. His gaze followed the line of prints. He stood and adjusted his collar. Then he came. Closer and closer. His eyes never wavering. His steps making a sharp crunching sound in the snow.

She wrapped her arms around her knees and tried to scrunch up very small. Her breath hissed from her lips. *He'll hear me. It doesn't matter. No—*

He was above her, so close that she could see the light glinting in his eyes, the drops of breath freezing on his mustache. She squinted her eyes, held her breath. Blood drummed in her temples.

A second passed. Then two.

No. No, no, no ...

He reached down.

She scrunched lower.

He pulled away the branch.

Stop!

His hand came down, grabbed her arm, and yanked her from her hiding place.

***

I love him. I, who have no right to love, no right to be loved. I never have. Not really. Yet, it has come to me now. Now, when I have lost everything, even who I am. Now, when my flesh is twisted and my skin puckered and sore. Now, when I can no longer hide, yet cannot be free. And still it comes to me. Love, pained, gentle, wrong. Love, in the face of a man who sees my scars and does not hate, who touches me and does not recoil.

And yet, I know what I am. And I know he deserves better.

The snow sloshes under my boots as I hurry away from him. I can feel him there, watching me. I can feel the question in his eyes, the hurt in his heart. Does he think that I fear him, and that's why I run? Or does he know that it is not him that I fear, but me? The betrayal of my own heart. The masking of the monster in the water.

I turn down a knoll, and I am lost to his sight. I am alone again. Alone, and cold, and afraid. What will I tell him? What will I do?

Tomorrow. I promised to go back tomorrow. And then, perhaps, I will know. Perhaps by then I can silence the monster within.

I find the creek again, and I pause by a frozen pool along its bank. I have been here before. Here is where I first looked at my reflection and saw what I had become. Here is where I knelt and could not weep. Here, I first knew that life had changed forever.

So I look again. But now there is only ice covered with snow. Only whiteness and flecks of broken twigs. No longer can I see myself in the water. No longer does it tell me what I am.

I stand and look toward the sun. God took my life. And now I can take it back again. I will. I must. After all, I have spent my entire life hiding truth from those who care for me, my whole life disguising my pain. It is no different now.

No different ... except for him.

He deserves better.

I step away from the bank. A scream pierces the air. Chills pimple my skin. I look up. Something is there. Through the trees. A flash of blue. A movement. And a face that ignites my fear.

* * *

Stupid girl. Lars' fingers dug into her flesh as he jerked her from the hole in the snow. She tried to pull away. He tightened his grip. Her eyes, like wide saucers, stared up at him. Her mouth moved as she whimpered words he could not understand.

"Shut up." He wrenched her arm.

She screamed.

He pulled back his hand and slapped her face.

She screamed again.

Then somehow, his hands were around her neck. Squeezing, shaking. Words spat from his lips sent bits of spittle spraying over her cheeks. "Stop. Stop it!" Fury raced through his veins, into his fingers, constricting them.

Her mouth opened. Breath whistled through her lips.

Let go. He heard the whisper in his mind, but he couldn't obey.

Her legs buckled.

Finally, his grip loosened.

She dropped to the snow. Her head tipped back, and she looked up at him with eyes that pierced his very soul.

His gaze fell to the marks on her neck. *I'm sorry. I didn't mean ... I didn't intend ...* "Why couldn't you just stay in Duluth? Why did you have to come back?"

For a moment, she didn't answer. Then she spoke, her voice high, quick, trembling. "You can't make me disappear. I ain't mist. I won't vanish." She leapt to her feet, took a step to dash away.

He grabbed her and yanked her back. Her sleeve tore. The seam shredded. Just like before. So like that other time. Too like it.

God help me ...

29

It came. Like a black shadow spilling from the trees. A black creature, with a black cape flowing behind it. Just like the image from Ellie's dreams.

It came. Right at them.

Ellie bit back her shout. Mr. Jensen didn't see it. He couldn't. The creature was behind him, moving fast. And silent.

She twisted her arm in his grip. Pain shot to her shoulder.

"Don't fight me, girl."

It was just behind him now—the thing, the monster, the ghost. Its arm rose. For a second, its teeth flashed in the blackness of its face. "Let her go." The words shot from beneath the hood of the cape. Then a fat stick crashed down on Mr. Jensen's shoulder, glanced off his arm.

He fell. Snow flew up as his chest impacted the ice.

And she was free.

For a moment, the creature turned toward her.

Ellie froze. Her eyes grew wide.

"Are you okay?" A voice grated from beneath the hood.

Mr. Jensen groaned.

The creature turned back. It raised the branch again. Then it stood there, trembling, waiting.

Ellie took a step backward. A thousand questions came to her mind, but she spoke none of them. Instead, she raised a hand to her face and touched the place where Mr. Jensen had struck her. Her cheek still stung. And her neck still hurt. If he hadn't let her go, if he hadn't stopped squeezing just at that moment …

Mr. Jensen rose from the ground.

The ghost-man stepped back. "Stay away from her. From us."

His eyes narrowed. "You. You'll pay for this."

Then a strange thing happened. The ghost-man laughed. A rough, wild sound that raced through Ellie's nerves and tingled along her skin.

"Pay? Never. Never again."

For a moment, they faced each other.

Then Mr. Jensen lunged toward the creature.

It swung the stick. And missed.

Mr. Jensen grabbed the cape. The hood tipped back. He dropped his grip. "What? You're, you're a woman."

Ellie gasped. A woman. But then …

The creature lifted her chin. "And you're nobody. Nobody at all."

Fear blazed across Mr. Jensen's face. "No. It can't be …" He backed up.

But before he could get out of reach, the creature lifted the stick and bashed it against his head.

Mr. Jensen crumpled to the ground. And didn't move again.

The creature stood over the figure of Mr. Jensen. For three full seconds, she didn't move. Then she pushed her foot against his side and rolled him face up.

Ellie stepped closer. Mr. Jensen's eyes were closed, his cheeks pale. But a wisp of white mist still hovered over his mouth.

The creature lifted her foot and pressed it into his chest. She leaned over and spoke in a voice so harsh that Ellie shivered. "You will never touch me again. Do you hear me? Never!" She straightened and looked at Ellie. "Come quick. Back to town. He's only out for a moment."

Ellie stared into the creature's face. Twisted, misshapen, horrible. Like someone had formed a face in clay then mashed it all up.

The creature, the woman, put out her hand toward Ellie. "I'll take you back to town."

Ellie glanced at the hand, delicate, small, and scarred. "I can't go back there. I don't want to go back. I want to stay with you."

"Me?"

"Please."

Breath left the woman's mouth in a rush. And then her eyes filled with tears. "Oh, Ellie ..."

Ellie's pulse quickened. The woman knew her. Could it be, could she be ... did she dare hope? "Mama?"

The tears spilled down the woman's cheeks. She shook her head. "No. Don't—"

Behind her, Mr. Jensen stirred.

***

Arla wrapped her arms around herself and watched as Nils' wagon lumbered away down the street. She rocked back and forth on her feet and waited.

Then he turned in his seat, grinned, and waved at her.

She giggled and waved back. *Gracious, I'm as silly as a schoolgirl.* Cold bit at her cheeks, but she didn't mind. There was a warmth inside her that no snow, no ice, could cool.

She and Nils had stood there on the porch for probably half an hour, just talking, and remembering stories from long ago. The good stories, the happy times. But behind her, the locked door of Ellie's room waited, and the girl on the other side of it.

Nils' wagon slipped out of sight. Arla sighed and opened the door. She would have to go in now, go in and face Ellie. Alone. As it should be, at least this first time. It ought to be just the two of them when she confessed her weaknesses, asked forgiveness from the girl she had wronged. It would be hard telling Ellie what she'd done and why. But it would be okay. God would help her, and somehow it would turn out all right. She'd made a lot of mistakes. So many. But things would be different now. God loved her, and so did Nils. And they both knew the truth.

Arla closed the door and started toward the kitchen. She'd make a little tea, then get Ellie, and they'd talk. Afterward, they would figure out what to do together, how she might adopt Ellie proper. God would give wisdom, just as he gave pardon—and love. She stoked the fire in the stove, then put water in the teapot and set it to boil. Next, she placed two cups and saucers on the table, and beside them a plate of gingerbread cookies. She picked one up and nibbled the edge. Gingerbread. She smiled. Nils loved gingerbread. *Thank you, Lord, for Nils, and for your love. Help me know what to do. Help us both.*

She smoothed her skirt. This time, she would do things right. Lars Jensen wouldn't stand in her way. And she wouldn't let shame keep her quiet. She dropped some tea into the water, then turned toward the hall. "Eleanor. Ellie dear, I'm home."

No one answered.

Arla brushed her hands against her skirt and stepped into the hall. "Ellie?" She moved toward the girl's room. "Oh no."

There, the door stood open, the jamb split, the handle askew. Bits of broken wood lay scattered over the floor.

Arla rushed into the room. Ellie was gone. Her gray dress was on the bed, her bedcovers mussed. She hurried to the bed, picked up the dress, and pressed it to her chest. *What happened here? Where is she? God …*

She stood in the middle of the room, clutching the dress, not knowing what to do, what to think.

Then a floorboard creaked behind her. She turned.

And there in the doorway stood the black-garbed creature from the hills.

* * *

The sun shone in Lars' face. He blinked. Snow seeped into his waistband, melted, and trickled down his hip. He lifted his head and shook it. Pain shot through his temple. *Crazy woman. Vicious. And ...*

The sun slipped behind a cloud. He shivered. *It can't be her. She's dead. She has to be.*

This morning it had all seemed so simple. Get the girl, send her on a train to St. Paul, where the Coles would pick her up and keep her. Then go back to the comfortable, respectable life he was used to. Prepare for Leif's interview, run his businesses, plan his campaign for mayor. Simple. Easy. Good. But somehow, everything had spun out of control. He didn't get the girl, didn't send her away. And now, worse yet, a monster had found him. A monster who somehow knew his sin.

Lars sat up and put his hand to his head. Something warm and sticky gathered at his hairline. He touched it, then looked at his fingers. Blood. Of course. He grimaced. It wasn't much. Just a little blood. Just like before. Only this time he wouldn't care if others saw. He dabbed his fingers in the blood, then rubbed them on his pant leg. This time, he would show the wound and make her pay for it. No matter who she was.

He gripped a handful of snow in his fist and made it into a hard ball. Why was it that every time he tried to fix a problem he ended up multiplying it? And it was always a woman's fault. He crushed the snowball and allowed the bits of ice to trickle through his fingers. It couldn't be her. But what if it was? That thing, that misshapen mass of humanity could ruin him, ruin everything. Like a demon from the past, she had arisen to accuse him. Arisen from the dead.

Lars stood on shaking legs and tilted his face toward the sky. Only God could have done this. Only God could raise a person from death. He turned up his collar. God was paying him back for his sin. He hadn't forgotten, hadn't forgiven. Melted snow dripped into his shoe. *It's not my fault.*

But it was. He blamed Agnes, he blamed his mother. But they were dead, gone. Only he was left. Only him to carry on the remnants of their sin. He looked at the dark-rimmed clouds, heavy with moisture, at the bits of blue sky painted with gray. A sky that wanted to be blue, to be clear, full of light. But the darkness invaded, the grayness spread, the sun vanished. *That's what's wrong with me.* He meant to be a good man, meant to do right and be respectable. But sometimes, just sometimes the darkness came, and he lost control. With Winnie, and then with Rakel, and today, almost, almost with the Hansen girl. Yes, something was wrong with him. And now, the whole world would know it, unless he could stop that she-devil in disguise.

"It's not my fault."

The sun came out again, blinding him with its brightness. The vision of a black-haired beauty danced before his eyes. He closed them and rubbed his eye sockets with his palms. How could such beauty be turned to ugliness? He shuddered. Someone should put that thing out of its misery. No one ought to live like that. Scarred and broken, disfigured, despicable. Living like an animal in the hills. It wasn't natural. Wasn't right.

He leaned over and brushed the snow off his pants. Then he turned and squinted against the glare of the snow. There. The monster had come out of the trees right there.

He strode toward the opening between the branches. Then he squatted down and pressed his fingers into an indentation in the snow. Her footprints were still clear in the ice. He looked up, followed the line of prints with his eyes. They led west. He straightened and set out after them. He may have lost her and that Hansen girl, but he would find out where she lived, where in this godforsaken wilderness she had been hiding. Then tomorrow, he'd do what needed to be done. Or maybe not him but Robert and the boys. Yes, that's what he'd do. He'd tell them the monster was on the rampage again, and after the girl. Just like before. He'd tell them where to find it, and let them take care of the problem quiet like, without his having to be involved. That way, he could keep his distance. From her, and from the past that she embodied.

Lars followed the prints as they wound through the trees and stumps, over a knoll, down a hill, and then to a clearing. A clearing with a farmhouse in the middle and smoke curling from the chimney, darkening the sky. Lars paused and leaned his hand against a tree trunk.

Strom. He had taken her in. Sheltered the monster.

This changed everything.

* * *

She stands before me, her hair grayer now, her eyes softer. I see the fear in them, and the horror. She drops the dress in her arms, and I see her tremble.

"What have you done with her?"

I look at the splinters of wood on the floor, the shards of a door broken. She thinks I did this. She thinks I am the monster. I want to hate her, but I cannot. I am a monster. But he is more of one.

"Where is she?"

I gesture for Ellie to come.

The girl moves from the hall behind me. Moves around me, stands at my side.

"I'm all right, Mrs. Anderson. I'm back."

The woman's eyes slip from me to Ellie. "Your cheek." She steps closer, then stops. "What are those marks, child?"

Ellie touches her face. "It weren't her. It was him. But she saved me." The girl tilts her head, looks up at me, and smiles. Then she tucks her hand into mine.

Warmth floods me.

"Her ... she?" The woman whispers the words, chokes on them. Then again her eyes are on me, probing, questioning, filled with fright.

I neither confirm nor deny. I just stand there, with a kaleidoscope of emotions raging through my soul. Hope and fear, dread and doubt, anger and sorrow. Memories of pain, tendrils of shame. And then I speak. "Keep her safe. Until—"

"I will."

My eyes catch hers and hold. Not like last time. "Not like before."

Her eyes widened. "No ..." It is not even a whisper. It is a prayer.

She moves toward me. Her arm reaches out.

I drop Ellie's hand, turn, and run.

30

She was beautiful, lying there with her eyes closed, her mouth ajar. Arla touched Ellie's hair with her fingertips. She couldn't bear to wake her. Not yet. *Sleep, child, dream that you're safe and happy and home.* Arla leaned over the bed and listened to the quiet rhythm of Ellie's breathing.

The night had been a long one, with Ellie sleeping next to her, and Arla jumping at every sound. But they had made it safe until the morning. And now it was time to decide what to do.

Ellie sighed and rolled over.

Arla stepped back. Her nightdress brushed against her bare ankles. Then she paused. *No. Not again.* She stared once more at Ellie's cheek, at the strange discoloration on the fair skin. Slowly, carefully, she reached out her index finger and traced the mark.

Ellie shivered and whimpered in her sleep.

Lars Jensen. He had done this. He had dared.

Arla's fists wadded into tight balls. She whirled and strode to the fireplace. She threw in a couple more logs, then paced back and forth in front of the flame. He couldn't be allowed to get away with it. Not again. Not this time. But what could she do? The word of a child against the word of a man? No one would believe the girl, just as they wouldn't have believed Rakel. Arla stopped. Rakel. Yes, that was it. Arla narrowed her eyes. Ellie wouldn't be the only one to accuse Lars Jensen. Rakel had accused him too. Accused him even from death through the words of her journal. But then the journal indicted Arla, too. It witnessed to her own failings, her own fears, her mistakes and weaknesses. If she showed it, everyone would know what kind of woman she really was, and what she had done to Rakel. And somehow she knew they would not all be as understanding as Nils Heg.

I don't care.

But she did. She had always cared.

I've left that behind. The fear. The masks. I've changed.

She looked at the journal, sitting there on the table near the bed. A simple book, small and plain. Yet its pages held both promise and pain.

Lord, help me.

Arla laid her hand on the book's cover and closed her eyes. She had the journal. And she had Ellie. Two witnesses against the evil of that man. But it wasn't enough. She knew it. *Lord, show me what I must do.* She opened her eyes.

The fire crackled. Ellie stirred in the bed. Shadows flickered over the walls.

Arla frowned. Where was the sudden conviction? The certainty that told her what to do? *Lord?*

She walked to her wardrobe, opened it, and took out her best Sunday dress. Today. Whatever she was going to do would have to be done today. Before it was too late. Before Lars Jensen could act again.

Arla put on her dress, then sat at the dressing table and fixed her hair. She looked at herself in the mirror. The wrinkles were deepening at the sides of her eyes, and there was more gray in her hair than was there last summer. "I am old enough." She whispered the words to herself. "I am old enough to not be afraid of that man." Or of anyone. But she was. She still was.

Arla laid Ellie's church dress over the chair and then returned to the journal. She picked it up and held it in her hand. Then she opened it one last time and turned to the final page.

IT'S COMING. I HEAR IT DANCING ON THE ROOFTOP. I SMELL IT RACING DOWN
THE HALL. IT IS COMING FOR ME. FIRE. LIKE ELIJAH'S CHARIOTS TO BRING ME
HOME.

Arla shuddered. Was this, then, the last thing Rakel had done?
Written these final words as the fire roared around her?

I WILL DIE HERE. I KNOW IT. I SAW MAMA RUNNING AWAY. THERE IN THE
SMOKE AND ASH, I SAW HER LEAVING ME.

Tears gathered in Arla's eyes. She dashed the water away and continued to read. The words grew bigger, sloppier, as if Rakel had scrawled
them in a final rush.

I DON'T HAVE MUCH TIME NOW. I WILL LOCK THIS JOURNAL AWAY IN THE BOX.
MAYBE IT WILL SURVIVE. IT IS A STRONG BOX.

AND IF YOU FIND THIS, MAMA, IF MY WORDS SURVIVE, KNOW THAT I
DON'T BLAME YOU. I FORGIVE YOU. FOR EVERYTHING.

I'D BETTER LOCK THIS AWAY NOW. THE FIRE IS HERE. IT'S KNOCKING AT THE
DOOR.

I LOVE YOU, MAMA.

The journal ended there. Arla stared at the final words until her
vision blurred.

Thank you, Rakel. Thank you, God. She straightened her shoulders.
"I will find a way. Somehow, I'll find a way to make things right." She
glanced at Ellie, then tucked the journal into her handbag.

* * *

They know. And I can feel their hope. I can taste their fear. That is what I am to them now. Both a dream and a nightmare. A lost wife. A phantom mother. A daughter devoured in flame. I cannot be them all.

So what do I do? Where do I go? Something in me tells me to run. To head north and never look back. But a promise holds me. I said I would return today. I owe him that much.

So here I am, with snow slipping under my feet and my shadow splashing like black ink before me. A bird chirps. Ice melts from darkened branches. I stuff my hands deep into the pockets of my coat and walk on.

But what will I say when I get there? How will I explain what I've done? What will he believe? What will he not? And how could he still want a wife who looks like a monster?

God, is it wrong to want to be loved?

It made so much sense to retreat, to hide, to become their ghost in the hills. It was supposed to be better to be their myth, rumor and no more. But I didn't count on the loneliness. I didn't count on love.

I see it now, as I could not before. It's not the scars that matter; it's who I am, inside. I have encountered evil and endured it. I have been clothed in pain yet lived to tell. That is what life is. There is sorrow, and injustice, and sin. There are scars that cannot be erased by time. I wear mine on my skin. They wear theirs in their hearts.

Is there hope for us? Is there hope for healing?

I close my eyes and listen for the wind. It touches me, caresses my face, lifts the veil of my pain. I want to be whole. I want to be healed. I want to be loved.

Who are you?

The question comes on the breeze. And I do not answer. I know I will have to face it. I know I will have to be true. But not today. God, let me have one more day ...

I open my eyes, and there is his house before me. A hundred yards between me and a dream. It could be mine. If only ... I sigh.

Behind me, a branch cracks. And a voice comes. Harsh, low. "There it is, boys."

I turn.

And they rush toward me. Four men. Six. Branches in their hands. A scythe, a club, and—I bite back my scream—a rifle shining in the morning sun.

"No, please."

Faces I know, twisted in hate.

"Stop."

"Get him."

"Don't let him go."

"Easy there."

Voices, like a flock of crows, pecking, beating my flesh. A flicker of the blade. A stick raises. They come at me, surround me. I cannot breathe. Cannot see for the blur of men.

Hands grab my arms, my shoulders, my wrists. I twist, pull. A flash of metal. The gun swings. Pain sears through my gut.

The hands are on me again, tearing, clawing. I fall. Snow splashes up my nose, into my mouth, muffling my cry.

A foot shoves into my side, rolls me until my face is against the snow.

"Tie it tight. Jensen said it was dangerous."

"Don't let it talk."

A knee slams into my back. My arms are jerked behind me. Rope tears at my flesh, bites into the scars at my wrists.

"Please, don't. I'm a—"

A hand shoves into my head, buries my face in snow.

I taste the cold, and the warmth of blood. And then there is only the darkness. And in it, a familiar fear.

***

Josef hobbled back and forth in front of the window. She wasn't coming. And maybe he was glad. At least he should be. But he still peered out the window every few minutes. He still kept smoothing his hair and straightening his collar. It was crazy. He'd spent half the night going over every detail of their times together. Her subtle gestures, the way her head turned just slightly to one side when she spoke. The strength of her hands. The hint of humor. And the words that pierced his soul.

It wasn't Maggie.

In the darkest part of the night, he'd decided that. Maggie wouldn't have lived as a hermit in the hills. Maggie wouldn't have built a shack or learned to hunt or dragged a man miles through the snow. What woman could do those things? Not Maggie. But this woman had. She had done all that, and more.

She had changed him. Made him better. Somehow she had found a place for herself in their lives, in his heart, in her own right.

So now what was he to do? Confront her? Tell her he knew she wasn't Maggie after all? Could he bear to bring her more shame? Or should he live with the lie? Pretend she was his wife, take her into his home, and have the specter of Maggie, of the hidden truth, always between them? No. She had lived behind a veil of lies for too long already. A person couldn't be happy like that. Pretending, hiding, covering the truth with a cloak of black.

God, what would you have me do?

Funny that he prayed now. She'd helped him there, too. He sighed and peeked through the shutters for the tenth time that morning. Still, nothing. No one. Maybe she was afraid to come. Or maybe she was ashamed.

"What do you think, Em? Is she coming?"

Emma rolled over on her blanket and crawled toward him.

"Oh no you don't." He picked her up and set her on her feet. "You're walking now, remember?"

She swayed back and forth once, then toddled toward the door.

Josef scooped her up and stood her in her crib. Then he handed her a bottle.

She plopped down and began to drink.

"You just wait—"

A shout came from outside. He tottered toward the window. Nothing. He limped to the door and flung it open. No one was there. Sunlight shone off tiny beads of falling snow. Josef squinted and held his breath to listen. Was she here? Was she coming?

No. He grabbed his crutch and coat, stepped out, and closed the door behind him. Men's voices, muted and harsh, drifted from somewhere in the trees. He glanced back at Emma.

"You be a good girl. I promise I won't go far." Not like last time. He wouldn't take that chance again. He shrugged into his coat, tucked the crutch under his arm, then hurried toward the sound of the men's voices.

Minutes later, he found them. Robert, Hans, and other men from town stood in a circle among the trees. One held a stick in his hand, another a rifle, another the curved blade of a scythe.

"Hey, what—"

Robert turned toward him.

And he saw her. There between them. A black cloak. A splash of red blood. A crumpled mass lying facedown in the snow.

He dropped his crutch and fell forward. "What have you done?"

Robert's hand shot out, grabbed him. "Careful, Strom. It could break those ties."

Josef yanked the lapel of his coat from Robert's grip. "Are you mad?" He spun and dropped to his knees beside her. Then gently, he turned her over. "Are you okay?"

The woman didn't move.

He glared up at Robert. "What did you do?"

"Nothing it don't deserve." Robert crossed his arms. "It attacked a girl. Beat her."

Cold twisted in Josef's gut. "No. That's not possible."

"We're taking it in. It's gotta pay for what it done."

Two men took hold of Josef's arms and tried to pull him to his feet. He shook them off. "You can't. I won't let you."

The scythe flashed in Hans's hand. He stepped forward. "Out of the way, man."

Robert reached down and placed his hand on Josef's shoulder. "It's a monster, Strom. You don't need to protect it."

Josef turned his head and looked down at the woman in the snow. A trickle of blood oozed from the side of her mouth. He leaned over and wiped it away with his thumb. "No. You're wrong."

Her eyes fluttered open.

He looked into them, so full of pain, so full of fear and sorrow, that he could hardly breathe beneath the weight of their gaze. "She's not a monster." He brushed his knuckles over the scars on her cheek. "She's my wife."

31

Lord, I have waited my whole life for this moment. My whole life waiting to look into the face of one who loves me. To hear those words and to wrap myself in them. I have dreamed. I have schemed. I have hoped and lost all hope. I have hidden my tomorrows in the deep shadows of my being and watched them burn away. And yet, he is here. He looks down at me with eyes filled with tenderness, soft with compassion.

And I hear him claim me, make me his own. Despite the scars, despite this face, he has called me his wife. I bask in the sound of it. I bask in the dream. Cling to it in my heart until I almost forget, almost believe it can be true.

Lord?

I wish this moment could go on forever. I wish there were no difference between truth and lie.

He reaches down, unties my hands, lifts me to my feet.

If he knew. If he really knew …

But he doesn't need to. Nobody does. Ever.

I touch my fingers to my chest and know this moment cannot last. Know that one day this vision will fade. But not yet. Please, Lord, not today …

He takes my hand in his own.

Dare I believe? Dare I think that someone could love me? Now. Even now.

"Josef …" I whisper his name.

Voices murmur around us like a hundred insects, chewing at the corners of my dream.

"You sure, Strom?"

"It ain't a woman."

"Can't be."

"Lawd, what a nightmare."

"Glad it ain't my missus."

The voice of Robert Larsen rises over the rumble of the others. "Don't matter if it's a woman or a man. Wife or monster. We've got to take her in. She's gotta answer for what she's done."

Josef's hand tightens on mine. "Answer to who?"

"Lars Jensen."

Lars Jensen. My breath quickens at the name. Jensen. They had said it before. I should have known. Should have guessed that he would not rest until he made me pay. I drop Josef's hand and back away. I won't face that man. I can't. He will steal every dream. Destroy every hope.

Behind me, a rifle cocks.

* * *

Lars shivered, though he wasn't cold. He adjusted his tie. The scar on his neck was bothering him again. His collar chafed at it, reminding him of things best forgotten. Reminding him of her.

It'll be over soon. They'll find that monster woman. They'll do what needs to be done.

He rubbed his fingers over the rough skin at his neck. *It can't be her. It has to be her. I don't want to know. I have to know.* He shivered again. Something was wrong. Something he couldn't put his finger on. Around him, folks sat in the pews just as they did every Sunday. Old Gertie Hedding banged on the new piano and squawked out a song like some old biddy hen. The preacher's wife sat with her back ramrod straight and her bonnet so stiff he could drop a brick on it and it wouldn't bend. The twins, Gunnar and Gregor, squirmed in their seats and sniggered behind raised palms. Everything was as it always was. And yet, it was different.

The preacher stepped up to the pulpit as the music ended. His eyes scanned the congregation and came to rest on the spot where Robert Larsen usually sat. "David said, 'I was glad when they said unto me, Let us go into the house of the Lord.' But I see there are some missing among us today." He cleared his throat. His gaze flickered to Lars.

Lars looked away. Robert should have been back by now. Had he found the woman? If he had, what had he done to her? And what about Strom? Surely the man wouldn't protect a monster. Surely he would step aside once he heard what that creature had done. Once they all heard. Soon. Soon, this would all be behind him.

"Let us turn to the Word of the Lord."

Lars flicked a bit of lint from his pant leg.

The preacher's voice tumbled from behind the pulpit. "And ye shall know the truth, and the truth shall make you free."

Lars' gaze snapped back to the man. Did he know? He couldn't. No one did.

"The good Lord says those very words in the book of John, chapter eight, verse thirty-two." He held up his black Bible and thumped his palm on the cover. "Truth and freedom, friends. The two things the human heart longs for. But what do they mean?"

Another chill swept down Lars' spine. Not today. He didn't want to hear these words now, not when somewhere out there everything hung in the balance. He sat up straighter. Beside him, Leif shifted in his seat.

"Sit still, boy." Lars spat the words under his breath. He didn't need Leif calling attention to them, not now anyway.

Leif scowled and crossed his arms.

Lars glared at him.

The preacher continued. "We think that lies will help us. We think that no one will ever know."

Crazy words. He wouldn't listen. Truth. What was truth anyway? It was what the strongest man claimed it to be, that's what. And he aimed to be that man.

"But someone does know."

She knows. Lars coughed.

"Jesus knows, and he says—"

Jesus. The preacher was talking about Jesus, not Rakel. Not that Hansen girl. Not even the Hinckley ghost.

"The truth will free us. And don't we all want to be free?"

Free. The word twisted in his mind. Did he want freedom? Yes. No. Not at that price. He didn't want truth. He just wanted peace. And that would come just as soon as that monster was dealt with, and the Hansen girl was sent away. Then truth wouldn't matter. Truth wouldn't hurt.

"We need but come to the Lord and—" The preacher stopped. "Yes, Mrs. Anderson?"

Lars turned in his seat. Near the back of room, Arla Anderson had risen from her pew. She stood there, her hands clasped, her face as white as ice. And she was staring right at him.

***

Arla's mouth went dry. Her hands shook. And still she stood there, staring at that awful man in his black Prince Albert suit, his creased silk tie, his mustache trimmed and precisely waxed. He was perfect. He was everything she had once admired. But not anymore.

He lifted a hand and smoothed his mustache. He touched his tie.

Every eye turned toward her.

She straightened her shoulders, tilted her chin.

His eyebrows raised slightly, waiting.

But the words wouldn't come.

The preacher stepped from behind the pulpit. "Mrs. Anderson, are you all right?"

Lars Jensen's gaze slipped from her to Ellie and back again. Then he turned away.

Heat flushed her face. Her breath quickened.

Whispers pattered around her.

Beside her, Ellie shuddered. "What are you doing, Mrs. Anderson?"

Perspiration dampened her blouse. "What I should have done long ago." But how would they believe her? Even she hadn't believed. Not really. Not until she had read the words herself.

Arla's hand slipped into her bag. Her fingers tightened around the journal. Rakel would have her say. Even now, even when it was too late to make amends.

Ellie reached up and gripped her arm. "Mrs. Anderson?"

"I'm setting her free, child. Opening the door, and setting her free." Arla pulled the journal from her handbag. She raised it so all could see. *It's your turn, Rakel. I'm sorry it's come so late.* "Here is the truth, Reverend. About Rakel, about me, and about the man who hurt her."

Her eyes bore into Lars Jensen's back.

Slowly, he turned back around. "Sit down, Arla."

Her voice faltered. "Not this time, Lars. Never again."

"I'll tell them." His gaze raced over the congregation.

Arla swallowed. "I don't care."

"They'll know what you are."

She clenched the journal tighter. "Let them know."

His lips pressed into a thin line.

Arla turned toward the people. "Fifteen years ago, I had an affair with that man." The words came out in a rush. "But that is not the worst thing I've done. I locked my daughter in a room, and the fire came, and she died there."

Someone gasped.

"I have pretended to be what I am not. And I won't pretend anymore." Arla looked around at the shocked faces, the condemning eyes. People she had known all her life, people who had respected her, trusted her. Their gazes slid away from her now. Except for Nils. She spotted him there on the far side of the room. He smiled, and nodded. And Arla knew she was not alone.

She turned and looked the preacher right in the eye. "I make no excuse for my sins, Reverend. My daughter needed me, but instead I locked her away. I locked the truth away. But no longer." She stepped out of the pew and walked up the aisle toward the platform in front.

Lars stood.

Arla paused and stared into his face. "Will you tell what you've done?"

His eyes narrowed. "I don't know what you're talking about. I've done nothing wrong."

She nodded. "Then Rakel will have to tell it."

She opened the journal and handed it to the preacher.

"What's that?" Lars' voice cracked.

"A testimony to my sins. And yours."

The preacher smoothed the page with his hand, then read it silently. His jaw tightened. A moment later, he looked up. "Is this true, Jensen? Did you do these things to the Anderson girl?"

Lars' voice raised. "I don't know what scheme this woman is trying to devise—"

Arla cut him off. "And what about Ellie? Will you deny attacking her as well?"

Heads turned toward Ellie. She lifted her hand and brushed her fingers over the bruise on her cheek. Murmurs fluttered through the crowd.

Lars licked his lips. "She told you I did that? I didn't, of course. I saved her. From the monster. From the one you all call the ghost in the hills." He pointed at the people. "I told you it would attack your children. And it has. And now you want to blame me?" He jabbed his finger into his chest.

People moved in their seats. The murmurs grew louder.

Leif leapt up. "That thing has tried to attack Ellie Hansen before. Remember? It ain't Papa's fault. He just wanted to—"

Ellie stood on the pew. "You shut your mouth, Leif Jensen. Ain't it bad enough that you shot me? And now your papa wants to keep me quiet. You won't get away with it. Neither of you. I'm gonna—"

"Silence!" The preacher's voice boomed over the congregation.

The muttering ceased. Ellie gulped. Leif sat back down. And Arla and Lars glared at one another and were silent.

A hand touched Arla's sleeve. She glanced down. The preacher's wife looked up at her. "Sit down, Arla."

She shook her head. "No."

"Please."

The preacher coughed. "There are two witnesses against you, Lars Jensen. What say you? Did you hurt those women?"

Lars stood straight, tall. He faced the preacher, then turned to the congregation. "Two witnesses, you say? Credible witnesses? I think not. One is dead. One is a child," his glance fell on Ellie, "and easily confused."

The preacher nodded.

Arla's stomach twisted. No. They had to believe. They had to. *Lord, please …*

"If there's no one else to accuse me, then I say we forget this whole fiasco." Lars slapped his hands together and smiled. "I will hold no grudge. Mrs. Anderson is a grieving woman. And we all know the Anderson girl was disturbed, wild. Who doesn't remember the girl's crazy ways?"

Whispers trickled through the crowd.

"No. She wasn't—"

Lars raised his hand. "You said your piece, Mrs. Anderson. Now let me say mine. I am a good man. I've served this community well. It's that monster in the woods we have to worry about. It's the one who attacked Ellie. It has to be stopped. And that's what Robert Larsen and his men are doing right now."

Bile rose in Arla's throat as many in the congregation leaned forward and nodded.

"So let's stop accusing one another when it's that monster—"

Arla shot forward. "No. It's you—"

Lars' voice rose to a shout. "Look at them, Arla Mae." He thrust his arm toward the people. "They know it's that creature's fault. They know. That's why there's no one else accusing me. No one—"

The door slammed open.

Everyone turned.

There, in the doorway, stood the monster itself.

32

"I accuse you." The words, harsh and rattling, rang through the room.

Lars' breath stopped in his throat. *The fools.* What had they done? Why had they brought her here? Hadn't he told them to take care of the problem out there in the woods?

The door opened wider. There stood Robert Larsen and his men, with Josef Strom and his baby beside them. He had done this. It was Strom's fault.

The creature, hooded and in flowing black, glided down the aisle toward him.

Someone screamed, a child cried, feet scraped against raw wood. A dozen men stood.

The black figure seemed to have grown taller, more deadly. It stopped just yards from him. "I accuse you." It said the words again, low this time, like the swish of a knife blade across a stone.

He shuddered.

The room grew quiet.

His heart jumped in his chest.

The preacher stepped to the front of the platform. His voice shattered the silence. "Who are you, sir?"

For a moment, the creature looked up at the man, then it turned back to Lars. "Don't you know who I am?"

Lars licked his lips. But words wouldn't come.

The creature stepped closer. Eyes shone beneath the hood. Light and shadows played off the twisted flesh, the grotesque features. No one would believe a person like this. They couldn't. It was a monster. A freak. A thing that crawled out of nightmares and didn't belong in the day.

Lars swallowed and found his voice. "How dare you. You, you ..." He turned his head toward the people and thrust his arm toward the creature in black. "I told you it was a monster. Look at it. It's the one who attacked that girl. And it'll do it again."

Someone whimpered. Another sobbed.

The monster's chin rose. It reached toward him with a hand scarred and horrible, like the claw of a demon summoning him to the pit. Its finger extended, pointed at his chest. "You will tell the truth, Lars Jensen. No more lies." The voice rasped across his nerves. The creature moved forward.

He stepped back. "You get away, get away from me."

It paused. A sound came, low and brittle. A laugh, eerie beneath the folds of the hood. Then it spoke again. "Get away? Now you want me to get away? You don't know how I've tried."

A picture flashed across his mind, of Rakel trying to escape him. In a blur, he saw her black hair, her thrashing arms, the fear in her face that matched his fear now. He cleared his throat. "I never meant to hurt you." It was barely a whisper, a near-silent admission that maybe he had been wrong.

Her shoulders sagged. "Didn't you?" Her tone softened. "Or are those only words meant to placate the crowd?"

"No."

She studied him for a long moment. "Strange, isn't it? I've been afraid of you for so long. I've cowered, I've kept silent, I've hidden the truth away and thought if I only ran far enough I could be free of you. But I can't be free. Not yet."

He glanced at her and saw the shadow of tears gathered in her eyes. "And then the fire came, and it took everything." Her voice lowered. "Except for you. I became no one and everyone. And yet, still, I could not escape you." She shook her head. "Everything that journal said about you is true. Everything Ellie accused you of happened. I was there. I know. I've always been there."

Lars shuddered. "Rakel?"

"I am not Rakel."

He steadied himself against the back of the pew. "Then who?"

"It's time for the truth, isn't it? For both of us. Then we can both be free." She reached up and gripped the top of her hood.

"No." Lars breathed the word. "Don't."

She pulled down the hood. "You were never a successful businessman in the East." She unwrapped the scarf around her head. "You didn't make your money importing goods from around the world." A lock of long hair tumbled from the covering. Light hair, and not black. "You stole your money from the newspaper you worked for." She dropped the scarf to the floor. "You're still wanted in New York." She reached up and unbuttoned her cloak. "And that knife on your wall isn't even your own." The cloak fell from her shoulders and landed beside the scarf. "You are a criminal and an outlaw. I will fear you no more."

Thoughts froze in Lars' mind. Fears. Questions. Doubts mixed with the horror of the truth. Rakel wouldn't know those things. No one did. Except Agnes, who was dead, and also ... But it couldn't be. She was dead too. He saw the body. He saw ...

She pushed back her hair and faced him full on. "Do you know me now?"

He looked into her eyes, narrowed and blurred with tears. Gentle blue turned hard. Familiar eyes. Eyes that he'd always loved. "You aren't ... You can't be."

Her hand reached into her pocket. She lifted out a necklace and held it up in the light. The silver glinted in the brightness. Then she threw it at his feet and tore open the top button of her shirt. She pulled back the neckline. And there, on her sternum, the shape of a cross was burned into her flesh. "I am."

Leif rose beside him. His voice quivered. "Sis? Is that you?"

***

Ellie held her breath. It all made sense now. The creature in her dream. Mama's call. And the dress that hung in her closet. And she knew what Mama would have her do.

Voices erupted around her, whispers and gasps.

"His own daughter."

"She ain't the monster. He is."

"He done it."

"I can't believe it."

"Poor girl."

Ellie touched Mrs. Anderson's sleeve. "I've got to go now."

Mrs. Anderson glanced down at her. Tears shone on her cheeks. "It's not her. For a moment," she sniffed, "for just a moment I thought, I had hoped …"

Ellie patted her arm. "I know, Mrs. Anderson. I hoped too."

Mrs. Anderson put her arm around Ellie and squeezed. "I love you, Ellie Jean. I'm so sorry."

Ellie smiled. "I know. I love you too." She hugged Mrs. Anderson around the middle. "We're gonna be all right, aren't we?"

Mrs. Anderson dried her tears with the back of her hand and sniffed again. "We are now, I think. Yes, we are now."

"I've just got one thing to do. For Mama. I've gotta go."

"Where?"

Ellie grinned. "I'm going to get Mama's dress. 'Cause it's a freedom dress. Mama told me so. It's the last thing she wanted."

Mrs. Anderson leaned down and kissed Ellie on her forehead. "You do that, Ellie Jean. You get that dress. And then maybe all of us will find our peace."

Ellie squeezed Mrs. Anderson one more time, then she slipped from the pew and hurried out the door.

***

The question dies and is swallowed by scores of voices. All whispering, wondering. A gasp. A cry. Someone breathing with a harsh rattling. That one is me. I turn and look at them all. And then comes silence. In that moment, no one speaks. No one moves. The air quivers with a thousand unsaid words, a hundred unspoken queries. I tremble beneath the weight of them. I shiver beneath their stares. I have done it. And there's no turning back. I have stepped from their dreams and become real. I have shattered the illusion, unveiled the mystery.

But I am who I am. It is time to face that now. I am who no one wants me to be.

So I stand here, with head bare, scars unhidden. I stand and bear the truth before them all. I know that Josef is lost to me now, and Emma, too. But I have made my choice. I will live this life God has given me. I will live with the scars and with the pain. I will be who I am, even if they hate me for it.

I look at my brother and nod. I look at my father and see him, clearly, as if for the first time. And what I see is not a monster, but a man. Just a man with eyes wide, mouth open. "Winnie?" He whispers the word as if he has never spoken it before. He breathes it like a blessing, and like a curse.

I raise my hand and touch my cheek. The skin is rough and puckered. And I know the creature he sees. "We can't hide anymore, Father. We can't pretend to be who we are not."

"But, but I saw ..."

"They know now. The truth about us both."

"You're alive."

He cannot believe. Even now, when I stand before him. When I've shown my proof, revealed my heart. I drop my hand to my side.

Footsteps come behind me, men striding down the aisle. The same men who hunted me, captured me. For a moment, my heart thuds in my chest. Then they are past me. They swarm around my father, grab his arms, pull his hands behind him. They glare at him with grim faces, eyes hard and narrow. They believe Ellie now, and Rakel. And they know what my father is. They know what he has long been.

Robert Larsen nods at the reverend, then he turns back to my father. "You'd better come with us." His voice rumbles like boulders hitting water. "I'm betting there are some folks in New York who'll be wanting to see you after you've answered for what you've done here."

Father blinks. He glances toward the door, then back at the men. He cannot escape. And even if he did, they would find him. They know that he is a thief and a coward. They will make him face his past.

They pull him toward the aisle, toward me.

I stand there, unmoving. And then he is beside me. I tremble with his nearness.

He stares into my face. For a moment, the breath chokes from me. I have stood here before, face to face with his anger, eye to eye with his hate.

But his features are soft now, his eyes sad. "My Winnie. My daughter." He looks away, as if he cannot bear to see me. "You were such a pretty little girl."

I turn aside. Even now, even like this, he can hurt me.

"That's enough." Someone growls the words behind me.

Father moves closer. I back away. Then he stops. His voice grows quiet. "You hid from me."

I glance up at him, but cannot meet his gaze. "I can't hide anymore."

He shakes his head. "Why? You know I always loved you."

His words surprise me. And what surprises me more is that I see he believes them. And that knowledge touches something in my soul. I have tried to escape him for so long. I have hated. I have feared. And yet he doesn't know what he's done to me. He doesn't understand that the scars he sees are only a reflection of the hurt within. A father should know. A father should see.

And then I understand. He is no father. Not like a father should be. I have never believed he loves me, because he hasn't. He is not able. But God is able. And yet I have not believed that he can love me either. I have looked to him as father, and have counted him like the man before me. But God is not Lars Jensen. He does not claim love, and then abuse. He does not send fire to punish or flames to inflict his fury.

And yet, the fire came. It came and, I catch my breath, it set me free. It made me new.

The men yank my father back. They pull him toward the door.

He looks at me, with pain in his glance, fear in his features. "Winnie …" This time, my name is a plea. "Please."

But I cannot reach out to him. I can only watch him go.

"Forgive me."

And I find that I can. I am his daughter, but I am not his daughter. He hurt me deeply, worse than the fire had ever done. Yet, in this moment, I see that the scars are not who I am. They do not define me. I am not a monster. I am just a woman. "I forgive you, Lars Jensen. I forgive you for everything that you are."

He closes his eyes. Thank you. *His mouth forms the words, though he doesn't speak them aloud. And then they take him out the door. It closes behind them, and he is gone. He is finally gone.*

Someone tugs at my sleeve. Ellie is there, with a gray dress draped in her arms. I brush my knuckles over her cheek. "I'm sorry I am not your mother. She was a good friend."

Ellie grins at me. "Mama loved you, and she would have wanted you to have this." She hands me the dress, and I know it for what it is. They had all worked so hard to save me—Nora with the dress, Maggie with the train tickets, and Rakel who would have gone with me. They would have given their lives to free me. And in a way, I suppose they did. They, and God, and the fire that swept my soul.

My throat closes as I hug the dress to me.

"Winnie?"

I hear his voice, soft, questioning, beside me. And I remember that he has lost much this day. I glance up at him. "I'm sorry, Josef. I'm so sorry that I'm not Maggie. I wanted to be. I wanted it so much."

He smiles and touches my face. "Shall we start over, you and I?"

I lift my chin. "My name is Winifred Jensen. I am who I am."

He steps forward and looks me full in the face. Looks at my scars, sees the ugliness, the pain, the hurt. Then he cradles my face in his hands. His eyes sparkle.

"You know, I never did like the name Esau."

He leans toward me. And there, in front of everyone, his lips touch mine.

Epilogue

September 1, 1895

It has been one year since the fire came and changed my world. Today, the town gathered at City Hall to remember those we lost. I wore the dress Nora made, and laid flowers on the death trench. It is covered with grass now, green with new life. And as I dropped the petals, I thought about the fire that came and laid bare. But the fire didn't last. We lost much, but life came again. And hope with it.

So now, I sit here on the porch Josef made. I look out over the fields. The crop is rich this year. Corn, oats, wheat in record numbers. Potatoes as big as a dog's head. Emma toddles in the yard. She glances up at me and giggles. I open my arms to her and call her to me. I stand. She runs to me. And I sweep her up in my embrace.

She opens her hand, and I see a tiny daisy squished there.

"F-ower, Ma-ma."

I take it and kiss her. Then I close my eyes and savor the moment. I have found my dream. I have known such sorrow, have endured such pain. But

God has restored my soul. He has healed me and made all things new.

Out in the fields, I see Josef walking through the stalks. He pauses and waves at me. I stand on tiptoes and wave back. He has told me that the rumor of a ghost in the hills remains. Only those who were there that morning know the truth of who I am, who I was. So the rumors persist, rumors of a German immigrant who was burned in the fire and now lives in the woods. Some say he's Russian, some say he doesn't exist all. I will let them believe what they will. I know the truth. I know where I have come from, what I have been. And I know what I have become.

I am Winnie, just Winnie, loved by God even through fire. Loved too much for him to leave me in my pain. And I know that even though I will always carry the scars, inside I am healed of wounds far more deep, far more ugly than those the fire caused.

Emma pats my cheek. "Down, Mama. Play."

I smile and release her. In time, I will tell her of Maggie. I'll tell her of a gentle woman who fought through fire to save her. And I will tell her to close her eyes, feel the breeze. For I know that sometimes, when the wind blows just right over the fields, I still smell the fragrance of her perfume. And I know that in her way, she saved me too. She, and Nora, and Rakel.

I close my eyes.

I listen to the silence.

I see through the darkness.

I wait. I remember. And here, in the quiet in-between place in my heart, they live again.

Historical Note

On September 1, 1894, one of the worst fires in history ravaged east-central Minnesota. It was the first firestorm in Minnesota history, destroying six towns, including Hinckley. Descending on the towns like a red demon, the fire consumed 400 square miles, killing 418 people in four hours. The maelstrom of flames caught the townspeople unaware. Five hundred were saved on the Eastern Minnesota train to Duluth, with the bridge over the Kettle River disintegrating into the fire only minutes after the train passed. Another hundred were saved in the gravel pit, where they desperately poured water on each other to keep their clothes from catching fire in the intense heat. Three hundred more were rescued on a second train, which backed up to Skunk Lake, five miles north of Hinckley. A few others were saved in potato patches, water barrels, and by sheer grace. After the fire, the townspeople rebuilt their town, but in the midst of rebuilding, a rumor began of a hermit in the hills—a person severely burned, disfigured beyond recognition. The identity of this person was never determined, and the "ghost" remains to this day a mystery, a myth, a shadowed figure whispered about in tales passed from grandparents to grandchildren. So the question remains: Who was this "monster in the hills"?

Veil of Fire was inspired by the stories passed down to me through my husband's great-great-grandmother, who moved to Hinckley just after the fire. And while I've tried to paint an accurate picture of the Great Fire, *Veil of Fire* is a fictional story. As such, I've introduced characters and events that are not part of recorded history. There was no Arla Anderson, no Ellie, no Josef, no Lars. But there was a town full of people who survived the fire, who rebuilt their lives afterward, and who never forgot what happened on that day. And there was a person burned in the fire, a person who lived the rest of his (or her?) life as a hermit in the hills. Today, that individual has turned more myth than monster, a nearly forgotten mystery swallowed by the modern world.

But you can still visit the Hinckley Fire Museum and see coins, dolls, and artifacts from the fire. You can read the stories, view the old photos, and wonder what it must have been like.

And, if you are lucky, you may get a glimpse of a black-cloaked figure hiding in the shadows of yesterday.

Invite Marlo Schalesky to Your Book Club

Transport your book club behind the scenes and into a new world by inviting Marlo Schalesky to join in your group discussion via phone. To learn more, go to www.cookministries.com/readthis or e-mail Marlo directly at bookclubs@marloschalesky.com.

If you would like to use *Veil of Fire* in your reader's group (study questions are available online at www.cookministries.com/veiloffire and at the author's Web site), or if the story touched you in any way, Marlo would love to hear from you. Please visit her Web site at www.marloschalesky.com and send her an e-mail at marlo@marloschalesky.com, or you can mail a note to her at the address below.

Marlo Schalesky, Author
c/o Cook Communications Ministries
4050 Lee Vance View
Colorado Springs, CO 80918

Author Interview

How did you start writing? What was your first piece of writing like?

When I was thirteen years old, I wrote a poem on the bus on the way to school. It was about an old tree, forlorn and desolate, standing alone in a field. I read that poem at every recess, tweaked it, polished it, and for the first time felt the thrill of how the written word can convey profound beauty. That day, I fell in love with writing.

Shortly after that, I told my mother (with all the angst of a newly turned teenager), "I will just die if I don't write!" So naturally when I grew up I decided to get my degree in chemistry! And, oddly enough, I didn't die. I enjoyed chemistry. But always that desire to write was with me in the back of my mind, saying "Someday, someday."

Someday finally came. I started writing articles for various magazines and submitting proposals for book projects. I thought it would be easy to get my first book published, but it took years of writing and honing my craft. And more than that it took giving up my dream entirely. I had to come to a place where I didn't have to write to be content. I had to let go of that strong desire and embrace God's will for me, whether that included writing or not. Only then, only when my dream had given way to God's plan, was I offered my first contract. Only when writing became worship could I do it the way God wanted it to be done. And I've been writing books ever since.

Why do you write fiction?

I LOVE A POWERFULLY TOLD STORY. I LOVE CHARACTERS THAT PRESENT REALITY AND TRUTH THROUGH THEIR LIVES AND STRUGGLES. I LOVE TO SEE THROUGH OTHER PEOPLE'S EYES, TO FEEL WHAT THEY FEEL, TO EXPERIENCE LIFE IN A NEW AND DIFFERENT WAY—I THINK WE ALL DO. THAT'S WHY MOVIES AND TELEVISION SHOWS ARE SO POPULAR. FICTION IS GREAT ENTERTAINMENT.

BUT FICTION IS MORE THAN THAT. IT HAS THE POWER TO CHANGE LIVES. BY LIVING VICARIOUSLY THROUGH THE CHARACTERS, BY ENCOUNTERING THE TRUE GOD EVEN IN A MADE-UP PLOT, I AM TOUCHED, CHALLENGED, CHANGED. I SEE GOD IN NEW WAYS. MY VISION IS BROADENED, DEEPENED. AND I DISCOVER TRUTH WITH NEW CLARITY. FICTION LAYS BARE THE IMPERFECTIONS OF MY SOUL, STIRS MY DOUBTS AND QUESTIONS, AND DRIVES ME INTO THE THRONE ROOM OF GOD. AND THAT'S WHY I LOVE WRITING FICTION.

WHILE WRITING *VEIL OF FIRE* IN PARTICULAR, I CAME TO UNDERSTAND MORE FULLY THAT GOD'S LOVE CAN'T BE MEASURED BY MY SUCCESSES AND FAILURES. I'VE ALSO LEARNED THAT GOD IS WRITING MY LIFE'S STORY. AND SINCE THE BEST STORIES HAVE CONFLICT, IRONY, AND PLENTY OF ACTION, I SHOULDN'T BE SURPRISED WHEN MY LIFE TAKES AN UNEXPECTED TURN AND MY FAITH IS CHALLENGED ONCE AGAIN.

AND SO I HOPE THAT MY READERS TOO WILL BE CHANGED AND CHALLENGED THROUGH THE POWER OF STORY. I HOPE THEY WILL BE ENCOURAGED TO PERSEVERE THROUGH DIFFICULTIES, TO PRESS CLOSER TO GOD, TO NOT SETTLE FOR THE EASY ANSWERS BUT WRESTLE WITH THE TOUGH QUESTIONS OF LIFE AND FAITH, TO DIG DEEPER WITH GOD.

Why do people remember a story more easily than a sermon?

BECAUSE GOD HIMSELF IS PRIMARILY A STORYTELLER. ALL HISTORY IS THE STORY HE IS TELLING—THE STORY OF HIS LOVE, HIS CARE, HIS PURPOSE FOR

US. AND OUR LIVES ARE STORIES TOO, THE STORIES HE ENTWINES WITH ALL THE OTHERS TO SHOW US THE DEPTHS OF HIS LOVE. WE LEARN, WE OPERATE, WE LIVE IN THE REALM OF THE STORY OF OUR OWN LIVES AND HISTORY. STORY IS THE WAY WE WERE CREATED TO LEARN AND CHANGE. AND SO, IN THE STORIES WE TELL THERE IS A POWER TO REVEAL TRUTH IN WAYS THAT SLIP PAST OUR DEFENSES TO IMPACT OUR SOULS. A STORY MOVES TRUTH FROM AN ABSTRACT CONCEPT TO A CONCRETE EXAMPLE. IT MAKES TRUTH REAL. IT HAS THE POWER TO CHANGE US, ESPECIALLY IN THOSE AREAS IN WHICH WE ARE MOST RESISTANT TO CHANGE.

What do you hope readers will take away from your book?

WHEN WE WERE CHILDREN, WE BELIEVED IN MIRACLES. THE IMPOSSIBLE WAS ONLY A PRAYER AWAY. FAIRY TALES WERE REAL, AND DREAMS WERE FREE. WHERE DID WE LOSE THE ABILITY TO TRUST? WHEN DID WE STOP DARING TO BELIEVE? WHAT HAPPENED TO US?

LIFE HAPPENED. FAILURE, DISCOURAGEMENT, PAIN, LOSS. SOMEWHERE, SOMEHOW, LIFE BURNS US ALL. AND WE REALIZE THAT THIS LIFE WE LIVE IS NOT THE ONE WE ONCE DREAMED. THE REALITIES OF LIFE SCAR US. DOUBTS RISE. FEAR WHISPERS THAT HOPE IS GONE. AND WHAT WAS ONCE A SIMPLE FAITH CAN FAIL IN THE FACE OF THAT FEAR.

IN THE MIDST OF LIFE'S DISILLUSIONMENT, CHOICES APPEAR. DO WE RETREAT? HIDE OUR HURTS FAR FROM PROBING EYES? DO WE EMBRACE BITTERNESS AND CYNICISM? DO WE USE DECEIT TO TRY TO OBTAIN OUR GOALS? DO WE GIVE UP, GIVE IN, FORGET THAT WE EVER DARED TO DREAM?

OR IS IT POSSIBLE TO REACH THE HIGH PLACES OF FAITH IN THE LOW VALLEYS OF LIFE'S REALITY? CAN WE STILL LIVE A LIFE OF BOLD FAITH, OF FIERCE HOPE, WHEN FAIRY TALES DON'T COME TRUE? HOW DO WE LIVE THIS LIFE THAT GOD HAS GIVEN US WHEN IT'S NOT THE LIFE WE DREAMED?

THESE ARE THE QUESTIONS I WANTED TO EXPLORE IN *VEIL OF FIRE*. THESE

ARE THE QUESTIONS THAT UNDERLIE EACH CHARACTER'S JOURNEY IN THE AFTERMATH OF THE GREAT FIRE OF 1894. SO, FOR THOSE BURNED BY LIFE, FOR THOSE WHO CARRY SCARS THAT CANNOT BE SEEN, FOR THOSE WHO HAVE RETREATED FOR FEAR OF MORE PAIN, THIS STORY IS FOR YOU, THIS JOURNEY FROM THE HIDDEN PLACES OF PAIN TO A NEW HOPE IN THE UNHIDDEN TRUTH OF CHRIST'S LOVE.

Which character in the book is most like you?

NONE OF THEM, AND ALL OF THEM. I BASE NO CHARACTER ON MYSELF, BUT THEY ALL REFLECT A LITTLE OF ME—MY QUESTIONS, MY STRUGGLES, THE ISSUES THAT HAVE SHAPED AND MOLDED ME. IN *VEIL OF FIRE*, THIS IS PARTICULARLY TRUE FOR THE HERMIT IN THE HILLS. JUST AS THE HERMIT QUESTIONS GOD'S LOVE, BELIEVES "I AM ESAU, UNCHOSEN, UNLOVED," SO I TOO HAVE STRUGGLED WITH THOSE SAME FEELINGS, DOUBTS, AND QUESTIONS. I HAVE CRIED OUT TO GOD, "WHY DON'T YOU LOVE ME?" FOR THE HERMIT, IT WAS A QUESTION BORN OUT OF FIRE, ABUSE, AND DISFIGUREMENT. FOR ME, IT WAS A QUESTION THAT CAME OUT OF FAILURE, INFERTILITY, AND MISCARRIAGE. SO, IN MANY WAYS, THE HERMIT'S QUESTIONS ARE MY OWN, THE ANSWERS MINE, THE EXTERNAL SCARS REFLECTIONS OF MY INTERNAL ONES, AND IN TURN, I THINK, SYMBOLS OF THE SCARS OF US ALL.

What actors would you picture playing the hermit and Josef in a movie?

I SUPPOSE I WOULD CHOOSE JODIE FOSTER TO PLAY THE HERMIT IN THE HILLS BECAUSE SHE IS ABLE TO CONVEY DEEP EMOTION WITHOUT APPEARING OVERWROUGHT. AS FOR JOSEF, OF COURSE I WOULD CHOOSE RUSSELL CROWE BECAUSE I LOVE HIS ABILITY TO COMMUNICATE A CHARACTER'S INNER LIFE

WITHOUT NEEDING MANY WORDS. HE WOULD BE ABLE TO PORTRAY JOSEF'S DEPTH AS WELL AS HIS RETICENCE.

Which writers have influenced you most?

SOME OF MY FAVORITES ARE C. S. LEWIS, J. R. R. TOLKIEN (I WAS A LORD OF THE RINGS FAN EVEN BEFORE IT BECAME POPULAR!), FRANCINE RIVERS, CINDY MARTINUSEN, LAVYRLE SPENCER, AND PHILIP YANCEY. THEY'VE ALL INFLUENCED MY WRITING, LEWIS AND TOLKIEN THROUGH THEIR POETRY OF WORDS; RIVERS, MARTINUSEN, AND SPENCER THROUGH THEIR ABILITY TO BRING CHARACTERS TO LIFE AND TELL A GREAT, MOVING STORY; AND YANCEY THROUGH HIS ABILITY TO WRESTLE WITH THE DIFFICULT QUESTIONS OF FAITH AND LIFE.

BUT FOR THIS BOOK, THE GREATEST INFLUENCE HAS PROBABLY BEEN MY LOVE FOR THE MOOD AND MYSTERY OF *THE PHANTOM OF THE OPERA*. I'VE TRIED TO CAPTURE A LITTLE OF THAT MYSTERY IN MY HIDDEN HERMIT.

Describe your writing process.

FOR ME, WRITING IS PRIMARILY AN ACT OF WORSHIP. EVEN THOUGH IT'S FRAUGHT WITH DISAPPOINTMENTS, DISCOURAGEMENT, AND THE TEMPTATION TO JUST THROW IN THE TOWEL AND TAKE LIFE EASY FOR A CHANGE, I WRITE BECAUSE GOD HAS WOVEN HIS STORIES INTO THE FABRIC OF WHO I AM. THIS IS THE WORK HE HAS GIVEN ME TO DO, AND HE'S CRAFTED ME IN A SPECIAL WAY TO DO IT. SO, MY WRITING IS AN ACT OF FAITHFULNESS TO GOD, OF SITTING DOWN WITH MY COMPUTER REGULARLY AND SEEKING TO FOLLOW GOD'S LEAD, SEEKING TO FIND THE WORDS, THE STORY, THE VISION THAT HE HAS FOR ME ON THAT DAY.

THAT MAKES MY WRITING VERY MUCH AN ADVENTURE OF DISCOVERY OF THE TALE GOD WANTS TO TELL AND ALSO OF THE GEMS OF TRUTH AND

BEAUTY THAT HE HAS HIDDEN WITHIN THE JOURNEY BETWEEN "CHAPTER ONE" AND "THE END."

AND ON THAT JOURNEY, THE CHARACTERS OF MY BOOKS WILL TYPICALLY TAKE THE PLOT IN DIRECTIONS I NEVER EXPECTED. THIS HAPPENED WITH *VEIL OF FIRE*. WHEN I STARTED THE STORY, I THOUGHT THE HERMIT WAS ONE PERSON AND BY THE END, IT TURNED OUT THE HERMIT WAS SOMEONE ELSE ENTIRELY. AS I WROTE, I HAD TO UNRAVEL THE MYSTERY OF WHO REALLY WAS THE HERMIT IN THE HILLS. IT TURNED OUT TO BE A FUN AND INTRIGUING PROCESS FOR ME, AND I HOPE FOR THE READER AS WELL.

Can you share a particularly memorable encounter with a reader?

PERHAPS MY FAVORITE ENCOUNTER CAME VIA E-MAIL. A WOMAN WROTE TO ME WHO HAD GROWN UP IN A CHRISTIAN HOME. OVER THE YEARS, SHE HAD DRIFTED AWAY FROM HER FAITH AND COME TO THINK OF JESUS AS "OLD NEWS," STUFF THAT SHE'D HEARD A HUNDRED TIMES BEFORE. BUT SOMEONE HAD GIVEN HER ONE OF MY BOOKS. AND AFTER READING IT, SHE FOUND HERSELF CONSIDERING JESUS IN A NEW WAY. HE WAS NO LONGER "OLD NEWS" BUT "GOOD NEWS." FOR HER, A STORY OF GOD'S GRACE IN JESUS REMINDED HER OF THE FAITH THAT WAS MISSING IN HER LIFE AND ENCOURAGED HER TO START GETTING BACK IN TOUCH WITH WHAT SHE HAD LEFT BEHIND.

What is one fact about yourself that readers might find most surprising?

IN THE MIDDLE OF WRITING *VEIL OF FIRE*, I GAVE BIRTH TO TWIN GIRLS (AND STILL MANAGED TO WRITE!). NOW, AFTER ELEVEN YEARS OF INFERTILITY, WE HAVE FOUR BEAUTIFUL DAUGHTERS WHO KEEP THEIR MOMMY VERY BUSY AND WHO LIKE TO PUSH BUTTONS ON MY LAPTOP WHILE I'M TRYING DESPERATELY TO MEET DEADLINES. SO FEEL FREE TO PRAY FOR ME!

Additional copies of *Veil of Fire*
are available wherever good books are sold.

***

If you have enjoyed this book, or if it has had an impact on your life,
we would like to hear from you.

Please contact us at

RiverOak® Books
Cook Communications Ministries, Dept. 240
4050 Lee Vance View
Colorado Springs, CO 80918

Or visit our Web site
www.cookministries.com